EPIPHANY

For one, precious, crystallized instant, Olivier knew with perfect clarity that he was about to change the whole of his life. He knew that if he reached out for Julian now, there would be no going back—not to a perfect Belvedere, to a perfect Domiziana, to the perfect life he had constructed on his family's ashes.

The thought made him hesitate for just one second. And in that second he saw his life clearly, as it actually was. He saw himself living forever in the lonely splendor of a castle that was no longer his home. Having to remind himself to kiss a wife whom, even now, before their marriage, he knew he did not love. Trying to hold on to a family that had long ago fragmented to find happiness elsewhere.

And worst of all—most frightening of all—trying to do all this without Julian near.

He reached out then. He pulled Julian close.

BOOK YOUR PLACE ON OUR WEBSITE AND MAKE THE READING CONNECTION!

We've created a customized website just for our very special readers, where you can get the inside scoop on everything that's going on with Zebra, Pinnacle and Kensington books.

When you come online, you'll have the exciting opportunity to:

- View covers of upcoming books
- Read sample chapters
- Learn about our future publishing schedule (listed by publication month *and author*)
- Find out when your favorite authors will be visiting a city near you
- Search for and order backlist books from our online catalog
- Check out author bios and background information
- Send e-mail to your favorite authors
- Meet the Kensington staff online
- Join us in weekly chats with authors, readers and other guests
- Get writing guidelines
- AND MUCH MORE!

Visit our website at
http://www.zebrabooks.com

THE LION OF VENICE

Deborah Johns

ZEBRA BOOKS
KENSINGTON PUBLISHING CORP.
http://www.zebrabooks.com

To Matthew—
You are simply the best

We are knights of France. If the sky were to fall, we could uphold it upon the tips of our lances.
—Sir Philippe de Mézières, 1396

CASTLE

CHAPTER ONE

Olivier, destined to be the last of the great warrior lords of the Ducci Montaldo, frowned as he broke the heavy gold seal of the letter.

" 'Tis from England, my sister Francesca," he said by way of explanation, looking up. The women, who were clustered decoratively about him, acknowledged his politeness with polite nods of their own and then turned with renewed attention to their tapestry work. But the thought of a letter from Count Olivier's illustrious English relations tindered a swift spark to the dry brush of their imaginations; it was a mark of their high station and careful breeding that they were able to keep their eyes demurely lowered. Especially when it was noted that the letter had been considered urgent enough to be carried all the way from the Ducci Montaldo castle in Tuscany to their palazzo on the Grand Canal in Venice. Even in this year of Our Lord 1395, the roads that reached out from the Veneto to the rest of Italy were rife with brigands and wild animals, no matter how diligently the Count's Gold Company patrolled them.

Therefore, a useful soldier sent out alone upon them brought important word indeed.

Important enough to cause Ginevra, at twelve the youngest of the four Venier daughters, to risk her mother's wrath by glancing again towards the burnished blond giant who sat beside her father. As always, she thought Olivier Ducci Montaldo the most gloriously handsome man she had ever seen, with his golden hair and magnificent eyes. Ginevra sighed. Olivier was a famous knight. And he had lived such a romantic life that it hardly seemed fair that her sister Domiziana—no virgin—had managed to snare him. Or almost to snare him.

Domiziana must somehow have sensed this last thought, for she pitched her sister a hard look before drawing a thread from her packet. Ginevra obediently lowered her gaze and began picking the delicate outlines of a white unicorn.

For some moments the only sounds in the main hall of the palazzo were the crackle of the fire and a discreet rustle as the Ladies of the Venier threaded silk through canvas. They worked in silence, for they all knew it would be left to Luciano Venier, their husband and father, to speak for his family.

"Not bad news, I trust," he said.

Olivier glanced up, his turquoise eyes clouded. "I don't know," he said, and then smiled belatedly. "Actually, I'm not sure it even concerns me."

"Not something to do with your mother, I hope?" the Contessa Claudia spoke sharply, her arthritic fingers momentarily forgetting to play at their tapestry. The last thing the Veniers needed at this late date was for something to go awry with the Contessa Ducci Montaldo. But it would be just like her to ruin everything. French born and bred, Blanche de Montfort Ducci Montaldo had always been one to capture attention, particularly when that attention concerned her eldest and best-loved son. But Claudia had her *own* eldest and best-loved to think of—and Domiziana's was a betrothal that begged a quick announcement.

"No, not Mother," Olivier answered as he folded the parchment once again. "It seems my ward, the Lady Julian, is on her way from Harnoncourt Hall to join me at Belvedere."

The Lady Claudia held her face in stern neutrality at this use of the word "Lady" to describe Julian Madrigal. "I imagine she's come on a courtesy call. After all, your generosity to her is noted throughout Europe," she rejoined sharply.

Olivier's handsome features hardened, though his feelings for Julian were not without nuance. "Hardly generosity unwarranted," he answered mildly, "when one considers that her mother saved my life."

"Yes, yes, of course," twittered the Lady Claudia as she deftly worked at picking up her botched stitches. "And how fortunate for us and for Italy that that woman—that *she* succeeded so splendidly in her mission."

Another error, thought Ginevra. She tried not to show her own quickened interest as she struggled to recall the whispers she had heard. Ah, yes. Now she remembered. People said that Julian Madrigal's mother was Aalyne de Lione. And that Aalyne de Lione was a witch.

Outside the granite walls of the palazzo a lone bird suddenly trilled, grateful perhaps to be perched on one of the few espaliered trees where green remained. Winter could be harsh in Venice, cold and damp; Ginevra fervently hoped this little creature would make a speedy way southward before times got cruel.

But the Veniers kept their palazzo—impressively situated on the Grand Canal beneath the very shadow of the newly completed Cathedral of San Marco, as Luciano Venier was wont to tell anyone who would listen—welcomingly warm. Especially when Olivier Ducci Montaldo was expected. This heat was calculated to mark their prosperity, as was everything else about their splendid residence. In the lengthening shadows of this November day this glowed exuberantly in the sheen that bounced from its gold fixtures and newly frescoed walls; its fabulous French tapestries and rich carpets which had been recently carried along the Silk Route to rich and powerful

Venice and then straight to the palazzo of the rich and powerful
Veniers. Even at twelve, Ginevra was shrewd enough to know
that their wealth—the very *Europeanness* of it—was one of
the reasons that Lord Olivier had inclined towards their family.
Others might think it was because Luciano was first cousin to
Antonio Venier, the head of Venice's ruling oligarchy, but
Ginevra thought she knew better. She had watched as Olivier,
wealthy himself, looked about at the evident signs of their
riches. She had seen him as he touched and smelled and breathed
in the atmosphere of their palazzo. He was a famous man
and powerful in his own right. Under his leadership the Gold
Company, that legendary mercenary army which had been
founded by his English brother-in-law, Belden of Harnoncourt,
had grown from strength to strength until now almost the whole
northeast of Italy was under its protection. But Olivier's legend
had not been made in Europe. It had been built in the East, on
foreign battlefields and in the prisons of the Sultan Bayezid.
He had been away for a very long time and terrible things had
happened both to him and to his family in his absence. It was
true that the troubadours sang of his exploits—and yet when
they did, tragedy chorused through their songs like a dirge.

Now he was reluctant to leave the comfort of the Venier
home and he let this reluctance show upon his face as he rose.

"I had best start my journey back to Belvedere before vespers
sound," he said. "I have a hard ride before me. My sister's
note said also that an emissary from our kinsman, the Duke of
Burgundy, accompanies my ward and that he brings a message
from his liege lord. And, of course, the nursery must be seen
to. The Lady Julian will have need of it."

"Nursery, indeed," snapped Claudia Venier once her husband and his guest were safely out of hearing. " 'Tis beyond
imagining what fools men be. Why, that girl Julian must be
well over twenty now and she should have been long married,
had not even the combined forces of the Harnoncourts and the

Ducci Montaldos proved vain in finding a husband for their little infidel foundling.''

"Julian is not an infidel, she is schismatic." The Lady Domiziana corrected her mother shortly, as she was wont to do. "She is Christian. It is said she was born in Constantinople after her mother's escape. Constantinople remains under the Lord Jesus, if not under his pope. But Aalyne must have already been pregnant when she fled. Julian was her protection. It is against decency to burn a carrying woman—even when that woman is a witch."

"Infidel or schismatic, what does it matter?" her mother retorted. She was so distraught that she had momentarily forgotten that her two youngest daughters, Luisa and Ginevra, were still in the room and all ears to hear about the notorious Aalyne de Lione. At this moment, Claudia cared nothing for them and their maidenly sensibilities. Her life had shriveled to the fervent wish that Domiziana's official engagement to Count Olivier be quickly and irrevocably announced. Sometimes she was convinced that she breathed only for this. And with reason. That very morning as the Ladies of the Venier had walked through the open market, two old crones had dared to give them the sign against the evil eye. It seemed that everyone was doing it. Domiziana, though still beautiful at twenty-six, had already buried two husbands and a betrothed—and worse, had produced no living child throughout all of this activity. The people of Venice were beginning to whisper that she was cursed and, thus, her family with her.

If anything, their real blight was that they had no sons to help them stoke the fame of the noble name they bore—and blazoned forth with much less money than even the best of their friends might suspect. The Veniers were wealthy but their wealth was new and had been brought in along the Silk Route. Venice was not as snobbish as the rest of Italy when it came to trade, but like most cities which had direct dealings with the vagaries and rampages of the sea, it was mightily superstitious. Advantageous matches were still needed for Luisa and Ginevra.

Luciano, usually the most indulgent of fathers, had already hinted that if this proposed marriage did not take place soon, Domiziana's discreet retirement to a convent might be the best solution for them all. But Claudia could not accept this. The very idea of her beautiful daughter packed off and buried alive in some faraway exile, of Domiziana subject to penances and rough clothing, was more than Claudia could bear. No, she could not bear it.

And she would not.

"What does it matter if she is an infidel or a schismatic?" Claudia repeated. "With that mother, with that lineage, she is hell-bound no matter what she calls herself. Besides that, she's ugly and bad-natured. Not a trace of laughter anywhere about her. She was already like that when Olivier brought her back with him from the East and she's more than likely grown into an evil-looking, darkling woman. Especially since she did her maturing in England." Claudia's voice made 'England' sound like 'hell.' "Bad natured and serious. Why, I've *never* seen her smile. They say the Countess Francesca is quite fond of her—but then everyone knows that Francesca of Harnoncourt is a saint. As you would be, too, if you had had Blanche de Montfort for your mother. Still, it's a wonder that neither your betrothed nor his brother-in-law has seen fit to place her in a convent long before this."

"Olivier is not yet my betrothed," Domiziana replied. She, too, had seen the two peasant women in the market that day: she had seen the way they had shrunk from her. They had been dirty, smelly, and foul and yet they had looked down on *her*, a Lady of the Venier, a niece of the Doge. She reached under her edge of the tapestry and pulled forth a small, filigreed-gold looking glass. Ginevra watched as her sister stared at her reflection, at the blond hair that was only now beginning its fade, at the cheeks that needed rubbing with currant juice to help in their blooming, at the long lines that had started to etch their way from her nose and along the sides of her mouth, at the whisper of webbing that already framed her winter-gray eyes. She raised long, jeweled fingers to her throat and stared at herself impassively.

"A convent," her mother repeated querulously. "I've no idea why they've not tried a convent."

Domiziana glanced up from the mirror, her face shrouded in the cold look which her own family knew quite well but which Olivier had never seen. "They tried," she answered. "But Julian would not hear of it. She has no use for the veil."

Olivier Ducci Montaldo urged his horse to a gallop as he crossed through the marshy peninsula that separated the Veneto from the rest of the Italian mainland. Behind him an honor guard of ten of his best soldiers—therefore the best that the Gold Company had to offer—easily kept the pace he set them. On his own, he would have set off to Belvedere with just one man as escort, but Luciano would not hear of it. The Veniers worried for his safety, and although Olivier knew theirs to be a solicitude not entirely devoid of a certain selfish interest, still he allowed himself the luxury of hearkening to their worry. He had been away for a long time and held captive in a place where no one—or almost no one—cared for his safety, and the thought that now someone did was calculated to warm him.

How young he'd been when he had first so carelessly ridden away from Belvedere—young and heedless. Barely twenty then, but headstrong and determined to be away from Tuscany and home. He had gone off happily to join forces with an unknown French prince against an equally unknown but encroaching infidel. Leaving his peace behind him. Because that was just what he had done. After the first prince there had been another, and another infidel. Like many of the noble knights he knew, he found himself constitutionally unable to resist the combination. War was a drug, strong as myrrh; he'd reached for it greedily with his hands and his sword and his heart. He'd had ten years of addiction before he'd been captured and sent to die a slow death in Bayezid's prisons while at first his whole family and then—after the deaths—his mother and sister alone slaved in vain to raise his outrageous ransom. Olivier had thought himself doomed to languish forever, when suddenly his illustrious brother-in-law, Belden d'Harnoncourt, arrived to lead him to freedom. With Aalyne's help, of course, and with Julian's. The bitterness he still felt about those years shocked him—as it always did—and he spurred his horse ahead to escape it. But he could never get quite far enough.

Aalyne got what she wanted. I took her daughter. She's been paid in full. Yet he sometimes wondered, especially as he rode down lonely, night-drenched roads like this one, if he would ever be able to pay that debt in full. If he would ever be truly free.

But he would not allow himself the luxury of those thoughts now. His way might lead back towards Belvedere, but his shrewd eyes narrowed as his mind moved towards a closer object. A note had been attached to the parchment from his sister Francesca and this addition had been sealed with the colors of a man whom Olivier did not know, but of whom he had heard. Indeed, there were few in Christendom, or beyond, who had not heard of Sir Gatien de la Marche.

Since the Battle of Poitiers in 1356, England and France had been openly kicking at each other's wounds in a continuous war that seemed destined to drag into the next century. That under these circumstances the Duke of Burgundy should send his most famous knight through half of civilized Europe with an appeal to the Sire of Harnoncourt in Cornwall, sniffed of trouble. But that Olivier's illustrious brother-in-law should then dispatch de la Marche to Tuscany—and that Sir Gatien would come—reeked of high perturbation indeed! Life had long ago firmly rammed its cynicism into Olivier's spine but he was not one to worry the inevitable into manifestation. He knew that, given time enough, the important questions had a way of answering themselves. Still, he thought, it might not hurt to get a considered impression of the man before they actually met. If nothing else, the Burgundian knight's arrival might bespeak peril for Venice. And when mighty Venice—with her strategic port and her rich trading routes and her strong but embattled connections to the East—was in jeopardy, she had a tendency to pull the rest of Italy into danger with her.

"Cristiano!"

He called over his shoulder and instantly Cristiano of Salerno, his second-in-command, was at his side. The Italian was a huge man, dark and threatening, his face disfigured by some long-ago sword in some long-ago war. But he was good and capable, an excellent lieutenant. Cristiano had squired under Olivier's father, the Old Count: he had ridden beside his brother-in-law, Belden of Harnoncourt, and now he had returned to serve once again beneath the crisp turquoise-and-white flag of the Ducci Montaldo. Cristiano had been at Belvedere for the arrival of Gatien de la Marche, and he had immediately taken it upon himself to carry Francesca's letter to Venice. He was no fool.

"What did you think of the Knight de la Marche?"

Cristiano shrugged, a brief movement in the dark. "He is French." Silence. "He is a well set man. Light hair, gray eyes. Looks younger than he should to have made the reputation he has. And his is a good reputation—for a Frenchman." Cristiano had his doubts about the French and had no hesitancy in voicing them even though Olivier Ducci Montaldo, through his mother, was half-French and cousin to the Duke of Burgundy. "But a good enough man. Doesn't talk much. Keeps company mainly with himself and with the few other Burgundians he brought with him. Not too fond of himself, the way the French seem to be. Of course, he's here to ask for your aid so it behooves him to be upon his best behavior." Cristiano paused. "The Duke of Burgundy will need your help if he hopes to mount this Crusade."

Olivier said nothing. But of course he knew that Gatien de la Marche came on a mission of Crusade. He had known that even before reading Francesca's letter, at least the part of it that he had not shared with the Veniers.

"Who hasn't heard the rumors?" Cristiano continued. "I

think even the milking maids in the village know what's sparked this knight's coming. They call the Sultan Bayezid 'Lightning' and say the Ottoman have dared their way through half of Eastern Europe until now they bang at the Balkan gates. And once they are entrenched that far into Europe—well, there is nothing that will keep them from the rest. You know Bayezid, don't you, Count? Know him personally?''

"Yes, I know him,'' Olivier replied.

"Then you'll know that his is not an idle threat. At least Sir Gatien doesn't take it as such. Bayezid is bringing trouble with him from the East. The priests are upset because he converts people to his religion. The princes are angry because they are always itching to fight. The desire for conquest flows through their veins with the force of lifeblood. And they will fight anyone who presents himself—as long as there is gain involved.''

He paused and for a moment there was only the hypnotic beating of hooves against packed earth and the huddled sounds of the dreaming forest that surrounded them. But for an instant, Olivier thought he heard something. A murmur of hooves further off in the trees that did not quite move with their rhythm. He felt a tightening at the nape of his neck. Though morning was dawning, it was still too dark to make anything out. He looked behind him at the reddening sky, but saw nothing.

When Cristiano spoke again it was in a voice that had grown low and secretive. "They say he has garrisoned the fortress of Nicopolis. You know that city as well, don't you? Isn't it where you met the Lady Julian?''

My mother. Your promise.

"Yes, I met her there. At Nicopolis.'' Olivier was surprised the word had not caught in his throat.

It was useless to try to think about anything else now, and he knew it. Olivier had no intention of going back to the East, no intention of engaging his army with that of Bayezid just because the Duke of Burgundy willed it. The Gold Company's duty was to Venice, not to France. *But if Bayezid takes the*

Balkans . . . If he threatens Venice's trade routes up the Danube and through the Dardanelles. . . .

"No, I've had enough of it." Olivier heard the words in his own voice but a stranger might just as well have spoken them. He urged his horse forward. He would not look back. He'd buried the past behind him. Sealed it there with his blood.

Olivier reached up to touch the place where Domiziana had kissed him good-bye as they crossed near Venice's Bridge of Sighs, touched it as he would a talisman. "Domiziana." He said her name aloud, not like Julian's name that he kept buried deep, deep within him in parts of his soul that he would rather forget.

Again he heard the muffled sound of hoofbeats—distinct this time. He could make out only a lone horse—and he frowned.

"Strange."

"Because," Cristiano continued, "though the Knight de la Marche is suave and even a bit reticent, despite himself he shows a particular interest in the fortress of Nicopolis—almost as much interest as he shows in the Lady Julian."

Cristiano heard a sharp intake of breath. He shifted in his saddle to face Olivier once again and hear what his Lord would say to this interesting piece of information about his ward. And as he did, his eyes bulged wide in horror. Olivier had slumped forward. The black shaft of an arrow stuck from his shoulder and stood out in relief in the faint light of the new day.

"It is only a glamour. It cannot touch me, it cannot hurt me unless I allow it to. It is only an enchantment," Julian whispered as she pressed her nose against the leaded pane of the donjon's window. Below her the fertile hills of Tuscany heaved languidly towards heaven, ready to enchant any unwary soul that might find itself wandering upon them. They looked merry and mischievous even while the trees upon them shivered in the wind that whistled through this cold winter's day. Lovers they were— Tuscany and Heaven.

But Julian was a Wise Woman. And she knew that she was open to the magic of this place, and therefore must be careful of it and of everything that formed part of it. Throughout all Europe people talked of Belvedere and of its bewitchments; minstrels sang its legends. Everyone knew that the castle of the Ducci Montaldo was enchanted and that its memories could bind. They whispered of the ghost of Count Piero and his three tragically dead sons who called out to random strangers along the road and welcomed them—and then would not let them go. Julian herself had felt it call to her as she had ridden with the Knight de la Marche on their long journey from the severe coast of England toward this land of fragrant cypress and undulating Mediterranean pine. Despite herself she had remembered what Aalyne had taught her. Julian had looked around her, watched the trees and learned from them. *We are evergreen,* the Tuscan trees had whispered. *We remain bright with the promise of springtime even when the skies above us spit forth winter's snow.* Julian had thought their lesson scant comfort at the time and now that she was actually at Belvedere—actually at the place to which she had fought so hard to return—she thought it even less so.

The priest beside her shook his head, calling her back from the hills to the laboratory once again. Calling her back to her purpose. Julian could see his eyes twinkling beside hers, reflecting back at her from the newly gleaming glass of the donjon's window. Glass that she had cleaned with her own hands.

"Are you not happy to be back at Belvedere?" Father Gasca de Loran chided. "For so many years it was your home."

Not my *home,* Julian thought savagely. *Never* my *home.*

After the dark years, this room, hidden away in the highest reaches of the largest donjon, had been filled with fought-for love and hard-won happiness. Ghostly laughter echoed all around her. Francesca with her husband. The cooing of their two children, the first of the longed-for Harnoncourt boys who had been born here. Francesca's mother, Blanche, flirting with

her beaux. Even the servants always happy, always pregnant.
But if you were never really part of all that love and laughter
and yet had to sit while it buzzed and circled all around you
. . . Yet, sometimes Julian would look in Olivier's eyes, would
read his carefully passive face and think that perhaps he had
felt the same way about the laboratory and that was the reason
he had left it to molder away on its own. That he, too, had felt
left out and estranged. But then maybe she was wrong. Olivier
was different. Probably he had always been different. He did
not share the family passion for alchemy and science. He had
not spent his time in prison studying as Belden of Harnoncourt
had—or as she herself had, for that matter. He had seen nothing
good about the East. From the first day he was captured, Olivier
had lived only to escape.

But she couldn't say this aloud to this kindly priest. Padre
Gasca would never have understood what she meant. He knew
what the Ducci Montaldos had done for her. He knew the love
they'd shown her. Olivier, Francesca, even Belden d'Harnoncourt. Always beside her, always helping her.

And yet. . . .

"I meant the laboratory," she said, smiling through the lie.
"I'd forgotten what a mess it had been left in."

"Ah, yes, the laboratory," echoed Gasca. He, too, turned
from the hills back toward the tower room that encircled them.
"It is a bit of a catastrophe. Obviously it was overlooked in
the general restoration."

"But Olivier's hand has not reached up the stone stairs of
the east donjon," she said to the priest, sensing his unease and
wanting to soothe him. "For some reason or other my guardian's industry did not extend itself to the old laboratory."

It had been six years since she had last seen this sky-high
room. Six years since Belden of Harnoncourt, heeding the call
of his liege lord, Richard II, Plantagenet, had left the Gold
Company, his famous mercenary army, in the capable hands
of his brother-in-law, Olivier Ducci Montaldo, and had returned
with his young family to England to put down yet another

Scottish rebellion. It had been six years since Julian had last
seen her beautiful, turquoise-eyed guardian. Six years since she
had planted a chaste kiss of farewell upon his cheek. But in
all these six years she had not passed six hours straight without
thinking of him.

''Indeed,'' she repeated. ''This part was obviously forgotten.''

The rest of the castle had been so restored and refurbished
and gilded and polished that Padre Gasca, who had once stood
trial at the Papal Court of Avignon and thus was no stranger
to luxury and the pleasures obtainable with a goodly supply of
gold, had silently gasped as its heavy oak doors swung open
before them. And he knew that he had not been alone in his
assessment. Trained as he was in observation, he had seen
Julian's small face, light with wonder, and the speculative
narrowing of Gatien de la Marche's shrewd eyes. It was certainly obvious to anyone that under Olivier's lordship the fortunes of the Ducci Montaldo were once again experiencing a
sharp rise. There was a gleam and smell about his castle that
only riches could afford. But the fact that the new count had
hunted down and brought back every tapestry, every silver
vase, even every piece of everyday pewter that his family had
sold while he was in prison, was obvious to Gasca alone. Of
the three of them, he was the only one to have known Belvedere
in its glory. Now once again, in their former places of pride,
hung the unicorn tapestry, the beaten silver bowls and pitchers
Olivier's mother had brought with her as part of her dowry
from France, the carpets from Provence, the long chests of
fragrant cedar wood. All returned, all exactly placed. Gasca
felt his blood chill. Knowing the Ducci Montaldo history, and
especially Olivier's part in it, he found the restoration of Belvedere quite troubling.

Now Gasca nodded, smiling. His walnut-colored eyes lighted
once again. For of course, this was obviously true, even to him.
The east donjon, home of the Old Count's laboratory, had been
left to shrivel into decay, its skulls to rot, its parchments to

molder, its memories to be hidden away. The collection of
Etruscan coins and pottery shards found and carefully hung
upon its walls by the five Ducci Montaldo children so very
long ago while the old priest and the Old Count stood by
laughing, had been left to fall off and shatter into the dust.
Julian had never known the others, but if she listened and held
her breath, if she ceased to worry and to think, and especially
if the old priest and his powers were with her, she could hear
them still. She could go into his heart and bring them to life
with the love she found here. Olivier, Piero Two, Luca, Marco,
Francesca. She could bring them back to life and their father
with them—their father who had been Gasca's great friend.

"I can see them all," he had whispered to Julian when
she had first returned. "Five children then—and now but two
remaining."

Francesca, far away in England—and Olivier, moving closer
with each passing minute.

He glanced over at Julian as she dipped her hands into a pail
of hot water and started earnestly scrubbing. She had grown
into a beauty, little Julian, though no one would have suspected
it when first she'd come from the East. She still had the same
sun-touched skin and clear green eyes. Beneath her shapeless,
soiled white apron he knew her woman's body curved well—
forgetting his vows and the silly superstitions that had been
drummed into him, he had watched her movements with a
trained, scientific eye. Julian had indeed become a beautiful
woman. Olivier would not fail to notice this. Her dark hair was
pulled back in one long plait that reached to the small of her
back. She wore no wimple, and this made the little priest just
vaguely uneasy. Olivier had grown conservative lately, as rich
men do. He might not like the way Julian had been trained,
the freedom she was used to. He might try to change her.

"I think we could do with a maid," said Gasca mildly,
glancing up at the cobwebs and the dust and the streaks of
mildew on the graying walls. "There must be someone free to

help. What about that girl the bailiff gave to serve you? Surely she could be doing her share.''

''You mean Sabata? She would be helping—she wanted to. I sent her down to the village. She was worried about her young brother. He's got a wet cough, she said, and it's early in the year for that. We're not yet even to St. Martin's Day and the new wine and the chestnuts.''

''The child must have a mother. She shouldn't have left you alone.''

''*She* didn't leave me. I insisted that she go.''

But it was obvious that Gasca would not be so easily placated. ''Still, it isn't proper that a lady of the house should soak her hands in sheep fat soap,'' he insisted.

''I'm not the lady of the house,'' said Julian, smiling up at him as she plunged her hands into the scalding water. ''And it is the least I can do.''

''Why don't you go to see to the brother? With your knowledge, you could help with the cough. Your mother was good with herbs. And we are not so far from France: the climate is near to what she would have grown her plants in. You can probably find what you need here. Why don't you go to the village to see what's about? Take the herbs. You might help.''

Suddenly a late ray of sunlight flashed through the window, catching Julian in its beam.

''No, no,'' she said, too quickly. Sunlight haloed her dark hair and the lie was all about them, twitching in its morning gleam. ''I know nothing of those matters. I know nothing of witch ways.''

''They aren't witch ways,'' replied Gasca mildly. ''This is healing. This is helping. There's a difference.''

''I have no knowledge,'' Julian repeated.

Behind her, Gasca looked up, startled. He held his peace but his mind flew to the six-pointed gold amulet that hung heavily from Julian's fair throat. He had known Aalyne, had met her once when his search for knowledge took him east. He thought of the rumors. He thought of the Magdalene. And he longed to cross himself.

"Besides," said Julian easily, "you are the learned man with herbs. Why, you were so famous—or infamous—for your knowledge of alchemy that the pope himself placed you under interdict."

"But that was long ago," cried Gasca, deciding to take her bait and lay his own questions aside. "Now I have been rehabilitated—at least by the Pope in Rome, the ally of the Church in England during this conflict which I believe will see me into my grave. In any event it was King Richard himself who appointed me to my seat at Oxford. Although whether this was for my merit or a spite against the French pope who had censored me—well, only heaven can give the sure answer to this bewilderment," He rolled his eyes upward with exaggerated piety.

"As though you cared." Julian laughed. "In addition to his royal pardon, the king gave you a post and a laboratory and the combination of these two conveniences has made up for many a past slight. . . .

"More than made up for," corrected Gasca.

". . . So that now even the monks at San Marco call you for consultation."

"And lucky they are to have me after their recent bad behavior," replied Gasca, idly scratching at his tonsure as he glanced through a sheaf of dusty parchments. "But their monastery is close by, not more than two hours away on a lively donkey. The food there is always good and fulsome and the wine even more so. I will be journeying in their direction tomorrow—as soon as I've had the chance to talk with Count Olivier."

Julian smiled as Padre Gasca bustled about among the dust and ruins. His hands automatically searched for parchments he had left behind and missed in the years they had spent in England. Life had gone well with him lately. Gone was the past, gone were his troubles in it.

"We'll have everything in order in no time," she said, looking around and matching his light tone. "We promised Francesca. She wants these things carted to England for Michael, her second son. She thinks he has a talent."

"As he does," the priest said, his eyes twinkling with good humor.

Julian lifted a jar that barely showed the movements of a preserved toad within its murky liquid. The toad's eyes stared back at her. One of them winked. She could have sworn to it. "We were lucky enough that the maids—in three, and crossing themselves at every bend of the staircase—agreed to carry the buckets and cleaning carts. And I've a feeling more than a few small coins will have to change hands before we find a man willing to carry them back down again. No one within three communes will voluntarily venture into the Ducci Montaldo laboratory. They've heard too many stories."

"Perhaps the Knight de la Marche will lend us one of his men," said Gasca innocently. "Or perhaps he'll even do the honors himself."

Julian looked up, astonished. "Gatien de la Marche would never stoop to such a thing. He is one of the First Knights of France, and a Burgundian to boot. They are noted for their pride."

"True, the Burgundians are notorious for their pride," replied Gasca. "But I've a feeling the great Knight de la Marche would stoop to help us—if you asked him."

He saw Julian's astonished face and the slow blush that sent peaches to her cheeks. She had a charming blush, Gasca decided. He wanted to see more of it. "I think he may have an interest in you. He is an unmarried man as well as noble and famous. You could do worse."

For an instant he was certain he saw fear skitter across Julian's face. "Impossible," she said before she turned quickly away from him. "He but sees a friend in me. Someone who knows something of these strange Tuscan ways." Gasca, noting the set look upon her face, decided not to beg the question.

And for a while this was enough. They worked well together.

Julian seeing to the heavy chores, the scrubbing and the scouring and the sorting of moulds and foul-smelling elixirs and tisanes: he looking at the manuscripts that had been left behind, easily distracted by them, and smiling. Occasionally he would say, "When the Old Count was alive . . ." Or "With Francesca and Belden we did this, ..." but mainly there was just a companionable silence. And after the mention of Gatien de la Marche, Julian was grateful for this moment of peaceful friendship and common purpose.

Because she was thinking of Olivier, it was all she could do to rein in her excitement. No one had told her that he approached, but she had known it, she had felt it. And when he came . . . When she spoke to him . . . Once he realized . . . She'd spent years watching for this miracle, years praying through her own fears that they would go back to Nicopolis. That they would find Aalyne—and that for once in her life strong-willed Aalyne would be made to tell the truth about herself and about Julian's father—and about the bond that had brought them together. But she knew that she must hide these thoughts from Padre Gasca. He had the gift. She sensed it in him. And he would know.

They worked on in silence. First, things got worse. Covered in dust there had at least been a sort of magic order to the room, a look of enchantment. Now that the laboratory was washed with water and pig-fat soap, it seemed dirty and foul. Hidden secrets that the peasants knew to avoid. But then, very slowly, almost miraculously, its appearance changed and got better. Julian could see traces of the room she remembered with such mixed feelings; she could almost hear the laughter in it once again. Beneath her touch the dozen mirrors that Belden of Harnoncourt had placed about so that his wife could find a remedy for her freckles—something that brought out their shared laughter—began to wink back at her from their niches on the wall.

Though not, she thought wryly, with the cheerfulness with which they had winked back at Francesca. Julian was a different woman. Darker of hair, darker of skin. Even the blue of her eyes was so shadowed that sometimes and in some lights, it seemed almost black. Her eyes startled people and she knew this. "Like shards of broken glass," Olivier had once said to her. Julian knew that she had none of Francesca's beckoning brightness. At best she sensed that she was cold and wintry. Far from what a man would want—or might even need.

"I can't help my eyes," she said. "I can't help what's happened. I can't help my face."

She couldn't help her looks. Couldn't help the eyes that life had given her. Couldn't help what they had seen. She turned again to the windows, even though they were the first things she had cleaned. She wiped away at imaginary smears, used her cloth to fight against non-existent dust. Anything to get her mind away from that room and the happiness that she had seen there, but of which she had played no part.

They were working like that when the cheering started. "The Count, the Count!"

Julian rushed to the windows, her heart hammering.

She forgot all about Padre Gasca in her excitement. She forgot that she mustn't let this clever man read her thoughts.

Below her the castle people were waving and shouting. The portcullis was raised and the drawbridge lowered. The flags were hoisted in welcome. She squinted forward and that's when she saw them. Not riding hell for leather as Belden of Harnoncourt had, but leisurely, even reluctantly coming on. Julian saw this and she frowned as she squinted through the glass. But then it didn't matter *how* he came but *that* he came, because she had glimpsed the black-and-gold banners of the Gold Company and over them, as they were always now placed, waved the bright turquoise-and-white flags of the Ducci Montaldo. Touched and brought alive by the wind.

Julian blinked once, twice, and then without her knowing it a brilliant smile transformed her, blushed her cheeks with roses, and turned her eyes into gems.

" 'Tis Olivier," she said breathlessly, dropping the rag she had been using. Not noticing it. " 'Tis my guardian returned."

She did not wait for a reply. She turned and ran down, her soft leather shoes barely touching the hard, high stairs that led from the donjon down into the main body of the castle of the Counts of the Ducci Montaldo. Her apron on, her face smudged, her hair loose from its ribbons, sheeting out behind her, wild and free.

"Olivier," she cried. It never even entered her mind that her guardian might not be glad to see her.

CHAPTER TWO

Despite the pain that roiled up from his wounded shoulder, Olivier smiled as he guided his powerful destrier to a stop within the inner curtain of his castle walls. Behind him the great portcullis, newly oiled and with its brass hinges shining, clanged shut behind him, closing him in. Pages resplendent in bright winter silk bounded up to relieve the knights of their horses.

Olivier's household had been waiting for him and now they bowed and curtsied; the women wore crisp, spotless aprons, the men new livery fashioned to the famous Ducci Montaldo colors of turquoise and white. He noticed with a certain satisfaction that their clothes were free from stains and the telltale signs of mending. They looked just as they had looked when he had ridden away to his first crusade. Since his return, he had made sure that all who worked for the Ducci Montaldo ate fresh meat every Sunday and that they could hold up their heads and strut through Tuscany's winding byways now that the ancient house of the Ducci Montaldo was known throughout Italy for being on the rise once again. Olivier knew that they enjoyed the new prosperity as much as he did. They had told him so themselves.

It was a miracle, the peasants said, a resurrection. And they crossed themselves, remembering the plague and the deaths and the bad times that were all over now. Finished and done with.

Now, at last, they were happy. Olivier could read this happiness on their faces as he climbed down from his silk-skirted horse, as he handed the gold-shot reins to his squire and peeled off his soft kid riding gloves. He winced with the effort of it. Cristiano had dug the arrow from his shoulder, but the wound had got dirty from the road and there had been no way of cleaning it properly, and no medicine. But Padre Gasca waited for them at Belvedere and Cristiano had thought it best to leave further ministrations to the priest—a man well versed in the healing arts—and to the Lady Julian. It was taken for granted that Julian could help.

And there was also the disquieting fact that they had no idea who had shot at Olivier, or why. Not that the Lord of the Ducci Montaldo did not have enemies; any man in his position would have many. But his attacker had been a lone rider, bold enough and skilled enough to strike at first light. Someone who had disappeared into the shadows before Olivier's trained soldiers could track him. A man desperate enough—or well paid enough—to risk his own life in order to take that of a warrior who rode surrounded by his men. At least a partial puzzle this, and one that Olivier decided to keep to himself until more pieces came to light. He had warned his men to silence and he himself would tell no one else. Only Gasca—and, of course, Julian. For some reason he knew that she must be told as well.

His shoulder pained terribly but his smile held as he looked about the inner curtain of his fortress—at the banners and the brightly skirted horses, at the crisp list field and the sparkling new quatrain, at the last of the blooming geraniums as they shot their blood color into the morning mist. He called cheerful greetings to his people as he searched for the unknown face of Gatien de la Marche.

"Do you think the French are behind this?" Cristiano had asked as he straightened up from pulling out the arrow and wiped his bloody hands on a rag. It was well known throughout the Gold Company that the army's second-in-command put little faith in Gallic good intentions. Not after having served under the very English Belden of Harnoncourt. But Olivier, white-faced and in pain, had shaken his head. His soldier's brain could think of no reason why the Burgundians should attack him—yet.

"Welcome!" Olivier looked up to see his bailiff, Giuseppe Motta, lumbering towards him, one of his innumerable sons tucked against his ample hip. He put the child down gently before turning to his lord. "Welcome to Belvedere! Welcome home!"

"Yes, home," Olivier repeated, and his smile broadened.

The two of them strode through the courtyard, the bailiff struggling to keep up. Belvedere teemed with activity. At least fifty men had ridden in with Gatien de la Marche, Olivier thought shrewdly. They milled about in small groups watching him, and he could see the green-and-deep-red banner of the Dukes of Burgundy flying from the guesthouse. All was in order and he was happy to see that Belvedere, even with this many warriors added to its garrison, still functioned well. Servants were already busy raking at the gravel which had been disturbed by the arrival of the lord and his men.

Fifty men, Olivier thought. At least. There were enough of them to fill all Europe with gossip and he was determined that these knights of France would take the tale of his family's recuperated fortunes back to his mother's homeland. Troubadours would sing new ballads about the Ducci Montaldo and their tunes would be happy ones. Olivier had worked hard and suffered much to ensure that this would be so.

He turned to his puffing bailiff. "And where is my guest? Where is Sir Gatien?"

It was then that Olivier heard the high, light peal of a woman's laughter. The sound was something he had not been expecting and his hand automatically fled to the jeweled hilt of his sword—even though he was within his own castle, even though he was home. He spun towards the sound, his hand still on his weapon, his eyes widening as he stared at the two people moving towards him. This time they laughed together and for the oddest reason Olivier felt a stab of jealousy of their happiness, at the chaste intimacy of it. He was sure they had been told of his coming and, like everyone else, they were seeking him. But he was outside the circle of their shared laughter. He stood for a moment in Belvedere's shadow as he watched the two of them draw near.

The French soldiers parted a way before the couple and Olivier knew that the knight must be Sir Gatien and that the woman beside him must be his lady wife. Of course he had heard of the Knight de la Marche. Who in Christendom hadn't? He was as famous in France as Belden of Harnoncourt was in England. With the Sire de Coucy and the Comte d'Eu he was considered one of the pillars of French chivalry. His family was splendid. He was related to the King of France, as was Olivier himself.

But he's young, Olivier thought, staring at the tall, slim figure before him. He felt the full weight of his own five-and-thirty years. *Young to have such a famous history.* And yet a reputation had been made and a good one. His gaze traveled over the Burgundian, sizing him up. The knight's brown suede tunic was expensively cut and trimmed with gold. It matched the deep, rich color of his eyes and contrasted with the thick curl of his blond hair. His golden spurs jingled as he walked forward. In spite of his fame, there was something earthy and solid about Gatien de la Marche. His would have been a handsome face had not a deep scar jagged its way along the left side of it, cutting down from his eyebrow to his jaw. Olivier wondered, for an instant, how he had come upon such a deep disfigurement.

Then, the woman made some slight movement and Olivier found his attention drawn to her.

She was beautiful, very beautiful, though at first he was quite certain that he had never seen her before. He allowed himself to stand silently for a moment longer, watching her. He took in the swift glint of a pair of large, shaded eyes, the sudden music of her laughter, the long, straight sweep of hair. It was the rich color of birch bark and fell in one long wave to below her waist. Oddly, Olivier thought that he might give anything to run his hands through the fine gloss of that hair, and as he did he forgot the low throb of his shoulder for an instant and his fingers loosed their grasp on his sword. But then as he watched, transfixed and still unnoticed in the shadow, he saw the man lean forward to whisper something in the woman's ear and then he heard again the sound of their laughter. The woman threw her head back, lost in the merriment, and it was then that Olivier saw the small, six-pointed amulet that glittered at her neck. He recognized the Maltese Star.

And he recognized his ward. He told himself that he might not have known her without the aid of the little golden trinket, but perhaps he would have. Certainly, though she looked happy, the basic solemnity of her face had not changed. Nor had the guarded look within it. And she still possessed the wonder of those blue eyes, and small-boned structure, and the truly incredible cascade of her hair. No, Julian's essence hadn't changed, he realized, but she had ripened into it. She was most definitely no longer a child; and this was something for which the Count of the Ducci Montaldo was not prepared.

Julian, he whispered. *How beautiful you have become.*

They were so close now that she must have heard his words because she turned to him and smiled her radiant smile. He watched her face light with welcome, watched as she turned away from the other knight and rushed towards him.

"Oh, look, Sir Gatien, he's here!" She flung the words at the Duke of Burgundy's grand emissary as she rushed past him to fling herself at her guardian and pressed against him with the thoughts of a child enclosed within a woman's body.

Olivier's arms went around her and the soft fragrance of that glossy hair filled his nostrils and pricked at his memory. The high, light, summer scent of deep violets surrounded her, just as it always had as long as he had known her. It was a perfume he had grown accustomed to as they had made their perilous way from Nicopolis to the safety of Belvedere. She had snuggled against him in the dark then, alone and frightened, and he had told her tales of the West. Told her stories of her own country, France, and of England and Italy. But he had spoken most of Tuscany, which was to be his home again—*their* home, because he was responsible for her. She was his ward. He had filled her imagination with the thought of his castle, had told her it would be a bright and welcoming haven from which they need never depart. But, of course they had departed from it— she to England with Francesca and he, once more, to his warrior's life.

"Julian?" he whispered again, in astonishment this time, holding her close for just an instant longer. Then he became aware that silence had fallen all around him; he felt Gatien de la Marche move just a little closer. Protectively closer, as though, very subtly, he was forcing Olivier to turn to him.

My Lord Olivier," Gatien said as he bowed pleasantly.

"And my Lord de la Marche."

The spell broke and Olivier became suddenly aware that his arms held a grown woman, not a child, and that he himself was a man who was nearly betrothed.

"Julian!" His voice was sharp, the voice of one used to being obeyed. It echoed through the courtyard. "Have you forgotten yourself!" The feel of her had upset him—that and the memories that floated back to him on the wave of her violet scent. "You've lost your veil. You are dirty. You are not fit to be presented to Sir Gatien."

At first she seemed not to understand him. She continued looking up at him, her strange, dark eyes shining with happiness and with hope. "But Gatien has seen me looking much worse than this," she said. "We were on the road two weeks in coming here. And it rained. The one thing France and England share in common is their horrible weather. We slogged through black mud 'til Hastings and then through brown mud after reaching Calais. Only in Italy have we see the sun shine." She smiled over at the Burgundian knight for confirmation.

"He may have seen you in any number of conditions before," Olivier said, very softly. "But he's not seen you like this here, and you will dress as the lady you are under my roof. Now go to your chamber and await my summons. Don't come down again until you can act in a way and dress in a manner suitable to your station as a ward of the Ducci Montaldo." He laid special emphasis upon the word 'ward'.

Julian said nothing but he saw the high color of her cheeks gradually fade as she pulled away from him. First one step back, then two. She might just as easily have put the list field between them. Shocked silence prevailed, though no one was more shocked or more silent than the Count of the Ducci Montaldo himself. He couldn't for the life of him understand why he had been so harsh. As soon as the words escaped him, he wanted to pull them back. But it had always been this way when he was with Julian. He wanted to be grateful to her, and generous as well. As long as she stayed away. But when she came near him she brought Nicopolis with her—and for Olivier, Nicopolis had been hell.

Now he promised himself that he would order a new silk for her from Como. Domiziana had taught him that gifts were always appreciated, that they could obtain anything. He would apologize to his ward and make it up to her. Again.

Julian could feel de la Marche's sympathy and could hear the whispers in the minds of the others. She quickly lowered her eyes from her guardian's face and caught a glimpse of her smudged clothing. She saw how red her hands were from their day's work. If her apron and her hands looked like this she could just imagine the horror that her face must be. She had

seen the changes in Belvedere since Olivier's return and she
realized suddenly that a cool demeanor and a clean apron might
matter to him. *Must* matter to him. And she knew that she did
not fit into this new Belvedere which was so ordered and
brightly polished.

"My lord," she said, stepping back even further and making
a reverence. "I beg your pardon."

But the pardons were smoothly taken in hand by Gatien de
la Marche.

"You've no idea how excited the Lady Julian was to return
to Belvedere," he said, speaking to Olivier but glancing over
at Julian. "She talked of nothing but this moment from the
time we left Harnoncourt Hall. I went immediately to escort
her here because I was sure she would be watching for you
from the donjon window—and you were, weren't you, my
lady? Because it gives the best view of the Ridings. She told
me that one is literally able to see the hills kiss the sky from
the castle's top reaches. The Lady Julian talked of nothing else
for all the time of our travelling. She wanted to come back to
Belvedere and to her guardian. She wanted to come home."

"If you will excuse me, my lord Olivier," Julian said, "I
shall await your pleasure. I have letters for you from your
mother and your sister. And one from the Sire of Harnoncourt."
She bowed again, her skirts sweeping the courtyard stones as
she turned to walk away.

Behind her, she heard Gatien de la Marche's pleasant words.
"I know you must want time to freshen after your journey,
Lord Olivier. So with your kind permission, I shall escort your
ward to her chamber—where I'm sure a clean, fresh veil awaits
her."

He strode to Julian, took her arm, and smiled.

No, he's not particularly handsome, Olivier thought. But
then again, when he smiles. . . .

"I've not got a veil. I can't stand them," Julian grumbled
as Gatien led her from the Great Hall and up the cold stone
steps to the *piano nobile,* where she slept. "And he knows

that. He knows that Lord Belden hated to see women trussed up like Christmas goslings. Francesca never had to hide her bound hair at Harnoncourt Hall and neither did I. Lord Belden wouldn't hear of it and so it might as well have been forbidden.''

"Perhaps Lord Olivier believes you to have more of an innate sense of decorum in you than does his gracious but eccentric sister.''

Julian turned on him furiously. "The Lady Francesca is not eccentric just because she takes an interest in scientific matters! Her husband would challenge you to the lists if he ever heard you say so.''

De la Marche threw up his hands in mock submission. "I admire the Lady of the Harnoncourts and I greatly enjoyed my stay at her castle. It is a lively place, to say the least. One never knows when one is opening the chest in one's room whether it will contain the expected linen or the skeletal parts of a human leg that someone had inadvertently forgotten. Or when that horde of little-boy Harnoncourts will decide they need a living quatrain to joust against.''

"You are trying to take my mind from what happened," she said, looking at him sideways. "But there is no need for that. Lord Olivier hates me. I guess I've always known that, from the time my mother forced him to take me away. Once, I thought that things would eventually change, that they *had* changed . . ." Her words trailed off as she let herself be led up the cold stone steps to the noble floor. She felt that she and Sir Gatien had become friends as they traveled through the wintry horrors of England and France toward Belvedere, but she could never tell him how she loved Olivier. How she had always loved him. The kind Burgundian knight would think her a fool to care for someone who was so far above her.

"When my guardian sees me, he sees Nicopolis and the prison and the shame," she continued finally. "And he forgets everything else.''

So far, Gatien de la Marche had managed to keep his own feelings under tight rein, as befitted a knight on a mission from his liege lord to another knight's fortress. But a muscle began to work at the side of his mouth. "Belden of Harnoncourt told me the story. How could Count Olivier possibly forget what your mother did for him and what he owes you? He is a knight, after all, and a great one. This means his life and his sword are plighted to certain ideals. He has committed himself to live a life of integrity and love and honor—and thus he will honor the vow he has made you. He could not live with himself otherwise."

"But you don't know what it was like for him in prison," Julian exclaimed. "He's not like Belden of Harnoncourt. He hates the East and the Saracens: he made no effort to learn anything from them. He lived only to come back to Belvedere. And now he blames himself for what happened to his family. He thinks the deaths and the bad times were somehow his doing. At least Francesca thinks as much and the Lady Blanche does as well. Sir Gatien, please forgive me, but you were born wealthy and you are a First Knight of France. You have no idea what it is to suffer."

"Oh, I think I might," Gatien said. Light from a wall torch illuminated the scar that marked his face from eyebrow to chin.

Julian paused before the door that led to her chamber and stood before it for a moment, staring at the gleam of its newly polished brass catches. She thought of what the little Gatien had told her about the Battle of Mahdia—and what had happened to him afterwards.

"Yes, of course you know," she said quietly, turning back to him. "Of course you know."

But Gatien was smiling his warm, kind smile. "And it is because I know," he continued, "that I can assure you Olivier will maintain his promise. He must. He has no other choice. He gave you his word that he would take you back to Nicopolis to find your mother, and he will do that. You are not to worry about the hows and whens and wherefores. Let these work themselves out in their own time. They will—they always do. You have *my* word on that."

For a very long moment Julian allowed herself to believe him; she allowed herself to bask in the care and the promise that had come from this First Knight of France—the man who had brought her safely to Belvedere again and was fast becoming her true friend. For an instant she was released from her constant fear and she was happy. Genuinely happy. But then Sir Gatien bowed and left and she was alone again in that great, wide castle that was not her home—and yet, was the only home she had. Unless she could rescue her mother. Unless Aalyne could finally be made to tell her the truth. Unless finally—once and for all—she, Julian, would *know*.

How easy it was for a great and powerful man who came from a long line of great and powerful men to speak easy words of comfort to her. She wondered if he would have said the same if he had known her history—had known all of it and not just the marzipan portion that Belden of Harnoncourt had told him. No, she must do something. Somehow or other she must convince her guardian to honor his word. Because if she continued to remain a woman alone and nameless, with no power and no one to help her, she would be forced to tread the path that Aalyne de Lione—the Magdalene—had trod before her. And theirs was a path that had no use for signposts sweetly marked with directions to honor and integrity and love.

CHAPTER THREE

Olivier's feet crunched against new-laid thyme as he walked briskly through Belvedere's vast and lavish interior. Padre Gasca had slipped away on some mysterious errand to the monks at San Marco, so his injury had not been properly cared for. Cristiano had many virtues, but he was no nurse. The wound had been cleaned badly and dressed even worse, and Olivier knew this. But he had refused Cristiano's admonitions to call for the Lady Julian. He had not spoken to her since the day of his return, though he had seen her—often. He had even caught himself watching for her, which is why he had ordered her to take her meals alone in her chamber. He could wait for Padre Gasca. The priest could minister to his wound. It ached, but he had suffered worse. He had been frightened by his own reaction to Julian. He could not trust himself when she was near.

But now the sound of his golden spurs jingling against the fresh herb made him happy, as it had made him happy for the three days since his return. They had been three long—and sometimes boring—days of lavish entertainments and achingly beautiful meals and the early morning rituals of falconry and tournament. Everyone had drunk too much of Tuscany's famous red wine. But not even the lowest scullery maid believed that de la Marche and his warriors had happened by because they wanted to pay a social visit upon the Count of the Ducci Montaldo. Everyone knew that the eating and the singing and the gossip formed part of the elaborate, chivalric ritual that the two knights played as they circled and drew closer to the inevitable topic of the crusade. Even now, as Olivier hurried toward his meeting with Sir Gatien, he did not think of war. Instead he thought of his castle.

No longer did his steps ring out hollowly against the emptiness that had been the Belvedere to which he had returned five years before—a Belvedere that had changed too much in his absence. The only thing that had kept him alive in Bayezid's rat-hole of a prison was the thought of his family and his castle. For he was the eldest son, the heir, and so the expectation of Belvedere and the title had always been his. Not Marco's or Luca's or Piero Two's, but his. And they had been his responsibility.

But he had returned to a barren castle, its walls empty of tapestries, its floors missing their carpets, with no hint left of the gold and silver and laughter that had glowed within it. The only thing that had relieved the starkness of the whitewashed walls were the mirrors which his brother-in-law had placed about as a tease for Olivier's sister, Francesca—Francesca of the freckles and the endless attempts to fade them. But those mirrors had only flashed back to Olivier his own seared face, shocked at the wasteland that had been made of his home in his absence. He had hated those mirrors and done away with them all as soon as he reasonably could. He did not want to see his own wasted face—there was too much other waste about him.

Because, of course, he had come home to the news that his father and his brothers had all perished from plague within the same, swift summer's week—while he had languished in prison. In those early days, and in the first rush of his grief, it had seemed to him that all of the glory of the de Montforts and the Ducci Montaldos had been pawned and sold, not to the service of a noble end—he could no longer consider his own ransom a noble end—but for the mundane tasks of putting food on the table and ensuring the wolves were kept at bay.

And worst of all was the fact that no one else had seemed to care. Not Belden, the great and wealthy Sire of Harnoncourt; nor his wife, the Lady Francesca. Not even Olivier's mother, Blanche de Montfort. In the first days after his return he had sat silently by while the three of them laughed in those bare rooms and talked of Francesca's enormous pregnancy. She had been carrying the first of the four sons she would eventually present to carry on the noble name of her husband—just as her own mother had birthed four healthy sons before her. The three of them had petted and admired the child Julian and taught her English. Olivier's mother, a proud woman, had thought her particularly intelligent; she had admired her education and encouraged her to talk of science, which the child was reluctant to do. It didn't seem to matter anymore that Blanche was a countess in both France and Italy and that Julian was the daughter of a pyre-condemned witch. No one had seemed to mind that they were surrounded by the remnants of a broken-down castle, or that there were four fresh graves in the little wisteria-bound cemetery that hugged the castle keep. But Olivier had minded. He had minded terribly. He had vowed to reclaim the splendor of his castle and make the Ducci Montaldo name glorious once again. Because this was his responsibility, and what had happened had been his fault.

Now there was hardly a spot where his hand had not reached. He had replaced everything that the great warrior lords of his family had built before him and added to it. The Ducci Montaldo ate once more from plates of gold and drank their wine from silver goblets. The family tapestries had been hunted down and hung again after Belvedere's walls had been cleaned of their damp and repaired and frescoed in bright colors. He had hired

Dino Rapondi, the best and most expensive agent in all Italy, to hunt down his family's treasures and buy them back. Every one of them. And more.

No peasant had worked harder than he as he pursued the gold necessary to buy back his history. He and his army had fought battles throughout Italy and up into the Savoy and the lower reaches of France. At various times he had been under the employ of the Signoria of Florence, the great Gian Galeazzo Visconti of Milan and now the Doge of Venice. Rarely had he allowed himself time for a tranquil moment to enjoy the restored Belvedere. But it had been worth it, he thought now as he walked briskly towards his meeting with Gatien de la Marche. It had been worth everything.

He had written his mother of the changes, thinking that she would return to see the results of his efforts. As strong and vain and determined as she was, surely Blanche would rejoice in his accomplishments. He had caused the Ducci Montaldo name to shine once again, and he had done it for his mother— to make up just a little for all she had lost.

The Countess de Montfort Ducci Montaldo had answered back swiftly and applauded his efforts, but she had declined his invitation to return from Francesca's new home in England. If he had no real need of her, she was happy where she was and would prefer to stay there. Francesca needed her, what with all of her children and her studies and her husband to attend. And Blanche was happy. She had repeated this more than once. She was happy now and no longer needed the things of the past.

Olivier had been stunned. His sister, Francesca, had been born the youngest after four strong, dynasty-building boys. He—all of them—had always treated her as an afterthought, useful only to be wed off advantageously for the good of the Ducci Montaldo. Blanche, he knew, had been guiltier of this than anyone else. The beautiful Countess de Montfort had had little time for her daughter while she was growing up. She had been too busy tending to the needs of her sons. So it was odd that Blanche should now feel such a strong pull towards Francesca. But she did. It was one of the many ways in which life had changed during his absence. Francesca had even hinted that Blanche was seriously considering marrying once again, to an old English knight—Henry of Kent—who was from a solid but not an especially important family. It amazed and even angered Olivier that his mother should consider a marriage such as this, a marriage that would bring no political or monetary value to her family. It was this thought that spurred him on to his meeting with Gatien de la Marche—and to the Burgundian knight's inevitable request.

Because, after all the chivalric festivities, the time had finally come for them to arrive at the point.

"Crusade," Sir Gatien said affably. "As you well know, that is why I am here."

The two knights sat at the long trestle in the Great Hall. They were alone. In the background Olivier could hear the sounds which announced the elaborate preparations of the evening meal. Rich aromas drifted up from the kitchens and the long, polished tables, which reached out in a U-shape from his head dais, set with fine silver and gold. He caught the gleam from them in the light of the many torches that he had had lighted. The evening banquet would be delayed and his temperamental Neapolitan cook would be furious, but Olivier had sent word that he and his noble guest must not be disturbed.

"Indeed," Olivier said. "And against whom?"

The other knight put down his silver tankard. Olivier noted that the sweet spiced wine still filled it almost to the brim. His soldier's instinct had already told him that Sir Gatien was not behind the arrow that had found its way into his back. The Knight de la Marche did not have the face of a man who would order a jackal-assault.

"Against the Sultan Bayezid," answered Gatien. "The Ottoman Turks have already defeated Wallachia and taken half the land that lies between the Danube and the Bosphorus. Their armies sniff at the very gates of Vienna. In fact it was King Sigismund of Hungary who first appealed to his brother knights for aid against them. It is rumored that Bayezid has already given fiefdoms on European soil to a fair portion of his mightiest warriors, which of course means that his is no leisurely excursion. He intends to stay. Sigismund has called upon the support of the King of France and the King's uncle, my liege lord the Duke of Burgundy. They have listened to him and are prepared to come to his assistance. They ask your help as well.''

Olivier lifted his own tankard and drank slowly. He felt the keen aching of his shoulder. "Of course I feel for the plight of the Balkans. But I fail to see what interest this war—this Crusade—should have for Venice. And as *you* know, Venice is my employer and thus my army is plighted to her interests.''

A heavy log fell into the fireplace, scattering sparks and ashes. For an instant its light brought out the amused gleam in Sir Gatien's dark eyes.

"In fact you were not the first choice of my Lord of Burgundy," he answered amiably. "He first sent for your brother-in-law, Belden of Harnoncourt. *He* was first choice. But like any good master chef, my Lord of Burgundy has learned to cook with the ingredients that come to hand. And my Lord of Harnoncourt was persuaded that you might eventually come to hand.''

Olivier stared at him for a moment and then threw back his head and roared with laughter.

"So you think me pretentious, Sir Gatien?''

"Aye. But I think you also a good knight—a great knight—and every bit as good a general as your brother-in-law. You have proved that with the Gold Company. You must prove it again against Bayezid." The Burgundian leaned closer, his forearms planted firmly on the trestle between them. "Philip of Burgundy, acting of course in the name of his nephew King Charles VI, wished at first to ally the French and the English in the fighting of this Crusade as they fought together in earlier ones. Troubadours have sung for centuries of the Holy War that united England's Richard the Lionhearted with our own King Louis the Saint.''

Remembering his time in the East, Olivier said without ceremony, ''Much has changed since those days.''

''Indeed,'' responded the Burgundian. ''So said your brother-in-law. He argued, though quite mildly, that it was useless to try to unite France and England in a common endeavor. The time is not yet ripe. Too much has happened since Poitiers.''

''My already high esteem for Belden's astuteness grows with your every word,'' said Olivier. He poured wine from a silver pitcher. ''France and England have been intermittently at each other's throats since that great battle. And when was it, 1356 or thereabouts? Forty years of intermittent warfare, punctuated by dubious periods of back-biting, back-stabbing peace. Why, this very castle had to defend itself from French incursions less than five years ago. My mother's own cousin, the Sire de Coucy, came this close to taking Tuscany and uniting it to the Kingdom of the Two Sicilies. It was Belden himself who stopped them. His lack of sympathy for the French is well noted. He married my sister despite her Gallic blood, not for it.''

Gatien smiled and his face broke into a surprising nest of wrinkles around his brown eyes. ''Indeed, since the Battle of Poitiers, France and England have not shown themselves able to agree on the rules for a paging tournament, much less on the intricacies of waging Holy War. You know, of course, that in my country they refer to the English as 'goddams'? The goddams did this: the goddams did that. They hoist them up on their own most common expletive.''

''No, I didn't know that,'' said Olivier. Once again, he threw back his head in laughter.

''Your brother-in-law was most hospitable and courteous but very firm in his belief that this is to be a French crusade,'' continued Gatien. ''The English want no part of it. Belden of Harnoncourt actually seemed saddened by this turn of events, but it appears his services are needed within his own country.

He told me that there is trouble in Scotland—is not there
always?—and he is honor bound to attend to his duties there.
He suggested, however, that there might be gain for your Venice
within this Holy War. As had, I might add, that great master
chef, Philip the Bold, Duke of Burgundy.''

"And what might this gain be?"

The Knight de la Marche leaned closer towards him. The
scar along his face stood out vividly in the bright torchlight of
Olivier's Great Hall. "Venice might stand to lose much with
these Ottoman incursions into her shipping territories," he said.
"Her trade routes might be threatened, especially those of her
Black Fleet through the Dardanelles."

Olivier shook his head impatiently. "The Saracen is no sea
power."

"He does not have to be, if he controls the land that surrounds
the sea."

"Indeed," said Olivier thoughtfully. He reached to pour rich,
dark wine into Gatien's goblet, saw that it was still full, and
poured instead into his own. His shoulder burned incessantly—
and he could feel a noose tightening around his neck. "I see
you've brought a fair share of men with you."

Gatien's smile was broad, almost indulgent. "It was my Lord
of Burgundy's wish. He has many virtues, not the least of
which is that he wishes the world to know of them. And this
is best accomplished by sending out a mighty force under the
green and red of his colors. The journey into England and then
on to Belvedere could have been accomplished much more
quickly but for the press of men that my lord deemed necessary
in order to awe my lord of Harnoncourt into an alliance."

Olivier laughed. "Belden is not impressed by such a show
of power. Nor am I. The same decision has been made by both
of us. I cannot see Venice joining in a French crusade. Your
lord gave you much trouble for nothing."

De la Marche laughed. "It was at least worth the try—and
men have been known to change their minds. Or to be forced
to change them."

"Not Belden. He is nothing if not constant."

"As he can well afford to be. He had his employer—the King of England—to back him in this. Not all warriors are so fortunate. And when the knight and his employer differ, as sometimes happens—well, then it touches the knight to obey." Gatien smiled and Olivier watched it grow from something that was merely diplomatic to something truly genuine. "But I am happy with the results of my mission. I met the Lady Julian, and I brought her safely home."

Olivier was discomfited by the intimacy in the Burgundian's voice. He snorted. "I should think it would have been more trouble having to bring a young girl along. I am surprised at Belden that he would have imposed her on you."

"On the contrary," answered Gatien. "They had no wish for the Lady Julian to leave, especially your sister. They tried in every manner to induce her to change her mind. But she was determined. She said that you would want her here. She said that you had made her a promise. She said you would not have forgotten it."

Forgotten? How could he? He had only to close his eyes to see again the child Julian clutching at Aalyne. Begging and pleading to stay with her mother. And he could hear his own voice, fervent with fear, "We will come back for her, Julian. I promise you that one day we will come back." Anything to get her away—to get them away—before the Sultan's soldiers killed them all. And what did it matter what he said? What did it matter at all? He had had no doubt, and neither had Aalyne, that she would be dead before first sun. There would be no hope for her once the child Julian's husband, the great Dogan Bey, discovered just what she had done. He was the all-powerful governor of Nicopolis and, just as sure as cockcrow, he would have her killed.

Now Olivier raised an eyebrow and said aloud, "Ah, she said that, did she?"

"She was sure of it." Again Gatien flashed his pleasant,

agreeable smile. "After all, she said you'd given your oath as a knight."

Olivier said nothing. He nodded to Cristiano and Giuseppe, both of whom had been waiting his pleasure at a discreet distance. Soon the other soldiers would arrive, and the food. His interview with the Knight de la Marche was at an end.

And then after the meal, again there was Giuseppe, his arms loaded down with the castle's documents and ledgers. He came every night, after the others had made their drunken or semi-drunken way to their beds.

But Olivier's shoulder pained him and he, too, wanted his bed.

"But you've not been here in two months' time, my lord," admonished his bailiff. "And God himself knows when you will find your way back again. There is much that needs your attending. There are things which only the Count of the Ducci Montaldo can decide."

And so Olivier worked well into the wee hours, seeing to the kitchens and the buttery, corresponding with the monasteries and universities that pleaded for the rare herbs which Belvedere no longer produced. He dictated polite letters to abbots and scholars, informing them that the Lady Francesca had accompanied her husband to his castle in England and that, therefore, there was no longer anyone to tend the herbal gardens. No longer should they expect healing from Belvedere. He cursed the fact that he had no wife to attend to these matters and silently promised himself that he would declare and publish his marriage banns to Domiziana as soon as he returned to Venice. He was a fool to have waited so long. No reason in the world for it. Certainly this accounting and letter writing was no fit occupation for a knight and a lord.

Giuseppe sat before him, determined to attend to business, but nodding over his ledgers. Even the hunting dogs on the hearth had stopped their bone-scrabbling over the last of the bones, and lay dozing. Olivier could hear their steady, rhythmic snores. He wanted to join them. It was hard to concentrate on this idiotic but necessary business with his wound aching so— and the smell of violets surrounding him.

He was in the midst of dictating a reply to the neighboring monastery of San Dominico, explaining to them with as much politeness as he could muster why he could no longer sell them the herb they requested at the price they had come to expect, when suddenly he vaulted to his feet, kicking back his chair with such force that the noise reverberated through the Great Hall and started the dogs to yapping.

His shoulder burnt with the fires of hell. And he knew he could no longer handle the pain.

"Enough," he said irritably. "The rest can wait for another day. When is Gasca due back? He might have taken leave of me before quitting my castle."

"*Padre* Gasca," Giuseppe said with some dignity. "He's gone to seek out the monks at San Mario. He goes there often now—sometimes for days at a time. The peasants say he is getting old and has started to fear his Day of Judgment. They have not forgotten that he was put under the pope's interdict for his alchemic experiments. It is widely rumored that he was saved from the pyre only by your father's direct intervention. Now the priest takes his journeys—but he always comes back. He should be home any day now."

"He should have told me." Olivier said shortly. "He should have asked my leave." He felt like a child. But he knew he had only himself to blame. He had asked help from no one, not even from his bailiff. Not even from. . . .

Julian, he thought. But she must have the knowledge. Aalyne had it, and so must she. Still, he shook his head no. There were a thousand reasons why he should not seek help from her. His mind formed them readily—it was late, she would be sleeping, he had shamed her before the others, she was no longer a child. But then he smelled again the springtime of her clear perfume, felt the softness of her hand as she had put it in his, heard her laughter. And felt his own pain.

"Giuseppe, where have they put the Maid Julian? Where does she sleep?"

She had been put in Francesca's room. It seemed logical, Giuseppe had told him. His sister and his ward had always been such very good friends. Julian had been the family pet.

Olivier slowly mounted the stairs that led to her. All around him torches glowed dimly in their wall sconces. It was late now: their light was almost spent. But he did not allow himself to think about that and he did not allow himself to stop until he reached Julian's door. *Francesca's* door, he corrected himself. He raised his hand and knocked softly at it.

Of course there was no answer, but this did not stop him. Neither did the brief thought that he should look for her maid, that it was a mark of great disrespect to come to her alone at night. Sir Gatien would never do this, Olivier thought wryly. The Knight de la Marche would have treated her with due honor.

But he hurt and he knew that Julian could help him. He knew also that he could trust her. If he asked her to do it, she would never tell anyone about his wounding on the road. She would keep to herself the suspicion—now fast becoming a certainty—that someone had wanted him dead. After all, had he not kept important secrets for her?

Again he knocked and when there was no answer, he pushed through the door and blinked into the darkness. There was only one small candle burning. Its light was not helpful, at least not at first. He could not see Julian in the gloom but he knew she was there. He smelled her violets: he felt her warmth. There was a freshness to the air that hinted of sunshine, that reminded him, normally the least romantic of men, of the spring to come. But then his eyes adjusted. He saw a wooden prie-dieu and behind it a small icon of the Madonna and Child. The Virgin's soft blond hair glowed in the light of the candle before it. But he could make out no face, no comforting smile on the image. The room itself was far too dark.

Then his eyes made another adjustment and he saw the bed. Francesca's maiden bed, with Julian in it. He did not say anything, did not call out her name, did not waken her. No, he especially did not want to waken her—at least not yet.

Instead, he reached into the hallway and pulled one of the torches down from its sconce on the wall. He held it high for an instant, getting his bearings before making his way across his sister's room. He walked softly and slowly. His smooth leather boots made no sound.

Newly laid thyme and mint, still not dried, sprang to life beneath the press of his boots. He thought briefly again of calling a servant, one of the women. Surely there must be someone sleeping near, someone who could serve as chaperon for this child-woman who was under his care. Julian, an outcast and thus alive to any slight, would realize the impropriety of a man, even her own guardian, coming alone to her sleeping chamber. And staring at her as he was staring at her now.

She was lying on the bed, her body curled tightly into itself. She moved in her sleep and the sheet fell away from her shoulders. They were covered by the finest of lace.

He should never have come. The thought hit him with the force of ice water and made him realize that he had been wrong to venture to this room alone. Foolhardily wrong. He did not fully believe all the tales he had heard of Aalyne de Lione— that she was the Magdalene, the direct descendent of Mary of Magdala before her conversion, and the witch of witches for the warlocking Knights Templar. No, he didn't believe all the tales. But he knew for a certainty that she had been condemned to the pyre in France and had barely escaped with her life. He recalled the tales he'd heard of Julian's mother, and those things she could do to a man's mind if she took the notion. What a witch could do when she wanted something. A very old and deeply buried part of the Count of the Ducci Montaldos urged him to stride quickly from this room and bolt the door behind him.

But instead he whispered, "Julian." When she did not answer him, he repeated her name again, this time more gruffly. And he moved closer. It occurred to him that he could easily reach down and touch her bare shoulder, which looked as soft as clotted cream to him, but he didn't. Or he couldn't. Instead, he waited.

Until she opened her dark eyes.

"My lord," she said, rising slowly to a sitting position and pulling the dark blanket close to brush against the small Maltese Star at her neck. "I was not expecting you or I would have bound my hair."

She had made her small joke but neither of them laughed at it.

"I was kept busier than I imagined," he said. "I've sent your meals up because I thought you would be bored eating with only soldiers."

Actually this was true. He had had food sent up to her to spare her. He had stayed away from her to spare himself.

Julian clambered up in her bed, tumbling up amidst the jumble of her hair and the scramble of sheets that surrounded her. She did not smile as she looked up into the stone of his turquoise eyes—now more green than she remembered them—and at his face, craggy and handsome and hard, in the light of the flickering torch. Her face puckered in thought as she looked out at him.

"Something is wrong," she said. "Something has happened."

Olivier thought again of Aalyne, of her powers as a witch and he found himself unable to tell Julian why he had come to her. That he was in pain, that his wound tortured him, and that he needed healing. Instead, he guided the conversation to a different turn.

"You should have stayed at Harnoncourt Hall," he heard his own voice saying.

If she was surprised by what he said, she didn't show it. Indeed, her face relaxed back into itself and showed nothing at all. "I couldn't do that. You know why I've come," was all the answer she gave him.

"And more the fool you are for doing it. Did you not think that the roads are infested with brigands and murderers? If you had been caught, a fortune would have been demanded for your ransom. You are related to the wealthy Sire of Harnoncourt and all the world knows this."

"But the Count of the Ducci Montaldos is my guardian and the world knows that as well. It is he who guarantees the roads from Genoa and thus I felt safe upon them."

"Do not flatter me, Julian," Olivier said in his low voice. "You have changed a great deal since last we met but I don't want you changed in that way. You were a fool to come back to Belvedere and you've come upon a fool's errand."

"Has it now become foolishness to expect a knight to honor his word?"

Olivier shook his head. "I've no intention of going back to Nicopolis. I've been away from Italy far too long. My responsibility lies here."

She loved this man. She always would. But there was something in the tone of his voice that frightened her. Something that reminded her that she slept no longer in the safety of Harnoncourt Hall, but at Belvedere, and in Olivier's sister's bed.

"I have come because of your promise."

Across time and space, Aalyne's compelling voice whispered to her: *Know your enemy. Use him.* But how could Olivier ever be her enemy? He was her guardian and only she knew how much it had cost him to care for her. Julian shook the sound of her mother's warning away.

She watched through eyes that were now wide open, as Olivier first placed the torch in a sconce, and then reached out one long leg and pulled a stool closer to the bed. She continued watching as he settled himself lightly onto it. He grimaced and

again she felt the flash that told her something was seriously
wrong. But she could not see his face clearly and the insolence
of his attitude was not lost upon her. He, a knight sworn to the
rules of chivalry, to the protection of the weak, should never
have allowed himself the freedom of these liberties with a
woman alone, except in the gravest of emergencies. He should
have cared more for her honor. *Would* have cared more for her
honor, had she been anyone except the daughter of the witch
who had saved his life.

Anger smoldered at the back of her mind, but she left it to
linger there, unstoked. She sensed that anger would be nothing
more than a welcome distraction for this man, and so she steeled
herself against the easy temptation. As she had grown used to
steeling herself against so much more over the years. Because
somehow she knew what was happening was her fault. That
she had done something wrong. That *she* was wrong. Why else
would the Dogan Bey have hurt her?

Julian scrupulously followed her early training and said nothing as she watched Olivier's cold eyes rake over her. She was
happy that she had thought to gather the sheets around her;
happy that she had warm covers under which to hide. She
reached to pull the blankets closer and that is when her guardian
noticed the gold ribbon that she had tied to her wrist.

"Who gave you that?"

"Gatien. Sir Gatien bought it for me when we crossed from
England into France," she answered and without thinking
smiled at the memory. "He stopped at Pavia to pay respects
to the Visconti and it was fair-time there. Sir Gatien told me
a legend of a silken ribbon, and he thought this one would look
well in my hair."

"You've quite bewitched the Knight de la Marche," Olivier
said, and those cold eyes never left her face as he said the word
he knew she hated. "It is obvious he thinks you quite a beauty.
Though of course he would never say this out loud, at least
not to me, because I am your guardian. In my presence he
always speaks of you with great respect. He said you were

intelligent and perceptive. Maidenly. Of course, I did not tell him of the Dogan Bey."

Julian said nothing.

"Though, perhaps I should have," Olivier teased. "He talks so much of honoring vows. Perhaps he should know of certain promises that you yourself have made."

Still Julian said nothing, even as he leaned towards her. Nor did she flinch.

". . . But I didn't tell him of them." Now he was so close that she could smell the tang of wine on his breath, and the faint scent of soap and leather that had always seemed to cling to him, even in the Dogan Bey's prison. He was so near to her now that she could almost feel the whisk of his eyelashes against her cheek.

"You can tell him, if you want," she said. "I have honored my vows to the Dogan Bey. I always have. I always will. There will never be another man for me."

"What a waste that would be. They all love you, little Julian. My sister sends word that you are to sleep in her bed. Her husband cannot speak highly enough of you. Belden encourages me to take on this Crusade, you know. But of course you do know that. It's why you left the pleasantry of your home at Harnoncourt Hall to come again to Belvedere. Because you have your hopes."

"No, I came because I had your promise," she said softly. "And because Harnoncourt Hall is not my home."

But he continued on, as though he had not heard her. "And now de la Marche thinks you quite the beauty. You have bewitched them all."

"I am no witch."

"Is that so?" His fingers reached out to the Maltese Star at her throat. She could feel the warmth from his hand as it fondled the amulet, though he did not touch her. "I could never tell with Aalyne, you know. Whether she was a witch or just a very intelligent, very unscrupulous whore. A woman who knew what she wanted and got it. We men are simple. Sometimes it is hard for us to tell the difference between good and evil.''

''For you my mother was good,'' Julian said. She felt cold seeping into her as she moved just a little so that the Maltese Star shifted from his hand and was hidden by the lace of the white sheet. ''She saved your life.''

''Indeed, that she did,'' Olivier agreed pleasantly. ''But I'm not going back there. I'll not hold myself in debt to a condemned witch—a woman who was saved from burning only because she had you. Take my advice and forget your mother. She's dead by now anyway—at least if she was lucky. And you are young. You have your whole life before you. The Knight de la Marche is wealthy and three years widowed. I am sure, once this foolishness of crusade has finished, he will come to me as your guardian and beg me for your hand. Marry him and live happily. You can do it, Julian. You can forget the past.''

She stared at him in astonishment. ''No one can marry me— no one would want to. Not after what has happened. You know that better than I.''

''Yes, but we are the only two who *do* know what happened—at least the only two here in this part of Christendom. Take my advice, little Julian. Live your life as it has been presented to you. If not with Gatien de la Marche, then with someone else. Choose anyone you want, and I will dower you handsomely. As your guardian I urge you to forget what happened in Nicopolis. Forget it, and start your life again as I have done.''

Julian had always assumed that Olivier had talked to someone about his imprisonment. Either to the Sire or to another of his friends. But the bitterness in his voice told her that this had not happened. He had carried his hatred unrelieved, through all these years. And, despite her anger and her fear, she felt nothing but compassion for him. Because she had carried her burdens alone as well.

''Forget the promise,'' he repeated softly. ''Forget what is behind you.''

"She is my mother. And only she knows who my father—my *real* father—was. I must find her. I must help her," Julian said quietly, as he turned away. "I can't forget the promise to her. And neither can you. You promised. You gave your word."

"What else could I do?" he lashed at her. His fist slammed into the heavy wall beside her bed.

Controlled again, Olivier threw more words into this weighty silence "You were screaming. You were clutching at that woman—at your mother. If I had let you go on like that it would have meant all of our lives. Can't you understand that?"

Julian looked her handsome guardian straight in his face. And even though the tears flowed from her eyes and her voice trembled, she said to him, "But you promised me. You gave your knight's word and you must maintain it. If not for my mother's sake, then for your own."

Witch or no, she is not strong enough to withstand me in this, Olivier raged to himself as he made his way back through his darkened castle. *I will send her straight back to Harnoncourt Hall, where she belongs. Or I will order her to a convent. There is one in Picardy where she will never again see the light of day. How dare she defy me? How dare she quote me my duty? She is determined and willful but she cannot stop me in this.*

He smiled at this simple solution and then laughed aloud. The sound rang out hollowly against the stone walls. And suddenly Olivier realized that he had not asked Julian to help him, to heal him, and that his shoulder still raged with pain. And then from someplace well-deep inside him came the totally unexpected, insidious thought that never, ever—in all the years he had known her—had Julian laughed with him the way she had laughed with the Knight de la Marche.

CHAPTER FOUR

Julian often spoke with Olivier in her mind, said things to him that she could never have had the courage to say out loud. The truth was, she was frightened of men, and had been from any time that she could remember. Her experience of them, at least thus far, had not been the best. But she could and did talk to Olivier every night as she closed her eyes for sleep. It was the time when she most longed for him and when he was most hers. Talking to him—reliving—was her way of putting away the bad thoughts so that she could sleep. That night lived beneath her eyelids—and she had but to close them and it would pop out at her again—vivid, real, and true. She had long ago learned that no matter where she was or what she did or how she acted, it stayed with her.

"Do you remember that night?" she said to him now in her mind as his footsteps echoed away from her. "I was so frightened. Do you remember? And is it true, my Lord Olivier, that you were frightened, too?"

* * *

It all happened so suddenly. The tug from sleep, the dark
eunuch, the tunnel, the dread that had so quickly and so totally
enveloped her—and had never left.

Above all, there had been Aalyne's silken voice. "I will
have my daughter with me tonight. I will keep her about me.
She is too ill to be with Dogan Bey. She might infect him."

"Mother, I am not sick." But Aalyne had clapped a firm
hand over the flow of Julian's French words.

Their guard, an enormous eunuch, had frowned dubiously.
He was a cunning man but not very intelligent; he could not
understand everything that was being said. And yet it was
important that he did understand. He was a servant of the
wealthy Dogan Bey and his life could depend upon his knowledge. Red, from an unseen fire, reflected through his eyes and
Julian saw the hesitation in them. She smelled his nervousness
and fear. One wrong move and this man's head would roll, of
that there was no doubt. The Dogan Bey was a merchant but
he was also a great friend of the Sultan Bayezid. It was rumored
they shared secret plans for the city of Nicopolis.

But this was the Lady Aalyne speaking to him. And Aalyne
was the Magdalene, the warlock's witch. She had the power
and she used it now.

Without knowing it, the eunuch found himself thinking the
thoughts that the Magdalene wanted him to think.

*It was true that she came from the Christian land beyond
the mountains but she loved the Muslim people and hated her
own,* he reasoned. *Her own had tried to burn her at the stake.
Besides, she was a past favourite of the Sultan Bayezid and
now mother of the Dogan Bey's favoured one. They all knew
how much stock this wealthy merchant placed in his new child-
toy. He would want her nourished and cozened if she were ill.
And where better to be cared for than at the house of her
mother? The Lady Aalyne was nominally Christian. She lived
outside of the harem and this was just as well because many*

of the women in the harem were jealous of the Dogan Bey's attention. They might harm the child Julian if they had the chance. She was just twelve. And if anything should happen to her. . . .

On and on flowed the rationalizations that Aalyne ably fed into the guard's unwary mind.

His hesitation vanished. "Yes, Lady," he said, bowing very low as he let them through. "Tonight your daughter should be with you, not with the Dogan Bey or in the harem. It is best that way. You will take care of her."

Aalyne smiled at him as she swept past.

Julian was pleased. In truth she did not especially like the Dogan Bey, though she was his concubine. He had hurt her— more than once—and she had longed for her mother. She had wanted to go home. But now, the two of them did not go towards the herbal gardens and their own small house that lay tucked beyond, as Julian had expected they would. Instead Aalyne took her hand and led her more deeply within the granite palace, to parts of it that she had never before seen. Julian heard swiftly running water and smelled the stink of dampness. The rich embroidery on her gold silk gown dragged out behind her in the mud. She worried about this and wondered how she would explain the soil on her new garment. Muna, her nurse, would be angry.

"Mother?"

But Aalyne did not answer and her pull on her daughter was harsh. They hurried on and did not stop until they had reached the tunnel's end and found the men. There were two of them and Julian, who had been well trained in observation, knew immediately that they had been waiting some time for them and that they were frightened. Early on, Aalyne had taught her how to recognize fear. She had said it was the most important scent to notice. When fear was upon a man he could generally be made to do the bidding of a woman full in her power. It was very important to know this fact and to use it.

And one of these men was very fearful. Even in the dim light from their one, small torch, Julian saw his cold turquoise eyes look about him with an open hostility that marred the considerable beauty of his face. And yet Julian was immediately drawn to him. Something in her wanted to smile at him and soothe away his apprehension. Perhaps because she was suddenly so very frightened herself. Her hands, on their own, had clutched convulsively at Aalyne, and she would not look away from her mother's face.

She registered that the other man was quieter, larger, darker, but careful and keeping guard. She did not smell the same degree of fear on him. The two of them whispered urgently to her mother in French. They pointed at a distant light and one of them even clutched at her mother's hand. Julian did not know which one did this. She was too busy looking into Aalyne's eyes, holding onto her. Even in the great confusion of their urgency and even though they all spoke the same tongue, Julian—who knew her mother's language well—heard the difference in their accents and knew that they had all learned their French in different places and in different ways.

"This is the Sire d'Harnoncourt and the Count of the Ducci Montaldo," Aalyne said firmly, turning away from the men and to her child. "You are to go with them."

"We must hurry," whispered the tall, dark man, the one who had been introduced as the Sire. His words were quick, but his voice was not unkind. Still, Julian heard the command in it, and the insistence. She had been well trained to obedience, but she cried now at this order. She could not help herself. She would have promised anything, even to the Dogan Bey, to ward off what was coming.

Aalyne bent down to kiss her daughter as she tore off her veil and began to clean away the makeup from her twelve-year-old face. "You'll not need this now," she whispered, her own face brightly painted as she exposed Julian's fresh, young skin. But Julian continued to cry as her mother rubbed the silk cloth quickly and none too gently, as she wiped away the only life her child had ever known.

"Ama?" Julian questioned. It was her pet name for her mother. She had not used it in years. Ama and me. Me and my Ama, Julian had sung over and over again as the two of them had pushed on from place to place. Me and my Ama. In the great insecurity of her life she had clung fast to her mother, who had been the source of that insecurity, for the little stability she offered. However, she had revolted against using the power and her mother must have known this. Aalyne had trained her and cajoled her, but she must have known that Julian could never be the Magdalene. Her mother knew everything. And now she was punishing her: she was sending her away.

Julian started to cry out in protest just as Aalyne's hand brushed against the six-pointed gold star that hung from her neck. For the briefest of instants she thought her mother would tear this away from her as well, and she couldn't have borne that. She would have died. The star had been with her for as long as she could remember. Just then there was a sighing movement in the dim light, very near them. She *sensed* the presence of a third man—a man who was hunched and misshapen and stood near to them. He stood behind her mother and he smiled at her. She could have touched him with her hand. Julian wondered if the others could see him as well.

"I can't take this from you," Aalyne whispered fiercely, though her fingers gripped hard at the amulet, almost as though she would crush it if she could. "I've not the right nor the power. Only you can give back what your birth has given you. You must make that choice for yourself."

Aalyne's words caught Julian's attention once again, and it was only then that she realized that her mother was frightened. The smell of fear was on her strong and deep.

Suddenly, a wind whipped through the cavern, hissing against the dripping rocks and the damp. Julian felt its heat against her skin and she shivered. She looked about her, but she could no longer see the dark man. The smell of fire was all about them.

"Muna," she whispered. "I cannot go away without first saying good-bye to my nurse." Julian hardly recognized her own voice; she could barely pull the words out of her throat.

Aalyne was her usual, calm self as she answered, "Muna knows nothing of your leaving. This is for her own defense. If the Dogan Bey suspects her he will have her quickly beheaded—if she is lucky. Her hope is to know nothing. Her ignorance is her only safety." She could have been discussing the weather or the price of some small trinket that her daughter wanted.

There was death in that voice and Julian heard it. "I'll not leave you," she cried, and her voice was shrill, her clutching fingers frantic.

That was when the blond man—the one whom her mother had introduced as a count—spoke to her for the first time.

Yet when he said, "Look at me," Julian looked up at him. And when he said, "If you come with us quietly now, we will return for your mother. We will come back to Nicopolis one day, when the time is right, and we will take her away with us." She had listened to his words and gathered shards of hope from them.

"Do you promise me that? Do you give me your word of honor as a knight?" she questioned. Their gazes met, dark to light; and for just an instant she was inside of him and she felt herself fall like a smooth pebble into his soul.

"Yes," whispered the blond man, and then again, "Yes. I promise it on my honor as a knight." But he had been quick to look away.

Still, Julian had believed him and had calmed beneath the smooth assurance in his voice. She had given him her hand and she had trusted his words. They would come back. He had promised. And she had believed in him more than she believed in the goodness of the dark man who, Aalyne whispered to her, was rescuing them both.

"On my word of honor as a knight," the Count of the Ducci

Montaldo had repeated the words again, more forcefully this time, almost as though he needed to convince himself as well.

And as the three of them fled from the dungeon beneath the governor's palace at Nicopolis, Olivier's was the unwilling hand Julian had clutched as a talisman in the night. His was the promise she had believed in. And his was the love she had sought.

Do you remember, my Lord Olivier? Dear God, do you remember?

Someone had lighted a bright fire while she slept, and at first Julian thought Olivier had returned to her and that even now he waited for her to awaken. She lay quietly and let her mind savor the thought. But when finally she did open her eyes it was not her guardian she saw, but the young village girl he had given her as a maid.

Sabata cleared her throat. "The Count sends his regards and bids you make Belvedere a good morning. He urges you to enjoy yourself. He regrets that he has no time to give you himself, but he is busy with his duties about the castle." She stopped. It was obviously a speech that Giuseppe had given to her word for word, and one for which she clearly would have liked to know the meaning. That the Count and his ward spent little time together was something that was, by now, common knowledge throughout the castle. The reason for the strange hostility was still hotly debated all through the buttery and the lower kitchens. Sabata was a dark-eyed, dark-haired, round little village beauty who must have been all of thirteen. Normally she chatted harmlessly on and on about her village of Sant'Urbano and her betrothed and the life they planned to lead together once he was given an extra hectare of land to farm. Today, however, she was frankly questioning and Julian was determined not to satisfy her curiosity. She swung her feet to the floor, pushing back the tumble of her hair.

By her age I was already within the harem of the Dogan

Bey, Julian thought. But the remembrance of her time there, and of the man who had owned her, no longer called back pain to her. It had all happened so long ago, as if she had been another woman. There had been no man for her since.

Now she made her home with the Lady Francesca. She loved the little Harnoncourt boys as though they were her own. They were all the family she had ever known or would know— except for her mother. And perhaps for her father—if she could but find and claim him.

"And how is your young brother?"

This time it was Sabata's turn to want to scuttle away from the tide of conversation. "Fine," she said. "Getting better."

This was a lie. Giacomo still coughed and wheezed during the long nights and slept away his days. She had a young brother—the only son of old parents—who had been sick these weeks with a wet cough. They had applied to the village witch for help. Strega Elisabetta had taken their few half coins readily enough, but she had provided no relief. Lately, she had begun to pontificate about God's Will as it concerned the poor and helpless, and how this must be bowed to. Her runes had told her this.

Sabata's parents were frantic for their young son. But the witch Elisabetta—the only person within a day's journey with interest in aiding a sick peasant child—had sternly warned her parents against asking help of Julian.

"She is the Magdalene, the devil's spawn," she had hissed to them. "She will turn her evil eye upon him and undo all the good I've worked."

Sabata could see little good that the witch had done. Her brother coughed more: he was growing weaker. However, her parents had been insistent. No word to Julian, no asking of help from her. Sabata still cringed at the ringing slap her father had given her to insure that his words were obeyed.

"Oh, what a lovely cloth!" she said now, reaching for a change of topic and a new interest at the same time. "Did you bring it with you?"

Clothing. It was a useful wheel upon which to revolve a conversation and both women gratefully fastened onto it. The Sire of Harnoncourt had no use for veiled women and did not tolerate his wife and her ladies with their hair bound. For a moment she had forgotten that she was now outside the enlightened boundaries of his influence.

Sabata laid out fresh clothing and helped Julian from the bath. "My, what lovely things you have. A person never hears of nice clothes coming from England, only from France. This gold veiling is just the thing for your dark hair. I hope you don't mind me saying, but you have the loveliest hair. Rarely does a body see really beautiful hair as dark as yours is. Not in this day. At least not here in the north of Italy. We are more for blonding here—both the natural sort and the piss bleached."

"Piss bleached?"

"Ah, yes. 'Tis all the fashion," Sabata said with some authority. "Brought to us from France—at least so says the Lady Domiziana. She brings her own maid with her generally, a Savoy maiden from north, over the mountains. But when the fancy hits her, sometimes she will allow me to dress her hair. She said that fashionable women use goat's urine for the bleaching, and some of them will even pluck the hairs along their hairlines in order to raise it higher. Though I tried doing this once and the pain was enough to set me off fashion forever."

Talk of the dark blue velvet moved quickly onward to a discussion of the simple but costly tunics Julian had carried with her from England. It was well-known fact, bantered about through all of Harnoncourt Hall, how the Sire Belden was interested in the dressing of his beloved wife but she herself was not. It was common gossip how the great warrior lord would return home laden with fine fabrics and rich jewels that he had picked up in his travels. He had even employed a French dressmaker—who had a cousin in Paris who belonged to the Glovers Guild and had strong connections at the Court—to keep his wife in the latest fashion. Francesca would smile and thank him and stand patiently for her fittings, but in the end the velvet tunics

and silk underskirts and fine-spun shawls would find their way
to the heavy cedar wood chests in Julian's chamber.

They will look better on you, Francesca would say, her fresh
face curling into a smile with the ease of a warm cat curling
nearer a welcoming hearth. *Besides, you like them more than
I do.* This much was certainly true. Francesca, though still a
great beauty after the birth of four sons, had never been one
to care for lavish dressing. Her mix-matched clothes were the
bane of her husband's existence. But Julian loved prettiness,
loved fine things, and she was given as many of them as she
wanted. Her years in the Sultan's court had trained her eye—
and much more.

"... and then of course when that happens they will be
closing Belvedere for good."

"Closing Belvedere?" Julian realized she had not been paying attention. She looked up from smoothing her deep gray
tunic to stare at her maid.

Sabata also stopped smoothing out the white linen and lace
of the bed and nodded. "At least that's what my grandmother
says and she's worked here all her life. She knew the Count
when he was just birthed. Lord Olivier has not much love for
the castle, despite the money he spends here. And who in
Christendom could blame him—with its graveyard overflowing
with the bodies of his father and his brothers? Especially now
that both the Lady Francesca and his mother are in England
and 'tis well-known that the Lady Domiziana has no love for
the Tuscan countryside, she being a Venetian on both her
mother and her father's side for generations."

"The Lady Domiziana?"

"The Count's betrothed, or nearly betrothed. There has been
no official announcement yet, at least that we've been told.
Though they say she's anxious for it. She came once on a visit
with the Count, she and her mother. She's getting on a bit, but
she's still a beauty and rich and will bring him good connec-

tions. They say she is a niece of the Doge of Venice—just imagine!—and so from a powerful and wealthy house. But . . ." Sabata lowered her voice and quickly crossed herself, "There be many who say there is a curse upon her because she's buried two husbands and one betrothed already. Superstitious folk say this—though I myself am not one. Still, there be many who are, and her family being so very pious and with other daughters to marry off. There were rumors that there were plans to lock her away in a convent, so as to hide the family shame and put a stop to the speculation, had not the Count shown up when he did.

"She must be married and children delivered of her soon," said Sabata shrewdly. "Or else she is certainly convent bound. A person like me might love the convent and the thought of regular meals and clean linen—but not a person like her."

Julian did not turn around. She wanted to be sure that she had control of her face before she did. No one must know what she felt, for Olivier was betrothed, he was soon to be a wedded man. And onto the foundation of his stunning engagement was now building the edifice of his future wife's great beauty and wealth—and the prestige of her family. No wonder he had come to her chamber stealthily and alone last night. What had she to offer him? Why would he bother to keep his promise to her?

"Have you had dealings with her? Is she good?" She had turned back to Sabata and was staring at her. Cold winter sunlight flooded the room between them.

"As good as she has to be," said Sabata. As she spoke she kept her shrewd eyes upon Julian. There was no unkindness in them. "But growing scared. You can smell it on her. She must be married and children soon delivered from her if she is to stop the talk about herself and her family. 'Tis a wonder she found no pretext to accompany the Count—or that her mama did not find one for her. They both seem reluctant to have him out of their sight."

Julian nodded. She laid out a piece of Florentine lace and the two of them pulled out needles and silk cotton threading to mend it. They chatted of many things, but not of the things that most concerned them. Sabata would have asked the Lady Julian's help with a poultice or an herb that might be of aid to Giacomo. And Julian would have probed deeper into the character and the beauty of the woman who was betrothed—or nearly betrothed—to Olivier. Instead, they contented themselves in discussing the new battery of laying hens and the men who had come from Norcia to dress this year's pigs, and when it looked like the cook's assistant would be delivered of her first child. The breadth of their superficiality seemed limitless. But beneath it, all the time, as both her fingers and her tongue worked with equal energy, Julian thought of Olivier. She thought of his hands, of his voice, of his laughter. She thought of the sweet heat of his breath against her cheek. Ever since she had met Olivier, she had always been thinking of him. Even when she was not consciously thinking of him at all.

Days passed, but she was not called into his presence. He neither came to her nor sent for her. And, of course, there was no hint as to his promise. Julian watched him ride away from Belvedere each morning, prepared for the hunt, surrounded by his knights, his dwarfs, and his falcons. The bright banners and flags of the Gold Company and the Ducci Montaldo playing in the breeze above his head, shooting color into the sereneness of Tuscany in winter. Sometimes the Knight de la Marche was with them and sometimes not. If he remained at Belvedere he would send a formal page to Julian and ask to escort her on some small excursion through the surrounding parish. Once or twice she said yes. Once or twice he made her laugh. They were together only in the daytime. At night he joined the other waiting warriors and their joviality and singing rose up to Julian as she ate her meal alone in Francesca's maiden-chamber.

No part of Belvedere and nothing in it was forbidden to her, but she noticed that, systematically and without comment, the simple daisies and chrysanthemums she had picked and placed about were stripped from their pewter vases. The tapestries she'd brought with her from England were taken down and secreted she knew not where. The fresh herbs she'd had strewn about the castle's cold stone floors were swept away and replaced by different ones.

CHAPTER FIVE

"Tsk, tsk, tsk," clucked Padre Gasca.

Outside it was past gloaming, but there were torches and candles aplenty burning in the private chamber of the Count of the Ducci Montaldo and a massive fire had been laid in the stone fireplace. Olivier had wanted light. He had wanted Cristiano to watch the priest as he made his diagnosis; he had wanted to assure himself that no mistakes would be made. His main concern—aside from the pain, which was fierce—was that he could not see over his shoulder to watch the priest himself. He did not like the thought that his own healing would be so far out of his control. It was true that Gasca had been a great friend of Olivier's father. The two of them, and then Francesca with them, had worked long hours in the laboratory that the Old Count had had built into the furthest donjon. But Cristiano, though fond of the Lady Francesca, had not quite trusted the experiments that were conduced there. And Olivier never had.

"This is as fine a festering as I have ever in my whole life seen," continued the priest as he bent over Olivier's wound.

He seemed totally oblivious to the hostility that danced around his head. "It is a classic example of all that can go wrong if one leaves a wound too long without proper care. One rarely sees a festering this deep anymore, even among the peasant classes. Even they have the intelligence to seek out a doctoring monk, or even a witch, when one is needed. I only wish I had students here from the medical school at Salerno to observe it. But perhaps I should send word to San Mario. They might have a cenobite or two who would be interested in viewing the case."

"Just get on with the healing," growled Olivier. "It should have started days ago had you not disappeared."

"It *could* have started days ago," agreed Gasca. "Had you thought to call upon the Lady Julian. Though she is a natural healer, she has learned her skill from the Lady Francesca, and from me as well. I'm sure she would have helped you had you thought to ask her. You could have spared yourself much pain."

A wave of irrational irritation swept through Olivier as he thought how he had gone to Julian, had been alone with her within her chamber walls. And how he had refused to let her know what had happened and to ask her for help. Still, to this moment, he did not know why he had done this, and had continued to suffer on another day and another night until finally Padre Gasca had returned of his own accord. But Olivier contained his irritation at himself, so that it did not erupt out and spill over onto the priest. He was in too much pain—in too much need—to argue when it was only God's truth that was being presented to him.

The anger that he turned towards his physician was half-hearted at best. "Priest, believe me, had I my sword this moment I would gladly run its cold steel through your even colder heart."

The words held no force. Beneath his sun coloring, his face had grown white with pain, almost as though the bright, livid welt that sat on his shoulder had pulled all of his life's energy into itself. He felt himself to be as querulous as a swaddled babe. Every time he opened his mouth he was afraid that great, wrenching cries might tumble forth unannounced and he would be forever disgraced.

"Then in my prayers tonight I must remember to thank God that you have not the use of it," answered Padre Gasca mildly. "Nor will you have in the future, unless we can set things to right again and quickly. I imagine it is quite useless to remind you that, if you would not seek aid from Julian, then you could at least have sent for me."

"We had no idea where you were," said Cristiano, his own face taut with concern. "And you were gone one half day, three whole days, and three nights."

"Pshaw! Giuseppe, the bailiff, knew that I was at San Mario. All the servants knew it. Once I saw the count safely returned I thought it best to slip away. My lord Olivier is kind enough to shelter me when he is absent. I did not want to make myself intrusive in his presence."

No one said, but they all thought, how the sight of the priest might bring back memories to Olivier. Memories that he would just as soon forget.

"We did not want to call attention to the attack by deeming the wound serious enough to call for you, at least until we find out the culprit," Olivier said.

"But we will discover him," Cristiano said. "Eventually. He will say a false word or make a mistaken move. Or he will try again."

He? thought the priest with a smile. But aloud he said, "Yes, surely he will not rest until he obtains what he wants. And certainly what he wants is the Lord Olivier—or to be more precise, his life. That much is obvious."

"But if something is not done soon, I will have no life left to give him," said Olivier shortly. His shoulder blazed and he craved relief. "Can you do something or not, Priest? That is all I need to know—and, of course, what you will need to competently complete your task. If you can do nothing, then call me a real priest. I will not pour my final confession into the eager ear of a monk who makes no secret of his interest in alchemy or feels no shame at the fact that he was once brought under interdict by the pope at Avignon.''

"Of course I can do something," Gasca answered. He rose from his study of the wound, stretched to the accompaniment of an enormous cacophony of creaking bones and sighs, then came around the bed so that Olivier could look him squarely in the face. "As with most cauterizations, this one will cause you great pain while it is happening and then you will heal. You should not have suffered through so much alone. As I have said before, and will say again, you should have sent for me. Or you should have called on the Lady Julian. She would have helped you. But I will help you now."

Julian again, and again Olivier ignored her. "Tell me what you need," he said to the priest.

He looked over at Cristiano and nodded, making sure that his lieutenant would do the priest's bidding whether he trusted him or not.

"The normal things one needs in this case to make a poultice," the priest said mildly. "Onions, bread, a little fresh milk. And, of course, bring me a young maiden from the village. She will be most important."

Olivier saw Cristiano's lip curl in disgust. Olivier could almost see the twin thoughts of *magic* and *superstition* form themselves in his mind. And when Cristiano spoke, he spoke for both his commander and himself. "What need have we for a young girl—a virgin—in a sick room? You are reputed to be a healer. Why do you wish strange help?"

"Oh, I did not ask for a virgin. I asked for a maiden—an unmarried woman. And she is not for *me*." The priest looked amused at the suggestion. "She is for the Count. His, unfortunately, is a truly great festering. A painful occurrence. And to cure it will require even more pain. Belvedere at this moment is filled with foreign soldiers whose first loyalty is to their own foreign king. They might be tempted, perhaps, to forget the pain their bodies have certainly felt. They might laugh and carry tales if they were to hear the Count of the Ducci Montaldo cry out in pain.''

He emphasized this last word with a delicately pious shudder. Behind him, the huge wood fire crackled along merrily towards its own demise.

"Your cries might echo through the castle," the priest continued, "to ears that are, perhaps, listening for but should not hear such weakness. I have found that having a maiden about to hold the knight's hand often helps him to hold in even the most warranted of screams."

Cristiano grunted. "An old wives' tale if ever there be one. 'Tis beyond credence the idea that a virgin can draw out a man's pain. Not even my mother—who is an old wife—would believe such a story."

"It is not his pain she takes upon her," said Padre Gasca, casting one more curious glance at the bright welt of Olivier's wound. " 'Tis his pride she draws forth. There are few warriors in this world who will allow themselves the luxury of crying out while staring into the face of a damsel. This was a truth—not a tale—even before such things as medicine or healing priests or even old wives existed. A man's pride, in this case, often proves to be his discretion. Now, instead of criticizing things, which actually don't concern you, I suggest you hie yourself to the village and bring me back a maiden. And make sure she is comely and fair."

Olivier watched as Cristiano, clearly unconvinced, turned to him for confirmation. The Count of the Ducci Montaldo shrugged, wincing from the effort. And then, suddenly, he heard his own voice say, "Fetch me Julian. I will have no village virgin near me for this. 'Tis an operation that has need of tact and discretion. Fetch me Julian. Bring me my ward."

No one was more startled by his strange request than he was himself. And no one hid it better.

* * *

Julian would not let herself be disappointed. Every morning she rose from her bed just as she had always done: she washed herself, dressed, tended her needlework and her flowers, made lists and packed crates that would be waiting for Padre Gasca's return. She gathered all the herbs and medicines that they would need to send on to Belvedere. And she prayed that Olivier would change his mind.

She woke early, went to bed early: during the day she clung closely to her chamber fire.

Since the night Olivier had come to her bedchamber, he had not once sought her out. It was almost as though he had said what he had to say and there was no further need of discussion. So Julian did what life had taught her to do. She remained silent and watchful. She bided her time. Every morning she went immediately to the laboratory to attend to her duties. What free moments she had were spent with the Knight de la Marche. She disdained to question him about Olivier's activities. She would not stoop to pry and show her ignorance. She did not want her new friend to know that she was isolated and ignored by her own guardian.

She continued to do the castle's mending with Sabata and to talk with her about idle things. Still, she was grateful for her maid's company and, quite without prying, she learned a lot. But there was a problem brewing and Julian sensed it. Giacomo grew worse and, despite the cuffings from her father and the vague threats from Elisabetta the strega, she was not quite ready for bowing and accepting a cruel inevitability—at least not yet. She continued to rage and pray and search for someone or something that could help her brother. Julian held her breath as the little maid told her the story, afraid that Sabata would apply to her for healing. Afraid that the girl had heard some vague tale of the Magdalene and she would think that Julian could help her. This was the one thing Julian would not do for her because she was afraid to do it. She listened as the child talked of her brother and his cough. She knew from what Sabata said that the boy grew worse and she wanted to help him. She knew just what to do. She thought of the row of wooden perfume bottles filled with essence that she kept near her bed. She thought of the roses from the plains beyond Nicopolis. Nevertheless, she did not want the others to think her a witch and she did not want to *be* a witch. She would have no help from the Magdalene. She could not use what her mother had taught her—not even for good. Too many times in her young life had she seen good intentions turned into evil and willful desires. So when Sabata talked of her brother, Julian's heart ached, but she held herself silent. She vowed to pray for the boy—and she did—but she could have done more.

And she didn't.

Julian was in her room, staring into the fire, when the knock came. She did not turn towards it. She assumed it was someone bringing water for her evening bath. She had grown up in the East where the idea of a daily bath was not uncommon, as it was not uncommon in the castles in which she had lived—in Francesca's home and in that of her brother. She heard Sabata scurry to answer the knock and heard the door open. She expected all of this, but what she did not expect was the particular voice she heard and the words it spoke to her.

"My lady, come quickly," said Cristiano. "The priest has returned and he has need of you."

It was really Olivier who needed her, Julian realized as she entered his chamber. The room was brightly lighted and for a second she stood within the doorway, blinking, getting used to the brilliance. Of course, she had never entered his private chamber before this. She had never been invited. A fire blazed and the candles were lighted. The room was austere. There was a large bed covered with furs, a simple trestle table, a few wooden stools. Nothing else. None of the luxury that characterized the rest of Belvedere, not even the painted icons and prie-dieu that simple religious practice demanded. There were no tapestries warming the walls of this cool room. In fact, this chamber's austerity reminded Julian of the laboratory. This impression flashed into her mind, to be just as quickly forgotten as her eye found Olivier.

Dressed in a simple white linen tunic, he was on his feet to greet her. He stood erectly but his face was chalk-white and Julian could tell he was in pain. Suddenly she realized he had been in pain the last time she had seen him as well—that time two nights before when he had come to her room. She had felt his pain when first she had awakened and had seen his large form looming over her. When she had smelled the welcome scent of him and smiled. Then he had started to speak to her, to frighten her, and she had forgotten that first intuition.

Now she would make no guess as to his situation before he himself explained it to her. She would not let the Magdalene do its work.

"My lord," she said, sweeping into a curtsey.

"I see you've braided your hair behind you," he said. It was obvious that by now even he knew she was vain about the long, dark ripple of her hair. His lips were white and tight with pain as he spoke. "Though 'tis still unveiled. Yet at least a start has been made to your obeying me." He narrowed his eyes and stared at her intently before continuing. "It seems I do have need of you, indeed. There is a festering on my shoulder—a wound that I have not properly cared for. The priest thinks I will be a better patient and not cry out should there be a maid here with me while he cleans and dresses it. He feels, I believe, that the shame of showing weakness before a damsel should stifle any scream."

His ironic smile came out as a grimace. They both knew that he had gotten to his feet and struggled into his tunic for just this reason. His pride could not bear that he should be seen as weak and helpless. She saw the pain in his eyes and around his lips and she wondered again how she had missed it before. How *could* she have missed it, when she loved him so? But that was in the past. She reached out to help him and he took her slender, strong fingers gratefully within his own.

"Aye," she said. "You do have need of someone. And so I have come."

There was no doubt that he was feeling better. The priest had been right to suggest a woman's touch. He himself had been right to insist on Julian. She had removed the tunic from his shoulders without hurting him, which in itself had seemed nothing less than a miracle at the time. He had been burning with pain and with fever, and he could not imagine that she could get him out of his tunic without hurting him: it had certainly nearly killed him getting it on. But she had done so and he had somehow found himself lying on his bed with both of his hands in hers. Tightly in hers. They were hands, he thought, which he had never seen flutter ineffectively or nervously pick.

Julian knelt before him, beside his bed, and looked into his eyes. He could see comfort in them and something else as well. Hurt. Perhaps fear. It was strange to think of Julian as being fearful. It was strange to think of Julian at all. He rarely did, he realized with sudden clarity. And that in itself was odd. She was, after all, his ward. She had saved his life. He *should* be thinking of her, and with gratitude. Actually he knew very little about her and none of the small things that were so important, such as what made her laugh and what irritated her and what she lived for and what she dreamed. Even if she had been his enemy he would have made it his business to know all of these things well before now.

Perhaps her eyes could tell him something, he thought dreamily. They reminded him of the sea as he had seen it once long ago in Brittany, during his paging days. The color had been just this deep tone of blue and had suggested this same sense of depth. It was a calm sea, but it had not seemed peaceful. He had stood upon it, on the rocks, and he had wondered at the secrets—wrecked ships and even bodies—which might be hidden beneath its placid surface. That was how he thought of

Julian now—calm, but not peaceful. Hiding something at her depth.

Normally he was not a fanciful person, but the pain, and now the blessed prospect of relief from it, had given his mind a sudden turn. He let himself reach down into the depths of those eyes, searching for the place where he knew she was hiding. He found, a little to his surprise, that he could do this. He would find her there one day, hidden deep, deep within herself. He knew this. He also knew that it was important for him to find her, to discover her and lay bare her secrets.

But that was for another time. Now he looked into Julian's eyes, he held her hands, he did not cry out as the priest began his work.

"All finished. And a good job I've made of it if I must say so myself." The tone of Padre Gasca's voice told his three listeners that though he praised himself, he was not above hearing others do the same and they murmured their assent. Satisfied, Gasca stood back, admiring his handiwork, and then walked around so that Olivier could once again see his face.

The Count of the Ducci Montaldo imagined that the priest did this out of habit in order to reassure his patients, but Olivier did not need reassurance. He knew the worst was over and that he would feel pain for a few days—and sometimes this pain would be intense—but then he would begin to heal. He had passed a turning point. He had felt pain before, and he understood it.

Despite this knowledge, it was a moment before he was aware that he still gripped Julian's hands and that he must be hurting her. He let them go slowly, so that the rush of blood back into them would not hurt her. It was only then that he was conscious of still staring into her blue eyes and that she still stared into his. He slowly let that grasp go as well until he could once again see her hands, raw and grooved, where he had gripped them. He must have hurt them terribly. He stared at her long, slim fingers as he realized that he had never let them go once through the whole ordeal. He felt a strong urge to hold them to his mouth—to hold them *in* his mouth. To chafe them and warm them, so that he could take away the hurt for her as she had just now taken away the hurt for him. Instead, he docilely let them help him into his white linen night tunic and turn him gently over into the softness of his bed.

"Here, my lord, drink this." The priest bustled over with a pottery mug filled with something vile but warming. Olivier drank it down, and over its brim he watched as Julian settled him beneath his fox skin rugs. The room was alive with the odor of spring violets, and with the scent of the woman Julian. Olivier smiled at how the sweetness of Julian's violets had swept away the stench of his festered wound. He didn't know why he was thinking about Julian or why he wanted her near. Some part of his brain realized, and realized quite clearly, that it was Domiziana, his nearly betrothed, who should be filling his mind and bringing him solace. He put his waywardness down to pain and drugs and let himself drift along on this pleasant, unexpected current. Tomorrow he would reform and think the practical thoughts that became a Count of the Ducci Montaldo. Just as he had done every day since his return from the East. He would become that man again tomorrow—but not tonight—and things would go back to the way they had been. What harm could just one night's thinking do?

He watched silently as Julian fluffed his pillows, as she straightened his linen sheets one last time and poured fresh water into a silver basin. He watched her as she smiled shyly over at him—and as she turned to leave through the heavy oak door of his chamber. And then—just as it had happened before—he, more surprised than anyone else, heard his own voice saying something that his mind had not consciously planned.

"I will be alone with my ward. She has skill in nursing and she will attend me. The rest of you may leave and take your rest." It was his best Count of the Ducci Montaldo voice, the one he used to command.

The others nodded—the priest with a small, secret smile on his lips. Bustling about, he said only that he would revisit his patient at cockcrow. He would cancel his planned return to the monastery until he was assured the Count was better. It was the least he could do.

Olivier could tell that Cristiano was not content to leave him. His lieutenant was still worried after the attack and would probably pull a stool and wait outside the door, in case he was needed. He would not like the idea that Olivier would be left without guarding and in the hands of a young woman, especially after what had happened along the Ridings. Cristiano knew all about Julian and, more importantly, knew what they said about her mother. He did not relish leaving his commander with a reputed witch, a woman who would undoubtedly know how to protect herself no matter how innocent she might look.

Olivier was aware of his lieutenant's opinion, but he motioned his dismissal anyway and, despite his misgivings, Cristiano left. The door closed behind him with a thud.

"Sit here," Olivier said to his ward.

Julian settled into a chair beside the bed. She moved it close, though he had not given her permission to do this, nor had she asked. Actually, she had not said one word to him since she had come and agreed to hold his hand and to help him. She seemed to know what he wanted without the need of idle chat. Olivier smelled her spring violets. He remembered how she had laughed with Gatien de la Marche, and selfishly now, he wanted some of that freshness and laughter for himself. He wanted to apologize to her for coming to her chamber alone and treating her without respect. But at the same time he wanted to kiss her. To plunge his tongue deep within her mouth and see if there was a welcoming for him as well. In his drugged and wearied state, he knew that in the end he would do both of these things.

Just as he knew that one day he would discover her secret. Just as he knew that one day, she would discover his as well.

For now, the Count of the Ducci Montaldo took his ward's hand and held it, gently this time. Then he closed his eyes and he slept.

CHAPTER SIX

In the days that followed, when Julian's life brushed against Olivier's, she strained to hear within his talk of warring and falconing some clue that he had at last turned his thoughts towards the crusade, but she never did. Since she'd held his hand and helped with his healing, he had taken to treating her with great respect. She was seated on his right at mealtime and he reached continually towards her to make sure that her wine glass was filled, and that choice pieces of meat and fowl and preserved fruits were heaped upon her plate.

"You're much too thin," he said. "It must be that foul English cooking you had at Harnoncourt Hall." Gatien de la Marche, French to the core and fresh from the trial which his British mealtimes had been to him, nodded in sage agreement.

She realized, of course, that Olivier carefully orchestrated their few encounters and that it was his purpose never to be alone with her, and so she was most careful with him. She wore the neck of her gowns high and her dark hair pulled neatly back into a veil. She did not speak of healing. She did not mention Nicopolis. Each morning she watched from the don-

jon's now-sparkling windows as he rode away on that day's
sport attended by his knights and his pages and by his hawks
and falcons. More times than not, Gatien de la Marche accompanied him, and she would stare as all their bright flags and
banners ripped away from her and disappeared. The empty
hallways of Belvedere Castle echoed her loneliness.

"Looks like drizzle," Sabata said from behind her. She
pushed listlessly at the pail and rags that they were using to
tidy the last corners of the laboratory. Since the first days
when she'd been so frightened—of both Julian and the sinister
atmosphere of this large upstairs room—she'd changed considerably. Now she asked questions about the parchments, brought
an Etruscan coin that she had found with her betrothed to place
it upon the wall with the others, even managed to clean the
collection of frogs that danced sluggishly about in their preserv-
ing liquid. Today, however, she seemed pale and her steady
hands worked only intermittently at their task. More than once
Julian caught her glancing anxiously past the castle windows
to the village of Sant'Urbano which lay in its shadow. Julian
knew the reason for these quick glances though she tried to
push the knowledge away, tried with frantic activity to make
up for Sabata's worried lethargy. She worked feverishly, hiding
behind a mountain of her own activity as she boxed herbs and
glass bottles that had been labeled and then carefully wrapped
in old linen sheets. She could *almost* ignore Sabata's anxious
glancing, but not quite.

" 'Tis your brother, isn't it? He's not better."

It was a statement, not a question, and Sabata was quick to
respond. "Oh, he's terrible, terrible," she cried, immediately
dropping everything to clutch at Julian's hand. "Oh, my lady,
he's doing so poorly. He's got a fever and doesn't know where
he is half the time. We've tried everything, everything that
Strega Elisabetta told us to do and still he feels no better."

"Have you sent for the monks from San Mario? They are
well-known for their healing arts."

"Aye, we've sent word for them but the Abbot sent word

that it might be days before one of them could make their way
to Sant'Urbano. There is a late pestilence near them and they
say that they are needed in villages within their own parish.
We are poor folk, and not worth the inconvenience of winter
travel." Her voice was vinegar-bitter. "Oh, if only the Lady
Francesca were still here. She would know how to help us. She
would want to help us."

"There has to be someone else," Julian insisted. "Someone
nearer at hand who knows the healing arts."

"You, my lady." There was anguish on Sabata's face but
determination as well. She reached out and took Julian's hand
and held it tight. "Everyone says you know the old skills.
Everyone says you inherited them from your mother."

"I have no skills," Julian said quickly, turning away. She
snatched her hand back and drew her arms close to her sides.
She felt the compassion she had felt for Sabata and for her
brother evaporate before the force of her own fear. "I cannot
help you with this. What you heard was rumor and nothing
more. I know nothing of healing. I know nothing of the old
ways. However, it's senseless for you to stay on with me. I
can finish what little there is to finish by myself. You go to
your family. They will have more need of you than I do."

Sabata hesitated, caught in a battle between her own need
to be with her family and her determination to bring Julian to
them so that she could help her brother.

"I've seen you myself, Lady Julian," she insisted stubbornly.
" 'Tis the talk of the kitchens how the Lord Olivier was sick
and awfully pale and then you went to him one night and then
the next day, magically, he was well again."

" 'Twas Padre Gasca who helped him," retorted Julian,
angry now. " 'Twas the priest who got him well, not I. Send for
him at San Mario. He will come when he knows the urgency."

Sabata was too frightened to be stopped by Julian's fear.
"Lady, if you can and if you don't help my brother then you
are a witch indeed and everything bad they say about you is
true!" Before Julian could say another word, the girl turned

on her heels and fled from the room, slamming the heavy oaken door behind her. For what seemed like hours, Julian stood where she was, listening to the sound of the maid's footsteps echoing down the donjon steps.

"It doesn't matter. I can't do it. I cannot allow myself to do it," Julian whispered urgently. She looked down to see that she'd clutched her hands so tightly that her fingers had drawn blood. "I've worked too hard to get away from all of that. I'll not be drawn back into it now." She had to think of her duty to Aalyne before anything else. A promise had been made to her mother and she must see that it was maintained.

Still. . . .

She went back to her work with a vengeance. She packaged, she washed, she labeled. But the donjon's coldness pressed against her, pressed *into* her. Worst of all, now that Sabata was gone, the ghosts of the Ducci Montaldo came out to dance. She heard their laughter and she saw, once again as though they were still near her, Francesca with her two children, the Lady Blanche, and the old, wise priest. People who were not frightened to do what was right and to follow their heart.

And she saw that child Giacomo as well. Sabata had only brought him up to her once—he had sickened soon after her arrival from Harnoncourt Hall—but now his face came back clearly to Julian. She found this strange because days and even months and weeks could go by when Aalyne was only a blur of golden hair and fairness to her, when she was only a whiff of roses. In her mind her mother's features had become as soft and white and melting as snowflakes. You could never hold them, not even in memory. Instead, with this boy Julian remembered everything. She saw the dusky blush of his cheeks, saw his dark eyes and the sheen of his straight hair. She heard herself say to him, "Don't play with rusted things," just as though she were repeating the words now.

She saw the frantic face of his sister.

Someone must help him or he'll die.

"Well, maybe just an herb," Julian thought. Her eye automatically found the row of rosewood bottles she had painted during her first, frightening days at Belvedere and then left in the laboratory when she had moved on. "There might be something in Francesca's garden which might help." She was surprised that she had spoken aloud and that the laboratory seemed to approve her last words and echo them back to her. *Help, help, help.*

Now that her mind was made up, she pulled off her apron and ran down the stairs, her footsteps much lighter and more determined than Sabata's had been. Just this once, she thought. 'Tis not right to let this child die when I've helped the lord of the castle to heal. And she *had* helped Olivier, she realized suddenly. Even though Gasca had done the herbal work, her presence had somehow been needed, just as it was needed now. The rightness of the thought carried her onward, but it did not rush her. Aalyne had trained her in the small preliminaries of the Power. The first of these was listening. One had to wait, to hear, to feel. One could not trust one's own impatience. One had to trust the Power.

Without thinking, Julian cocked her head to listen and knew that there was time left for the boy—not much, but enough— and that she must give patient way to this time. She had a task to perform first: someone waited for her. Someone she must speak with, something she must do before she could make her way to Francesca's garden. A small task, really—and then her aid could be freely given. She caught herself—Julian Madrigal, a woman not known for smiling—as she smiled.

Like Olivier, she did not know her own words until she heard them.

"My mother was a witch," Julian heard herself saying to her great friend the Knight de la Marche. He had been waiting for her, as she had sensed he would be. They walked within the inner curtain a little behind the castle main and along a gravel pathway that, in June, would be alive with wisteria and a plethora of small, fragrant flowers. It was not summer now. Belvedere's grayness loomed up all around them—a little darker than the sky, a little brighter than the wintry hills. It was well past the midmorning hour of *primes* but still the fog held fast.

"At least I think her to have been one," she continued softly. She would not stop, now that the first words had been spoken for the very first time. "I don't know what it means exactly, being a witch. I do know that she had a power and she used it. And she used it to hurt people, though of course that wasn't her intention and she always denied that people suffered because of her. They were hurt anyway. If they didn't do what she wanted, if they were too strong, then she hurt them."

Gatien said nothing. Not yet. Instead they walked slightly apart, not touching. The wind whipped their cloaks and their hair about them. It came from the east, behind them, and Julian's face was half-hidden behind the blowing shreds of her dark hair. The bluster did not seem to matter: she did not seem even to notice it. She had kept her gaze studiously down upon the pathway before them since he had happened upon her and asked her for this time. She had nodded once, twice—quickly and reluctantly. He knew, of course, that she did not want to be with him, but he was determined to talk with her. He had not seen her in six days. Not since the morning he had quite unexpectedly watched her come forth from Olivier's chamber at dawn. It had been a bad few hours for him until his spies had told him that the Count of the Ducci Montaldo had been mysteriously ill and that his ward had helped him. However, he was taking no chances and had determined to talk to Julian first, and then to her guardian about her. He had already wasted a great deal of time at Belvedere, had delayed again and again his return to Burgundy and he knew that his liege lord would be fuming. The duke would surely be watching for him and had probably already sent out informants. It didn't matter. Gatien knew he had no news of moment to report. Though he was out of his bed again and supposedly on the mend from his sudden inexplicable fever, the Count of the Ducci Montaldo had not made up his mind. But Gatien had made up his.

"A witch," Julian repeated.

"But how could you know?" he said very gently. "You were so young. You left her when you were but a child. How could you know what it was she was really doing, or why she did it, or how?"

"Because I was supposed to do the same thing myself." She looked up very quickly and Gatien felt the full strength of her deep, dark eyes upon him. He blinked once quickly as she continued. "She was the Magdalene, you know. Not an ordinary witch. She was supposed to pass her knowledge on to me. It had been done thus for generations—since time's beginning."

He loved Julian and so he did not want to scoff at what she obviously took as serious, but he was also young and could not quite help himself. "A legend, that. Aalyne's way of making herself important and raising her prices. There is no mention of a Magdalene in any witchcraft legend, at least not until her time. The stories begin with her."

"But she always existed and the gift was passed down from mother to daughter. Different women, but the gift was the same and the power with it," said Julian. She did not seem fazed by his indifference. She was used to misunderstanding and, anyway, she knew what she knew. "There was never any need to make her presence known before. She just lived and did what she was supposed to do and there was protection for her in it—at least until the destruction."

"You refer to the banning of the Knights Templar," said Gatien crisply. Despite himself, he was growing annoyed. He was impatient to get on with what he had to say to her, and he did not want to hear these things that he had already heard for years in old ballads, when troubadours were either too bored or too tired to sing of new gossip. Aalyne's trial and her flight would always serve. Everyone from Picardy to Constantinople sang that the beautiful Aalyne was a witch—and even a great witch—and that only a miracle had saved her from the stake

years ago in Lyon. This should have no effect on her child. He
would not believe what Julian was telling him. He thought she
was making excuses even to herself for her refusal of him.
Because even though he was determined to ask what needed
asking, he was already sure that she would refuse him. And he
knew that the reason would have nothing to do with witchcraft
and legend, with good and evil. It had to do with her emerging
from Olivier's chamber into the morning light, tired and
drained, but with her face radiant. Oh, no, what would stop his
having Julian predated the snake's bringing cunning into Eden.
It was an enemy that would need all of his patience and skill
to better.

Julian was in love with Olivier. But Olivier was nearly
betrothed to another, and a rich and powerful 'other' at that—
and therein lay Gatien's hope.

"Yes, to the Knights Templar," Julian said. Again she graced
him with her quick look. "But they were always around and
they were called other things before that. During the first crusades, when the world was in chaos, they thought the time was
ripe for their entrance into the world. They thought they no
longer needed to keep themselves secret. They found out otherwise."

"You are referring to the Disbandment. But that was almost
a hundred years ago—at the beginning of the Schism and the
establishment of the second papacy at Avignon. Pope Clement
V fulfilled the wishes of the King of France who was his
protector and the guarantor of his earthly power. As always,
Philip the Fair of France needed money and the Templars had
it." Gatien shrugged his shoulders, bored with this and anxious
to get on with his own affairs. "The verdict of witchcraft given
against them had nothing to do with sorcery and everything to
do with a precarious list in the ship of French finances. The
Templars would still be alive and respected as the Knights of
St. John Hospitaler are today had they not been so astute in
amassing a fortune that the king needed."

Julian went on as though she had not heard him. "According

to what my mother told me, they were warlocks and the Magdalene was their own witch. She enriched their power with her own and hers was formidable. She was called the Magdalene because the first of our race came from the small thorp of Magdala—the same village as that Mary who went on to become a saint. We were very different from her—perhaps we were from another part of the village." Julian stopped for an instant and smiled, but this smile quickly faded. "And of course the men were always with us. The world has always been a hard place for women, and they were our protection. As we were theirs."

"But the Templars are all dead. Even if this absurd legend were true they would be no use to you now," Gatien insisted. "King Philip killed them all, from their Grand Master Jacques de Molay on down. They were outlawed and tortured and burned throughout Christendom—most of them in Paris on pyres struck up right before the Cathedral of Notre Dame itself. He confiscated everything they had and made his state and his family rich from it."

Despite himself, Gatien hesitated at this. He remembered what his father, a young squire at the time, had told him about the burnings.

"You are thinking of the curse," said Julian mildly. "You are thinking of Jacques de Molay. How when he was already burning, with his hair crackling around his head like a devil's halo, he turned to the king who had once been his great friend, turned to the man who had called him to be godfather to the royal princess, and cursed Fair Philip's family down to the thirteenth generation. He vowed that he would meet both Clement and Philip before God's judgment seat within the year. The King was a hale young man himself and had a pride of sons. Yet within seven months of Molay's words both he and the pope were dead. Strangely, unaccountably—but most certainly dead. After him, one by one, Philip's three sons took the throne and died one after the other, aged, 27, 28, and 33. Not one of them left a male heir. The Capetian dynasty withered beneath the Templar curse and was no more.''

"Surely you cannot believe all of this. It happened a long time ago. There were no records. The whole area of superstition and secrecy—this is what legend thrives on.''

She reached up and pulled the small starred amulet she always wore from beneath her cloak. The gold of it seemed strangely out of place on the silver of that winter's day. "This is the Maltese Star,'' she said. "It is the emblem of what I am. Jacques de Molay wore one just like it, only larger as befitted his position. It was seen on the burned husk of his body but then it disappeared. They say it looked untouched by the fire and that it—glowed. They say my father—whoever he is— wears the Maltese Star of Jacques de Molay and that I will know him by it. I want to know him.''

"Why?'' asked Gatien. "When you can have your own life? When you can marry me and be my Lady?''

She had known this was coming. It did not take the power of a Magdalene to read it in his attention to her, in his courtesy. Love was always trickier to read than fear, but still it left its traces. And she knew that she could find no trace of it in herself, at least for this kind man who stood before her. She raised her gaze and looked at him as she shook her head.

They stood silently for a moment, staring into each other. Even the wind about them seemed to have fallen into its own stillness. Then Gatien took Julian's arm and together they continued on with their pleasant, friendly promenade.

"I will not push you about it,'' he said to her. "At least not now. We will talk of other things. I must tell you that I am most anxious that a decision be reached soon about this Crusade. I, for one, am quite looking forward to going to the East.''

Julian stopped in her tracks to stare at him, astounded. It had been a long time since she'd heard anyone say anything kind about her home. "Whatever in the world for?''

"Belden has talked so much about it, for one thing. He loved it there, even though he was being held for ransom. Said he had learned a great deal from the Saracens, especially about medicine.''

"That's true," Julian answered doubtfully. "They are very far advanced in those matters."

"Belden said you knew a great deal as well. He said you were a born healer."

She wanted to ask him if the Lord of the Harnoncourts had actually said "healer" or "witch," but she didn't. Now that thoughts of love and marriage had gone from it, their conversation had taken on the frosty tones of the day around them, at least for her. She pulled her cloak tighter, as much against this as she did against the wind. "I know a few things," she said. "A very few. We were Christian and so allowed more freedoms under Muslim rule, but I was raised in the harem of the Sultan Bayezid—and then that of another man. Not many men were allowed into the harem, and so women had to learn skills to help when help is needed. The doctors taught me things.'' Julian did not add, *My mother didn't. There was no time.*

Gatien reached down and patted the fingers that still held tightly to his arm. "You'll have to tell me about it. I want to know."

"I don't want to talk about it. I don't want to talk about what happened to me in the past," she blurted. "Talk about yourself, first. Tell me what happened to your face. Not just vague murmurings about the Saracens in Jerusalem, but how they hurt you—what you felt. And then we can talk about me."

She pulled her arm away, shocked that she could even have anything so horrible inside, shocked that she had said such a cruel and terrible thing, and especially to this man who, not a few moments before, had asked her to be his Lady. Who had offered to take away her bastard status and replace it with a name that was renowned throughout Christendom. Her fingers flew to her mouth as though to keep other strange and horrible things from tumbling out.

To her surprise, Gatien looked at her levelly. "I don't mind talking about it," he said. "I used to, but I don't anymore. It happened on a small expedition to Jerusalem. There was nothing extraordinary about the mission or what happened to me during it. The Saracens are excellent swordsmen, and the one who got me was good. Not so good that he killed me, but good enough that I'm called upon to remember him every time I look into a speck of glass. Olivier fought in that battle as well, though I did not know him then nor did he know me. I was disfigured: he was captured. I sometimes wonder who was worse hurt.''

"Oh, Gatien. I'm so sorry. I don't know why I said it. I don't know what came over me.'' Julian suddenly realized how frightened she was to lose the only person who had seemed her friend in this strange place. It was true he wasn't Olivier, could never *be* Olivier to her, but he had been kind and she suddenly realized how important that small thing was.

"Now I *could* say there's nothing to forgive,'' he said slowly, not giving her the instant absolution she had come to expect from him. "But I won't say that. One day, though, I'll recall to you that you once said that if I told you my story first, then you'd tell me yours. Not your mother's—yours. I won't hold you to that promise now. Not now, but someday, when you're ready. For now we'll just be friends who don't talk about certain things.''

Julian smiled her relief and nodded. Secretly she knew that that day would never come.

"Now,'' Gatien said, briskly changing the subject. "Tell me what you plan to do with the rest of your day. I didn't see the Count ride out with the others, but I'm sure he's gone, which means there are at least some hours before the evening meal. I've reports to send on to the duke, so I won't be able to spend the afternoon with you, as much as I'd like that. Perhaps that's just as well, as I need to be on my best behavior so that in the end you will change your mind and marry me. Tell me about your own plans.''

"I thought I might tend the herb gardens,'' Julian said. "The Lady Francesca asked me for some specific perennials that are missing from her collection in England. There is not much that can be done in winter—the ground is like stone, but I thought to try anyway."

"The land looks sere about here now." Gatien glanced upward towards the steel sky. "Not much growing."

"I can try," Julian answered. "I promised. And then my maid Sabata has a young brother who is sick and shows no sign of improving. I thought I might pick a helpful herb for him as well."

Gatien smiled and the whole of his face seemed to fasten around that smile. It occurred to her that his smile was the first thing she had noticed about him, and that she saw it now much more readily than she saw the scar on his face. Julian hadn't smiled before, but she smiled at him now.

"I thought you had no use for healing," he teased.

"Oh, this is not healing," she said quickly and with a blush. " 'Tis but helping. The parents already have a wise woman helping them and she wants no interference. And I have no wish to meddle. I just thought to bring them some rose bark, if I can find any with still a bit of green to it. I've seen them use it for congestion often in Bulgaria, where Nicopolis lies. It always seemed to help."

"Perhaps," said Gatien thoughtfully. "If the rose bark is wielded by the right hand, and if that hand is yours."

Julian opened her mouth to protest, but just then a beam of sunlight broke through the clouds and bounced against the turquoise-and-white flag of the Ducci Montaldo that billowed over their castle. Julian stood on tiptoe, pointing to it, and then she clapped like a child.

"See, Gatien? Just look at that. 'Tis a sign—a great sign from heaven! We're going east. I know it! We were talking of Nicopolis just then and God has shown us the way!"

"Aye, little Julian, 'tis a great sign from God. Now you go to your gardening and let me be off to somehow write to the Duke of Burgundy that we're sure we're off on crusade, because God Himself has sent a ray of sunshine to tell us so!"

* * *

The gray soon closed in once again around her ray of sunshine. She turned purposefully away from it and towards the wicket that led to Francesca's garden. She had trained herself early on not to look at things she didn't want to see. Instead she turned to the plant enclosure and the good she could do within it.

Belvedere stood high in the Tuscan hills, but it had escaped the first winter frosting. A few wisps of geraniums still peeked wistfully from terra-cotta pots. There would be every chance that the ground below in the hidden garden would be workable. She needed very little from it—a few withered branches, a little sap of rose. Surely that much would be available. She pulled her dark blue cloak firmly around her.

Julian found that even after all the years in England she remembered the way. She had learned it well in her time at Belvedere and she was beginning to realize to her dismay just how much easier it was to learn things than it was to forget them. She found the wicket door and smiled without humor at how much it recalled to her. She remembered even the screech it made as she pulled it open, and she remembered the pathway beyond it and the feel of dry leaves and branches against the soft leather of her shoes. How often she had passed this way with Francesca, talking to her and laughing as they hunted some strange herb or gathered honey or spring flowers. How different those outings had been from those with her own mother. She and Francesca had joked and laughed as they set about their way. With Aalyne there had been no laughter. *They are all against us and we must win.* The herbs she'd picked with her mother had been serious things: they had often been deadly. Julian looked up to catch hoarfrost caressing the trees just above her head. She pulled her cloak closer and hurried on. In the early afternoon sunlight the way to the herbal garden meandered downward, overgrown and almost covert, but still discernibly a path. Someone had trod upon it recently and Julian decided that the children must play down here, even though they were warned not to by their parents. The Count had expressly forbidden it.

Perhaps it was because she had spoken so much of the past that she could not now seem to shake its ghost. It was as though Aalyne were beside her, urging her on. She could feel her mother's arms around her like a vise, could smell on this autumn afternoon the full summer heat of the attar of roses she always wore. It was strange and even frightening how much she felt her mother's presence as she walked Francesca's path, but feel it she did.

Give that silly girl her hankering. What she wants is so little, really—the life of her brother—and you can do it. You can give it to her. You have the knowledge. You have the Power. Give her that one thing—and she will give you everything else.

"But I don't want power. I don't want power over anyone." Julian's words fled from her mouth on a rush of cold steam. Above her head, tree branches met and hugged themselves in the raw wind.

She walked on quickly, only pausing to cross herself and say a quick prayer before the Ducci Montaldo cemetery. Its small stone cruciforms marked the family dead for three generations, since the time the great warrior Luca had founded Belvedere as his legate fortress. She had visited it often with Francesca, who had told her the whole of the story. She could talk to Julian, and Julian had been trained to listen.

She knew that Francesca's beloved father and all three of his warrior sons were sheltered in this sacred ground. They had died of plague and been buried here amid the peace of ivy and wisteria. They were said to haunt the castle, to come out at sunset with a shouted welcome. Julian had never seen them, though she had tried often enough. She had no fear of ghosts— indeed she had welcomed them with the fervor and loneliness of her fourteen-year-old heart. Only living people frightened her.

Their sister had talked often about her brothers, had laughed

about them and done good imitations of them. Even Blanche,
their mother, and Belden, who had known them all, could speak
of them, though Blanche did so rarely and haltingly and still,
eleven years after their deaths, with tears in her eyes. There
had been dark whispers that their deaths had crazed her and
sent her to wine. But gradually, very gradually, Blanche had
got over it. She had gone on.

For the first time, Julian realized that she had never heard
Olivier speak of his brothers. Olivier, the eldest of them, had
been imprisoned under the Sultan Bayezid when plague came
to Belvedere and so had escaped the fate of the whole male
portion of his family. Now they were only ghosts, guarded by
their simple stone crosses. Julian, trained to look upon the
ground for needed herbs and flowers, saw that the ground before
the churchyard was many-tracked and that the tracking led
within. She would have to tell Sabata to scold the children. If
Olivier knew they were playing in the churchyard he would be
angry.

She almost passed the garden. Unlike the pathway, it showed
no use and had obviously been left to meander and overgrow
since Francesca's departure. Not even Padre Gasca had
remained to tend it. He had gone to England with the rest of
them and found a protector in Richard II. The king, happy to
have within his court someone put under interdict within enemy
France, had graced Gasca with a teaching chair at Oxford. The
priest had only returned with Julian, and then reluctantly.

The garden had once been lush, but now all that remained
were a few dried rosemary stalks and impressions of dead and
forgotten oregano and thyme plants, all laid out within the
graying web of a hemp-string wall. Beyond it, deserted honey-
combs whistled in the wind. Honey had been a mainstay of
the Ducci Montaldos during Olivier's imprisonment. Under
Francesca's loving hand, Belvedere honeys were carefully elab-
orated and had become justly famous all the way to the Muslim
world. Upon his return, the Count had ordered that all the bees
be freed to the fields and pastures. He had cut back the haw-

thorns and the teasel that they loved. Belvedere was to be once again a warrior fortress, not a home for healing. He had made this point quite clear.

He had not, however, been able to cut away the atmosphere that had bred the bees and their honey. Julian put her nose down and sniffed the earth. She smiled. She could help that child Giacomo, and she would. She would allow a little—just a little—of the Power to flow through her. The thrill of healing was upon her. She would open herself and listen. Just this once.

Of course, she hadn't meant to work through the afternoon. She had brought no one to help her. Yet there was something so familiar about this place, so wildly welcoming after the cold perfection of Belvedere that she lingered.

Julian pulled the last weeds from the patch and tried to put the child from her mind. Elisabetta would handle it, she told herself, yanking and pulling. If not, she would go herself, but tonight after the dark had fallen. No witchcraft was needed to save young Giacomo—and thus no need for Aalyne's power and no need for the skill she had passed on to her daughter. Julian tidied the last of the herb rows, plucked dead leaves from the ornamental geraniums.

"Simple herb work and nothing more."

The wind whipped the words from her mouth.

She bent lower over the blighted plants in Francesca's garden. She pulled them and mulched others with the straw from her hemp-string basket, yanked at them energetically, pulling out good roots with bad. She didn't notice. Her mind was miles away—with other people in other times.

She had no idea how Sabata had known she might help. They had never seen each other before and the maid was too young to have heard of the Magdalene's legend. Why should she have heard it—it had all happened so long ago. It had been the same with Aalyne, at least at Nicopolis. People had just seemed to sense her power and they had come to her for it. Julian remembered the scene over and over again from her childhood. The knock on the door, the crossing of silver on the palm, the relief given. At least for a time.

It was the caw of a raven that called her back. Julian jumped when she heard it: the sound seemed much too close, just beyond her shoulder. She shivered, but when she saw the bird, he was far up the hill. Still, she finished and looked about her in some satisfaction. She'd tied the last of her herb row and the ornamental geraniums. These had been particularly hard to tidy: they had run riot and overgrown themselves. Weeds had matted their woody stems to the ground. She had managed to trim and neaten them anyway, cutting them back to ready them for the summer's growth.

There was nothing left of what must have been the string hedge that had once ordered the garden and confined it from the surrounding woods. Francesca would be pleased with her, of course, when she told her, and the priest would as well. More importantly, the work was done and done to her satisfaction. She had even gathered the pine cones that she needed, and had found some useable rosewood. All would be ready if the sick child still required her help. For the first time since she had sat with Olivier, she was content as she turned back to the pathway and the castle of Belvedere.

All around her swirled the early whispers of that strange Tuscan fog that was nothing at all like what she'd known in England. There, one could see the mist rising from the ocean, rising from the cliffs and from the meadows. It came from the earth and carried something of earthiness with it. From miles away one could see it coming. It didn't sneak up. Here the mist rose up from the ground, but it seemed to descend from heaven as well, and it came quickly, almost as though it wanted to frighten. But, aside from the one important issue, Julian was not given to superstition. And besides, the Magdalene was not superstition: she knew it to be fact. Nevertheless, as she neared the Ducci Montaldo cemetery, she again raised her free hand to cross herself and prayed quickly for them, as she had always seen Francesca do. The hemp-string basket with its pine cones and its rosewood rocked back and forth comfortably against her thigh. She listened to her own footfalls. She listened to the natural silence. And her sighting of the man seemed just as natural as well. He seemed, in his own way, to be part of the picture.

He was standing just within the boundaries of the ossuary, beneath a gnarled wisteria that had been seared by many wintry winds. She walked closer, not muffling her footfalls, still not frightened. Still finding something natural in his being where he was. She was curious, that was all. His back was to her. Then his cloak caught the wind just as the raven cawed and it wrapped about him like full-blown wings. At least that's what it did in Julian's suddenly full-blown imagination. Words tumbled back into her mind with pell-mell speed—admonitions and muffled whispers about highwaymen and brigands and what they might do to a woman alone. She'd had that done to her before: she wanted no part of it now.

I must get away. Her feet were moving silently even before the words were fully formed. *Got to get away. Must hide.* She thought again of the raven's strange cawing, and even more than the sight of the strange man before her, this made her heart hammer and her hand shake.

Now, of course, since she was determined to be quiet she found herself making more noise than she ever had when the sight of this man had seemed so natural to her. Her feet crunched against the dry cypress covering on the path. The rattle of her pine cones could have been heard in Florence. And so it didn't surprise her that the man heard them as well and that he turned to her.

At first she was so relieved to see Olivier Ducci Montaldo's face that she started running towards him, waving her hand, and feeling her hair stream out. She had actually gotten quite close to him before his face and his eyes really came into focus, before she could see the taut pain that no arrow wound had etched around his mouth and the look of hatred in his eyes as they found her.

That look, those eyes, that hard, cruel mouth—they stopped her in her tracks and brought a flush of blood to her cheeks. They brought recognition and remembrance, cold as ice, to her mind. She had seen that look before—in Nicopolis when she had first met him, and even sometimes when he thought no one was near him at Belvedere—but she had seen it. And she had known what it meant. Hatred was something she had once felt herself and so she knew that Olivier hated her. She didn't know why he did—but the fact that he did was as plain to her as the hills around her or as the raven's nighttime call.

Still, she had her training, her careful education, and she fell back upon them now.

"My Lord Olivier," she said as she lowered into the safety of a deep reverence. The pine cones in their hemp basket jostled gaily against her thigh. The raven was silent.

He did not acknowledge her greeting or her graceful curtsey. He did not ask her where she was going or what she was about. He did not offer to escort her back to his castle. Instead, Olivier stared at her, stared into Julian Madrigal's soul with eyes as hard and dangerous as glass shards.

"It's not my fault." The anger in her shout stunned her. She wasn't even sure she had said them until she heard them push their way out again. "It's not my fault. I didn't kill them."

She clapped a hand to her mouth in horror and then she turned from him to make her own way—but not to his castle. Instead, she followed her own path to the village of Sant'Urbano.

CHAPTER SEVEN

Once she had disappeared, Olivier was filled with remorse. Julian had saved his life, and not only at Nicopolis. Padre Gasca had told him that the festering of his wound had been serious. Had it not been cleaned and cared for that night, there would probably have been dire consequences. This the priest had said only this morning and with a certain emphasis that left no room for doubt. Certainly Olivier did not doubt him.

And he had wanted Julian beside him, with him, as the priest began his painful probe. He had called for her, insisted on her coming, even over the look of consternation on Cristiano's face. She was the daughter of a witch and probably a witch herself, and still he had wanted her. Needed her. Still now, he had but to close his eyes and he could remember the threading of her long, slender fingers through his own. He could smell her flowered scent. It was not lost upon Olivier that he was nearly betrothed to a lady of the Venier who would bring him position and wealth and the children he desperately needed to carry on his name. Julian could bring him nothing. Quite frankly, she had nothing to give except what he gave her him-

self. And yet when he'd had most need of a woman, he had
not thought of Domiziana at all. He had thought of Julian.

He had wanted Julian.

There was something in her that continually took his thoughts
to places where they had no right to linger, to places that were
just beyond the stern rules of chivalry he had set for himself
upon his return from the Dogan Bey's prison. It had been this
way since the first night when he had gone to her chamber—
alone—as she lay sleeping. That first night when he had returned to Belvedere. She loved him. He was no fool and so he
knew this, just as he also knew that she would get over her
young girl's infatuation with him. And probably with the aid
of the Knight de la Marche, who seemed quite diligent in his
intentions to help her do just that. Olivier, who prided himself
on adherence to the knightly vows his family had taken for
generations, found that he could not leave this one woman
alone. Even though her presence in his life was a continuous
prickling, reminding him of what he had had and had lost. And
what he had been and had lost as well.

Olivier looked up and grimaced. This conundrum could be
puzzled later, but for now he must look for his ward and beg
her forgiveness. Once again, he must find Julian and bring her
home.

She hurried past the wicket that swung loosely back and
forth on its rusted hinges. Automatically she reached to lock
it behind her but then realized that, of course, Olivier had come
this way. She remembered the trodden earth in the cemetery
and knew that this had not been his first visit there. And she
had seen the hatred in his eyes when he looked at her, a hatred
bred of that churchyard and the reproach of those silent white
crosses. *Your people held me while my brothers died, while my
father's body swelled up and his skin blackened.* It was no use

to try to tell him that they weren't 'her people', that she had been held just as much a captive as he was. All she knew was that she must run free of that hatred.

And so instead of going back towards the castle and the safe hiding of her own small chamber or the laboratory where most people were too frightened to tread, she turned towards the village.

She hadn't been in the little village of Sant'Urbano since her return, but she had heard its church bells chiming out the hours of prayer—primes, sexte, compline—the hours that people lived their lives by. The bells had not changed, but then nothing changed in Tuscany. Nothing ever would. It seemed to stretch out eternally, one fecund hill following another, majestically glowing beneath an evergreen mantle of Mediterranean pine and cypress. Her feet found their own rhythm. They had not forgotten the way.

And once in Sant'Urbano it would not be difficult to find the tiny house of Sabata's parents. It would be one of many tucked into the eaves of the larger stone houses on the outskirts of the village and near the planting fields. It was easy to see that poor people lived in these cramped spaces, but their dwellings were still flanked by bright pots splashing color into the dusk, by wine jugged in the glazed black and deep red pottery of the region, and by herbs and fruits netted and strung along the windows with their flax panes.

A cheerful picture—except there was no one on the streets. Instead they were strange and eerie and silent. Julian saw no children playing: she heard no laughing men on their way home from the tillage. And most ominously of all, she saw the care with which clean straw had been placed on the lane's packed earth, as though the town had already prepared itself to mourn its young dead. Julian shivered as she had shivered when she heard the raven's caw. She hurried on.

So preoccupied was she with her mission that she might have missed her sighting of the witch. As it was, she caught

only a glimpse of a bent shape that shadowed into the darkness.
The figure skulked around a corner, but Julian could still feel
the heat of Elisabetta's gaze upon her. Strega Elisabetta—who
was jealous of her skills and undoubtedly fearful for her place
within the scheme of this poor village and for the pittance of
bread that it brought her. Julian had known women like this
in the past, had pitied them even, but not tonight. Tonight she
had glimpsed Olivier's hatred up there on the hill and it had
left her with her own fears to deal with. Her own fears—and
her anger. She threw that crystal anger towards the skulking
figure that dogged her steps.

"Well, you'll not have him, you black cat," Julian whispered
furiously, but loud enough so her words echoed back from the
village stones. "You'll not have him. You'll not have him."
She clutched the parcel of pine cones close against her breast,
loving the way the prickly ends pushed into her. Like a baby,
like a child. She carried light, not darkness. For the first time
ever she was beginning to understand the difference. The vari-
ance between the two was beginning to work its luminance
into her mind and into her heart. She carried life, not death,
and the newness of this thought prickled against her. Her steps
quickened and she found herself running towards the child.
Suddenly she knew exactly where she was going—where she
needed to go.

"Thank God you've come," cried Sabata. She had been
waiting—Julian could tell—and she rushed forward, almost
throwing herself into the Magdalene's arms. "Elisabetta has
doomed him. The runes have spoken, she said, and there is no
hope. God is taking him from us in punishment for some sin
we've committed. We will learn from this and be better next
time—that's what she said. But what have we done? How have
we sinned? My father says the sin must be mine. He says
that I've dirtied myself with my betrothed and brought God's
vengeance upon us. I didn't mean it. I swear I didn't mean it.

I would take back all the kissing and the touching—I swear I would—if God would take this curse from my brother. If it weren't too late.''

Tears rolled down her cheeks, almost but not quite obscuring the livid marks laid upon them by a heavy hand. There was very little left of the fresh-faced maiden Julian had seen just that morning. She reached out to soothe Sabata's matted curls.

"Shhh. Shhh," she said soothingly. She was calm now; all of her own agitation had flown. She stroked the girl's hair back so that she could look directly into her eyes. "Find me your mother and then take me to your brother. I've brought herbs and simple things that will help him. I've brought healing."

Olivier found the streets of the village torch-lighted and teeming with his people. He had expected as much, which is why he had come alone, save for one young page who carried the bright turquoise-and-white banner of the Ducci Montaldo, and why he was very simply dressed. Only his golden spurs and his heavily jeweled sword—and of course the fact that he rode a stallion, though he had but to traverse barely a mile to reach the gates of Sant'Urbano from his castle—gave away the nobility of his knighthood. He had chosen to ride beneath his family's colors rather than those of the Gold Company that he commanded because these were his people; this was the home his family had defended for generations. He needed to feel that the villagers realized this fact as well, at least if he were going to help Julian. And he wanted to help Julian. That is why he had come.

He saw that not everyone was happy to make way for him. He could feel their curiosity turn to distrust and even darken into something else. These were witch-burning times and the story of the Magdalene was well-known. And it was not the only one. There had been many whispered charges of sorcery against Olivier's sister Francesca before his return, and Cardinal

Archangelo Conti had even had them drawn outright, at Rome, against her husband Belden d'Harnoncourt. Conti was gone now, burned to death just hours before he could burn Belden, but the Inquisition he had planted within Italy still continued to flower. Julian was senseless to have come on such a fool's errand—and he knew exactly why she had come, had known it as he paced through most of the night and watched in vain for her return to Belvedere. Of all the times for her to take up Aalyne's damnable skills. What if that poor child should sicken further—or worse yet, die? If he hadn't been so horribly afraid the others might beat him to it, he would have loved to throttle Julian himself.

And then there was the troubling fact of his own wound. The arrow that had caught him had been sure and well aimed— not meant to kill but to give clear warning. He was sure of that. Why? Warning of what? Many of his own people were good bowsmen—he had trained them himself. The Ducci Montaldo had good relations with their peasants, but there had been serious revolts in both England and France in recent decades. Not in Italy, at least not yet. But then one never knew when the spark might strike tinder here as well. High taxes and poverty were universal blights.

Olivier spurred his horse lightly forward. He kept his head high and his hand away from his sword.

One man stepped out ahead of the others. He stood big and burly in the Count's way. Not young, thought Olivier, glancing down at a bald pate ringed with white hair. He recognized Ezio Moro. He had aged, but was still obviously a bully and, like all bullies, had been quick to make his calculations. He must have decided that the Count's dark-eyed ward was not Ducci Montaldo bred and so a bit of his reputation could be built on her head. "You'll find that witch with the child," he said sullenly. "Working her heathen arts when what he needs now is a priest from San Marco who will help his young soul from this foul life to the next."

Olivier glanced at his page, who was staring in open-mouthed indignation at the peasant's effrontery, and very slightly shook his head.

"My greetings to you as well," said the Count equably. "I take it you refer to my guest, the Lady Julian, and that you know where she visits."

"Visits?" said the villager. He snorted, then looked around to see that his audience was with him. "Visitations might be the reality of it—from the devil and his like. At least where that black-haired temptress of yours is concerned. She's here, all right, and with her heathen ways."

A muscle began to work in Olivier's jaw but he said nothing. His gaze moved swiftly over the scene to see a quick escape route for his young page should he need it. He cursed himself for bringing the boy along.

Other villagers had started to join their leader. They blocked the light from the little house at the top of the stone steps.

"He's had enough of witches' spells, that poor child," said another man as he drew nigh. "He's had our witch and she's not helped him. We told her so ourselves, but she would have her own way in this. Got the mother out and made that woman force her husband into her letting her in. We wanted no heathen putting her hands upon this child. 'Tis a village child and we'd a right to have our say. That witch Julian wants to bring the devil in right around us, to sneak it past us in the night and infest it here. The Strega Elisabetta we know. She'd not spit upon the plate she eats from. But this young witch—what's to stop her tormenting us? What's to stop her selling our souls away?"

The man had been drinking and Olivier remembered that drinking men always frightened Julian. It was one of the things she'd told him on their long journey back from Nicopolis. He hoped that this brute had not come near her. He hoped that she had not been terrified of him.

Well, if so, she would soon be avenged. Olivier had not wanted to show force with his people, but there seemed to be no way out of it. Not with the ugliness of the crowd and the lateness of the night. He had the very real conviction that he was going to have to battle his own way through, though first he would have to find a safe route out for this most unfortunate of pages, and he had to locate Julian. That was essential. The thought of her forced him to hold tight rein on his temper as his hand eased closer to his sword.

"No heathen witch will practice here," the man began again but then they were all surprised by the sound of a woman's cry and her weeping.

Olivier, not usually a man given to impulse, surprised himself by forgetting all his training and leaping from his horse. He tore right through the men and by the time he reached the top of the narrow stone stairs, his sword was drawn and at the ready. He didn't need it.

"Put that away," Julian hissed at him as she poked her head from one of the oaken doors. "You'll frighten the mother if she sees it. She's not crying from pain but from joy. The fever has broken. The child will live."

Afterwards.

Well, he would think about that for a long time and he knew it already. He would remember the way Julian had shyly moved aside so he could enter. He would remember the sheepish look of the father and the radiance on the face of the mother and sister. He would remember the bruise on that girl's face and what this could have meant for Julian. He would remember the absolute sweetness of that child Giacomo with his newly pink cheeks, who had reached out his small hand for Julian. He would remember the brightness of Julian's answering smile.

Yes, above all, he would remember Julian smiling.

"My lord," said the mother. She swept into a deep reverence that seemed to bring the others to their senses as well. They bowed in their turn as the excited woman continued. "She saved my boy. She had us build the fire hot, even though it was nightfall and time for its dying—that's what the old strega told us. We must keep strictly to the rhythms of nature. We must turn out all lights in the night." She paused for an instant and turned to her husband with a look of triumph. "It was hard for us to change our known ways, but the Lady Julian wanted the fire hot and we did it. We did what she told us to do."

Now the tears started. "And she made our boy well," she whispered. "She put a pot of water on the boil—a great huge pot it was, you can see it steaming still—and she cracked pine cones and threw them in it, and rosewood, too, and rose nectar. She said there was much healing in the rose—there always had been. She told me soothing stories about the roses 'cross the mountains from the land where she grew up. She had me bring a clean flax hanging to fling over the pot and the two of us took turns holding our Giacomo over the waters. Holding his head near it so that he could pull in its goodness. She wouldn't give him to anyone else, only to me. We took turns. And then he coughed . . . Our Giacomo coughed. . . ." She tried to continue but couldn't. It was Julian who finished for her.

"He hacked up the miasma," she said simply. "And then he started to improve."

Afterwards.
He would think of these things later, probably over and over again, and the thinking would be pleasurable but would probably bring anger and remorse with it as well. That would all come later.

Now—well, for now he had Julian near him and that was all that mattered. She had righted the things she had used and made sure the child was truly mending before she had allowed him to lead her away. She walked beside him, so tired she was babbling, but still excited and happy. She was smiling at him as he led his horse and they walked together through the early morning mists. It had been years, he thought amazed, since he had actually walked the road that led from the village to his castle—if, indeed, he had ever walked it at all. He was a knight, after all, and therefore born to his saddle. A knight unhorsed was somehow considered vaguely unmanned. But that didn't matter to Olivier this early morning. He had wanted this time with Julian to last and he had known that riding would take him to Belvedere much too soon. He had already sent his page back to the castle to rest.

"And then I remembered that I did know something and that it might help. . . ."

Olivier nodded. He watched her lips as they told him her tale. He was transfixed by them, couldn't seem to take his eyes away. No trace remained of the bitter look she had flung at him near the graveyard, and for this he was grateful. He had grown used to her adoring ways and he liked them. He hadn't liked her anger. No, that wasn't true, he corrected himself. He hadn't minded her anger—he just hadn't wanted her angry with him. She wasn't now. He could see this in her smile, hear it in her too-excited chatter. She wasn't laughing yet, at least with him, but he knew she would eventually. For some reason it mattered to Olivier—and mattered greatly—that one day she would laugh with him the way she had laughed with the Knight de la Marche.

It *mattered* to him that she should laugh again.

It seemed perfectly natural to him to take her hand into his free hand and to edge her near.

She stank, he thought with wonder but no revulsion. His fastidious Julian smelled of hard work and sweat and anxiety. Her hair was matted, still damp with the steam she'd breathed in and out, over and over again, with young Giacomo. And he could smell fear on her. She had been afraid. Of the village? Of the Magdalene? He didn't know—and it didn't matter. In the end she had not let the fear stop her. She had done her duty anyway.

Duty?

Well, he wasn't about to do his. He wasn't about to think of Domiziana or his obligation to his young ward or even of the complications that his actions were going to bring into his life. He shook his head. He moved those thoughts right out of his mind. There were other notions that needed heeding.

He wanted Julian. He needed her near. That's all that mattered—that and the fact that he knew she wanted him as well.

He was determined to kiss her and had been determined to kiss her for some time. Just once, he thought. Something in him was determined to see what it was like.

He stopped walking, he let the reins fall, he drew Julian near.

Yet as his lips parted and he bent down to kiss her, he saw indecision deep within the pools of her dark eyes. He felt it in the stiffening of her hand. Not given to hesitation when there was something he wanted, Olivier made himself hesitate. He let himself hover. He let himself listen for an instant as an early robin sang its morning greeting into the air.

There was time. She would kiss him. He knew this, in a very male and self-satisfied way.

This was Julian, and he was her lord.

And she did, indeed, move to kiss him; unweaving her hand from within his, to bring her fingers up to his lips and gently trace their outline. He tasted rosewood on her fingers and the sap of pine. They were soft against him. *She* was soft against him as she opened her mouth to him and drew him in.

"Olivier."

The Count of the Ducci Montaldo felt himself swell to meet the hot, sweet sound of his own name being whispered within his own mouth. She shifted within his arms and then moved cautiously, and somehow chastely, against him as her embrace pulled him closer. As her tongue drew him near. He felt himself becoming saturated with Julian—with her woman's smell, with the softness of her, with the brush of her still-damp hair as she cradled against him—and he would have hesitated now in his turn, but he couldn't.

Because something unexpected and warm had shot through him, something that melted a frozen part of him that he hadn't even known was there.

He had to have Julian. He had to have more.

And so he was startled when he felt her draw away from him. Startled and just a little confused and even angry. That is, until he followed her gaze and looked upon the red-faced page who was trying to get his attention, the bright turquoise and white of his new livery splashing the only color into what was promising to be a very gray morning. He couldn't remember the boy's name or his lineage, but he was so furious that he made a decision to send him immediately packing, even if he turned out to be the son of King Charles himself. But he was aware of Julian's restraining hand upon his forearm and the calm, sweet smile she had turned upon the page. Olivier could not allow himself to be outdone in courtesy by his own guest. This boy needed a reprimand and a small lecture on discretion but he would get these later, and in private.

"Tell me," he said crisply, but he did not move away from Julian: he did not take his hand from her shoulder. Instead, it was she who edged away from him.

The page dropped into a deep reverence, then cast a shy glance at Julian before turning back to his lord.

" 'Tis Sir Gatien who sent me for you, Count," he said. "An urgent missive has arrived from Venice saying that Count Luciano Venier is bringing you word from the ruling Doge. Urgent word—important enough that the Count must personally carry it. He has been travelling through the nights and should reach Belvedere quite soon. He would have already arrived, but he brings his family with him."

"His family?" Olivier did not have to look at her to know that Julian had drawn away from him. He could still feel himself enfolded in her essence: he could still feel the heat of her kiss on his lips. The page was nodding, calling for attention.

"His family?" Olivier echoed his own words once again. He could feel Julian take another step away.

The young page bobbed his head up and down in assent.

"Sir Cristiano said I was to tell you most emphatically that the Count brings his wife and two of his daughters with him," said the child. "The Maid Ginevra—and the Lady Domiziana."

CITY

CHAPTER EIGHT

She was genuinely beautiful. Even though Julian didn't want to admit this, she was forced to as she watched the woman who was nearly betrothed to the Count of the Ducci Montaldo enter his castle of Belvedere. Olivier's back was to her and his broad shoulders partly blocked her view, but Julian could see enough to know that Domiziana Venier was, indeed, a comely woman, and comely in a way that Olivier would notice and approve.

Because she was perfect.

Julian, stretching up on the tips of her toes, could see her rival as she pulled off smooth kid gloves and brushed at the specks of dust that had managed to become attached to her pale ivory riding cloak. The very thought that she traveled winter roads in pale ivory was in itself daunting. Julian marveled at Domiziana Venier's perfection and she envied it. And Domiziana had not come alone, as she herself had come, or with an escort of men that would raise more questions than it answered. Domiziana's family surrounded her. There was a mother and a father. There was the odor of perfume and rich oils. The

servants, who had accompanied them, clucked about solici-
tously. There was even what could only be a younger sister.
She had the Venier fair coloring and light eyes and their small,
fine bones. Julian saw the girl smile over at her and, without
thinking, she smiled back. There was mischief in the look the
girl tossed her and Julian would have liked to investigate this
impishness further. She knew she wouldn't. She was too jealous. She hated herself for it, but she knew that she was.

She remembered how she had arrived at Belvedere—both
times—with her cloaks streaked with mud and her hair stringy
and lifeless and dirty, because she had refused to wear a veil
for her journey. She worked hard at it, but she had never
managed even to near this acme of perfection. She had nothing
at all in common with this ephemeral vision before her—a
cloud-like image of pale hair, pale eyes, and purity. The two
of them—she and the Lady of the Venier—had obviously made
their way along very different roads before arriving here. And
it was Domiziana's way that Olivier would wish to traverse.

With all the power of the Magdalene that was in her, Julian
knew that the woman before her would be the new Contessa
of the Ducci Montaldo. She had been born and bred to this,
just as Olivier had been born and bred to make a woman like
this his wife.

Julian held back just a little, hoping that she would be ignored
as she stared.

As he strode into his castle to welcome his guests, the only
thing Olivier hoped—but he hoped this quite fervently—was
that his face did not look feverish. Not when he must go over
and receive the Veniers. Not when he must face his nearly
betrothed and greet her. And he must do this with the smell of
another woman still about him; with the feel of her lips still
fresh upon his own. He could tell by certain uncomfortable,
but still pleasurable, movements of his body that his desire for
Julian had not yet completely abated. Olivier had taken certain

vows as a knight and, though times had changed and he knew that he had changed with them, he still took seriously the promises he had made in his youth. One of these was to guard womanhood, to protect it, and he knew he was failing in his mission on at least two counts.

He was kissing—trying to seduce even, if he were truthful with himself—a woman whom he had taken on as a charge. A woman who had a witch for a mother and so probably had certain knowledge. He would give Julian the benefit of charity in thinking that she had used no strange power over him. Yet, she was Aalyne's daughter and could easily have enchanted him, even without meaning to do so. He could not fully accept this idea, even as he smiled at the Veniers and welcomed them. Julian was a puzzle—but Domiziana was not.

She was the woman to whom he was nearly betrothed: she was a noblewoman, the niece of his employer. Moreover, she belonged to a family that had been especially kind to him since his return and to which he owed much of his present good fortune. He had plighted to Domiziana and he must have her. This fancy that he had for Julian would pass. He knew it would. Julian was a witch, just as her mother had been before her. She could incite men, even *excite* them, just as he had been excited by her these last days. In the end she could not hold them, and he would not allow himself to be held by her now.

Olivier made sure there was a smile upon his face as he strode into his castle. "My Lady of the Venier," he said, bowing over the Contessa Claudia's outstretched hand. She twittered towards him, her thin eyebrows arching even further towards the far-off goal of her fashionably plucked hairline. She had shaken off her wimple as she walked in the door and she still held it in her arthritically gnarled fingers. The fact that she had not immediately tossed the cloak to a servant meant that, indeed, her family carried important information.

"My lord." The Contessa Claudia was so bursting with her news that she spoke even before her husband.

She was most certainly a tiresome woman. Olivier literally

always felt more tired around her and he hoped quickly but
fervently that the Contessa Claudia's hold upon her daughter
was not too firm. He could not quite appreciate the thought of
having her constantly underfoot at Belvedere. He wondered,
even now, what he would do with her for the few days that
they should all be together at the castle.

"My lord," she repeated, curtseying low.

Olivier watched the women of the Venier as they admired
his improvements at Belvedere. He listened to the Contessa
Claudia's idle prattle about their journey: he endured her complaints concerning the discourtesy of the other travelers they
had encountered along the Via Pellegrina—"My lord, they
almost drove us altogether into the ditch and we had our colors
prominently displayed. They could see that we were part of
the nobility. You have no idea what we suffered."

Catching her mistake—for it was the Count's duty to see to
the safety of the roads—she smoothly complimented him, and
more than once, on the fact that although discourtesy might
have been rampant, brigandage was not. A poor, defenseless
woman could feel herself safe these days as she traveled through
country controlled by the Count of the Ducci Montaldo. She
simpered when she said this and batted her eyes. She was ever
so grateful to God that this was so.

Olivier's future relations handed their travelling capes to
maids and adjusted their veils and headpieces. They had brought
the sharp, cold wind of winter in with them; it was wrapped
all through their clothing and in the brisk and brittle way in
which the mother spoke. He recognized the sharpness of winter
in the urgency that shone through Luciano Venier's eyes and
in the faint line of perspiration that shadowed his lips. He
noticed how they quickly glanced at him and then smiled. The
two things did not happen simultaneously, he noted. First they'd
glance at him and then they'd turn quickly away. Only then
would they smile. He watched Luciano Venier watch him.

Olivier thought, ironically, that he hadn't noticed how cold
it was before. Not when he had walked home with Julian and

buried his face in the damp mantle of her hair. Not when he had kissed her. Not now when, despite all the activity around him, he still smelled her glorious perfume. He thought of her and wondered about her—and surprised himself by feeling no guilt. In the end, something would happen, because it had to. He was a man who had plighted himself to another, to a woman who would help him carry out the duties that had been left to him. He forced his mind back to this fact, to the exclusion of everything else. He had his responsibilities to his family and to Belvedere and its people. He had shirked them once and the result had been disastrous. There was a graveyard filled with the bones of his brothers to remind him of that. No more thoughts of Julian, he told himself firmly as he again turned to his nearly betrothed. He would give his young ward to the Knight de la Marche. Olivier had no doubt but that Sir Gatien was in love with her—and that she was a very lucky young woman to have someone of that caliber who would love her and take her for wife. Julian brought no fortune or family with her. She brought no name.

Luciano Venier cleared his throat delicately, but there was enough of a command in it to quiet his wife's twittering.

"My Lord Olivier," he said, striding over and holding out his soft hand. "I hope you don't mind this intrusion. I bring you important word from Venice. My cousin the Doge has entrusted me with it—he thought me best for the task. And naturally, my wife and daughters *would* accompany me. They insisted they would not burden me and hold me back—and indeed they have not. Though Domiziana has managed to take a small chill."

This was both an imparting of information and a subtle rebuke and it had its desired effect. Olivier remembered that he had not properly greeted his nearly betrothed. He turned to her now, cutting off her father in mid-sentence.

"Lady," he said as he bowed to her.

She was as lovely as ever. Still tidy, still unruffled, though he noticed that her face was pale. Probably the fatigue of her journey and not a fever, he thought, dismissing her white skin and the drawn look about her mouth. A good rest would put her back to normal again and she would have one within the comforts of Belvedere. He had had all the mattresses filled with the very best goose down and there were fur rugs and lavender-scented lace-and-linen sheets to cover them. She would rest in one of his beds and become herself again.

He noticed that she was staring at a bowl of winter flowers that Julian had placed beneath a tapestry. It was a simple beaten silver urn filled with evergreen branches and a few late-blooming chrysanthemums. He saw disapproval on Domiziana's face and recalled that he, too, had disapproved of Julian's flower choices when first he had returned. He had thought them too simple for the restored grandeur of Belvedere. Now he realized that these would have to be got rid of, and he found himself reluctant to do so.

The Lady Domiziana curtsied to him and then smiled her shy, sweet smile. Olivier felt remorse settle on him like a blanket. *She* was his contessa, this confection that stood before him. She was perfect, a fitting woman to take his mother's place as the Contessa Ducci Montaldo and the chatelaine of Belvedere. He took it as a miracle of God that she had come when she had. Otherwise . . .

No, he could not allow himself to think again about what he had done with Julian or what else he had wanted to do with her. But the thought of his ward had caused him to remember his manners. He stopped and turned back.

"Lady Claudia, you remember the Lady Julian Madrigal?"

Claudia's hesitation lasted only for the briefest of instants. It could have been missed, but everyone knew that Julian had not missed it. It was Luciano Venier, however, who strode forward and rescued his wife and daughters from this embarrassing moment.

"Yes, of course, we remember the Lady Julian," he said with an extreme show of heartiness, but then found himself daunted in his turn. Should he bend to kiss Julian's fingers or not? Julian was not a married woman: at least he had never heard of a marriage, which he now thought odd, considering her beauty. On the other hand, he certainly didn't think she still remained a virgin. Not at her age—and not with Aalyne de Lione as a mother. Everyone knew that Aalyne was a witch and a whore. It was not that Luciano Venier had never met women of her ilk—or at least of her mother's—but he had met them under different circumstances. They had been much more intimate, so to speak.

Julian solved the delicate dilemma by holding out her hand to him but smiling over at the Contessa Claudia.

"My lord and lady, of course you would not remember me but I remember you both well. In addition, the Count has spoken highly of you and of your great service to the city of Venice." This last was a lie. Olivier had never spoken one word to her of the Veniers, she suddenly realized. What she knew had come from other mouths.

Her manner is good, Olivier thought. She is just modest enough not to offend. He found himself slightly amused and curious to see how she would handle the next part of this delicate situation. He was still feeling the lightness of being with her and of sharing that one kiss—a kiss for which he would have to apologize. He should have told her about Domiziana. He cursed himself for his negligence—and for his selfishness. To kiss her without first telling her about his almost-betrothed was unconscionable. She may have been Aalyne's daughter, but she had helped him and saved him—and she had done both of these more than once.

The effect of her kiss had surprised him. It surprised him as well to realize that the person to whom he wanted and needed to make an apology was Julian, and not Domiziana.

"Oh, Lady Julian, I've so especially wanted to meet you." The youngest of the Venier daughters, ignoring strict etiquette, now moved out of her sister's shadow. Ginevra was her name, Olivier recalled. She had the Venier coloring, which was to say she possessed no coloring to speak of. Both sisters shared the same light hair and light eyes, but what was ethereal on Domiziana bordered on plainness in the sturdier Ginevra. This probably went far in explaining why, at the advanced age of fourteen, she was not as yet bespoken.

Still, the Veniers were wealthy and their family powerful—someone would bid upon the Maid Ginevra's hand, of this Olivier had no doubt.

"I came along especially to meet the Lady Julian Madrigal," she said and she was smiling radiantly at Julian. "I think it is so wonderful that you were named for a song."

The Count of the Ducci Montaldo spent his day closeted with Count Luciano Venier. The Doge's cousin had brought news that was expected, but not welcomed. Olivier emerged only for the evening meal and only because courtesy to the Veniers demanded their host's presence. His humor was not good.

It became increasingly worse throughout the meal. The Veniers had brought their own servants with them from Venice, including their own cook. This man—a *Frenchman,* Olivier thought with some disgust, forgetting his own French blood—had done nothing but disrupt the serene life of the castle since his arrival. At least this is what Giuseppe the bailiff had told Olivier as soon as he had emerged from his marathon meeting with Luciano. There had been complaints and hysterics. There had been swift sniffs and the obstinate stamping of feet. There had even been shudders at the quality of the Belvedere honeys and cheeses. The bailiff turned crimson with indignation as he recounted this, acting out the small Frenchman's actions with his huge bulk. The Belvedere cook had quit in a huff. He was already packing his satchel to seek refuge with the same monks at San Mario who had been trying desperately for years to pry his secret recipe for hare in a sweet almond sauce loose from his reluctant hands. It was known by all that bribes had been offered and piously refused. The profane even gossiped that the good Brothers had sent up novenas to heaven in furtherance of this great intention. Of course they would be more than happy to shelter the newly freed Belvedere cook. They would think his arrival an answer to prayer.

"And where is the Countess Venier?" demanded Olivier. He had an almost uncontrollable urge to stamp his own foot.

"Resting from her journey," answered an impassive Giuseppe. "And her daughter with her. They instructed their servants to tell your servants that they are not to be disturbed."

He was very, very careful not to meet the Count's eye.

"Then send for the Lady Julian," snapped Olivier. "She will know what to do."

He could count on Julian. She would take care of this mess.

She did, of course, just that. Giuseppe had trotted off, deeply relieved, to place the whole farrago in Julian's hands and she had seen to it, just as Olivier had known she would. The cooks were each placated, the Great Hall polished in readiness for its illustrious guests, the servants calmed and feeling important. As he smelled the aromas of the culinary masterpieces that were soon to grace his table, and looked about at the perfection that surrounded him, Olivier knew he should have been thankful and happy. He should be grateful to Julian.

He wasn't.

He had been immediately aware of her as she stood, motionless and silent, at the Hall doorway, her hand looped through the arm of the Knight de la Marche. Olivier was surrounded by a hive of Veniers, buzzing and swarming, but he was not thinking of them. He was not thinking of Domiziana, who was drawing his attention to the sugared date her long, thin fingers were drawing to his mouth. Instead his thoughts were on Julian and the fact that she touched the Knight de la Marche. It was obvious that Gatien had come to escort her to the meal, though Olivier had not given him permission to do this. Nor had Gatien asked.

Julian had stood in the doorway for a long moment without smiling as her hand played with a cloved orange. He suddenly remembered that this was thought to be a warder against the plague. She wore something loose and green that hid her body and yet, as she began walking slowly towards them—towards him—it moved as she moved, in and out. Olivier grew uncomfortably aware of the outline of her legs as she walked across the long hall to greet him. The silk of her gown made a slight swishing sound as she neared. He could hear it despite the chatter and clinking of glasses that surrounded him. Her hair was parted in the middle and it curtained around her shoulders before beginning its free fall to the small of her back. It was totally without ornamentation. It needed none. Olivier caught himself staring at that hair, watching the torchlight dance around and through it. Julian caught his eye but did not smile. Instead she tossed her head—just a little—but enough to let him know that she realized that he had been staring at her. Enough to remind him that he had kissed her once and, if stark truth were told, he would kiss her again. And again.

He owed her an explanation, that much was certain, both for what had happened and what was to come. But a part of him rebelled against the fact of his own bad behavior and wanted to portion at least part of the blame onto his ward. Domiziana would never leave her hair like that, he thought. She would always be correctly veiled: she would always behave in a way that would never shame him. That was why she would make him a perfect Contessa, and Julian would not. He reflected, with not a little smugness, that only an indifferently raised woman would let her hair ripple so obscenely and seductively down her back.

And yet, despite himself, he also remembered how, when he had been in need, Julian had come and helped him. How she hadn't been afraid of his blood or his pain. How all the order that he saw about him was the work of her hands.

Olivier sipped his wine as he watched her make her reverence to him and then seat herself gracefully beside Gatien de la

Marche. The Burgundian was obviously quite smitten, though
he made a stalwart attempt to hide it. There was no gainsaying
the light in his eye and the solicitous care he took of her. Nor
the way that, without being obvious, he kept her involved in the
steady stream of his conversation so that no one—least of all
she—could realize how completely the Lady Domiziana and
her mother ignored her. He found himself staring at Julian's
lips as they smiled, as they pursed around a word, as she opened
them wide in laughter. He looked down to find his fingers
tracing their outlines against the smooth wood of the trestle
table. He wondered why Gatien had not as yet come asking
permission to pay his court. To his absolute amazement, Olivier
found himself to be quite envious. The thought settled on him
and called for another deep pull at his tankard. He brushed
aside another of Domiziana's sweetmeats, barely remembering
to smile at her as he did this. It wasn't that he was jealous of
Julian. They had shared one brief aberration of a kiss, and now
they would go back to their separate lives. He—certainly—
with Domiziana. She—he hoped—with Gatien de la Marche.
Nevertheless, he found that he was jealous anyway of his ward
and his Burgundian guest—of their friendship, of their laughter,
of the little world they made together and from which he felt
excluded.

Unaccountably, his wound had started to ache again after so
many days, when he had thought himself on the mend. He
wanted to ask Julian . . . Just exactly what could he possibly
ask her, seated as he was between his nearly betrothed and her
mother? That her wish was to come true? That he was about
to be forced to honor his promise and return to Nicopolis for
Aalyne?

The Lord of the Ducci Montaldo turned to the Lady Domiziana Venier. He took the silver wine carafe from a servant and
showed his nearly betrothed the courtesy of filling her glass.
He noticed that she was pale, and that tight lines had etched
themselves around the edges of her mouth. He chided himself
for not having noticed this before.

"You must be tired after your journey," he said to her and there was concern in his voice.

"Not tired," chided the Lady Claudia. There was enough reproach in her tone to make Olivier realize that his scrutiny of Julian had not gone unobserved. "My daughter is delicate and she has picked up a chill on the road from Venice. She should never have made such a perilous journey, and would not, had she not been so anxious to see for herself that you were well cared for."

She cast a telling glance in Julian's direction.

"Of course . . ." she continued.

The Countess Venier might have continued along this path indefinitely had not Olivier turned to her daughter. "You are ill? Why did you not tell me? I would have sent for one of the monks from San Mario for you."

"They would not have come for a woman—they hate women," Domiziana snapped. Then she softened her words with a delicate smile. "I have only taken a chill and then, of course, as mother said, the voyage was tiring. I will see no celibate priest but if you have a Wise Woman here, someone versed in the healing arts, perhaps she might be persuaded to come to me."

"Of course Julian could help you," Olivier said. "She is quite skilled in the healing arts. There is a child, the brother of one of the castle servants. . . ."

"No, no." Domiziana reached out long fingers to stop this line of thought. "I could not trouble your ward in that way. A village Wise Woman is all I need. Someone who might know a light draught."

Just then Julian laughed and Olivier thought of Strega Elisabetta. He had seen her holding tightly to the village shadows when he had come for Julian and he knew she had been hiding in fear for her life. One never knew when a witch failed them if the people would turn against her and she would be cast forth—if she were lucky. Unaccountably, he felt pity for the old woman. The strega had used her skills well for Sant'Urbano.

through the years. She had brought the village through its share of winter phlegms and miasmic humors. Surely it was not her fault that Julian had helped the child when she herself had not been able. Besides, Julian would be going soon and the village would once again have need of its traditional healer. Better to stop any muttered cries of witchcraft. Better to show that the strega was still in the Count's favor.

"Perhaps I know someone," he said slowly, wanting to help. "I will have her sent to you tonight."

Olivier waited impatiently as the meal progressed. The combined effort—and rivalry—between the two cooks had served to make this a memorable event. He realized that he would be expected to praise it and he did so. He praised the peacocks that had been plucked clean and then re-feathered after careful braising. He found kind words for the delicacy of a small brookfish steeped in butter and stuffed with bread and herbs. He could not say enough about the salad greens topped with oranges from Sicily. In his life he had never eaten such exquisitely ash-roasted vegetables. The oil that glistened upon them might have come from Caesar's own olives: it had just that touch of empire about it.

Fortunately, words failed him when they wheeled in the flaming boar that had been roasting on an enormous spit since peace had returned to his kitchens that morning. He clapped with the others but was grateful not to have to come up with more words of exclamation. It was difficult to find them when he had not really tasted one thing from his silver plate as he tried to keep himself from glancing towards Julian.

There was more clapping and stamping as his own cook glided in carrying a mounded confection of lemons and preserved berries. The Venier chef, not to be undone, pranced quickly after him with a beautiful marzipan *torta* of the Ducci Montaldo banner replete with its famous turquoise-and-white coloring and its high-flying doves.

Io porto la pace. I bring the peace.

The simple motto had been spelled out in a conceit of finely spun sugar. Olivier could not remember a time when these words had not been deep in his family's blood.

He whispered something first to his soon-to-be mother-in-law and then to his nearly betrothed. He could not remember what he said to either of them. And then when the moment came, he rose.

"As you all know," he said into the silence that had immediately surrounded him. His voice was pitched low, but it was heard. "Our brother knight, Sigismund, King of Hungary, is being besieged at his borders. The Ottoman Sultan, Bayezid, has ventured forth from the boundaries of his natural and lawful suzerainty and has set his eye upon Europe's eastern lands. He has eaten so far into Christian land that now he threatens the very gates of Vienna itself. He must be stopped."

Olivier had not meant to give a rallying speech—there would be plenty of time and need for that later—but tumult greeted his words. The foot-thumping and banging of pewter and silver tankards that had come to represent the start of war greeted him on every side. The time of waiting was over. He could almost hear the sizzle of tension pervade the room. His men shouted their relief that the decision had been made, if not yet officially announced, and knights of Gatien de la Marche shouted with them. Olivier allowed himself to look toward the Burgundian only to find that his face was impassive. He was not joyfully greeting the successful completion of his mission. At least he was no longer giving his full attention to Julian. For an instant the two warriors stared at each other in silence, and then Olivier continued on with what he had to say.

"However, my own first loyalty is to mighty Venice," he said, "to whose welfare my own life is plighted as well as the lives of the men of the Gold Company. Venice must want this war in order to release me to it. She must need it for her own defense." He paused, and then let his voice ring out once again. "Just today, Count Luciano Venier has brought me direct word from his cousin Doge Antonio and Venice's ruling oligarchy that the city has decided to defend the Christian cause. She will fight beside the armies of Charles VI of France and his uncle, John the Fearless, Duke of Burgundy. She is sending her Black Fleet and our own Gold Company to aid King Sigismund. She will fight beside his forces against the Sultan Bayezid in Holy War!''

Olivier sat down to pandemonium. He could hear the shrill voice of the Lady Claudia as she shouted something to her husband. He could feel the parchment touch of Domiziana's fingers as they sought his own. But the noise and the confusion were only peripheral, a covering. They would let him find Julian again, would let him share this with her.

Both of them knew just what this decision would mean to them, just where it would take them.

"To Nicopolis," she whispered.

"To Nicopolis," he said.

CHAPTER NINE

The night had not yet reached its culmination. The room was flush with war talk and his men had rushed him, so it was a moment before Olivier actually realized that Luciano Venier, excited and more than slightly drunk on heavy Tuscan wine, had risen unsteadily to his feet and raised his tankard high. Without thinking, he found himself moving towards the man to stop him, at the same time knowing that it was already too late.

Not like this. Not now.

Out of the corner of his eye he saw the Lady Claudia beam brightly and Domiziana blush and prettily lower her gaze.

"In the name of the Venier family," Luciano said. He stopped, reconsidered, and then began once again. "In the name of mighty *Venice*, I thank the Count for his defense of our city and for his admirable constancy to its cause. My own may sound faint praise but it is steeped in personal rejoicing as well."

His smile was broad and magnanimous; it verged on the angelic. His arms opened wide to welcome an Olivier who was hurtling towards him. They looked to all the world, and especially to the knights gathered here, like two men replete in healthy alliance. Claudia had planned it this way. She had insisted that the announcement be made now, right after the call to crusade. And Luciano Venier had never argued with his wife.

"I don't think my lord of the Ducci Montaldo would mind," he said, holding onto Olivier with both his hands, "that I divulge a secret that has been long decided upon. Our two families are to be united. The Count has asked for the hand of our daughter, Domiziana, in holy marriage. They are to wed as soon as he returns from crusade."

Once again, a wall of cheer surrounded him. Olivier closed his ears against it while his eyes searched frantically for Julian. She was no longer there, but Gatien de la Marche still lingered. He was in the midst of a group of knights who thumped him on the back as they deprecated the Sultan and his men. Cowards. Infidels. They would yield like pig-fat to the thrust of French steel. The crusade that they cheered was still months in the future, but already the glory of it was destined for France. Olivier smiled ruefully at how his friend King Sigismund would be pushed to one side, how any intelligence the King of Hungary might have about the Sultan—who was, after all, his ancient enemy—would be arrogantly dismissed as unimportant to France. This is how it had always been. This is how it would continue to be. There was nothing he could do about it now.

Because *now* belonged to Julian.

He was aware that Domiziana had stepped up to take her father's place beside him. She smiled at him and Olivier was uncomfortably aware of the mask of his answering smile.

Because *now* belonged to Julian and he had to find her. He had to explain himself as best he could: God knew he would have the devil's own time doing it. He was having enough trouble explaining himself to himself. "Despicable" was the word that came most easily to mind when he thought about his behavior. It was not a word he would have used to describe himself just two days before, but he faced it squarely now. He had taken unfair advantage of a woman whom he had solemnly promised to protect and to cherish, and there was no way around his own perfidy. Luciano Venier's unexpected announcement had thrown cold water on any romantic notion he might have harbored. He was the last of the Counts of the Ducci Montaldo and he had family and duty and responsibility. He must tell Julian that his betrothal to Domiziana had been decided well before this, and that his marriage to her would be for the best— for all of them.

Still, the kiss they had shared had been his doing and he would take the sole responsibility for it. Julian might be the daughter of the Magdalene and the concubine of an eastern warlord they were set to vanquish, but she was innocent in this. And Olivier knew it.

"It was my fault," Julian said to him. She had known he would come to the parapet that crowned the laboratory to look for her and she had waited for him. It was difficult, but she had forced herself to turn from looking down into the valley to face him as she heard the door open. "I knew you were betrothed. I should never have kissed you."

It was a clear night for winter. Stars. A fat, full moon. Just the hint of a cold north wind. She did not allow herself to shiver in it. She did not allow herself to look away.

"Julian, how could you know? I didn't know myself. It was something we had discussed. Certainly it was something we had even planned," he said loyally, not wanting to sully the reputation of the Veniers in any way. Not wanting to make it seem that they had taken advantage of the situation. "But the official announcement ... We've not even as yet discussed dower or bride-gift. How could you have known when I didn't even know myself? Is this some of the Magdalene's doing?" He smiled down at her, teasing, but she was having none of it.

"Sabata told me—and she told me very early on," said Julian. "All of the servants knew that you were nearly betrothed. But I wanted to kiss you and I let myself do it."

She nodded quickly—one, two. "I wanted it. I've always wanted it. Just kissing. Nothing else. I've had the rest and I didn't like it."

"And I wanted it, too," Olivier said. He was amazed at how her truth-telling pulled the truth from him as well. "At least the kissing—and probably the more as well. If there had been time. If I had been able to trick or cajole you into having me. My behavior was unconscionable. Inexcusable. I beg your pardon for the way I treated you, Julian, and I swear on my word as a knight that nothing like that will ever happen between us again."

"Because you love the Lady Domiziana?" she said simply.

"Because she is to be my wife," he said. She noticed that his bright turquoise eyes had shadowed. They were not as dark as hers were, but neither were they as light as they had been. "You know part of my story, Julian, but let me tell you the rest."

He reached reflexively to take her hand and then drew back. They walked together to the very edge of the rampart and stood looking out.

"I was trained for war," he began softly. "And after a while I grew restless without it. I was sent to Picardy to page with my mother's kinsman, Eguerrand de Coucy, when I was but seven, and from that date onward war was my life and my blood. Just as it was for my father and my younger brother—but more so with me. I seemed constitutionally unable to enjoy the peace I spent my life fighting for. The last time I rode away, which was the last time that Europe fought in the East, my mother pleaded with me to stay at Belvedere. She had had a premonition, you see. She begged me on her knees to stay—but of course I wouldn't heed her. I didn't have to. I was a knight and a man. I could do as I wanted."

"You would have died as well had you stayed."

"Then at least I would have died with honor, and with the rest of my family." He still would not touch her, but he was standing so close that the slight wind flapped at their separate cloaks and mingled them as Julian's laugh rang out.

"The rest of your family?" she said and there was deep irony in her voice. "What about your mother? What about your sister? They were alive, you know. They were left. What would have happened to them if you had died with the others?"

"The same thing that happened to them anyway." Olivier's voice was mild as he said this but his eyes flashed. He was the Count of the Ducci Montaldo, after all, and not used to being contradicted by a slip of a girl—especially when that slip of a girl was the ward to whom he had come seeking forgiveness. Had *humbled* himself to seek her forgiveness, he thought with growing indignation. Julian was not behaving herself correctly at all.

"The same thing that happened to them anyway," he repeated. "They managed by themselves with their honey and their herbs, and then the rich and powerful Belden of Harnoncourt came and solved all their problems by marrying my sister."

"You fool," said Julian. She looked at this man she had always loved with utter amazement. "You don't know anything. You don't understand. Your mother was *prostrated* by the deaths. She blamed herself. She was the one who insisted that the old woman be sheltered within the castle main that night. She was the one who said that all poor pilgrims should be fed at the castle table. And she did it for you, Olivier, as some sort of a penance to keep you safe and bring you home."

" 'Tis not true what you're saying." Now his anger blazed as well. "You don't know anything about it. You weren't even here."

"They talked to me about what happened," Julian retorted. "Francesca did, and your mother as well. The Lady Blanche drank because of the deaths. Every day, all day—she couldn't let go of the guilt. Francesca said she was never without her silver goblet and her red wine. But they got over it. *They* got over it. They faced their problems; they went on. Belden would be the first to tell you this himself. *He* didn't save Francesca—if anything *she* saved *him.*"

"You're lying," Olivier said, his voice dangerously low. "They wouldn't have told you anything like that. My mother was born a de Montfort: she was a member of one of the great families of France. Certainly she would never have confided in a. . . ."

"In a what?" prompted Julian. She, too, was whispering now. "In a witch or in a concubine? Which of these definitions calls forth your strongest objection, my lord Olivier? It is, in truth, only you who object. The problem is yours—it does not belong to either your mother or your sister. They found they could talk to me, and so they did. They did not find that they could talk to you, and so they didn't."

Olivier was so angry that Julian could feel the vibration of his mighty struggle towards at least a semblance of temper control.

"You forget yourself, Maid Julian," he said finally. "You forget whose castle you inhabit and who has the say over everything in your life, down to and including whether or not you will continue to stay here—or be packed off and convented with first light. You have obtained that for which you came. My employer, the city of Venice, is sending me to Nicopolis on crusade. There I will honor my promise and inquire as to the well-being of your mother. If she is alive and wishes to accompany me, I will bring her back to Belvedere and then send her on to wherever the two of you wish to establish yourselves. I will pay for all of this and I will continue to maintain you generously, just as I have done in the past. I will take on the support of Aalyne as well. This is my duty to both of you, and the very least that my honor impels from me. I have offered my heartfelt—*heartfelt,*" he repeated with conviction, "apologies for having taken advantage of your youth and your dependence upon me. You may rest with the utmost assurance that there will never, never be any type of intimacy between us again. I am betrothed and soon to be married. What I did was without excuse and, again, I take the responsibility for it and I ask your forgiveness. But Julian . . .''

He leaned towards her then, so close that she could feel the whish of his breath against her face as he said, ''Take heed that you do not ever speak to me of my family again. Do not speak of those times. Do not speak of the deaths.''

Then he turned from her and slammed through the parapet, leaving her alone in the night.

''I'm not frightened,'' Julian mumbled aloud to the sleeping hills, and the moon and the stars. Her teeth were chattering so hard that she could barely force the words through them, but she did this anyway, once again—this time longer and stronger.

''I but told him the truth and I'm not frightened.''

''What was the name of that damn abbess?'' cursed Olivier aloud as he hurled through his castle. Only her name eluded him; he had perfect recall of the rest. He remembered her warted face and her sly, ingratiating smile. He remembered how cold the convent had been when he'd been forced to accept its hospitality just that one night—a night that had been so terrible and inconvenient that the thought of it would undoubtedly accompany him to the grave.

As he had learned to his dismay, a mild winter in Picardy could make the rigors of a Tuscan November seem like a frolic in Egypt. Olivier shivered again at the memory. There would be only ice to wash in, and beans with onions three times a day. There would be no oranges from Sicily, no marzipan castles, no roasted partridge or boar. The bread would be black—except, of course, for its occasional moldy-green speck—and they would dress Julian in dark gray wool.

Not fine wool, either, he thought with some satisfaction, but something rough and still smelling of sheep. Julian would itch—oh, how she would itch! Olivier smiled as his mind lingered to savor the image of his ward scratching feverishly.

She'd learn to appreciate his kindness, he reasoned. She'd soon regret what she'd said. Who was she to say that his sister and his mother would tell her things that they would not tell him? That his sister and mother could talk to her when they could not talk to him? This was impossible, out of the question. He was the Count of the Ducci Montaldo, the head of their family. They *owed* him their confidence.

And yet . . .

And yet—he had talked to Julian himself.

The unwelcome thought settled on him before he could push it away.

For the first time, he had confided in someone about what it had been like for him to come back to a dead castle, about the guilt he had felt.

And that someone had not been Domiziana, his soon-to-be wife.

"No," Olivier said aloud. He was no longer thinking of the great and horrific tortures that could be inflicted by overzealous nuns upon a recalcitrant Julian, but of the years he'd spent in the Dogan Bey's prisons, dreaming and plotting the wonderful life he now held within his grasp.

"I must help Domiziana."

He would send immediately for the Strega Elisabetta, he decided. She would come; she was not one to mind the lateness of the hour. Nor would the Veniers mind, not once he had explained how worried he was about his betrothed. He could at least honor his promise to Domiziana. He could send the strega. He could do it this night, and the witch would bring healing and peace.

No, all of them would be happy.

Julian could not sleep. She would close her eyes and then wait for them to open again. The weight of her hair on her

pillow was too hot for her, even though it was November—
almost December. The silk of her night tunic twisted heavily
around her tossing body. It was useless. She could not sleep.

She heard the winter's wind breaking against Belvedere's
towers as it shivered through cracks in the mortar. What was
left of the night closed in about her and she knew there would
be no rest for her this night in Francesca's maiden-bed. She
wanted so much to be sweet and docile and pious, to rise above
her dubious origins. But the anger was there and it terrified
her. It rose up of its own accord from some stream hidden deep
within her and she seemed to have no control over it.

She had been furious with Olivier. She had shot words at
him, words aimed with a sure marksmanship to wound.

He hurt me, a part of her whispered.

That didn't matter. She had known he was not free.

Her eyes felt tight and dry, the inside of the lids like sanded
paper, as though she had been crying for days or even weeks.
In truth she had not shed a tear. What was there to cry for?
Was Olivier not going back to Nicopolis? Was he not being
forced to keep his promise to her? Had not the Lady Domiziana
brought them this word? She, Julian, should be pleased.

She thought of the Countess Blanche and of Francesca and
Belden and their four lively sons. She would be happy so see
them again—because, of course, Olivier would want to be rid
of her, now that the Lady Domiziana was here. Her presence
would be a constant reminder to him of the kiss that they had
shared and he would want to put this thought firmly from his
mind. Julian did not have a vast experience of men, but what
she had learned from them had been telling.

Once again she raised her hands to her lips. And this time
when she closed her eyes she slept and she dreamed.

*The five-year-old Julian had shared her mother's prison. She
had shared the stink and the damp and the once-a-day bowl
of gruel. After seeing the Inquisitors come and go and listening
closely to what they said, she had asked her tortured and
battered mother if God might not save them.*

"Not God," laughed Aalyne, the beautiful Aalyne whose loveliness not even the Inquisition itself could destroy. *"Not God. Others might, at least if I still serve their purpose. If not—well, I've no sorrow. I embraced the Power and I used it. And the power brought me far."*

But not far enough, reasoned the child as a rat skittered across their slime-slick floor. Not far enough to save us from this. Naturally, she could not say these things aloud.

Julian looked on as her mother hunkered deeply into a licefilled robe and went to sleep. She, the Magdalene, had slept like a child as her own child watched and reasoned.

Aalyne's was the only life that Julian had ever known, but she thought there might be a better one. She thought it was possible to help people and not have them turn on you in the end. Something told her this, although she'd never seen this evidenced. People who Aalyne had helped the most had oft-times been among the first to call for her death. Julian remembered Solange and Pierre and Evian. How they had begged her mother for help—and how in the end they had turned against her.

Now the full moon shadowed her mother's pyre through the window and onto the prison walls. Tomorrow would see the burning of the Magdalene and half of the countryside was rumored to have come to Lyon for the burning. The people, especially those who belonged to the merchant classes, were rumored to be delirious with anticipation of the promised spectacle. Everyone was happy, it seemed, except the child Julian. She was determined to save her mother.

Except she had no idea how this could be accomplished. With nothing better to do, she recited the prayer a kind priest had taught her. She heard the words as they rang through her mind.

Help my mother. Help me. Free us.

And that is when the man had come, wrapped in a black cloak and limping. He had simply opened their cell door that night and walked in. Julian had looked on, her already enor-

mous eyes growing wider still with amazement. There had been
no guard with the man and he had carried no torch. The cell
had seemed suffused with moonlight and Julian had no trouble
seeing him at all. Aalyne had awakened and tried not to show
her relief but it had been there anyway. Her bloodied and
bruised face had quirked upward in a grotesque smile.

"Master," she had said, and then more softly, "Husband."

Julian had grown attentive then, her mind alert. If this man
were her mother's husband might he not be her father as well?
The thought warmed her and she wanted to please him, wanted
him to want her. Wanted him to take her away from this horrible
place and take her home. She smiled at him and rubbed the
straw from her dirty, matted garment. She pulled at her dark
hair and wished quickly that it were blond like that of her
mother. She knew she did not smell good and this bothered
her. She wanted to he beautiful like Aalyne, so that this man
would want her. She wanted him to give her a home.

The cloaked man had not seemed to need persuading. He
had paid little attention to Aalyne; instead, he had come straight
to Julian. He had leaned over her. She felt the caress of his
soft fingers as he lifted her face, felt the burning of his silver
eyes as he looked into her.

He had smiled and nodded.

The three of them had walked from the prison that night.
Julian with her mother and the strange man who was her
mother's husband—and her father, she thought. They had
walked free from that French prison, with its hundred guards
and the people already sleeping on the ground who had come
for the circus of her mother's burning the next morning. He
had left them at the gates, but the two of them—Julian and her
mother—had remained alive to make their leisurely way to the
East and the court of the Sultan Murad, Bayezid's predecessor,
and to a sort of freedom.

From that day onward, Julian had thought the strange silver-
eyed man the answer to her prayer—and yet she had feared
him. She had instinctively recoiled from him when he had

placed his dry fingers on her cheek and had marked her as his possession.

It had been years since Julian had thought of this man. She thought of him now.

CHAPTER TEN

Domiziana liked the witch from the beginning, though of course she could not show her this. It was important for a Venier to keep a safe distance from servants; this was something that the Lady Claudia had always very carefully emphasized. The old woman was obsequious and she stank. Domiziana thought this something that could be easily remedied. Every inch of the strega's dress was covered with handmade amulets and figures. Little wooden fetishes hung from brass posts at her ears. She was outrageous. However, a bath in oil, some new garments—really, what could these cost? After that she could keep the old woman around her always. She needed someone near.

The Lady Domiziana was bored with her mother and frightened of her father. Even on the night of the announcement of her formal betrothal, he had asked why Lord Olivier had not seen her to her chamber and had left this important task to her parents. It was true that chivalry was all-important and proper respect a necessity, but this lack of initiative on Olivier's part did not bode well. She did not need to be reminded that Olivier had not seemed beside himself with a desire to kiss her and that he had spent an unseemly amount of time staring at the child Julian—who, most obviously, was no longer a child. Domiziana sensed danger in these coupled occurrences, and she was no fool.

"He seems to be well taken with that ward of his," Luciano had said. The threat of the convent rang through his voice.

Claudia had cited Domiziana's illness. She had cajoled her husband and then bullied him and in the end he had gone silent. The warning had been thrown out just the same and it had remained with them as a shadowing presence.

No, Domiziana was glad to be ill and confined away from both of her parents. She hoped for something contagious that would keep them at a distance indefinitely. And she found the ministrations of this wicked, little old woman quite amusing. The witch made her laugh and she was starting to feel better. As a matter of fact, she had not felt this good in a very long time. The strega has put her under goose down coverlets and between crisply clean linen covers. The room smelled pleasantly of spices and herbs. She did not ask her embarrassing questions about why the Count of the Ducci Montaldo did not love her. She did not expect her to be beautiful and to perform.

"So you are the village Wise Woman," Domiziana said. It was not a question.

The old woman nodded and smiled. She hadn't a tooth left in her head.

"So then, Wise Woman, tell me what it is you do."

"Ah, many things, my pretty. Many things."

Domiziana pulled herself slowly up in her bed. She settled in among dozens of lavender-scented linen pillows that the Veniers had carted with them from Venice. One never knew the state of civilization beyond the Veneto, and so it was always best to be prepared. She was fascinated by the old woman sitting before her—and by what the old woman might know.

"For one, I have a particular gift with romancing men— with making them get on to doing it, if you take my meaning," the old woman said. Her eyes shone shrewdly. "Especially if the man is found to be mistakenly in thrall to another. I know how to win him back."

There was a sharp intake of breath from the bed and the old witch cackled. She knew she had Domiziana's full attention now.

Olivier's Betrothed.

For the briefest instant, fear overwhelmed Julian as she stood before Domiziana's door. She wished fervently that she were anywhere else, but most especially she longed to be back in her own room, in *Francesca's* room, with its virginal simplicity and its bright, clean smell of new herbs and cedar woods. She had come to pay reverence to the Lady Domiziana and she knew that the chamber would be stifling hot, its air cloying with heady spices and the incense that sparked up from flames within the grate. The witch would be there as well: she always was now. Elisabetta and Domiziana had become inseparable— at least according to Sabata, whose knowledge of castle goings-on was nothing if not comprehensive. She crossed herself when she mentioned the strega: Julian had noted this more than once. The others might think Elisabetta harmless but Sabata didn't. And neither did Julian.

She shook the foreboding away. She reminded herself that she had come to see the Lady Domiziana. She wanted to know more about the future wife of her guardian. It was true that she had been summoned, but she could have refused. Since the day when she and Olivier had argued, then kissed, then argued again—or when *she* had argued, then kissed, and then argued again—her life seemed to have disintegrated into one long argument with her guardian. Certainly, Julian thought ruefully, she had proven herself well able to take on his betrothed as well.

However, Domiziana was still quite ill and keeping to her bed. There was something in Julian that wanted to help her, that *needed* to help her. She wanted to make up for the kiss she had stolen—and the knowledge that she would have stolen more of them had she been able.

She wasn't able. Olivier avoided her, just as she avoided him.

Julian raised her hand to rap upon the heavy wood door and was promptly admitted. Domiziana slept in the traditional chamber of the Countesses of the Ducci Montaldo. Blanche had slept in this room and Olivier had been born in here. It connected to his. The Veniers had insisted upon it, Sabata whispered. They were great sticklers at holding to marks of their rank. "Though they've not much money," the young girl had said. Obviously she had wanted to tell more, but Julian had feigned disinterest. It hurt her to hear anything at all about Domiziana, and, for some reason, most especially the bad things. She could explain this to no one and she didn't.

There were no smaller beds trundled about as there usually were and had been in the time when Blanche was chatelaine of Belvedere. Normally maids or young ladies slept with the mistress but there was no trace of even a pallet for Domiziana's personal maid. The Countess Venier had asked to be placed far down at the other end of the Noble Floor. Claudia had said she had a weakness for a hill view, but the hills that could be seen from that high and barred window were anything but picturesque in the sere of winter. Her younger daughter, Ginevra, must have been given other quarters as well. Belvedere was a great castle and held accommodation for many. Space was no problem, and it was obvious to Julian that Olivier wanted no chaperonage for his bride-to-be.

Three servants, dressed in the br ht nd expensive colors of the Venier family, stood upon the threshold of Domiziana's chamber and ushered Julian inside. The Lady Claudia stood close behind them, hovering between Julian and the thin figure on the bed.

"It is too hot in here," Julian said. "Deathly hot." She was reminded of the sick boy in the village and the stifling heat of his small peasant hut. She noticed that Ginevra sat in the room also, far to one side, diligently working at her needlework in a candle's light.

Beside the bed, Elisabetta huffed up alertly. She had been ousted once from the village: she had no intention of letting that happen again, and this time from even more comfortable quarters within the castle. But it wouldn't. Not with what she was teaching Domiziana to do. Not with the little dolls they had hidden away.

But perhaps it was best to seek assurance.

"She'll not help us," grumbled Elisabetta. "She's a sly, selfish beastie and jealous of her power. She won't share even a bit."

"You may leave us as well," Domiziana said to her and waited until the door closed once again.

"My daughter is ill," said Claudia. "It might just be a slight thing, a fatigue of the journey. Yet this is Belvedere, after all, and there are other things to be considered. This castle has a tainted history. I shouldn't want to take chances."

"If you talk of the plague then there is no danger," Julian said. She knew of the deaths but she never thought of Belvedere as tainted by them. "What happened here, happened long ago. It was a fluke."

"Still . . ." said the Lady Claudia. She waved a heavily ringed hand and the servants departed. Once they had left, the countess again turned her attention to Julian. "I have heard you are the daughter of a great witch and that you may be one as well."

Julian's face froze at this, but Domiziana's mother hurried past the look. She took her hand and led her further into the overheated chamber.

"It doesn't matter to me what they say of your mother," she said quickly. "I have no interest in Aalyne, other than the fact that speculation about her guilt and the stake that was expected for it can fire discussion at a flagging meal table. However, I am interested in you. They say you have the Power: the servants tell me that you have cured both the Lord Olivier and a child. My daughter needs you for that power. She wants you for it.''

"You have Elisabetta,'' protested Julian. "Her skills can cure what ails the Lady Domiziana.''

"Oh, we don't need you for the healing,'' Claudia sang out. "That proceeds well. We have need of you for something else.''

"Come here,'' said Domiziana. "Bring that stool closer to my bed. I have something to show you.''

She raised herself amid the snowy white linens and furs that covered her. Julian noticed that a piece of tapestry was neatly folded on the bed, and she could see the vague outlines of a hart upon it. Claudia also moved closer. Only Ginevra stayed away, but she looked up from her needlework for an instant and her eyes were bright with mischief.

"They want you to play the witch for them,'' she chirped from her corner. "They want to know what is to happen—and what they can do about it.''

Claudia whipped furiously about. Her face had gone quite white. "How dare you say such a thing, Ginevra! We have no intention of asking the Lady Julian to put her skills at our disposal.''

Julian did not miss the "Lady'' that Claudia had attached to her name and she heard the breathless anticipation in the Lady of the Venier's voice.

She followed her gaze to the cards that sat upon the trestle table close beside Domiziana's bed. She had never seen such a beautiful set of the tarot and she said so.

"We had them painted in France,'' Claudia whispered. In her eagerness she touched Julian's arm. "In Lyon, and then someone sent them on to us. They do the best of this kind of work in Lyon, at least that is what we have been told. Wasn't that your mother's city? But the problem is, we have no real idea what to do with them. How to read them. We thought you might . . .''

She let her request trail away naturally in the perfect manner of a well-bred and noble Venetian lady. A relative of the Doge himself—at least through her marriage. She did not want to offend Julian, at least not this day. And Julian knew this. The Ladies of the Venier had no time to waste in silly games of effrontery. Not when they wanted and needed their fortunes told.

A log fell into the fire and sparked blazing cinders in the grate. The smell of incense was overpowering, but not as offensive as it had been before. Julian had grown accustomed to the odor; she almost liked it. She found herself moving towards the cards.

They were beautiful—much more beautiful than her mother's well-worn set and her mother's had been a gift, though a very secret one, from one of the Sultan's advisors. Soothsaying was just as strictly condemned in the Muslim world as it was in the Christian. But still it existed there, just as it did here. There were always fearful people about who would pay to have their fears stilled.

The backs of the cards were painted indigo, which was one of the most expensive colors to manufacture. The pigment sat thickly on the rich, slick surface of the paper. The fronts were figured in gold and Julian had no doubt that the gold was real. Other colors had been worked in as well—cardamom, scarlet, and a deep black—but it was the gold one noticed first. Perhaps because it possessed the vitality of something almost tangibly active. The cards lay neatly spread upon the table and the urge was strong in that hot room for Julian to reach out and touch one, just one. To turn it over.

Touch me. Feel me. Turn me. Loose the Power.

Another log caught fire and settled comfortably into the grate.

Julian had been with her mother many times when Aalyne had questioned the cards, when she turned them over and over in her hands and lovingly caressed them. Rarely had she been allowed to stay when Aalyne read the cards for a paying client. These had been serious occasions, very carefully composed.

The Magdalene always dressed in silks and jewels and she received in a room filled with flowers and a variety of suggestive smells. She made certain to appear as someone who knew a great deal about the finer points of life. No use to look like a crone, for example, when one was being asked for help with romance. What could a crone know about love?

Aalyne was like this when there were clients about.

When her mother read the cards alone—ah, this was something different. Something that Julian had seen, something that had frightened her. Especially when her mother could clearly see what the cards meant—could read the death and destruction when there was no longer a need to couch them in words that did not frighten or offend. Aalyne had clutched frantically at the cards then, and she had let her hands tremble. Sweat had poured down the deeply etched lines of her face. No thought had been given to which gown to put on and which jewels with it. Aalyne had been disheveled. She had been shaking.

This was her mother. This was a true witch's life. When the Power was upon her, it used her as it wanted.

Ah, but the Power . . .

Now, the golden snake on the cards seemed to wiggle—just a bit. Julian felt her hand stretch out. Beside her, the Lady Claudia gasped.

And then there was a bump from the next room, the very slightest noise. It had obviously been made by the Count of the Ducci Montaldo or by one of his men. It didn't matter. It had been made. The spell was broken. The Lady Domiziana let out her bated breath in a hiss as Julian moved her hands back to her sides and away from the cards.

"I know nothing," she said, looking away. "I can help you with traditional healing, with herbs and medicines. I can do the things I learned to do in the East. But I know nothing of these cards. I know nothing of what they can do." The lie did not come easily to her, but she persisted in it anyway. "I cannot tell you what will happen for you in the future. I cannot change the future for you."

But they wanted someone who could.

* * *

"Did you see her face?" whispered Domiziana. Her voice was swift and breathless and there was heat in her face. The door had barely closed behind Julian but the three women in the room huddled together. Even Ginevra put down her tapestry work and took a place closer to the bed. "Did you see how her eyes changed from blue to green as they looked upon the cards?"

"A change in the light," the Lady Claudia said and it was very evident that she wanted to believe just this. "And yet . . ."

"But she knows something, does my little ward-to-be," said Domiziana, her eyes dreamy. "Only she does not wish to share it. She wants to keep her knowledge close to her bosom, just as the strega says. Or perhaps it is Olivier she wishes to keep to herself by using her trickings and her power."

Ginevra glanced up. "Julian does not seem the type to value artifice. Nor does she seem to need dupery to keep Lord Olivier. He appears fond enough of her to want her near, at least he does so to me. If this were not so, she would already have found herself well along the road back to Harnoncourt Hall. That seems obvious enough, knowing the Count's character."

Claudia bit back sharp words and calmed herself before she answered.

"Of course he is fond of Julian," she said to her youngest and least favorite daughter. "Her mother saved his life. He told us that himself in Venice. We mustn't forget that she is a witch's child. She saw something in those cards. I saw knowledge on her face and in her eyes."

Domiziana looked over at her mother and the two of them smiled as Claudia reached down to pull up her tapestry work.

"I am glad she said nothing to us about what she saw, if indeed there was anything at all to see, which I doubt," Ginevra said with uncharacteristic fierceness. "It is a bad idea to want to know the future and totally unnecessary as well. The Count is betrothed to Domiziana. He will marry her. You don't need strange cards to tell you that.''

Domiziana smiled from her pillows. "And yet they say that the Lady Blanche had horoscopes cast—and by the monks at San Mario, who are rumored to be holy men.''

Her mother nodded as she cut a strand of silk thread with her teeth. "The Lady Blanche is French and the French know about such things. Just look at Aalyne,'' she said.

"They say the predictions were most accurate,'' Domiziana continued. "They say, as well, that they were beautifully wrought. Things of beauty—much as are these cards.''

Ginevra snorted. "Accurate or not, the Contessa Ducci Montaldo saw nothing in those parchments that helped her to prevent the death of her husband and her three sons in the plague. They told her when to expect a good bee season and a far-off war, but they said nothing of the calamity that buried her soul. And 'tis always like that, I've heard. The stars tell you the trivia—the important things you must learn on your own. I put no store in them.''

"Then more fool you,'' said Domiziana sweetly. "You should take help where you can get it. I've seen no suitor slaying dragons for *your* hand.''

Claudia ignored this latest altercation.

"The Lady Blanche's was a great loss,'' she agreed piously. "Still she was left with a daughter and a son. The daughter is well married and the son will soon be. It was not noble of her to carry on for so long about the dead ones. Why, Ottavia Valli told me that she even took to imbibing wine in secret—and a great deal of it as well. I think this a perfect disgrace for a noblewoman of her level—and her pretensions. It makes one have one's doubts about our involving Venice with the French in this Holy War.''

"As if holiness had anything to do with this war,'' said Ginevra with a snort. "Everyone knows that Venice is involved solely for the purpose of protecting its trade routes. If these weren't threatened, Bayezid could take half the world *and* King

Sigismund and King Charles with it and we'd but murmur our condolences. We'd not lift a finger to help.''

"There was something when Julian moved towards those cards," Domiziana whispered, changing the subject. "You felt it, Mother. Even Ginevra felt it."

Her younger sister hesitated for a moment and then nodded. "There was something," she agreed reluctantly.

"She wants to keep it to herself," continued Domiziana. "She will not share her knowledge. But I know someone who will."

She pulled herself up amid her pillows and rang the little silver bell beside her bed. "And perhaps if Elisabetta is helpful, we might find a place for her in one of the caravans that will take us to Venice. She looks much healthier already. Cleaner, too. It always amazes me what marvels can be accomplished by a long soak in a hot bath."

"Domiziana . . ." Ginevra warned.

It was too late. The door that led into her sister's chamber was already opening before Elisabetta's stooped but triumphant figure.

Their mother went back to the serene wielding of her needle.

The Lady Claudia lay awake well into the night, listening to her husband's snores and thinking. When she remembered her youngest daughter, and above all when she was far away from her, she tried to love Ginevra. It was a mother's duty to love her child, and Claudia was nothing if not a dutiful mother. All of Venice knew this, and the haughty Venetians sometimes—but not always—forgave her low birth because of this.

And after all, Claudia reasoned, Ginevra was her youngest daughter, flesh of her flesh and also of dear Luciano's. And she, much more than her three older sisters, strongly resembled their father. She possessed the slim height and patrician features that had marked the Venier aristocrats for generations. The Lady Claudia's illustrious relations loved Ginevra.

But Claudia herself loved Domiziana.

Domiziana was her child—hers alone. Though of course she was biologically Luciano's and he knew it—otherwise nothing could have come of the gamble for Claudia except, naturally, her disgrace and eventual death. Her father would have had her killed when the pregnancy showed—and no one would have said a word in protest.

It was because of her calculated pregnancy with Domiziana that Claudia—who was from a good but not a noble family and lived in Venice, a city where only the nobility counted—had been able to wrest together such a glorious marriage. It was because of Domiziana that she was now a Venier and had been for so long that many people had forgotten her more humble origins. Those who had not forgotten chose not to remember them, at least publicly. Of course, Claudia knew that her own pretty looks had counted for much, as had her even prettier ways in bed. It was because she carried Domiziana that she had gotten what she wanted and she knew this. She would leave no stone unturned in giving her beautiful daughter what she wanted—and even so desperately needed—in return.

Yes, Claudia sighed as she angled close to her husband. She would take the strega with them when they left in two days' time. She would carry her into Venice. It was important to use any net when one would bag a lion.

Had she not proven this herself? And was she not happy she'd done so?

CHAPTER ELEVEN

The next night the two counts lingered late over their tankards.

"It was not as though the Europeans expected no trouble from the East," commented Luciano Venier. "We have fought crusades aplenty against the Muslims and for generations we have looked in that direction with a fretful and worried eye. But in truth the East, as we call it—vaguely and even mysteriously—lies far away, beyond a vast frontier of seas and mountains and plains. People who practice a different religion rule it. They are infidels and, as such, are automatically condemned to hell. Any priest or knight or mendicant peasant could tell you this."

Luciano pulled at his wine. "Quite good, this," he said. "Is it of your own vintage?"

He seemed pleased with Olivier's nod and drank again before continuing. "Therefore the problem of the East and the growing strength of the Ottoman Empire did not frighten people. We all thought that any problem with the Sultan could be dealt with quickly and summarily by God's own people in His own time. No, the preoccupation in Europe did not lie in a threat that lived beyond mountains or seas—it lay within the sacred boundaries of our own continent."

Olivier was silent He let the man speak.

"Since the Battle of Poitiers, nearly forty years ago—in 1356, France and England have smoldered and sometimes erupted against each other. In a dragging-on war, they quibble over borders and territories. They kept cunning ambassadors busy deciding who owed homage and reparation to whom, and who held rights to the seaport at Calais. These talented men could have more constructively spent their time numbering angels on pinheads. Naturally, lesser knights in lesser states cannot let these grave questions be settled without the assistance of their swords and the staking of their own plunder claims. And so the discord has spread. The land that Charlemagne once fashioned into a strong and united Europe has found itself fragmenting into smaller and smaller shards."

Olivier listened to his soon-to-be relation with acute attention. He had always thought Luciano Venier something of a buffoon, a minor member of a major family, who was under the control of his strong-willed wife. Still, what he was saying was interesting and Olivier encouraged him by joining in the conversation.

"But this didn't seem to bother the Europeans," he said mildly. "We are Christians; therefore, God is on our side. At least that is the prevailing rationale. It was always known that we would vanquish the infidel in an easy but glorious battle—someday. In the meantime, it is all that King Charles VI of France can do to keep his kingdom together and hold rein on his crafty royal uncles, the Dukes of Burgundy and Anjou. The only consolation he has in dealing with those two recalcitrants—at least in lucid moments when he is not engulfed in the madness that continually threatens him—is in knowing that his royal cousin, Richard II of England, struggles to maintain control of his own nobles. This is no easy task, especially when

he king is forced to deal with Thomas of Woodstock, Duke
of Gloucester, a born troublemaker if ever one lived.''

"Still their kingdoms were strong," said Luciano with a
cunning shrug. "And each of the kings went to bed at night
knowing that, by Divine Right, his own noble cause would
triumph handily in the end. The various battles gave occupation
to the knights, who seemed constitutionally unable to stay at
home anyway. They could have squabbled along amiably like
this indefinitely except for one determinant.''

Now it was Olivier's turn to shrug. "Italy," he said.

Luciano laughed. "They call us a 'landmass' for want of a
better name. They wonder aloud how one could call a place a
country when it is nothing more than a conglomeration of
bickering city-states and pompous communes who seem to be
in a constant state of internecine warfare. Hostilities between
Florence and Siena barely finished before fighting broke out
between Genoa and Rome. Bloodshed, squabbles, and a certain
sly diplomacy seemed to be the order of the day. Northern
Europeans, ignoring their own problems, shake their collective
heads at the antics of sunny Italy and wish fervently that they
could treat the whole country as nothing more than a cautionary
tale.''

"But they can't." Olivier laughed out loud.

Count Venier joined him in his merriment. "For one thing,
Italy controls the purse strings of Europe through its powerful
banking families in Lombardy and Florence—chief among
them, Gian Galeazzo Visconti in Milan. He is an astute man.
I admire him greatly. He became a legend in his own time
when he cleverly used the lever he exercises over a France
whose finances are ever precariously perched close to the abyss,
to wrest for his favorite daughter, Valentina, the hand of the
king's younger brother.''

"A situation that seems to have soured," said Olivier
thoughtfully.

"That this royal rogue has subsequently abandoned his bride,
preferring instead to take the Queen as mistress, has not seemed

to worry the doting father overmuch. Even though the luckless
Valentina has been publicly disgraced and accused of sorcery,
Gian Galeazzo is man enough not to appear overly concerned.
He has but smiled and murmured of God's Will, and has contin-
ued to treat with France—perhaps in more ways than one.''

Olivier did not share Luciano's high regard for the Visconti
ruler. He deftly changed the subject. ''It would have been
bad enough for Europe with our wily country controlling the
financial passages of this world, but we also managed to hang
onto the only direct route to the next one as well. The Pope
sits conspicuously upon his throne at Rome, and from Rome
he rules the world.''

''Naturally, it was not stated in just exactly this way,''
Luciano said, adroitly adjusting to this shift in the conversational stream. ''Strictly speaking, the Church is in charge of
men's souls and what will best benefit them. That is all. The
problem is that the soul is nebulous. Not even our greatest
alchemists have ever been able to see or weigh it. It might
include little, or it might include much. Our recent popes insist
that it encompasses everything—and this includes the temporal
world as well. Of course, many a powerful prince, beginning
with the Emperor Frederick Barbarossa, has disputed this thesis.
One by one these rulers have been brought, quite literally, to
their knees. Not only did the Pope exercise authority over their
immortal souls but he also wields the anathema as well. By
his word a village or even a whole land could go, in the space
of only one night, from being immensely prosperous to being
a pariah.''

''His is a power bound to make enemies,'' responded Olivier.

Luciano pulled again at his wine. ''So thought the French.
It was Philip the Fair who decided, when a pope at Rome seemed
inconvenient, to establish a papacy at Avignon. Naturally, as
it is within French territory, it is endowed with a French head.''

''The English, for their part,'' said Olivier, ''clutch with
determination at the throne of St. Peter in Rome. It has become
their possession.''

"This is common knowledge. Even poor peasants know this and recite their prayers according to the papal preference of their liege lord."

"Thus the Great Schism was born," Olivier replied. "And everyone, it seems, has found his own expedient side within it."

"And through all of Europe's frantic maneuverings, the Sultan Bayezid and his warriors, including the very able Dogan Bey at Nicopolis, observed these strange machinations, and planned and conquered and waited—as they grew ever more powerfully united," said Luciano with an air of conclusion. "This is excellent wine, indeed. Is there more?"

"Julian is not to come with us." The Count of the Ducci Montaldo was not only forceful in this, he was adamant. "Under no circumstances."

The Knight de la Marche, well-schooled in diplomacy, let his face speak while his lips remained silent. He raised his brow quizzically as he let his eyes glance towards the east. He sadly shook his head, and it was a full moment before he said, "As you wish, my lord." And another moment before he added, "Might not she be a help? Might not she make a difference?"

Olivier was not convinced. He would have gone back to a careful study of his maps had his guest been less noble, but chivalry only permitted him to say, "I cannot see what good my ward will do us in battle. She has much too light a frame to be of much use with a mace."

"I have no wish to see the Lady Julian anywhere near the battlefield in Bulgaria. However, I think we may have need of her in Venice."

"In Venice?" Olivier was surprised despite himself. He looked directly at the Burgundian across his parchment-stacked trestle table. The sound of hammering echoed into the Great Hall from the courtyard as the men from both their armies prepared for war. For a moment neither knight spoke.

"In Venice," Gatien repeated. "As you well know, this battle will begin well before we reach any foreign battlefield. Which reminds me—how is your wound progressing? I trust Padre Gasca is tending it well between his monastical pilgrimages."

Of course the Knight de la Marche would eventually divulge what his spies had told him—if, indeed, the Burgundian had not plotted the attack, Olivier surmised. The disclosure would only wait Sir Gatien's discretion.

"It—and I—proceed well," the Count said. "Our learned Franciscan is an able physician."

"And the Lady Julian a good nurse." Gatien smiled, but the light from it did not quite reach his eyes.

The two men stared at each other as Julian's name silently reverberated in the air between them. The set of Gatien's mouth told Olivier that spies had not provided all of the Burgundian's information. He had gathered part of it himself.

"Indeed," said Olivier, "my ward was good at what she did for me."

"As she will be in Venice as well." Gatien walked to the barred window, turning his back on his host as he did. "Let us not fool ourselves. We are in Italy and, without meaning offense to either your family or your country, we both know what that means. For every city or commune that will welcome this crusade, there is another that will use every means possible, and even some blatantly impossible ones, to see that this Holy War never takes place. Whoever wants to keep Venice from participating in a French endeavor has already tried to seriously wound you—if not kill you."

Olivier was listening.

"It might just as well be anyone," continued Gatien. "One would think automatically of the Sultan, who might want Venice neutral so as not to disrupt trade with Italy. It could have been someone in Venice who plays, perhaps, a double game. It could be Gian Galeazzo Visconti."

"What would he have to do with this?" Olivier's voice was

sharp. The notion of possible treachery from the Visconti had also lodged in his mind, and it had not been shaken. "He seems such good friends with the King of France. He is rumored to be supporting with his own money—something that rarely happens—this French adventure into the Balkan lands."

"He seems to be cooperative. He seems to be content," repeated Gatien. "Yet Gian Galeazzo is a man of many parts. Venice, whose land forces are under your command, recently defeated Genoa, which is under his protection. This would form a strong motive of retaliation, especially for a man not used to compromise, as certainly we know Gian Galeazzo to be. He had his own uncle Bernabo strangled in order to obtain the inheritance, as I am sure you must know."

Olivier nodded. Who did not know this? Gian Galeazzo, a secretive man, made no secret of it.

"I think his wish for vendetta might have little to do with Venice—and much to do with France," said Gatien. "And specifically with the King of France. You know, of course, that he had managed to marry his daughter Valentina to the king's brother and that she will be converted because she proves to be an impediment to that man's relationship with the queen, his brother's wife."

"I know that, yes," said Olivier ironically, remembering his discussion with Luciano Venier. " 'Tis much talked of—though I hardly expected you to talk of it."

"And that person will try again," said Gatien, turning back to face Olivier. "This much is inevitable. And if that person is the Sultan he will send spies to Venice, and not just a few. The city will be clambering with them, and one or two will need to get close to you. Julian knows Turkish, as well as many of the dialects and languages that are spoken in and around Bulgaria. She also knows Arabic, which is the language that the Ottomans use for their written communications. She would make you a useful secretary."

"I know those things myself," scoffed Olivier. "Why would I need a woman to secretary me."

"Because she is good with accents. It is one of her grea
talents. She can tell where a man comes from, not by the word:
he uses, but by the way he speaks them, even if that accent i:
covered over by years of crafty living in a foreign land. Her:
is a useful gift that might serve you well. Many will be coming
to see you in Venice as you prepare for war. It might be good
to have someone about who will know at least that they are
who they claim to be."

"I have already decided that Julian must return to Harnoncourt Hall where she is under the care of my sister."

"Then, for your own sake, I beg that you reconsider your
decision."

"For my sake?" asked Olivier. "Or for your own?"

The man whom Julian loved and the man who loved her
faced each other in silence for some time. Above them, the
banners that generations of Ducci Montaldo warriors had carried into battle hung from the exposed beams with the banners
of the men whom they had vanquished. They swished back
and forth, side by side, in a draft that eddied through the rafters.

"She will not have me," Gatien finally said. His voice was
quiet, controlled. "I have asked."

"Before you spoke of it with me, her guardian?" Olivier
didn't know why he was suddenly so annoyed. He hadn't
planned to be. Yet he found he was just as hostile as Gatien, and
with less reason. "And just exactly what was your request?"

De la Marche's smile was irony itself. "Why, holy wedlock,
of course. That is all I would think to offer to a woman whom
I value as highly as I value the Lady Julian."

"You would do this without speaking to me first, without
gaining my approval?" Olivier was damned if he'd let himself
be bettered by this Burgundian. He knew his faults—and most
especially his fault where Julian was concerned—but he would
not let Gatien be his judge in this. He was the Count of the
Ducci Montaldo and Julian's guardian. Her rescuer. If this
French barbarian had anything to reprove him with, then by
God he'd better spit it out.

Which is exactly what the French barbarian proceeded to do.

"Considering your promises to the Lady Domiziana and her family," said Gatien with exaggerated civility. "Even though she had not yet arrived at Belvedere, all of Europe knew of your intentions towards her. Troubadours sing, as you know. And they are most anxious to carry stories—especially love stories—from place to place. Considering the circumstances, I thought it possible that your mind might be too filled with the thought of your nearly betrothed—your *betrothed* now— to have space left for the contemplation of your young ward's future."

"Given the circumstances," Olivier echoed. Gatien's sword had certainly drawn blood with this last thrust and he would be given his point. Besides, there were merits to de la Marche's plan and Olivier, though angry, could see them.

"The Lady Julian will accompany us to Venice," he said finally. "After that, we will see."

"Everyone, and especially those who have fought against him, calls the Sultan 'Ilderim,' which means thunderbolt," Gatien said to Julian. "Did you know that?"

Julian could have answered that she did indeed know this and a great deal more about the Sultan Bayezid, as well as about his great Turkish commander, the Dogan Bey at Nicopolis, but she didn't. Instead she nodded once, very quickly, and hoped the knight would not pursue the matter.

The two of them rode a little ahead of the main caravan and were securely cloaked against the cold north wind—the Tus- cans called it the *tramontana*—which had been blustering since the party started out from Belvedere two days before. It threat- ened to blow against them until they reached the lagoons of Venice. The wind whipped fiercely at times, but it did not prevent little snippets of conversation. Julian was grateful for this and for Gatien's company. True to his word, Olivier had allowed her to accompany the Gold Company to Venice. He had formally sent for her and informed her of his decision in the Great Hall of his castle, and before his betrothed and her family and the noblest of his knights. But he had spent no time with her and whenever she had caught a quick glimpse of him, he had been either with his men or tending to the Lady Domiziana. Without Gatien, Julian would have keenly felt her isolation.

"It was Sigismund, King of Hungary, who first brought us the warning of him," the knight continued, as though he understood she did not want to speak of the Sultan who had been her mother's protector.

"I've heard of Sigismund," Julian said. "Count Olivier and the Sire of Harnoncourt have both spoken of him."

Gatien chuckled. "As well they might. They are all old friends. All knights are like that—either they've fought with each other or against each other. Bloodletting and camaraderie are the two main points of the occupation."

"The king is not actually Hungarian, is he?" Julian questioned. Her nose was beginning to run and she tried surreptitiously to wipe at it, hoping that the renowned warrior beside her wouldn't notice.

"When he first arrived to take the throne, his subjects called him the Bohemian pig," said Gatien, passing over a square of fine white linen. "But no one says that anymore. He is brother to Wenceslas, the Holy Roman Emperor. Sigismund has proven himself an able monarch in his own right. Much better than his brother, who is a drunkard. King Sigismund's is the last organized state that separates Europe from the threat of Turkey and he does not let the rest of us forget it. The Hungarians, for their part, do not need a lesson in memory. They well remember what it has been like these last years as the Mongols swept down to overrun the country, and have come to idolize their king.

"He is quite handsome and makes the most of his height and girth and a truly magnificent swath of dark hair—actually, its color is very similar to your own—which he wears long and curled. Of course, there is no end to the whisperings about such a fair and forceful man. When he left France after pleading his case to King Charles, many said his loss was personal to half the fair damsels at court.''

Julian laughed before she could stop herself, then pulled her face together and grew stern. "You should not say things like that to me, and I am scandalous to laugh at them.''

"No, indeed," said Gatien heartily. "It would only be scandalous if you did not laugh. You are an intelligent woman, Julian, and you know the world's ways without pandering to them. These are two of the foundation stones of your considerable charms and you should recognize them.''

Julian, who had spent the whole of her life defining herself as what she was not, now found it strange to have someone talk with her about what she was—or perhaps could be. She found the notion pleasant and wanted to stay with it a while, but Gatien was already back into the intrigues of his knight's tale.

"Of course, the king is still young, only twenty-eight, but he has already shown himself to be a capable warrior. He has fought off the Sultan's troops when he could, but Hungary is a small state and he needs the help of Europe if he is to protect his borders.''

"You yourself like him?'' Julian wiped at her nose again as Gatien shrugged. He used the motion to cuddle more deeply into his thick cloak, and then reached over to settle Julian's more closely around her shoulders. It was some moments before he spoke.

"I admire Sigismund. Any knight would. He is brave and learned and headstrong and foolish. This is the perfect combination for ensuring the continual turmoil all warriors crave. He lives to fight—as we all do. However, I am afraid that he does not use diplomacy when it would serve. When last he was in Paris he turned to examine a bone reputed to belong to St. Elizabeth, and said it could just as easily have come from a

cobbler. He said this quite loudly. The monks who had custody
of this relic—and charged half a silver florin to the faithful for
its viewing—were not amused. And that is to say the very
least.''

But Julian was amused, and she laughed heartily. Her deep,
rich laughter flew headlong into the wind as the army and its
bright, silk-covered wagons left Tuscany behind them and made
their way north and east to the mystery of Venice that lay
ahead.

CHAPTER TWELVE

The Italians called Venice *La Serenissima,* the Serene One, and Julian hated the city at first sight. She thought it smug and complacent, as though it looked down upon the rest of Italy from some lofty, ethereal height.

Not hate, really, she quickly amended, even though she had not and would never say these words aloud. But there was something here that did not attract her. With its mirror-like air of still silver, it looked uncomfortably like a place bewitched. It was not at all what Julian had expected, this city that shimmered silently into its gray-colored lagoons.

For one thing, Venice did not seem like the rest of the Italian peninsula at all: certainly it was not like the open brightness of the Tuscany that she had just left and that she loved. Tuscany always charmed her, with its inherent buoyancy and its promise of fun. Even its winter dormancy resembled nothing so much as a child taking a brief nap in preparation for new mischief.

Venice, instead, was a serious location and Julian did not like the grayness of its waters. She did not like the black-painted, flat-bottomed barges that lay silently waiting to carry them from the mainland to the loose fabric of islands that called itself a city. She did not like the way low wooden bridges knitted this fabric together.

Something in Venice did not bode well for her. Something would jump out from her dreams and catch her if it could. Julian knew she would not be happy in this place.

And yet she was meant to be here, and she knew this as well. She was the one who had pleaded with Olivier to come on this crusade. She was the one who had been determined that he honor his promise and rescue her mother. She had been willing to pay any price, so that events would work out as they were working out now. The thought made her shiver. She was, after all, the daughter of Aalyne de Lione, the Magdalene, and thus too much of a Wise Woman not to know that a price would be demanded for all of this largesse. Julian shivered as the barges made their slow and stately way up and over the watery byways that led to the Grand Canal. She had never felt this chilled at Belvedere, though actually, Tuscany was far colder. She was getting ever nearer to Nicopolis, but she had never in her life felt so far away from home.

Thank God for Gatien, she thought. He did not challenge her, he no longer spoke to her of marriage; he talked to her and he made her laugh. He was her friend, the only one she had ever had.

Venice, of course, did not seem to care about her new friendship. The city smiled its enigmatic, jeweled smile as the black barge flying the crested-lion banners of *La Serenissima* and the Ducci Montaldo slid through her still waters. As ward of the Count of the Ducci Montaldo and so by right a member of his family, courtesy decreed that Julian enter the city on the first of the ferries. She had been kept to the back, that was true, and quite safely tucked next to Ginevra, the youngest and least important of the Veniers. But Olivier was on this barge as well, and for Julian this was enough.

The Lady Claudia and her eldest daughter had been given positions of honor. They sat upon sturdy wooden chairs that had been especially brought from their palazzo. Fox skin rugs shrouded their legs. The Count Luciano Venier stood beside his wife and Olivier behind his betrothed. The Knight de la Marche, an especially honored guest, stood nearby. All of their positions had been carefully choreographed by the rules of chivalry, and Gatien had not been placed beside his good friend Julian.

The only thing giving an incongruous coloring to this gray day were the bright strips of silk hanging from the windows of various palazzi along the Grand Canal. These were colorful indeed—bright flutterings of red and blue and yellow and an especially vivid purple stood out in relief against the steely day of winter.

"These are from our friends," Lady Claudia said, waving a jeweled hand that took in the various brightly colored swaths. "It is the traditional way of welcome in Venice. We do our greeting with a certain flamboyant discretion."

They laughed at her witticism.

"Listen," Ginevra whispered to Julian, "Mother will now launch into a history of these lagoons. She has much to say about the Lion of St. Mark—the Lion of Venice—which is a local legend, and she will favor us all with the story, but her particular attention will be for the Knight de la Marche. Now that Domiziana is safely arranged, she must think of Maria." She shushed Julian's inquiry with a shake of her head. "No, you've not yet met Maria. She refused to leave her beloved Venice even for a brief sojourn in Tuscany. How my mother expects that she will travel as far as Burgundy is a question best left to the angels and saints."

Julian seemed to have lost the thread of this conversation and she said as much.

"My mother has seen promise in Sir Gatien," Ginevra quite readily clarified. "He is a man encumbered with both a great name and a great fortune. The only thing wanting seems to be a wife. My mother has very generously decided to rectify this lack by giving him the hand of my sister Maria in holy matrimony.''

Ginevra smiled, and Julian caught herself smiling as well.

"Well, indeed, he isn't married," she ventured, whispering so that the others could not hear.

"I know that," replied the Maid of the Venier. "As does everyone else. However, Maria is not the match for him. I am."

"You are!'' Julian's astounded face darkened. "Don't tell me Sir Gatien has forced himself on you. Why, you are just a child.''

"I am but few years younger than you," replied Ginevra with dignity. "Besides, the Knight de la Marche thinks himself already in love with you. It will take him a while to get over his disappointment, but in the end I will have him. I have loved Gatien de la Marche from the moment I saw him. He is mine.''

Julian opened her mouth to say something more, but Ginevra placed a finger to her lips. "Shhh," she said with exaggerated politeness. "My mother is speaking and we must listen."

Then she winked, and Julian had the strangest sensation that Ginevra Venier thought of her as a friend.

"We are seeing Venice as it was first seen by the earliest Venetians," continued the Lady Claudia. She settled into her chair. Julian, who was shivering in the January cold, surmised with sad certainty that their history lesson threatened to be a long one. She hoped the barge was drawing near to what her hosts called the Cá Venier, their palazzo which fronted on the Grand Canal. "Much of this water that we are passing over is actually shallow enough for a man to walk through, and yet it has protected us from invaders for generations. In fact, Venice was started as a haven from invaders."

The Countess glanced placidly around to see that she was being paid her due attention. Julian, gazing at Olivier through the shelter of her eyelashes, saw his bored face snap to interested attention as first Claudia and then Domiziana stared at him. The two ladies nodded approvingly. As they looked away, Olivier glanced up and then over to catch Julian's naughty smile. He grinned at her, and for just an instant that complicity united them as surely as a kiss. His gaze lowered to her lips and then flicked upwards, as if he had suddenly remembered who he was and what he was doing. But it didn't matter. Julian had felt the heat and the light from him and had responded with her own. It was a long moment before either of them looked away.

"A refuge," the Contessa Venier continued. "People came here from the Veneto mainland long before the Romans first arrived, because they thought that the lagoons and the marshes would protect them. . . ."

Julian remembered to smile and look interested but she was no longer standing on this wet, cold barge as it meandered through the slick water to the family's palazzo. She was back at Belvedere, feeling Olivier's hard muscles beneath her fingertips, tasting him for the very first time with her tongue. She remembered the freshness of morning that enclosed them as she had first opened her mouth to Olivier and then drawn him in. She remembered how secure she had felt in his arms and how, for the first time, she had thought where such kissing might lead. The thought had not been unpleasant. It had not frightened her. She had thought . . .

It didn't matter what she had thought or what she would think. What mattered was that Count Olivier Ducci Montaldo was betrothed to the Lady Domiziana Venier. This was the reality of this situation, and Julian, trained from childhood to face reality in even worse circumstances, would not let herself shrink from this now.

"He is in love with her. He will marry her." She whispered these words to the wind and to her heart. "The Lady Domiziana is everything that the Lord of the Ducci Montaldo has ever wanted." This was the way life went.

And, of course, she had always known this. In the excitement of knowing she would be included in this expedition, in knowing that she would be near Olivier still and that she could see him and smile at him, she had somehow thought that things would be different. She had allowed herself to spend hours thinking of him and reliving that kiss. She had seen no harm in this. After all, the most important thing was to rescue Aalyne. In the end she could renounce anything if she knew she had fulfilled her duty to her mother. She could renounce Olivier because he was pledged to another. As she had on many occasions in the past, she had counted on the force of her own strength. She had counted upon the fact that she could always make herself do the right thing.

What she had not counted upon, she was discovering now much to her chagrin, was the searing, daily pain of watching Olivier as he took exquisite care of the woman he loved.

Olivier was bored—bored almost to distraction. He had always harbored the furtive suspicion that the Contessa Venier was a woman whose brain did not labor under the burden of a heavy intelligence. Since accompanying her to Venice, he was now quite certain of this fact. Not that she was not cunning, he quickly amended. She was a very clever woman. Anyone could see that: perhaps he more than most. Yet there was something of the *arriviste* about her, as his mother would say. She was a little bit too charming, a little bit too perfectly dressed.

On the one occasion when the two contessas had met—which had happened more than a year ago at Claudia Venier's insistence—they had not got on well at all. Olivier still cringed at the memory of how perilously close to rude his mother had appeared. She had fiddled with her numerous and noisy gold bracelets, whilst the Contessa Venier waxed eloquent about the history of her marital family. She had yawned openly at the hundredth mention of "dear Antonio, our cousin the Doge." In the end she had even taken to sending down transparent excuses for her absence at mealtime. When her son, as head of both the Ducci Montaldo and the Gold Company, had reprimanded his mother for her incivility and reminded her that he was in Venice's employ, Blanche had shrugged her pretty shoulders and yawned her pretty yawn. Her famous eyes, the exact same turquoise as his own, had taken on a bored glaze.

"Let her think I am drowning myself in the nearest wine vat," she had said, joking about a part of her past life which Olivier still found hard to consider. " 'Tis probably what she's gossiping behind my back anyway. If you are determined to marry her daughter then do so, and with my blessing. Please don't make me a party to it. I cannot abide that woman."

Olivier, though furious, had thought it prudent not to argue. After all, Blanche de Montfort Ducci Montaldo was known to be a terrible snob.

But there was no gainsaying the fact that she loved Julian.

The thought hit Olivier with a force that he certainly had not been expecting. And of course it was true. Blanche, who was descended from one of the first families in France and who had crossed the mountains to marry a man who traced his august lineage back to the Roman Republic, had loved the child Julian from the start. She had played with her and petted her since the first day they had met. She had crooned lullabies to her and told her how lovely she found her family name.

"Julian Madrigal," she had said in her light, cultured voice. "How wonderful it must be to be named for a song."

As if taking on a name could give Julian a heritage, the Count of the Ducci Montaldo thought with some irritation. She had that witch mother: she had that unknown father—and that was all she had. Blanche had more than tasted poverty in his absence, and Olivier knew this. He thought she would have been as determined to put it as far into dead memory as he had been. He thought that she would be willing and eager to take up her old life again, to tolerate even more offensive women than Claudia Venier in order to rebuild the Ducci Montaldo family into what it had been in the past. But his mother seemed to have lost her ambition during the years he had spent as prisoner of the Dogan Bey, and so had his sister Francesca. They had no more use for the Claudia Veniers of this world.

They wanted Julian. They wanted her near.

And so did he, Olivier realized. So did he.

The feeling was not at all welcome.

What in God's name had possessed him to kiss her? Since then he'd not had a moment's peace. He would be studying his maps and he would suddenly smell violets. He would be supervising his men and the outrageous thought would come that perhaps he should ask Julian's opinion concerning their rations. He would see a sunrise or a sunset and be on the verge of calling her to share it with him. He seemed to think of her constantly, whether or not he was consciously thinking of her at all.

This had to stop. And he knew how to make it do just that. The Count of the Ducci Montaldo's face hardened around his new resolve as the barge bumped gently against the mooring that fronted the Cá Venier. He was a betrothed man with an intended bride who wanted him. This much had been made quite clear. He would go to Domiziana tonight. He would make love to her over and over again, if need be until morning. He would do whatever was necessary to drive the thought of Julian Madrigal out of his mind.

It was Gatien who handed Julian up the slick stone steps that led to the palazzo proper. A manservant appeared and reached out from the palazzo's door to help her inside and take her parcel, but Julian held it close. She had found special healing seeds in the laboratory and decided to carry them along. A war would call for much healing. It did not take a witch's power to realize this fact.

If he was curious about what she carried, Gatien did not allow himself to show this. Instead he took Julian inside the palazzo and quietly held her in conversation while the others disembarked. The sea lapped at the stone steps that led to the palazzo proper and Julian saw a water line that told her that the structure, although it seemed fairly new, had been flooded more than once.

"Is there no higher ground here?" she said, grimacing and holding onto her plants for fear that they all might be washed away. Anything could happen in Venice, she decided. The whole place was soggy and grim. "Could not the nobles have betaken themselves to a higher position? As it is they must find themselves conversing with the fishes after each spring thaw."

"It is as the Lady Claudia told us in her travelogue. To which, I might add, I am sure you paid the strictest attention," said Gatien naughtily. "The Venetians came to these islands in order to shelter themselves from the barbarians."

"There are no more barbarians now," scoffed Julian. Though they were her enemy, she knew the Ottoman Turks too well to consider them uncivilized. "You would think the idea of turning moldy might seem a greater danger than anything that might swoop down from the mainland."

Gatien laughed at this. He held to her arm as she made her slippery way up the stairs. "Of course they could have moved their city inland. However, that would have deprived them of a continual link to their livelihood."

"Their livelihood?"

"The sea."

And he swept his arm out to enclose the endless sweep of gray that led from Venice to the East.

Olivier handed his betrothed up the stairs to her home—soon to be his home as well. He reminded himself of this with a certain grim determination. He had admired the Venier palazzo from the very first day he had arrived in Venice, as head of the Gold Company. He had gazed at the Cá Venier from a perch across the Grand Canal and had thought it solid and strong. Dominating, even. It imposed itself upon its surroundings, just as he imposed himself. He had wanted it for his own, and had, in a certain sense, obtained it. Just as he had obtained everything else he had dreamed about while he

languished in the Dogan Bey's prison—and while his father
and his brothers died and life had changed his mother beyond
his recognition.

He had gotten what he wanted. Venice was his.

And yet . . .

Again he felt the uneasiness he had felt in the barge, when
he had looked at Julian and smiled at her and remembered. He
didn't know where it was coming from, had never felt it before.
He did not like this feeling.

He tried to concentrate on the Lady of the Venier as she
unfurled tapestries for the Knight de la Marche, laughing as
she said they had been in her own family for generations.
Olivier would not have been surprised to see flax price tagging
still sewn to the backs. Claudia Venier was a noisome woman,
and growing increasingly more so as he in turn grew more tired
and worried. He noticed her shortcomings with more clarity
since she'd come to Belvedere. Thank goodness Domiziana
had not taken on these less subtle attitudes of her grasping
mother. But then Domiziana was a Venier born. He would
always be able to depend upon her to act the lady.

Olivier had always known that he would marry well and that
he would marry a lady of stature, and in Domiziana he had
gotten exactly what he wanted. Just as he had with everything
else. He had escaped from the Sultan's clutches, he had restored
Belvedere to its glory, and he had found himself a suitable
wife.

"I am a most fortunate man," he said with determination,
as he promised himself yet again that this night he would seek
out his betrothed and bed her well—for both their sakes.

In contrast, Julian did not feel fortunate at all. It was true
that she, too, had gotten what she wanted. It had taken the
working of some truly incredible miracle to bring her to Venice,
but she was here, and she was nearer to her mother than she
had been since that night in Nicopolis when they had been

wrenched apart. All of this had been accomplished, certainly
with the help of a benevolent grace, but also through the force
of her own determined will. She had known she would accompany the Knight de la Marche to Venice—and she had done
it. She had known that, in the end, Olivier would be persuaded
to this Crusade—and this had happened as well. She had known
that he would honor his promise to rescue Aalyne—and this
had been repledged. In addition, there were only a very few
doors to a very few chambers separating her from Olivier. She
had never before in her life been chambered so near the man
she loved.

Yet she felt bereft.

Yes, that was the feeling that slithered through her. Loss,
dispossession, bereavement. She tried at first to put her bad
humor down to the chamber the Contessa Claudia had assigned
to her. The rooms had been wondrously impressive. They glittered with more silver and gold and polished wood than Julian
had seen since leaving the Dogan Bey's palace. Not even Olivier
had arrayed Belvedere so well. Julian had counted ten tapestries
in the main apartments alone, and they included every kind of
unicorn imaginable, as well as bright maidens and silver-haired
rabbits. The Lady Claudia assured her that the one she and her
daughters were then constructing—she tugged Julian over to
see it—was a replica of the very one that Queen Isabeau of
France was working, at that very moment, with her ladies.

"Though I seriously doubt that hers will end better than
ours," said the Lady Claudia with some smugness. "No one
wields a better needle than my Domiziana, aside from the fact
that everyone knows the very best threads are carded and colored here in Italy. Why, 'tis rumored that the queen has a
standing order with a Lombard dyer and that he only works
with silk brought from the East by Venetian traders. In the end,
our quality and colors are much superior to those obtainable
in France. One is born knowing that."

Julian had her doubts that the notoriously snobbish French
"knew" any such thing, but she thought it prudent to keep

sharp words hidden behind a bright and interested smile. It was
a miracle that she was here at all. She must remember that fact

She found her own assigned accoutrements less showy than
the main apartments below. That did not particularly surprise
or disappoint her. She had lived her life as a guest of other
people, even if those people had been kind, so she knew what
it was like to be fitted into the grander scheme that was already
in place before her arrival. This one was on the Noble Floor—
it would have been a grave insult to her guardian had she been
placed elsewhere—and was outfitted with the usual discards
of a distant renovation. Its furnishings were sparse and a little
splintery, and the red hangings and draperies showed the effect
of a somewhat prolonged mothy gluttony. However, there was
plenty of light. Julian thought, rather wickedly, that obviously
light was not something that made a good impression in Venice
because her hostess had failed to mention it as she catalogued
the Cá Venier's treasures. But she herself was happy with the
light. It brought possibility to many other things.

What she didn't like was being alone. There was only one
bed in the chamber—not that there was room for much more—
but still she had expected at least a small pallet upon which a
serving woman might sleep. What she had hoped was that she
would be placed with the Maid Ginevra. She liked the young
girl's saucy sense of humor and her frankness. When Ginevra
had talked of the Knight de la Marche it was almost like seeing
herself at that age—in love with a man and determined to have
him. Thinking that her love would conquer all obstacles and
that one day, one special day, he would be hers. Her will would
bring her this. Her fierce love would make him love her.

Instead . . .

Well, instead, reality was what it was. Some things she had
obtained: other things would never be hers. At least she could
redeem Aalyne, as she herself had been redeemed and given
her freedom. She could free her mother from having to make
witchcraft. She could free Aalyne from the burden of casting
spells. They would live together in a stone cottage. They would

dress in dark clothing, and go often to church, and they would be sober and respected and loved.

Everyone would forget the legend of the Magdalene. And in the end they would be allowed to forget it themselves.

This was all she had ever really wanted, she told herself. To be with her mother. To live a respectable life in which magic played no part.

A life in which Olivier played no part as well.

Because this was the reality of her situation and she knew it. She had faced the fact that he loved Domiziana and would marry her, had looked this grim fact right in the eye and accepted its truth. Life was for looking beyond, for going over. This was one of the lessons she had learned at her mother's breast.

But, oh, God, thought Julian as she looked around her bright and shabby room, as she leaned back so that her dark hair billowed over the slightly mildewed coverings on her bed.

Oh, God, she thought with an anguish and a fervor that surprised her. It was going to be harder than she'd ever thought to put her love for Olivier behind her.

CHAPTER THIRTEEN

"I came to get you," whispered Ginevra. "Everyone is resting. We can sneak away."

"Sneak away?" echoed Julian. She had been surprised to hear the knock on her chamber door and even more surprised to hear Ginevra's muffled voice behind it. She had wiped her eyes dry and positioned her lips into a smooth smile before she'd responded.

"Open the door and I will explain it all."

Once she was inside, Ginevra glanced about and shook her head.

"My lady mother could have done better by you," she said with some disgust. "I wanted you with me."

Julian shook her head and pulled out her gravest facial expression. "Why should the Contessa Venier place me with you?"

"Because it is customary to place maidens together. You must know that, though you are pretending not to. Probably you wanted to be with me as well." She looked shrewdly over at Julian. "My room is much better situated for viewing the city, but I must admit it shines not half so well with light."

"I like the light," admitted Julian.

"Then we will make this our room together, at least in the daytime. Mother won't notice what I am about—not with a wedding to plan. I can go and come as I please and I mean to go and come with you."

"Your mother may not like your keeping my company," said Julian. "I am not of noble birth. I am but the Count's ward."

"That's true," answered Ginevra. "And my mother is the most snobbish woman in Venice. Yet you are hardly a peasant and she would normally have placed you with me just to further content Lord Olivier. She is frightened of your mother, the witch. There have been witchcraft stories whispered about Domiziana—hers has not been a happy tale where marriage is concerned—and mother does not want all of the Veneto tittering that the marriage between my sister and the Lord of the Ducci Montaldo required any help other than God's to bring it to fruition."

"But the Lady Claudia brought Elisabetta with her from Belvedere."

" 'Twas my sister who insisted on making space for that witch and my mother, as usual, will refuse my sister nothing. She only insists that Elisabetta be kept well out of sight. Besides," concluded Ginevra as the light twinkled through her wide, pewter-colored eyes, "Elisabetta is merely a silly country strega who has found a rich vein which she intends to mine until it inevitably plays itself out. You are the Magdalene and that is an entirely different thing. That legend calls for a certain respect."

"I know nothing of witchcraft," said Julian wearily. Earlier she thought that she had found a friend in Ginevra, but now she saw that the girl wanted only what everyone else had wanted from her—relief from an itch, the curing of one of life's hurts. "I cannot help you to ensnare the Knight de la Marche."

"Oh, I will need neither a witch's nor a friend's help with that," said Ginevra, looking more than a little amused. "He is

mine already. He just does not know it yet. No, I've come to
help you. We are going away from the water and more into
the city. I saw the soft kid gloves you wore as we traveled.
They are a lovely color; really, I've never seen such a soft
buttercup yellow. And I thought you might like a small piece
of lace to match them. If we hurry we can just make the cloth
market before guild closing. Oh, what a joy it is to be back in
Venice again! You will love it here. There are so many little
treasures to buy.''

"Did I not tell you?" said Ginevra gleefully. The two of
them had left the lacemaker and were clutching their small flax
packages. "Was not that the most beautiful cloth you had ever
seen?''

"Yes," said Julian. She was already starting to sound a little
frightened, even to her own ears. "Perhaps the price was a bit
high?''

Ginevra managed to shrug her shoulders and shake her head
vigorously at the same time. "Nonsense. Count Olivier undoubtedly gave you money or else you would not have had
any. And if he gave you money he must reasonably have
expected that you would spend it. You have just spent it well.''

Julian must have looked doubtful because Ginevra laughed
again. "The whole purpose of Venice is to buy beautiful
things—else why would we send our Black Fleet to the East
to bring them to us? The city is built on more than 100 islands
spun together by a webbing of more than 300 bridges. At the
end of each bridge there is always a guilded craftsperson who
will make something wondrous from the glorious objects carted
back along our Silk Route. There are dressmakers and glovers
and perfumers and hose makers at every turn in the cobble-
stones. The heaven of this city is its shopping. You, Julian, are
bound to have a good time. I knew it as soon as I saw your
garnet ear-jewels on the first day we met.''

Julian's hand flew to her face. "They're not mine, not really.

I've never bought anything for myself before. The Lady Francesca just gives me her discards.'' Then she loyally added, ''Not that her clothing is not lovely. The Sire d'Harnoncourt always buys her the most beautiful things, but the Lady Francesca has other interests. She does not care for fancy tunics—she says they get in her way. Much less can she wear ear-jewels and bracelets when she has four sons that need attending—at least that is what she says. So the tunics and the small bangles were always handed on to me. 'Tis a vanity, I know,'' she added shyly, as though she were confessing a great sin. ''But I've always had a weakness for such things.''

''I knew it!'' exclaimed Ginevra, clapping her hands in their exquisite new gentian-blue gloves. ''A fellow pilgrim to the shrines of sartorial vice! Come along, we must make one more stop before vesper bells. There is a little man, a bit wizened maybe, but he does the most extravagant . . .''

Actually, it was three guilds later that Julian left the Maid Ginevra to haggle busily at prices with a master hoser. She was feeling that sick tightening in the stomach that follows a day of unremitting expenditure. At the same time she lovingly fingered her numerous flax packages and thought how much she would enjoy unwrapping her purchases with Ginevra in the privacy of her chamber. There would be more of the exclamations and oohing and aahing that they had indulged in for the greater part of what had proven to be a very instructive afternoon.

Julian had thoroughly enjoyed herself, but she had never before been so abandoned with money. If she were not careful she would have to ask her guardian for a replenishment for her neat purse of gold florins—something she had never done before and something she had no intention of doing now. In fact, the horror of the idea quite took her breath away.

The dreaded vespers bell had already sounded and Venice was snuggling down for its winter's night rest. This was accomplished much more silently than it was in Tuscany, and as she walked the cobbles of the streets, Julian could hear her own footfalls and the swish-swish of the lagoon water against the wood of the wharfing.

Nor was the city overly lighted, she thought. Of course, cooking fires and candles gleamed through the windows but the fog was rising. They would not be seen from afar. The streets of Venice reminded her more of alleyways than regular byways. They snaked together leading to bridges and water, and no one seemed to be about. Here on the lagoons of Venice the sea was secretive. It made no sound. Yet Julian fully realized that it was all around her—waiting and pervasive.

As she wandered about, she seemed to lose all sense of direction. She had no certain sense of where her feet would take her in this strange city. It continually disoriented and surprised her. Silvery, wintry Venice was so different from the rest of an Italy that seemed a confection of so much spun gold.

Perhaps that explained why she did not notice the man before he was upon her. At least that was the reason she gave herself. She had been thinking of her purchases, trying to work out the mathematics of her remaining coins so that they did not add up to the paltry figure she suspected; she had been trying to find her way back to the hoser's door.

Yes, maybe those were the reasons she did not notice the man. Surely he could not have actually arisen from the fog's swirling, which is what she immediately thought.

There was something about him, something in the way he walked deliberately towards her that both frightened Julian and locked her to her place. She could not take her eyes from him, from something hypnotic in his movements. It took her a moment to realize that this was because of his limp. Up, down, painfully slowly, the man clumped his way over the wooden bridge towards her.

Right towards her, she realized clearly, though she did not know him and could barely see him. His form was wrapped in long, black cloaking. It covered him from the top of his head down to the deformity of his feet. Or one of his feet—he was not totally crippled.

Julian, who at first had wanted to run away and had only
been stopped by the bulk of her precious bundles, stopped and
openly stared. There was something in that walk. She had seen
someone clump along like that before.

But where?

The man seemed in no hurry to give answer to her questions.
He paused, and Julian had the oddest feeling that he was staring
at her with his eyes that she could not see. And she wanted to
see those eyes, *needed* to see them. Aalyne had always told
her that they would tell her everything she needed to know.

In her eagerness, she took a step forward.

She felt the man smile. His halting footfalls started up again.

That's when she saw the Maltese Star. She had not seen one
since she had left Nicopolis; since she had left her mother. It
was hanging from a strong silver chain at his neck. The little
light that remained on the darkened street seemed drawn into
it, not reflected. For the first time, Julian was uncomfortably
aware of the matching amulet she wore at her neck. She had
not actively thought of that star since Olivier had touched it
when she had first come back to Belvedere.

And then she remembered.

"Master. Husband."

She heard Aalyne's worshipful voice and saw the slow pro-
gression of their liberator as he made his way across the dank
cell. She had been but a young girl and yet she recalled it,
recalled him. How could she not? This was the man who had
saved their lives.

Yet had he?

Her welcoming smile froze. How was it possible that he
would be in Venice some twenty years later, limping in exactly
the same way and coming inexorably towards her? It was
impossible. This was a spell.

The man seemed to know her hesitation, seemed to know
her thoughts as they formed in her head. And then suddenly
he was right before her with his hands outstretched.

"Julian, take this," he said. His voice seemed to sigh out at her. It seemed to love her. "Wait for me. I will be back."

"Julian! Julian!"

She turned back to the sound of her own name, but at first she did not recognize the young girl running towards her. It was only as she drew closer that she could put Ginevra's name to her face.

"I thought you had wandered off and that we would have to send the Gold Company to find you. The byways of Venice are notorious for sucking maidens into heaven alone knows what wild and delicious fates."

She was giggling teasingly, but something in Julian's face immediately stopped her laughter.

"Are you not well?" Her words were warm with concern. "Oh, dear God, don't tell me. . . ."

"Do you see the man?" Julian whispered urgently. She moved quickly aside so she did not obstruct Ginevra's view of the bridge. "Do you not see him?"

"What man? Where?"

Of course this virginal Maid of the Venier could see nothing of evil. And Julian knew that was what the man had been. His appearance had been meant for the Magdalene's eyes alone.

Or maybe she had been dreaming.

"What man?" Ginevra repeated, looking around. Then she bundled Julian close to her and smiled. "Poor Maid Madrigal is tired and distressed. It was selfish and wrong of me to take you for such a long adventure through the city on your first day. Venice can disorient even people who are trained to its strange ways. We'll go home now and have our meal with the others. The Count will be worried about you and will probably favor me with a great tongue lashing for my selfishness."

It was as she reached for Julian's hand that she noticed the flower—and Julian noticed it as well.

"What a lovely thing," she said, obviously charmed. "A white rose in winter. I've never seen one quite so large. Wherever did you find it?"

She smiled and bent to sniff at its fragrance.

"Julian," she gasped. "The thorn has cut you. There is blood all over your beautiful gloves and your packages. Poor dear, let me help you. Why did I not think . . ."

She was so busy clucking and soothing that she did not notice as Julian tossed the white rose, with great force, into the slick water of the lagoon.

"They say the Sultan Bayezid sends his dogs to hunt wearing diamond collars," said Domiziana at dinner. The room was warm, as it always seemed to be around the ladies of the Venier, and there was the lingering odor of incense. They had all eaten well just as, Julian suspected, they always would. Meals were not taken as cavalierly in Italy and France as they were in England. Here what one ate and how and when it was eaten was never something left to chance.

Indeed, there had been a surfeit of food and now, well past *compline,* the guests at the Venier table were only slowly making their way through the candied almonds and heavily sugared oranges meant to clear the palate. Julian longed for a piece of virgin fruit. She craved the taste of an orange that had not been sweetened or skewered or carved to resemble something other than what it actually was.

"Diamond collars. Can you imagine the decadence?"

The table was full, but Domiziana's low voice carried well. She had been placed between her father and her betrothed at the raised dais. The Knight de la Marche had been placed there as well. He sat next to the Lady Claudia and was the sole object of her attention. Naturally this positioning owed much to his exalted position as ambassador from a France which, overnight, had been welcomed to the bosom of friendship by a wily and determined Venice. Their established sea routes were threatened by the Ottoman and, if it took alliances and a Holy War to protect the trade that sustained them, then they were staunchly ready to pay that price.

Julian suspected that Gatien's new position also owed something to his availability as a prospective son-in-law for the Lady Claudia. She did not stop to consider what Luciano Venier might think of this. He seemed a most malleable man, thoroughly in the shadow of his wife and his powerful cousin the Doge. He rarely opened his mouth without mentioning one or the other. Julian looked over at him and smiled. His answering smile was quick and startled—but warm. She liked Luciano Venier. She hoped that life would continue to treat him well.

Her hand had been carefully bandaged by Ginevra. The Lady Claudia had not asked how she had been hurt, but she had relented a bit by letting the two girls sit together, though she had placed them below the salt cellars and well down at the end of the table. Neither of them minded this at all. Ginevra prattled and Julian answered her—when she remembered. The room blazed with candlelight, but the warmth brought the prickle of perspiration to Julian's forehead and along her back. She thought the Great Hall much too hot. Olivier seemed happy enough in it. He talked to his betrothed and to her mother, smiled and bowed to the others, and occasionally called something across the table to the Knight de la Marche. He would not meet Julian's eye.

This didn't stop her from looking at him and from thinking him the most beautiful man she had ever seen. His tunic was a deep blue that enhanced the color of his eyes. The simple gold embroidery on his tunic burnished his hair. All of the Venetian nobles at table were covered in rubies and diamonds and pearls, but the Count of the Ducci Montaldo was marked by his simplicity.

He does not need what they need in order to shine, thought Julian loyally. It never occurred to her that she was defending someone whom she had determined no longer to love.

Her hand ached and she remembered the man on the bridge—the evil man who had known her name and called her by it.

Never in her life—not even in the Dogan Bey's harem at

Nicopolis—had she felt so miserable. Never in her life had she
so much wanted to die.

But she couldn't die—not when she was so near to rescuing
her mother. Not when she was so close to restoring her life.
And after a while her days at the Cá Venier took on an inevitable
rhythm. She spent her mornings with the other ladies of the
house, gossiping over mending and fine-work, and occasionally
venturing out into the market or the small-houses, as they were
called, to search out something of value. Ginevra was ever avid
for these excursions, but Julian's slender purse and her deep
aversion to asking for florins from the Count of the Ducci
Montaldo put a natural damper on their shared enthusiasms.
Still, Julian found herself seeking Ginevra. She had never had
a friend before—except, of course, the Knight de la Marche.
More times than not the two young maidens sat together in a
corner alone, whispering and laughing and completely forgetting their needles until the Countess Venier would sharply
remind them of what they should be about. Julian had never
felt so young and irresponsible. She found that she rather liked
the feeling.

She did not see Elisabetta. After their experience in the
village and at Belvedere, the witch stayed well out of attention's
way. She had made the trip through Tuscany hidden in one of
the silk-covered wagons of the caravan. Julian had never yet
seen her at the Cá Venier but she knew the witch was near—
she *sensed* this—and that Elisabetta clung to the Lady Domiziana. And that the witch was working very hard.

Nor had Julian seen the dark man again, but she knew that
he waited, just as he always had. And she knew that one day,
in his own time, he would be back for her.

For now, Julian spent her mornings with Ginevra and her
afternoons riding with Ginevra's great love, the Knight de la
Marche.

"Don't you wish to come as well?" Julian asked her friend.

"We do nothing but cross over the lagoons and ride through the Veneto. It would be fun for you."

Ginevra shook her head vigorously. "Mother would never permit it. I am too young, and her mind is set upon Sir Gatien for Maria. She is very one-minded, you know. The only reason she allows you the freedom is that she has thought of no reason to stop you from it. You are, after all, the Count's responsibility and not hers. Besides," she said with a glint of mischief, "Sir Gatien will not even notice me while you are about. He thinks himself in love with you and he must get over his infatuation before he can discover the true love of his life."

Julian, who could never have discussed her love for Olivier with the same lightness, and so did not discuss it at all, shook her head at her friend's good-natured impudence. They were so different, the two of them, that sometimes she wondered how they could be friends at all.

She had to admit that she reveled in her solitary afternoon rides with the Knight de la Marche. She enjoyed the brightness of their skirted horses as they bounded through the winter-seared hills and loved the sound their bridle bells made as they jangled merrily through the cold air. She insisted that they hold their horses to a gallop for as much of the ride as they could. The noise and the exercise made her forget Olivier—or at least they usually did.

They had left their shared confidence behind them. Since that night on the parapet at Belvedere, he had maintained both his word and his distance. She no longer had any idea of what he wanted or what he did. Still, if she were not supremely watchful and careful, she would catch herself avidly watching for him—and she hated herself for her weakness. Hated herself for still loving a man who was betrothed to another, and wanted his ward only in secret.

"I hate Venice," she said one day as they walked their horses.

But Gatien, as usual, did not seem daunted by her irritation. "It is because it reminds you of the East, and the East was your home for so many years. You may be French, but I don't suppose you heard much good about your homeland from Aalyne.''

''And why should she have loved it?'' scoffed Julian. ''They didn't understand her there. They hurt her. They tried to burn her at the stake.''

''Indeed,'' said Gatien, deftly giving her his arm. ''But she went on, and she found a home and at least a makeshift calling in the East. And you will find much that is eastern in the Veneto. Most especially in Ravenna, perhaps, because the Eastern Empire made its mark there and the Byzantine Church found a sure footing. But the East is present in Venice as well. You will see this. You will come to know it and love it. Despite its somber aspect, this is a city of gamblers and explorers. They are people like you—people who have worked at mastering their fear and thus have become fearless. The Polo brothers brought back more than spices when they journeyed off to expand the markets of their city throughout the world. They also brought back a way of thinking and an atmosphere.''

That she was without fear? Is that what he thought of her? Julian wished with sudden fervor that she could tell this kind man just how frightened she actually was.

''But I can't help myself,'' she said, speaking of her quest for her mother but meaning her love for Olivier. ''It's been there too long—I can't give it up now. It's as if it's taken me over—bewitched me.''

She colored at what she had said.

Gatien did not seem to notice her slip. He smiled, and the whole of his face wrinkled into its customary snug fit around that smile. ''If the quest is still that active and deep within you, then you've no choice but to follow where it leads. You can't throw it away as though it were something superficial. You can't *decide* not to love Lord Olivier.''

Julian blushed and shook her head, but Gatien was already speaking through her protests. ''You can't force love away by strength of will. And you have always worked your will, Lady

Julian—perhaps too much so. You have to *grow* out of love.
You must become bigger until that particular pain becomes
smaller. You must *let* it take its proper place in your history
and in your life.''

Julian looked at him sharply, wondering how he had guessed
her secret and wondering, as well, what—or who—had taught
him this lesson. But she was afraid to ask, afraid that she would
betray more of her love for Olivier. The Knight de la Marche
was obviously too quick a man to play with. He also seemed
to know her too well. With the others she might be able to
pretend she was on a chastely noble quest for her mother, in
which her love for Olivier played no part. She might even be
able to fool herself with the half-lie of her selfless intentions.
She couldn't fool Gatien, and she knew there was no use to
try. He knew her purely and simply—just as had that man at
the bridge.

She was afraid that he must think her little better than
Aalyne—if that good. When she looked shyly over at him, she
found that he was still smiling.

She had a moment's strong urge to confide everything to
him—what her life had been like, what it had meant. She even
wanted to tell him of that man at the bridge and how he had
promised to come back for her one day, and how she was
afraid. But then she took a deep breath, and the moment passed.

She was heiress to the Magdalene, and even if this myth
meant nothing else, it meant that she could settle her own
problems, and that she could take care of herself.

''It doesn't matter,'' she said, walking ahead and keeping
her face to the wind so that her tears would dry before they
fell. She wanted no one to notice them. Most of all, she did
not want to notice them herself.

She was finding no joy in this journey to rescue her mother.
It was so different from what she had thought it would be.
There was nothing of the relief she had thought she would
finally have.

CHAPTER FOURTEEN

All that remained with Julian of Belvedere were its nightmares. These had grown more frequent and frightening and insistent in Venice, as though something in the city's silvery waters drew them forth and subtly molded them.

Frequently she dreamed of the same, strange, bundled-up and hobbling man she had seen on the bridge. This time, rather than a rose, he held out the Maltese Star to her. It was fashioned like her own, only larger and much more detailed. He moved his lips in a chant she could not hear, but which left her breathless with fright.

At other times it was Elisabetta who haunted her nights. She saw herself once again in the courtyard at Sant'Urbano, where up in a small room the child had lain dying. This time, in her dream, she did not stop with hissing at the witch. Instead, she threw the Power at her and the old woman reeled against the stone wall and crumpled down, down onto the street's cobbles. But this had not been enough for Julian and she had screamed at the motionless form, "Now you see it! This is the Power. This is what it does to you. Is this what you want?''

Over and over again the words had rushed forth while she stood there looking dazed and ashamed as the blood flowed from the cut at the old witch's head. Rationally she knew that there could not possibly be so much of it; yet it had flowed like a fountain. It was all she could see.

Or almost all she could see, for through its red veil she had also glimpsed two horrified faces. She saw Domiziana's mouth open in greedy astonishment, and she saw the look of disgust on Olivier's face. Most of all she saw that look. She watched silently as he, resplendent in the full black livery of the Gold Company, prepared to present his betrothed to his army. He handed a radiant Domiziana onto her horse with great care. He no longer looked at Julian; she no longer looked at him.

In her dream she thought quite clearly, *I am my mother's daughter. I am no better than she is and I will be doomed as well.*

She woke with a start. At least she wasn't screaming, but her hand had started to bleed again and it hurt. Still, she wanted to talk to no one. She wanted to feel nothing. She would take care of this new trouble, just as she had taken care of all the others in her past.

And it doesn't matter, she told herself fiercely. I have got what I wanted. We are going for my mother. I am happy.

A little blood could be quite easily stanched.

She re-wrapped the wound in a piece she tore from her private linen, but it wasn't enough. The blood continued to flow. She did not want to ruin her linen by tearing away at it. She had no desire to see either the Lady Claudia or the Lady Domiziana, but then neither did she have a great desire to bleed all over and ruin the Venier bedcovers. She had no private serving girl at the Cá, but she had seen many about. Even though it was quite late, Julian thought she could find one near

he kitchens. The fires needed constant attention, and it was
usually easier to have someone keep them going through the
night than to start them anew.

She opened her door and stepped out into the corridor.

There was no one about and there was no sound. The Cá
Venier seemed huddled deeply in sleep. A light glimmered at
her from the end of the rich passageway and she followed it.
She was confident it would eventually take her where she
wanted to go.

"Italian palaces are well ordered, all of a part," she told
herself, though she had a suspicion that the Cá Venier might
be different. It was then that she heard the low murmur of
voices as she hurried towards the glimmer of the light.

A portal was just slightly ajar and through it Julian heard
voices—two of them. There was a low word, and then an
excited giggle. Julian stopped. Without thinking, she caressed
the door's polished wood.

"And now what?" Excitement vibrated just beneath the
Lady Domiziana's whisper. "What do I do now?"

"Shhh," cautioned Elisabetta. "Just you be quiet, my lady,
and trust in me. I will show you."

Julian raised her hand and widened the crack of the door.
Its hinges squeaked a little in protest, but no one noticed—
certainly not the two women who leaned together, enthralled
in their task.

Domiziana bent towards Elisabetta with the conspiracy of a
lover, her silvery hair just grazing the tired iron curls of the
witch. Shadows from the fire's light played across their faces,
and Julian was momentarily sure that she had never seen either
of the women look so beautiful. Domiziana's lips were moist
and open. The hard lines had disappeared from around her eyes
and mouth and warm, bright color surged through her cheeks.
The witch, too, looked transformed by good food and cleanliness and the glow of firelight. Her eyes were bright and mischievous.

"Hurry. Hurry. Shape him now." Domiziana's voice was breathless, low with heat.

The old woman chuckled. "Patience. Did I not heal you? Are you not now well? I have promised you this man and he will be yours."

"But when . . . how?"

Elisabetta reached out a gnarled hand to caress the Lady of the Venier softly on her cheek. Domiziana had saved her, had brought her here and fancied her up. There was genuine affection in her voice as she said, "He is yours already. He has taken you as his betrothed before God and man."

"A betrothal is not marriage," grumbled Domiziana. "And he has not yet taken me. He has said that he wants me, but he has yet to come."

"This always works," said the old women shortly, slowly and lovingly fingering the dolls. "We women have been doing things like this in the dark through all our long history. We must. Our only power lies in what we can manipulate—and it has been like this ever since time began."

Domiziana nodded. She was a lady of Venice after all, and therefore had been taught from her swaddling how to wield a certain sly power. The heat of victory shone through her eyes.

Julian, mesmerized, thought of her mother and wanted to laugh. If Aalyne were here she would howl outright at this show. These women did not understand. They had no idea of the Power. They had no idea where it would eventually take them. Not even the one who called herself a witch—perhaps least of all her.

She knew she should let them know she was there. It was wrong to creep about and spy. Despite her good intentions, her eyes were still drawn to the small waxed object that Domiziana held in her hand—to the blond hair that straggled across its forehead, to its dark, rich cape, to the brightly painted color of its turquoise eyes. Domiziana's eyes shone. Her lips were moist.

A log pitched forward into the fire and sparks shot up to die in the night. It reminded Julian of the night she had first seen

he witch at Belvedere—when the ladies of the Venier had
olitely asked the daughter of the Magdalene to tell their future
n the tarot cards. It was such a strong and vivid memory that
or an instant it broke the spell and allowed fear to clutch
strongly at Julian. She remembered the dreams she had had of
he cloaked man who beckoned to her with the Maltese Star.
She remembered Elisabetta dying. Julian wanted to run away,
ust as she ran away every night in her dream.

But the unknown—and perhaps it was the too-deeply
known—pulled her inexorably forward and into Domiziana's
chamber. She sensed that even with the nonsense the witch
was doing, the forming of dolls and the bowing to a superstition
hat meant nothing—the Power was nevertheless here. She,
Aalyne's only daughter, could feel it in the air around her,
much as a dog might sense a burglar, or a cat a mouse. It was
ike an intrusion that had not perhaps been specifically wished
or, but was present just the same.

Something that called forth instincts that were older than
ime.

Yet a part of Julian wanted to laugh out loud at the gnarled
hands of the old woman, at her obsequious words. This witch
was no one to reckon with. She was nothing but an old poor
woman with a need to go on. Someone who used charms and
amulets and spells in order to wrest a coin or two from the
credulous poor. Someone who sensed there was something, but
did not know it. She was not like Aalyne, who had used the
Power as it should be used. She was not like Aalyne—who
had *known*. The Magdalene would have instantly realized that
Olivier was a man not to be trifled with. And that this little
game, which so enthralled Domiziana, would only wreak havoc
n the end.

Elisabetta laughed. "Come in, my pretty. I've been expecting
you."

Startled, Julian looked around to see that she had ventured
a good way into Domiziana's chamber. The heat from the room
eached out to engulf her. The air around her was full of the

Power, and she could smell pitch pine and the underlying fra-grance of myrrh. Julian had never liked myrrh.

"It won't work," she said simply. For the first time she looked Domiziana full in the face. "You will never have what you want from him if you do it in this way. You cannot impose your will upon him—he is too strong for that."

For an instant, Julian saw confusion in Domiziana's eyes, then fear and hesitation.

Elisabetta cackled again. It was distracting, as it was meant to be. "She wants him for herself," said the witch with mock indifference. "You saw that yourself, my little one, when I showed you how to read it in the bones."

"I cannot have him," Julian shot back. "If you read the bones they would have told you that as well."

"Or *he* will not have *you*." Elisabetta laughed, but her voice had grown shrill and fear had made her ugly once again.

"No, he will not have me," said Julian. "He has made that clearly known."

"He might still—want you," Domiziana murmured.

"Then what you are doing cannot change that. It would be his own choice, done in the freedom of his own will. These little tricks and mumblings can never change anything that has been rightly wrought."

Julian's eyes narrowed. She waited. She knew that Domizi-ana might very well reach out to slap her. The Power was in the air and many times in the past she had seen it take command.

"You've no business dabbling in these things," she whis-pered. "You do not need them."

She stood there, breathless, until suddenly Domiziana threw back her head and laughed.

"You were right," she said to Elisabetta, awe in her voice. "You said you could call her to you and that she would come—Julian Madrigal, the daughter of the most powerful witch in God's world. And yet she came to your beckoning, just as you said she would."

The old woman chastely lowered her eyes. " 'Twas not my

:alling that brought her here. I only knew that she *would* come.
The bones told me that—just as they've told me everything
:lse.''

But not how to heal a child, thought Julian with disgust.
They've never, ever told you anything of true benefit and use.

She would not let herself be distracted by the old woman.
Instead, she crossed the room to stand quite close to Domiziana,
:lose enough to feel the other woman's excitement. She, Julian
Madrigal, the daughter of Aalyne de Lione, forced herself to
move into the circle of another woman's feminine power.

''What Elisabetta is doing is wrong,'' she insisted. ''You do
not want Lord Olivier like that. You do not need to have him
in this way.''

''She wants him for herself,'' whispered the witch. ''You've
seen the plants she nurtures. You've seen their seeds. Who
knows what they are good for? She wants your man. And she
will have him if you do not heed Elisabetta.''

Julian paid her no attention. ''You will only be hurt in the
end. I've seen it. I know.''

''Wants him for herself,'' repeated the old witch.

''It will only hurt you in the end. It will avail you nothing
even now.''

''Avail her nothing?'' The old woman snorted. ''Why, you
yourself know the strength of the Power—your own mother
was the carrier of it. You cannot help knowing what it can do.
It is in your family, in your blood.'' She whirled around to
Domiziana. ''They were fatherless whelps, the both of them.
But Julian cannot help but carry on, no matter how hard she
might try. She may not want it, but her power is always with
her and, like a sleeping mad dog, it might spring up at any
time and bite. Why, she only wants to keep the knowledge
from you, Lady. Wants to keep it to herself and use her magic
to take away your man. She wants you convented and secreted
away.'' The old woman sighed. ''We have our tricks, too, and
we have our secrets. Tell her what we know. Tell her what the
bones have told us.''

"That you are married," Domiziana said with infinite sweetness. "And that your husband lives."

Triumph glittered from her silvery eyes.

"Then they have lied to you," Julian said. "I have never been wedded."

"Perhaps not wedded—but at least bedded."

She heard Domiziana's low, heated giggle as she turned to walk away. There was no use staying, no use persuading. Domiziana had already made up her mind. And at least the Lady of the Venier had been right in one thing.

She was made for bedding—not for wedding. The Dogar Bey had not married her. No one had.

And no one ever would.

"You've been hurt," Olivier said, looking at the neat bandaging that Julian wore on her fingers. The cut had been deep—it was not easy of healing.

"You may be assured that it will not affect my writing," responded his ward as she seated herself firmly into a low chair and put the writing board upon her lap. "I can perfectly well take down whatever you might decide to dictate, my lord."

"I am most certain of that," Olivier said. He was in a snappish mood. "And that you will serve as an able translator as well. The Knight de la Marche recommended you most highly. In fact, you are in Venice at his behest."

Julian ducked her head in reverence towards Gatien who sat beside the Lord of the Ducci Montaldo in the hall chamber that Luciano Venier had put at their disposition.

Olivier watched them wryly. "Don't tell me you've finally learned some respect," he said in answer to her careful politeness.

He was in no mood for banter. In the weeks since the Gold Company had arrived in Venice, he had barely seen Julian at all. He had been most careful to avoid her. Of course, he had been busy with the ruling oligarchy. The Venetians, like the

crafty merchants they were, wanted the maximum in trading
privileges from this crusade, while paying the minimum possible to participate. He filled his days with fulfilling his duties
both to his men and to the city of Venice—a tight line when
dealing with merchants who wanted to economize on everything, including the cost of their defense.

He spent his evenings with Domiziana. This was to be
expected, and he was proud of the fact that he remembered to
be attentive to her wishes. He had sent Cristiano to buy lengths
of ribbon and lace for her at the markets. He had sent a short
dispatch to Dino Rispondi, a Lombard agent, commissioning
him to buy small jewels and trinkets. He had even specified
that Rispondi should buy the very best. Other than that, he had
offered no suggestions. He would need these things, he was
sure of it, if he wanted to have a good relationship with this
particular wife.

Olivier was determined to have this.

He had schooled himself to be the model of propriety to his
betrothed. He had kissed Domiziana when she seemed to want
it, and he had given her a lock of his hair when she had requested
that as well. He had been conscientious, kind, and caring with
his actions. No one could fault him there.

Last night, at long last, he had gone to Domiziana and he
had loved her. He had spent hours with her, what had seemed
to him an eternity. And he had come away empty—no, worse
than empty. He had emerged from his betrothed's chamber
more agitated and alone than when he had gone in. He had
started to doubt.

And he had longed for Julian.

No, not for Julian, he quickly corrected. For her peace—for
the peace he always felt when he was with her. This is what
he wanted. It probably had nothing to do with her at all.

This morning he knew himself to be angry, though he would
never have called himself confused. How could he possibly be
so? Was he not the Count of the Ducci Montaldo, head of the
Gold Company and a leader of men? Why, only recently the

Venetians had taken to calling him the Lion of Venice, in honor of the mythological winged giant that had symbolized their city since its earliest days.

And how could a lion not know his own mind?

"Well then, I assume we may begin," he said briskly. His lips dictated statistics and questions, while his mind flitted back along byways where he had strongly forbidden it to turn.

He found himself, at his age and in his position, lusting for Julian. There was no other way to describe it, though it appalled him to think of himself with that word. Lust was something one was allowed to feel for any woman except those placed under one's care.

Yet—there was no other way to describe it. He found himself thinking of Julian in the most unusual instances. He would be talking to the Doge Antonio Venier, arranging for the ships of the Black Fleet that were to take them along the Danube, and he would suddenly savor the sweet taste of her in his mouth. *Feel* her tongue, silken and lovely, as it glided slowly back and forth against his own. He could remember the exact cupping of her breast. Her perfume clotted his breathing when she was nowhere in the room. He seemed to hear her laughter everywhere.

And the worst of it was that he could not, in truth, say that she had bewitched him. He knew something of such matters and knew that they pestered a man like the bite of a fly. What he felt for Julian was not an itch—something that needed immediate attention and then would come back to bother again and again. The craving he could have understood—after all, her mother was a witch and would of necessity have taught her many things—but what he felt for Julian had nothing of need to it at all.

There were moments—like this moment—when he would have given anything to hold her.

What *was* this feeling, he wondered. Could it be . . .

"This is terrible," he mumbled aloud. "This will not do."

"My lord, the prisoner has been summoned. Should we bring him to you?"

He had almost forgotten Cristiano and his mission to bring in the Bulgarian—a subject of the Sultan's who had presented himself at the Doge's palace of his own accord. But Olivier nodded to his lieutenant and motioned for Julian to bring forth a new, sharpened quill.

"This prisoner might help us," Olivier said. He welcomed the relief of an interrogation that would require all of his concentration. "He is Bulgarian, brought up near Nicopolis, and supposedly knows something of the land through which my army will travel. He claims the Turks enslaved him when he was but a child. He was made a Janizary and advanced smartly for quite some time, but then there was an indiscretion with one of the women in the Sultan's harem. She was killed, of course, but he managed to escape. It seems he wants revenge."

Already, and without seeing the soldier, Julian doubted his story. The idea that an escape from one of the Sultan's prisons could be so easily effected was a notion that she knew Olivier must mistrust as well. This man was probably no more than a planted spy.

Yet, perhaps she was wrong. She had been so before. She lowered her eyes and kept her hands busy with the arranging of her parchments and pens. She did not look up at the jingle of spurs as the Janizary was brought into the room, but she was aware of the swing of his body as he lowered it into a deep reverence. And she was aware of the scent of the East that accompanied him.

Still, Julian kept her eyes down as the Count of the Ducci Montaldo courteously but firmly dismissed the others, including his ally the Knight de la Marche, from his presence.

"I choose to have no others here," he explained in good but halting Turkish. "No one except one person to translate and to scribe."

The Janizary said nothing, but he grunted in agreement. The problem with spies was undoubtedly just as rife where he

served, as it was in the West of Europe. His guttural told Olivier
that they were both well-seasoned commanders, and thus both
well aware of this.

"Julian, please ask this man his name," continued Olivier
in his perfect French.

And it was then that she looked up.

He did not act as though he recognized her, but of course
he did. How could he not have? When she had known him he
had worn a younger, smiling version of the face that stared
back at her now. This man was not smiling. He looked at her
impassively, his dark brown eyes without expression, his sun-
browned face without any light of recognition. Yet undoubtedly
he knew her. He could never have forgotten it all.

"My name is Assen," he began. "I was born in Bulgaria—
as you call it—near enough to the great city of Nicopolis, but
nearer still to the small jewel they call Rachowa. My father
was warlord of his village and a Boyar, whose territory Murad
II, the Sultan Bayezid's father, devastated early on. We had
fought well, so we had to be especially punished. The Sultan
wanted no hint of insurgence. All the men of my village were
killed, and then the women were raped and their children
slaughtered before them. The women were finally put to death
last. I remember, even now, how many of them begged to die.
I saw everything, but I was spared."

"And what led to this sparing?" asked Olivier through
Julian's translation.

Assen shrugged. "I was spared by a bird's touch. The sword
was already pricking my throat when suddenly, in the midst
of all that carnage, a dove chose to swoop down and settle
upon my head. He was shooed and pushed at, but he would
not depart. The Sultan, probably sick himself of what he had
felt called upon to do, took this as a sign from God. I took
another meaning from the dove's presence. I knew deep within
that my father had sent that bird to me. If I had wanted I could
quite easily have seen his death-eyes staring at me—my father
whose bloody corpse still littered the campground and would

be left there to rot. I didn't look. I knew only that I was to live and I was to wreak vengeance." He paused. "I was five years old the day the dove settled onto my head."

And he, Assen continued, had served the dove well. First as a slave—but he was ambitious. He was also big and appealing. After all, he was from warrior stock. He watched the Sultan's troops as they practiced their maneuvers within the walls of the palace. He listened to bragging-tales of their battle prowess. He was always careful to offer them water, to be the first to take the bridles from the hands of a tired commander when he returned. Assen cleaned the soldier's wickedly curved scimitars and he sharpened them. He was always helpful. He smiled often. He did not go unnoticed. He made friends.

Eventually, just as he had always known he would be, he was asked to take his place with the warriors. Murad, and later Bayezid, had started to take non-Turkish soldiers into their ranks. They called these new men Janizaries and Assen was one of the first.

He was required to become a Muslim, which he was willing to do. The Christian God had not saved his father or his mother or his sisters. He doubted that the Muslim God would have bothered, either. One or the other, it was all the same to him. He, himself, would do what God had not done.

He had changed his name because they told him he must. He married a Muslim woman, a marriage arranged by the Dogan Bey himself. He had given Assen a highly educated girl from his own harem. His wife had been a virgin. She had been raised to run the household of an important man in the Sultan's empire. That she had been given to Assen said much of the Sultan's plans for the little Bulgarian boy who had been visited by the dove.

The woman, his wife—though he never mentioned her name—had given birth to Assen's four sons and two daughters. He had, of course, mated with the woman, but he had never actually touched any of his children. Not one of them. A strange, fierce pride shone through Assen's face as he spoke these words.

They were not his family. His family had been left to feed the vultures when he was five years old.

And through it all, he had continued to move forward in his profession of killing. He had grown quite skillful at it. He had proved himself invaluable to the Sultan on more than one occasion.

"If you were so valuable to the Sultan, then why has he allowed you to escape?" Olivier leaned forward quietly. Assen's gaze did not drop from his face. The two men were still talking through Julian, but they were speaking to each other. Her words were rushed and whispered as she translated.

"He did not let me escape. I am on mission," said Assen. A smile touched his lips, stopping just short of his eyes. Then even this brief light was snuffed. "You are aware, naturally, of Gian Galeazzo Visconti, the ruler of Milan and Pavia?"

"And of Genoa as well," replied Olivier with some irony. "I know him, but only in a manner of speaking. We have just recently defeated his forces at war. However, as so often happens, we now find ourselves bosom allies in this French Crusade. You are a warrior; you know the course of these matters. He was our enemy yesterday—today he is our friend."

"If you believe that, then you are indeed a fool," Assen continued. He seemed to feel no fear, though he was Olivier's prisoner in a city under his protection. "Gian Galeazzo is that most dangerous of all Italians in a country that abounds with dangerous Italians. He is a Visconti—a family that has never been known to take well to defeat. His is a true craving for revenge, and not just against Venice for her humiliating victory. No, for graver injuries and for more wounding reversals."

He paused for a second and drank wine from the silver tankard that the Count of the Ducci Montaldo had ordered placed before him. "You are aware, I am sure, that Louis Duc d'Orleans, the king's brother, has sought separation from his wife, Valentina?"

Olivier nodded.

"Good." Again Assen paused over his wine. "Then you

will know as well that the Duchess d'Orleans is Gian Galeazzo Visconti's daughter.''

"Of course," snapped Olivier. But he leaned forward slightly.

''Then the world must know that he has sought this separation because he is the lover of the king's wife. Queen Isabeau has decided that she must have her lover all to herself, and therefore they are sending Valentina to a convent. She is accused of using witchcraft on the king. You are naturally familiar with the Inquisition. Your own illustrious brother-in-law was brought up before it, if I recall.''

Well enough, Olivier assured him by a curt nod.

''Valentina's fate is already sealed. She is to be divorced and disgraced. The Visconti, with many machinations and much payment in bribes, will manage to have her life spared. However, she will lose her exalted position as a power within powerful France.''

"This is an old happening. The Lady Valentina, though innocent, has already been disgraced. And Gian Galeazzo said nothing. He is not a warrior, but he is nonetheless a pragmatist and took the humiliation of his child as a necessity of political life. He is more allied with the French now than he has ever been.'' Olivier's tone was mild, but his interest remained acute.

"The Visconti has accepted nothing. This slight weighs heavily on his vindictive soul. He has remained silent and good-tempered—waiting patiently for this moment of vendetta.''

Though supposedly he could not understand Julian's French, Assen smiled as she finished her translation.

For a moment the three of them sat in silence as the rest of the palazzo wrapped them in its sounds. Julian heard the clatter of dishes being brought from the storage rooms below, and she heard the prattle of the maids as they came in from their morning washing at the public well. In the distance she thought she caught the sound of Domiziana's voice and then a high squeal of laughter. Julian studied Olivier through the veil of her lowered lashes, and weighed his reaction.

Though she doubted that Assen, even with his well-trained soldier's eye, could see the change in the Count of the Ducci Montaldo, Julian could read it and she had respect for its meaning. The pupils of his turquoise eyes had narrowed into pinpoints, almost as though he were willing himself into Assen's mind. And once there, Julian knew, he would push and push until he had learned the truth behind what the Janizary said. Assen was skillful as well—no one knew this more than she— and he would pull back from Olivier to hide himself behind his words. Julian could feel the two strong wills as they mentally circled and studied each other. She could smell the friction of their heightened attention.

"And what form shall this revenge take?" asked Olivier finally.

"You know already," said Assen, still wearing that same agile smile. "His desire is to ruin this crusade. It is a Venetian endeavor and he wants the Venetians humbled. More importantly, it is a French endeavor and he wants the French humiliated—more than he wants anything else in this world. Just as he has been humiliated by them."

Olivier scoffed, but diplomatically. "Has the Lord of the Visconti no care for his immortal soul? This is a religious war, after all—a so-called godly effort to save the East from the Infidel. Will not Gian Galeazzo be risking much in his quest for this vendetta?"

Assen's small, black eyes glittered with life for the first time. Olivier's had been a rhetorical question and both men knew it. It could have no answer, because there was none. The pious peasants, who would actually pay for this crusade with their taxes, could perhaps be persuaded that their sacrifices were destined for a sacred cause. Perhaps the simple priests who served them would believe this as well. At least they would say as much. It would not be politic for them to entertain another, contrary opinion. However, the rulers of the land— and even a great many who governed the Church—would know differently. They saw a sure glimmer of gain before them, and they would content themselves with a more earthly reward from this Holy War.

The two warriors seated before Julian knew this. She shivered in the frosty complicity of their gaze.

"Tell me the rest of what you know," said Olivier simply. Assen smiled and began to speak again as Julian repeated his chilling words.

"In their usual labyrinthine way, the Visconti sent word to my master that they wished to be his very secret ally in this matter. They promised him important information for his trouble, and assured him that they would provide more—much more—in time. Bayezid is not a stupid man, and he was instantly suspicious when Gian Galeazzo quoted no price. He is noted, even in the East, for his avidity. My master knew the history of the Duchess d'Orleans and he took this as a sufficient explanation of why the Visconti did not call for bargaining coin. The Sultan, too, understands the value of family."

Again the frosty smiles flashed for an instant. They all knew that Bayezid, upon his ascension to the throne, had taken the customary Ottoman precaution of having his brothers strangled to death with bow wire.

"And your role in all of this?" asked Olivier.

"I have been sent by the Sultan Bayezid to meet with the Visconti in Parma. I am to be the emissary requested. At his court, my discretion is considered the eighth wonder. Am I not known to be discreet even with my own children? A cautious prudence is the virtue of choice for this enterprise. The Visconti are strong and vocal supporters of the French—and, more importantly, the French king owes them money. They would never want to make an open enemy of him—or of his powerful, debt-ridden state." Assen paused. "Gian Galeazzo put much store on that marriage. He is a taciturn man, but he loves his daughter to a fault."

Olivier's gaze never left Assen as he said, "Both the Duc d'Orleans and his brother, King Charles, were too young when their father died. They had the luxury of freedom without the

responsibility of it. They have made many mistakes, grave
mistakes. Still, d'Orleans was a fool to think he could thwart
Gian Galeazzo Visconti. He should have known better. There
is no doubt that the information you carry is intriguing,'' Olivier
added. He seemed almost to be talking to himself. ''It interests
me even more to know why you decided to bring it to me.''

Assen did not falter. ''Your blood hate against the Turks is
well-known. Yours, like mine, is a question of honor and of
death. I thought you might appreciate the goods that I came
selling.''

''Now, we have hit the base,'' Olivier said. He seemed suddenly relieved. ''Tell me your price.''

Just for an instant Assen hesitated, and within the harsh
wrinkling of this bitter man's face Julian saw, shining forth,
the five-year-old child he had once been. A child who had been
guilt-ridden at being left alive—the one allowed to walk away
from that devastated village.

''What I want,'' Assen said finally, swinging his arms wide,
''is a bit of light. A bit of freedom.''

His words hung feathered around them like the touch of the
dove that had once, long ago, settled upon his head.

''That man is lying,'' Olivier said quite calmly to Julian
once they were alone again. The normal light rain of morning
had stopped and sunlight prowled the cloud edges. Julian could
just glimpse it through the room's small windows. ''Do you
not think so, little Julian?''

She was surprised into looking straight into his eyes. Their
color had changed again, she noticed. They were green now,
very intensely so, and they were hard and wary.

''No, I do not think he was lying,'' she lied, but cautiously.
''Why should he? His story proves he has much to hold against
the Sultan Bayezid.''

''Or against someone else,'' Olivier said. ''That he would
not tell me the truth is understandable. We are, after all, enemies

who will soon be at war. Why *you* should lie to me is another matter entirely."

Again she hesitated, this time fatally so. "I tell no falsehood. I believe he has told you what he knows."

Olivier did not take his eyes from hers. He stood perfectly still. His face did not change. "Is it Aalyne you are trying to protect?" he asked thoughtfully. "Or could it be someone else? Yourself, perhaps?"

He looked away from her and back to the litter of parchments and maps upon his trestle. "If you are not lying to me, at least you are not telling me the full truth and neither is that mad Assen. A man like that does not set himself as a spy. He is too naturally fearless to play at sneak games. I also do not believe he is so indispensable to the Sultan that he would have been forbidden an indiscretion within the harem. No man is that essential. I must have the truth from him eventually—and from you as well—if I am to make a judicious decision on his offer. For now he can languish in the Venetian prisons. You may leave me."

Sunlight broke completely through the clouds in that instant. A ray of it rushed into the Great Hall, gilding Olivier's golden hair and setting his face in stone.

Julian lowered her eyes and gathered her quills and small sharpening knives and put them away in their lacquered boxes. She scattered fine sand on her parchments to dry them. She kept her eyes down and away from Olivier's. Her movements were slow and deliberate, but her mind raced.

She remembered the last thing the Bulgarian warrior had said as they were leading him away. Olivier had sent for his best soldiers, including Cristiano. They walked in the formation of an honor guard, but there was no one among them who was fooled into thinking that Assen was anything more than in bondage. They were at the door when Olivier's voice snapped out again.

"One last question, Assen," he said. "I am curious as to why the Sultan would choose you to plot his course with the

Visconti. You speak neither French nor Latin. And more, you are a simple man. You have not the aspect that a man as meticulous as the Lord of the Visconti would find, shall we say, reassuring. Why would Bayezid choose you for this mission?''

Assen had stopped, but he did not look back. ''It is the luck of my destiny,'' he said as he continued on through the door.

As the sounds of their footfalls were lost in the vast expanse of the Cá Venier, Julian knew that luck had played no part in Assen's choice, nor in the fact that he had presented himself to the Count of the Ducci Montaldo. She could see cunning in it; she could see skill.

Assen would be waiting for her visit. He would know it was inevitable.

But how she was to bring about their reunion was another matter indeed.

CHAPTER FIFTEEN

Her salvation presented itself from a most unlikely source.

"I have no intention of going to Carnivale," she said to Ginevra. The girl seemed intent on chatter just when Julian needed to think. "I hate tableaux and anything that requires a mask."

"Oh, a mask is not all that is required here," said Ginevra, not at all fazed out of good humor when there was the question of dress-up at hand. "That is only the beginning of it."

"The rest of it?" Julian hoped that her voice carried just the right tone of bored politeness.

"The whole point is to fool one's friends," exclaimed Ginevra triumphantly. "For you to be anyone else you'd like."

Julian was suddenly alert, as she had been upon hearing the words "fool one's friends."

"Tell me about this Carnivale," she said, putting aside her needle and turning with deceptive calm towards her friend. Inside she was fairly ringing with anticipation. "What do you do? How did it come about?"

Ginevra laid down her fine-work with a sheer sigh of relief. She had been needling at the silver horn of a unicorn for at least the past three days and had already been forced to pull the costly threads out six times. It was wearying to be so frustrated by something that she hated doing anyway, and she more than welcomed this new conversational diversion. She and Julian were seated alone in their usual corner. They would be able to talk on and on without being disturbed.

"I've no idea about the origins of the celebration," she said, settling into her subject. "Of course there is the religious part of it and all that. Carnivale takes place on the last day before the Wednesday of Ashes. They call it *Martedi Grasso* in the Venetian dialect. But the concept is the same throughout Christendom—one last fling of extravagant sinning before the penance of Lent begins."

Ginevra sighed at the thought of the long days of ribbon buying she would soon be forced to do without.

Julian's mind had fastened on another point.

"Extravagant sinning?" she echoed dubiously, looking over at Ginevra's chaste young face.

"Well, in a manner of speaking."

Julian, who did not view the loss of market excursions with the same degree of horror, merely wrinkled her brow and said, "Tell me more. I did not grow up under these customs."

"Poor you," said Ginevra with sincere compassion. "You've missed a great deal of fun. From what my sisters tell me, we are the only city in Italy to have made such a cult of Carnivale. Perhaps the idea is a version of something the Polo brothers brought back from the East. So much of what we now take for granted originated from there. Take our pasta, for example. . . ."

Ginevra mused on this for a moment while Julian struggled to hold onto both her patience and her tongue.

"No matter what its origin, Carnivale exists. It is here," Julian finally prompted.

To this Ginevra gave a nod of agreement. "Indeed it is, the most fun of the liturgical year. Better even than waiting for the

Befana at Epiphany with nothing but coals for your socks if you've happened to displease your parents.''

A serving girl passed with a pitcher of hot, sweetened wine to refresh the ladies at their task. Ginevra waited until she had completed her circuit of the chamber before she continued.

''The whole point is to pretend to be something you are not, and thus confound the others who try to guess at you,'' she whispered. '' 'Tis not a question of much strange dressing but rather of masking. You hide your face and the others must discover who you are. The masks are extravagant and wonderful. They are made of parchment molded and sculpted and then brightly painted. We will go soon to Rialto Market to choose one. You've not seen that one yet. The word 'Rialto' means 'high shore' in Latin, and the place is indeed one of the highest land points in Venice—which is saying precious little because the city is situated so low. My mother knows the most wonderful man there. Why, last year—without her knowing anything about it, of course—I was able . . .''

Julian, though she nodded and smiled and puckered her face at what she hoped were appropriate moments, had long ago stopped paying attention.

Martedi Grasso, Ginevra had said.

It was barely ten days away.

She would have to think quickly. She would have to plan well.

Julian laid her plans with infinite care, and she was helped by a kind fate. The question of Carnivale was broached that night at the evening meal. At first Olivier had wrinkled his nose at the notion. He had an army in the Veneto that was being prepared for war, he had told Luciano Venier loud enough so that Julian, at her far end of the long table, was able to hear him. He did not have time for frivolity.

Luciano had diplomatically reminded him that Carnivale was an important Venetian custom and that his army was in Venice's employ. It would do no harm and it might do some good, should the commander of the Gold Company be present at such an important occasion.

Olivier had seen the wisdom of this, but he insisted that everyone in the household go along—including Julian. Usually she put up a very staunch fight against social visits and occasions. Her aversion to masked evenings and tableaux—which were longed-for social occasions in Venice—was well-known. If the Count of the Ducci Montaldo was surprised at his ward's docile acquiescence, he said nothing. Instead, he insisted upon personally choosing her mask. She walked into her chamber late one afternoon to find a dead-white face upon her red bedding.

She stifled a scream.

Ginevra, who had come in with her, rushed to the bed in rapture.

"Oh, how lucky you are. 'Tis the physician's mask, one of the most prized."

"How can you tell one style from the other?" demanded Julian. The thing upon her bed looked nothing like a physician—unless he had been dead and bleach-boned for centuries.

"From the nose," said Ginevra matter-of-factly as she picked up the mask. " 'Tis traditionally long. That was to allow a place for fragrant herbs and potpourri so that he could keep out the miasma of disease."

Julian moved over, taking the cool paper mask in her hands. It was totally without expression, except for two beautiful oval slits for eyes and a pair of exquisitely wrought lips. There was nothing alive or human about it at all. It would serve her purpose admirably.

"And look, a note from the Count!" exclaimed Ginevra. She showed not the least sign of leaving Julian to read her missive in private. "Quick, tell me what it says."

Julian pried through the thick gold wax that bound the parchments.

I had this made especially for you, Olivier had written. *You earned it with your care of the child.*

Julian read his words aloud.

"What child?" Ginevra asked, just as her friend had known she would.

"A young boy in the village who had taken a fever. The Lord Olivier is too kind to me in his remembrance of it."

"He takes little time from his war preparations even to eat and yet he has found an opportunity to have this crafted just for you," said Ginevra, and then her voice turned fretful. "But the problem is he will know you in this. There will be no guessing at all, at least on his part, as to who you might be."

Exactly, thought Julian. And she smiled.

She had every intention of letting Olivier see her in his gift. His note, too, would serve her purpose well.

Julian's own ideas for her costume did not include masking, but they did include careful and secret planning. This she did with grave determination. She was perfect at her needlework; she was willing and anxious to please the Count of the Ducci Montaldo when he needed her writing skills or her translations. She was a paragon of docility with Olivier, so determined was she not to light any sparks of interest within his quick mind. She did not mention her mother. She did not mention his promise. And of course, more than anything else, she did not mention the Janizary, Assen.

She thanked him profusely for her mask and assured him— and everyone else within hearing—that she could not wait for *Martedì Grasso* so that she could finally, *finally*, put it on.

If she spent more time than normal conversing with the serving maidens, no one found this curious or took exception to it. She had been raised in the East, after all, and therefore could not be expected to act according to the rules of civilized society.

"If the Count, her guardian, says nothing of her strange behavior," said the Countess Venier to her daughter Maria, "then we must all bear with it. One would not want to vex him when he is under so much pressure. As you know, his destiny is now married to that of Venice.''

Maria, who was not yet spoken for and had seen Claudia's deft hand at work in Domiziana's brilliant betrothal, sagely decided to keep her mouth shut and to nod in acquiescence to anything her lady mother said.

Thus the days flowed tranquilly onwards—towards the culmination of Julian's plan.

''We will meet behind the palazzo, in the courtyard,'' Ginevra told her friend. ''From there we will walk to the Piazza San Marco, right before the Cathedral. Our friends will join us, either on the way or at the Square itself. Oh, Julian, do hurry and dress yourself. You are going to have the adventure of your life!''

For once, Julian did not doubt her.

She rose sedately from her sewing stool and feigned a polite, slow crossing out of the presence of the Lady Claudia and her daughters. Olivier was nowhere about. She had not seen him all day, and she was considerably grateful for that fact. Once out of the room she was anything but slow and aimless in reaching the confines of her chamber and the trunk where her secrets lay.

Her chest was where the servants placed it when Julian had first come from Belvedere. She had gone to some trouble to make it seem that no one had entered it since. Instead, she had gone through it herself by candlelight on nights past and rifled through its contents until her eye came upon that for which she searched.

She had never seen such a beautiful dress. Francesca had given it to her, though it was not a hand-down garment. Her friend had called in a French dressmaker especially to construct the tunic for her a few weeks before Julian left Harnoncourt Hall. No one could ever quite tell what the fey mind of the Lady of the Harnoncourts was up to. The garment, when it was nished, was perfect—and perfect for the Maid Julian. There was no doubt at all about that.

Julian sifted through the contents of the chest and was not long in finding her treasure. It was midnight blue and resplendent; even before she had pulled it out from its hiding place, she could see the light catch at its beading and make it gleam. The embroidered threads that danced through it were the exact color of Julian's chestnut hair. Where Francesca had discovered silk that so closely replicated Julian's eyes and thread that was shot with the gloss of her splendid curtain of hair, no one had ever questioned. They were not meant to. But Julian was more than pleased. This dress would do; its color would be dark enough for her to hide within.

"And I will look lovely in it," she murmured grimly. "Assen must think I am favored in this place."

There was a knock at the door and then two maids rushed through it. They were giggling and already swaying slightly with pent-up excitement, as well as from the extra rations of wine that Julian knew flowed freely from the Venier cellars this night. And no Venetian would be exempt from the merrymaking. Julian was counting on that. She was praying for it as well.

The maids—including the one whom she had so carefully befriended—brought filled beaten-copper buckets for her bath. The girls were so well into their festivities that more of the water puddled onto the floor than made it the distance to the tubbing that had been placed before the fire. The mess did not bother Julian in the least. She realized that if the Venier servants, who were usually kept well in line under the stern hand of their mistress, could be so deeply into the festivities so early in the evening, then there might be hope for her with Assen's guardians as well. She must believe that there was hope and that she would actually reach his prison—which lay across the dangerous Bridge of Sighs.

Julian smiled at the maid she had chosen. She noted once again the woman's height and hair coloring. She had been

drinking, but not as much as the others. She smiled back a
Julian now, in true friendship. Julian knew that her plan wa
not without its hazards, but she would take the entire blam
for any missteps. This servant would have nothing to fear eithe
from the Veniers or from the Count of the Ducci Montaldo.

She lay back in the perfumed tub, letting the deep viole
aroma lead her naturally into meditation. Her furrowed brov
relaxed more and more as the water around her grew cold an
her hands turned white and wrinkled.

Julian thought of the Power.

She would need just a little of it—just a very little—if he
plan were to succeed. Not the dose needed for witching, but
woman's natural dosage. Just enough to make Assen's guard
do what she wanted.

Hers was, indeed, a very *seductive* plan.

And she was most frightened by its very seductiveness. Sh
had seen in the past what had happened to her when a ma
took it into his mind that he wanted her—she had seen it firs
with the Dogan Bey and then with Olivier. She shivered with
shame at the remembrance of her guardian's kiss. The Doga
Bey had been a man when she was a child. He had chosen he
and taken her—with skill and desire and even with compassion
But not with love. This happened every day, in Christendom
and in the Ottoman Empire, to girls who were much younge
than she had been at the time. There had never been a question
of love between them. She was but performing her duty; he
was but fulfilling a need.

Instead, she had loved Olivier. Loved him still. And he had
not taken her, but he had kissed her. Kissed her openly and
deeply and lovingly when all the time, through every stroke of
his tongue and every whispering of her name, he knew that he
was sacredly pledged to another.

Well, 'tis only what happens, she thought now with a sigh
Without family and protection, and with a history behind her,
a woman is set back on her use of the Power. It is the only
thing that might help her in the end.

Julian sat up so quickly that water splashed over and sputtered into the fire. The women stopped their giggling and came to see what was wrong.

"Nothing," said Julian, a little too hastily. "I have lingered long at my bath and must be hurrying."

They nodded and helped her. Of course, they assured her, they understood. Julian hoped that they would put her trembling down to coldness and damp. That was not the reason for it.

She had thought Aalyne's thoughts—and she had thought them in Aalyne's own voice. It was her mother who had always told her that the Power was the only thing she could count upon—that it was all that could help her. But Julian, even as a child, did not agree with what her mother told her. She had only to look at Aalyne—who was ever only hunted or feared—to know that she did not want the life that this particular Power offered. Even if she had the gift—something she many times doubted—she couldn't help but think there was a better way to use it than by force.

This way had ruined her mother. In the end, it may have even killed her.

Julian shook her head away from this thought.

She took special care with her hair, sitting patiently as the maid worked through it and cooed compliments about its thickness and luster. Julian let the girl brush and brush until gold sparkled its dark chestnut, and then gazed in a piece of silvered-glass as it was lifted and wound about her head. She knew she was looking fine, and she was grateful for their efforts. They were complimenting themselves on their achievements when there was a quick knock on the door. Before they could even question its provenance, a richly clothed and masked man burst full forth into their midst.

This was such a singular sight, and so totally unexpected, that all the women—including Julian—squealed and grabbed at linen towels to hide their fully clothed bodies. It was then that their visitor squealed with laughter and pulled off a plumed velvet hat and gold, feathered mask to reveal himself—as the

Maid Ginevra. They all laughed and said that they had known who it was the whole time.

"Oh, what a terror you are!" exclaimed one of the serving women as she doubled over in laughter. "If I should only tell your mother . . ."

"If you tell my mother," began Ginevra impishly, "then might be forced to ask for the return of the quarter-florin I am about to gift you."

Again more squeals and laughter as Ginevra dug into her purse.

"Now off with both of you—the cellars are open. I will finish helping the Lady Julian. The night has already started and we must hurry if we do not want its finishing without us.'

One of the women hesitated slightly, then she, too, hurried forth at Julian's brief nod.

Her red hair tumbled down around her shoulders and the maids laughed and pinched themselves.

Ginevra struggled at rearranging the tangle of her blond hair beneath its elaborate velvet covering. She lost her balance and fell in a heap, just by good fortune landing upon the bed. "Oh Julian. Help me. I'll blind or kill myself struggling into this wretched covering."

"Then you should not have chosen a hat twice the size that you are," said her friend mildly as she gathered the velvet wrappings around Ginevra's head once again. "I thought you said the Carnivale included only masking, not costuming."

" 'Tis not costuming for me to present myself as a boy," said Ginevra, once again fully encased. "If I had had my choice, I would have been one. They've much more freedom than we have and can get on with things more easily. They needn't ask permission from mothers or nuns or older sisters for every breath they take. They can decide whom they want to marry and just ask. They don't always have to be waiting around."

"Ah, so we've come to the crux of the problem," said Julian. "I doubt anyone could do much getting about in those shoes. I've never seen such ridiculous pointed toes in my life—and

/ith bells on them. You will warn every mouse in the palazzo
f your imminent arrival.''

"They are the latest design from Paris," said Ginevra, lifting
er small, masked face. "We will see many more of them
rhen the French army returns from their triumph of a crusade.
'hey've promised to pass through Venice before returning
ome to glorious France. I heard my father and the Doge
iscussing it just this very morning. They will be rich from
illage and anxious to spend their money on the treasures that
'enice has to offer.''

Julian, who knew the strength of the Sultan and the ferocious
iscipline of his army, doubted that the French, even if they
nanaged to defeat him, would find themselves facing the pleas-
nt outing that many of them anticipated. Even a day facing
Bayezid in battle could swiftly turn a man's thoughts towards
firm inclination never to leave home and family again. She
lecided to keep her gloomy thoughts to herself. Ginevra was
n love with the Knight de la Marche, and so everything that
e did or that his countrymen did would be glorious to her, no
natter what Julian said, even to the wearing of belled and
ointy-toed harlequin boots.

"Thank St. Lucy and all the glorified angels that Gatien
vould never fashion himself like this," she murmured under
er breath. "And that Olivier would not as well."

"Did you say something?" inquired Ginevra as she looked
ip from Julian's silvered glass. She seemed serenely satisfied
vith the reflection of her ridiculous garb. "Oh, but I forgot.
Count Olivier sent me for you. We are ready to see the costumes
nd masks in the great piazza. What great fun we will have
onight!''

"He is back then," said Julian. She had hoped otherwise.
Ier work would have been much less fraught with worry had
he thought Olivier safely encamped in the Veneto with his
urmy for the night. There was nothing for it now. She linked
ier arm through Ginevra's, and the two of them set out together.

* * *

Luciano Venier, a stickler for detail and a man who keenly felt himself a most insignificant part of a very significant family had made sure that his palazzo, at least, claimed a commanding position, even if he himself could not. It stood firmly in the shadow of the new Cathedral and one did not need to cross water to reach it. However, Venice was such a water-loving city that it seemed a pity to be denied the pleasure of a lagoon crossing on the day before penance, so the Veniers had ordered their barges brought to the landing anyway. They bobbed back and forth amid the sound of laughter and lute-playing that drifted in from the various piazzas and byways of the city.

The barges, like the palazzo itself, were brightly decorated with silk banners and oil flames set in hollow copper canisters. The reflections from the many torches attached to the façade bounced off the water and made everything recognizable, even though vespers had long since rung and it was full night outside. But Julian, glancing quickly about her, was able to recognize everyone—not only all of the Venier family but many of their friends as well. Her heart sank as she snuggled deeper into her warm, fur-lined cloak. To make matters worse, a bright, round moon shone down upon her. It seemed full of a mischievous thwarting of her plans.

"And stars everywhere," she mumbled. "I might as well have gone on in broad day."

It was good she had already decided to present herself as herself. There would be no disguise in Venice on this Carnivale.

As if in confirmation of this thought, she caught Gatien's eye just as he absentmindedly reached over to the elaborately costumed Ginevra, who had managed to angle up beside him.

"Givvy, pull this cloak tighter," he said, bundling her up much as he would a child. "The water is freezing. You'll start your Lent penance in bed with putrid throat if you don't take a care."

Julian could not see Ginevra's face, but she would have had to be deaf indeed not to hear her groan.

They were a noisy group, their plumage and masks bright and colorful. Yet, Julian recognized them all. Luciano Venier, hidden behind the bright-red façade of a satyr, stood with his arm looped through that of his angel-faced wife. Their daughters clustered gracefully about them.

The second eldest, Massima, had come on a visit with her very wealthy husband in tow. His family was a pillar of nearby Ravenna and had become inordinately wealthy by supplying swords and seize engines to the emperor at Constantinople. He had obviously been sent posthaste to see if they could perform the same service for the Count of the Ducci Montaldo. It was rumored that the young couple was soon to move back to Venice, where they had hopes of finding a climate more congenial to newly made riches. The family had married its eldest son to the only plain daughter of the Veniers in the hope that he would eventually be raised to the Venetian nobility, and thus become part of the city's ruling oligarchy. The Italians were a litigious people and there was always money to be made from their various squabbles, if one could place oneself judiciously.

Naturally, a wife with the social cachet of Massima Venier had not come to them cheaply. It was rumored—and not only by the malicious—that Luciano Venier's main source of income was the selling of his daughters' fair hands to families that needed the cachet of his impeccable family connections. Whether this was true or not did not seem to matter to him in the least.

What did seem to matter was that there were plenty of people willing to buy a Venier, and to maintain their purchase appropriately. Massima was wearing a white mask that sported a diamond in the middle of its forehead. Her hand fluttered nervously to it many times—her interest seemed more drawn to it than to the man who had presented it to her. She barely nodded at Julian. Without the Count of the Ducci Montaldo there to protect

his ward, she did not see the need of showing a civility she
was very far from feeling.

Domiziana was there with her family, but Olivier was
nowhere about. Julian did not know if she should be happy
about this or otherwise. Ginevra had seen him; she had said
that he had sent her especially to bring down his ward. It would
have been good to know just exactly where he was; on the
other hand, that would have meant that he would know her
actions as well. In the end she decided to accept his absence
as a gift from a kind fate. He had never been one for gay
festivities. She would have to watch for him and be careful of
her back. Everyone else had seen her and would testify to this.
If she disappeared for an hour or two there would be no one
to note it in the general confusion. Olivier was probably with
his men, busy with his parchments and his maps. Aside from
Gatien de la Marche, he was the only one who seemed to be
taking this crusade seriously.

Julian went inside for an instant and listened. No, she could
not feel Olivier. She did not think he was near. She knew that
even if he had been, she would still have had to play out her
risk. Assen would have to be released soon. If he chose to
believe him, the Count of the Ducci Montaldo would have to
send him on to Padua and the court of the Visconti. If not,
Gian Galeazzo, a man who had been born both cunning and
suspicious, would grow even more so. And any advantage
Olivier might have gained from Assen would be lost.

But first Julian would have to see him. They were old friends.

She had no fear that she would find him drunken or sleeping.
He was a Muslim and would not be taking part in the pre-Lenten
festivities. Besides, like the Count of the Ducci Montaldo, he
was not a festive man.

The evening air, usually so humid, was crisp with the promise
of snow as the barge docked before the great Cathedral.

"Come with me, Julian," cried Ginevra. It was obvious she

had gotten over her snub from Gatien. "Take these coins. We scatter them to the poor who are waiting for us. It is the custom and the way that we guarantee our salvation on this night when devils romp."

She giggled and Julian laughed with her, but she took care not to get too close. She would need her freedom. She must be ready. Already the *compline* bell that confirmed nighttime had started to peal.

Their group swelled as it moved along and inhabitants of the other grand palazzi, their friends, joined them on their way to Venice's main square. Julian heard music from a pipe and a nearby burst of sudden raucous laughter. Other laughter joined in. They passed the stalls that were a traditional part of the whole Carnivale celebration—peasant women selling steaming iron bowls of polenta, a man scooping roasted chestnuts into paper cones, an astrologer plying his handmade charts at a table beneath the shadow of the Cathedral. They passed the stone façade of a cloistered monastery, its windows tightly shut against the dangers of this night—they were the only walls along their path that had not been festooned with banners and torches. The building stood forbidding and grim amidst the general revelry. Images floated through Julian's mind—of the prison she was soon to enter and of the cruel crusade this frolicking city would soon face.

The sounds of the *Dies Irae,* the Gregorian chant for the dead, bubbled up from deep within the monastery to hang like crystal on the night air. Julian glanced over to see Ginevra crossing herself as a shadow passed over her face. Then in an instant she was happy and giggly once again as she flirted openly with a son of the powerful Manfredi family, under her father's watchful but indulgent eye.

It was Carnivale—and everything was possible on *Martedi Grasso.* Julian prayed fervently that this would be so. She touched the purse tucked into her threaded gold girdle and felt the coins jingling against her fingers.

And then she saw her chance.

Claudia's thin lips beamed brightly at an enormous group of people. There was talk and laughter and a round of new introductions.

Ginevra said, "This is our guest, the Lady Julian Madrigal. She is the ward of the Count of the Ducci Montaldo. She and I have become dear friends."

"Ah," said the young girl who was the object of the introduction. She was dressed in bright red and had taken her mask off in order to cool her excited face. "Perhaps she can tell our future. There do not seem to be many true witches about, at least not this year. My mother found a soothsayer in the outer Veneto who is rumored to know everything, and this woman foretold a great marriage. My mother just assumed it would be that of the Lady Domiziana to the Count of the Ducci Montaldo. As he rides to war soon, they might wed before the sailing. Oh, if only God would permit that to be soon. For such a great occasion the Papal Legate will surely release us from our Lenten penance. . . ."

"Yes, yes," agreed Ginevra with true fervor. "Domiziana is the most wretched sister that anyone could possibly imagine, but one could even wish her well if she were the reason for a Lenten lifting."

"Indeed, I hate Lent," agreed her friend with equal earnestness. "No cakes or sweets for its whole forty days."

"And no riding the hillsides."

"And no color on clothes. Only black dresses. . . ."

They were off into a mournful litany of the horrors they would have to endure for the next forty days. Julian, as she slipped away, knew she would not be missed.

Unexpectedly, she found herself caught within the nettings of another conversation. Claudia Venier reached out to grab her as a large-bosomed, heavily jeweled dowager tittered into what would obviously be a very scandalous tale.

"Did you not hear of it—why, everyone has. Troubadours call the episode the *Danse Macabre*," began this eminent presence. "My dear, it was the very nearest of tragedies. A notorious courtier—a great favorite of Queen Isabeau's, or so I've heard—was about to enter into her second marriage. You know what a time for ribaldry that is, and especially in a country like France that has no sense of propriety. Of course, the king and queen were invited. . . ."

"I know the story," squealed Claudia. "It happened in January, on the Tuesday before Candlemas Day. And the woman in question—a lady-in-waiting—was about to celebrate her third time, not her second. She had already been twice-widowed—can you imagine?"

The Lady of the Venier said this last with enthusiastic gusto, obviously forgetting Domiziana's marital history, though the arch look on her friend's face showed that this lady had not.

Julian let her footsteps lag further and further behind until a whip-line of children lashed through them, laughing and holding aloft paper strips that caught the wind as they ran. They provided the cover she needed. She slipped even further behind, slid into an alleyway—and then she was gone.

CHAPTER SIXTEEN

By now the population of Venice was all in its piazzas. She could hear voices floating from the *Campo di Santa Maria Formosa*, the *Campo di Santa Maria Zobenigo*, and the Field of Saint John and Saint Paul. There was no sound from anywhere else. Nor was there much light. She made her quick way through the glow of a few wall torches that had been placed by the Guard. But this didn't matter. In daylight she had paced out the path to Assen's cell, over and over again. She knew the way by heart.

And the serving girl, too, was where she had been told to be. She stepped out from the shadows as Julian neared her. They smiled their relief at seeing each other.

"The Veniers are still within St. Mark's Square," Julian whispered. "They will probably stay nearby; it is the most fashionable place for festivity. But hurry—one never knows for certain. Say nothing. Be sure you are seen."

The woman nodded.

She looks intelligent. She will do, thought Julian with some relief.

If the night went awry, it would not be this woman's fault.
The purse of coins that she carried changed hands.

Quickly Julian tore off her fur-lined cloak and her mask.
She gave them to the woman, and took hers in return. They
said nothing as they swiftly redressed and went their separate
ways.

"I've come this far," Julian chanted to herself as she ran.
"I've come this far. I've come this far. I've come this far. And
I can't go back."

She shivered in the strange, crystal air and she remembered
the promise of snow. There was nothing but darkness all around
her and the occasional sounds of something small that scurried
out of her way as she hurried along the damp cobbles. She did
not want to know what made these furtive, scurrying sounds.
She could not stop to look around. She had chosen her pathway.
She must follow it to its end—and right now it was leading
her to Assen, whose cell lay across the Bridge of Sighs.

" 'Tis all the devil's doing as well as our own bad luck that
put us upon this duty on this of all nights," sighed Roberto
Mori to Clemente Asso as they each looked with equal distaste
around the damp, depressing walls of the city dungeon.

Most of Venice's prisoners had already been granted clem-
ency by its Doge. Though it was still deep into its festivities,
the city also held a wary eye to its collective soul and the
virtues it would be called upon to take on the morrow. Better
to take a first step upon charity by freeing the usual prisoners
in advance. They would be rounded up again in a few days'
time, but for now at least some conscience-assuaging effort
had been made.

Only one inmate had been remanded to their care. They had
been told to watch him carefully but were assured that he would
give them no trouble. He was an infidel. He would not drink;
he would not demand a feast and complain when it was not

;iven. Above all, he would not try to escape. He had no place
n Venice to go.

Instead, Roberto had had more than his share of Martedi
Grasso invitations.

He was an ex-soldier, the holder of a small pension that the
oligarchy had granted him for youthful valor. He was also a
man of some little property on the small island of Murano. In
fact, the only thing he seemed in great need of was a wife.
And there had been many a woman determined to supply this
lack during the festivities that closed Carnivale.

He had always been one to need a firm hand, the women
told each other. He was not the type to keep himself in check.
Indeed, it was just past compline bell and already the sour wine
was beginning to stink upon his breath.

His companion, Clemente Asso, was younger and brighter—
and therefore more cautious. "You had best keep your mouth
closed against the Count, old man, or you will be joining that
one in there." He was a native Savoyard and the music of his
native French still trilled faintly through his voice. "The Doge
has no real care for who is in or who is out of there."

Roberto shrugged. He was Venice-born and bred and he had
the native's lack of respect for the exigencies of communal
laws. He was fast becoming too drunk to move, but was not
yet so drunk that he could not pass the earthen jug over to his
companion.

"At least we've this," he said. "My sister grows the grapes
herself in Tuscany. She married a lad who farms for a lord
near San Gimignano. They are known for their wine in Tuscany.
I've sampled the world over and never found a better batching."

Clemente noted that he was having a decided difficulty in
keeping to his seat. But—drunk or not—he'd be a witch's
broomstick before he'd let this snobbish Venetian think that
there existed a Savoyard who could not hold his wine—not
that this wine was worth the headache experience had taught
him would shortly be his. His vision might have doubled, but
he was still sharp-witted enough to know that what he was

drinking in no way compared to what could be got for a lead
pence at home.

Still, it was probably best to be diplomatic. One never knew
with these hot-blooded Italians. "Do you think we should offer
him some?" he said, nodding towards the solid oak of the cell
door. "After all, from tomorrow on, there will be little enough
true drinking until Easter."

"Wouldn't do any good," Roberto said, showing him a
bleary eye. "He's infidel, you know. Don't drink. They never
do—against their religion."

"Pity." Clemente looked genuinely sorrowful for a moment
and then he brightened. "Maybe we should try to convert
him?"

"I'd convert for this fine wine and you could bet my faint
chance at heaven upon it," responded his newfound friend.

They were both laughing uproariously at this pungent witticism when the knock sounded. At first they could not place it
but when it rang out again they both looked in slack-jawed
wonder at the outer door. Finally, Clemente stood and stumbled
his way to the portal. It took him a moment to figure out its
simple latchings, but then he pulled it aside—to disclose the
Lady Julian Madrigal.

Her efforts at a careful toilette were paying off, Julian noted
with satisfaction. She saw stupor shade both men's bleary faces
as she entered their dank room. And within herself she saw
what they saw: the sensuous flexing of her beaded bodice; the
shining, straight sweep of the hair she had unloosed as it curtained down to the small of her back; the hint of moistness on
her cheeks and in her eyes.

'Twas but a woman's cunning she had used in her dressing,
but this was proving power enough.

She spoke before she could be questioned. "The Count of
the Ducci Montaldo has sent me to see to the needs of the
prisoner Assen who was born Christian, but has committed the
mortal sin of denying the Christ. For this, a priest is to be sent

to him upon the morrow. I speak his language. I am sent to prepare him for that visit.''

Both guards knew the Lady Julian Madrigal. They knew that she came from the East and that she was the Count's ward, and they knew that she served him as secretary. Still . . .

Roberto was not so wine-drunk that his eyes did not narrow at this. ''We were not told to expect anyone. Lord Olivier has sent no word of a visit.''

Slowly and silently, Julian reached within the folds of her tunic to pull out a fragment of expensive white parchment. Roberto took it from her and studied the seal, turning the paper over and over slowly in his hand. Finally he broke the sigil and stared down at the official wording—which he could not read. He had no intention of letting this fact be known, either by the Count's strange ward or by the arrogant young Savoyard who shared this watch with him. Roberto only hoped, and prayed to his seven patron saints, that he was holding the parchment right side up.

He was not.

The missive was passed on to Clemente. ''What do you think?'' Roberto asked with a grunt.

Clemente, in his turn, studied the parchment with profound care. '' 'Tis the Count's seal,'' he said at length. ''And written in his own hand.''

Of course it is, thought the Count's trusted secretary. She had resealed the letter herself. It told of her Carnivale mask.

'' 'Tis the Count's seal. Clearly written in his own hand,'' Roberto echoed abruptly as he moved towards the locked and bolted door. He could not let this young Savoyard—who had just enrolled in the Gold Company and was a bastard from France—get the better of him. It just couldn't happen. ''We must open to the Lady Julian, as it says.''

''I must see him alone,'' Julian prompted. ''The priest will hear his confession, but I must prepare him for it.''

They nodded. They both understood that it was important not to come between a man and his sins.

* * *

"Are you my father?"

Clemente had put an extra torch to the wall before leaving, but its light only served to accentuate the shadows. Still, Julian could plainly see Assen sitting on his small straw cot. Waiting for her.

Though obviously not in the mood to answer questions. Instead, he said, "I knew I could count upon your coming and I thought this might be the night that you would choose. You were always reliable—a serious girl of your word. 'Tis good to know that the West has not changed you overmuch, my little Julian."

She noticed that he had not called her a "Lady"; this said much about him and about what might lie ahead.

" 'Tis good to see you again, Assen," she said, moving towards him. "I am happy that God has once again allowed old friends to meet."

"I seriously doubt that," he replied. "Or else you would not have been so quick to leave so many of them."

When he laughed—as he so rarely did, but as he was doing now—Julian could see what her mother had seen in this man. She could see why Aalyne had loved him for years.

"But I did not leave you, and certainly I did not leave my mother. I left the Dogan Bey."

"It is the same thing. At least, *he* took it to be the same thing."

"Because he is a man and his pride could never have admitted that I could leave."

"You meant much to him. You were his favorite. . . ."

"I was a child of twelve years," Julian said quickly, not wanting to hear the excuses Assen would give, not wanting to think about them. "It was wrong what he desired of me."

She remembered the words that Francesca had whispered, night after night, when Julian had first come to Belvedere and the nightmares had gripped her.

It wasn't your fault. It wasn't your fault. You were a child. They were the adults. It was not your doing. You were only a child.

Now, Francesca's dear voice, saying her kind words, reamed through Julian's mind like a song.

It wasn't my fault.

"Your mother seemed to think you had age enough," Assen scoffed. "There are many women married and conceiving at twelve. Noble women, even. You weren't the only one so used."

"I wasn't married," she answered quietly. "I was not protected."

They spoke in French. Despite what he had said to the Count of the Ducci Montaldo, Assen was quite proficient in languages. He spoke at least six of them well. He had known that Julian would never betray him to anyone—not even to Lord Olivier. He had felt no fear of this: he felt none now.

"Six years since you left us," he said. "We all wondered what had happened."

"Were there reprisals?"

Assen laughed again, disposing of yet another of her questions.

"You've grown beautiful," he said thoughtfully. "Less like your mother. More like yourself. I remember your hair being lighter in Nicopolis. Chestnut color it was and still is, but it's deeper now. And, of course, the body has changed. Yes, the body has changed considerably from that of a child's. The eyes, though—they're the same. As is the look they always wore."

"The look?"

"Of something hunted and wary," he said. "Of something determined not to be caught."

"Were there reprisals?" Julian repeated.

"After you left?" Assen snorted. "Of course there were. Your leaving wounded the Dogan Bey in his pride as well as in his lust. Not only was he deprived of a new toy—but he was also deprived of the rich ransom the Count of the Ducci

Montaldo's relations would have eventually provided. He almost erupted in two when it was known that the eminently wealthy Sir d'Harnoncourt was the one who had led the prisoner free. The Dogan Bey seemed to believe he'd been deprived of two fortunes at that point. Naturally there were heads that rolled.''

"Whose?" she whispered.

"The eunuch' s. The guard is always the first to be eliminated. He is, after all, the one who lets the trouble in. One thinks he should have done better—and in your instance this was certainly true. The eunuch paid too little attention to the gossip of Nicopolis. Everyone knew that Aalyne was a witch, and that a witch can mold and persuade. He should have known, when he let you free, that he was thinking Aalyne's thoughts and not his own. But he didn't." Assen sighed an exaggerated sigh. "Then again, no one fears a castrated man, and they should. There is even a colorful story about the origins of this very haven of Venice and the eunuch, Narses. He commanded the armies of the Emperor Longinus. Unfortunately, the emperor's spoiled and beautiful wife had no use for him . . . Eventually, of course, Narses had his revenge.''

"Who else suffered?" Julian pressed, fighting the impatience from her voice. It would not do to be overanxious with Assen.

He sighed. "You are right. It is a boring story. Even though, in the end, Narses had a most sweet revenge." There was a pause. When he continued, his voice had changed. "Servants were killed. Lesser women in the harem, whom the Dogan Bey either thought had known something or whom he wanted to make riddance of for some totally unrelated reason. Like most warriors, though he grieved you excessively, he let your disappearance serve his purposes. He cleaned his house thoroughly by using your broom." Assen, the soldier, shrugged at this bloodshed.

"And my nurse?"

"Blinded. She was an old woman and obviously knew nothing. The Dogan Bey decided to be merciful.''

Julian shuddered. Tears scalded her eyes but she blinked
em back. She'd come too far to be stopped by tears now.
And my mother?''

"Ah, Aalyne." A shrug, a raised eyebrow. "No one knows
hat befell her in the end."

"But you must know," insisted Julian. Her voice was rising.
he could not help it. "You were her lover. Surely you, of all
eople, must know if she is still alive."

"Tell me why I *should* know," said Assen. His voice was
a amused growl. "I had all I could do to escape from the
ebacle with my head still firmly upon my shoulders. The
ogan Bey trusted no one. He was firmly convinced that I had
ayed a part in Aalyne's belated show of motherly solicita-
on."

Julian had gotten control of herself once again. "And just
ow did you escape? Tell me that, Assen. It was no secret that
ou were my mother's lover. You had been together since
efore I was born. In France, as I recall, when the Sultan sent
ou to Paris on mission. Or that's what they said. It was even
amored by some that you were my father. That you *are* my
ather." She paused. "Surely the Dogan Bey must have sus-
ected you. And suspecting you, he would have had you tor-
ured."

Assen's dark eyes betrayed nothing more than polite interest.
hey intimated that Julian could easily have been talking about
omeone else, not him. He certainly could have had nothing
o do with the accusation on her lips. Julian saw his gaze flicker
ver her expensive gown, the softness of her jeweled hands,
he long, dark flow of her unveiled hair. She saw him gently
niff, and knew that he smelled privilege on her clean body
nd on the scent of her perfume. He smiled an enigmatic smile.

"He could not kill me, because he needed me," Assen said
imply. "He needed my knowledge. As most men—at least
nost warriors—do."

He shook his head in mock commiseration. "You've not yet
edded your great love, have you, little witch? Your mother

would have by now. You know that. That is, if she had trul
wanted or needed him. Aalyne let nothing slip from her tha
she truly wanted.

"Yes, Aalyne always got what she wanted," Assen mur
mured. "You look just as tense, just as unhappy, and I'll warrar
you've not yet got what you want—nor see that much chanc
of getting it."

"Then that means we have much in common, Assen. Nov
tell me what you know of my mother." The bantering had le†
her voice and now it left his as well.

"She could be alive. She could be dead. I've neither see
nor heard from her since I left Nicopolis—and that was si
years ago. She was always under the Sultan's protection, bu
accidents can happen." He shrugged. "The Dogan Bey is gov
ernor of Nicopolis—a city that will probably soon be the foca
point for Holy War. Why don't you return to your home, Julia
Why trust this to your guardian? Why not ask the Dogan Be
yourself, face-to-face, what he's done with your belove
mother."

"Because I have promised the Lady Julian that I would se
to Aalyne's welfare. I have given her my word, and I inten
to maintain it."

Neither of them had heard Olivier come in. At least Julia
hadn't, and the quick, astonished look on Assen's face said tha
he, a man who missed little, had missed the Count's entrance a
well. But he was too used to keeping control to lose it now.

"Ah, the great Lord of the Ducci Montaldo," he said wit
a laugh. "Betrothed to one woman, but bewitched by another
And with no less than a Holy War to prepare for. By Allah,
declare, is there to be no end to this one man's preoccupations?'

Olivier refused to be provoked. "Julian, leave us," he said
"I will deal with you later."

"Then *I* will not deal with *you* at all," said Assen mildly
"At least without the presence of your beguiling ward. Stay
with us, dear Julian. Pull your stool closer. As you said, w
are old friends and we have much to discuss."

"Don't let him provoke you, Julian." Olivier was massive
side her. He wore no mask and was dressed simply in the
ld-trimmed, black suede tunic of his army. His presence
ought freshness into the dankness of the room. Assen seemed
tent on ignoring it.

" 'Tis a pity, Assen," Olivier said, stepping further into the
om and motioning Julian to the one chair, "that you did not
ck up a command of French manners with the ease with which
u seem to have picked up the speaking of their tongue."

"And what might you mean by that, my lord?" The Jani-
ry's tone was deceptively pleasant.

It did not fool Olivier. He fixed his eyes on Assen. They
one cold and green in the torchlight. "That one should natu-
lly expect treachery from a traitor."

Silence crackled between them for a second and then Assen
ughed.

" 'Tis true that I am traitor to the Sultan," he said. "There
no harm in that—I am proud to be so. Proud as the devil.
s for the rest—why, even you, my Lord, with your cold
estern blood, can understand my longing for revenge. Is it
t this that fuels your pledge to defend Venice, and not this
nsense about Holy War? 'Tis the specter of your father and
ur brothers that drives you. 'Tis the belief that, had you not
en so cruelly detained by the Dogan Bey, you might somehow
ve managed to save them from God's wrath. We have much
common, you and I. Given another occasion, we might well
ve been friends."

"We can still be friends," said Olivier softly. "We can, as
ey say, share our information."

"Ah, but I've already shared mine," said Assen in mock
solation.

"Not all of it. Not by half."

"Meaning?"

"That you have told me how Gian Galeazzo Visconti spies
r the Sultan. You have not as yet told me which of my own
ople spies for Gian Galeazzo."

Another might have missed the flicker that passed acros:
Assen's face, but Julian had grown up with him. She had opene
the door to him—sometimes night after night—so that he coul
enter into her mother's house. She had studied him too ofte
and too well to miss the light that was there for an instant, an
then just as quickly gone.

"I have no idea what you are saying. If you have troubl
with the loyalty of your men, then I fail to see where I migl
be involved with it."

"I said nothing of my men," said Olivier. "I spoke of b
trayal."

"And you think there is not a man of yours who woul
betray you?"

"I am certain of it. The loyalty they all have to the Gol
Company has been well tried. All of them have served wit
fortitude—first under Belden of Harnoncourt and now unde
me."

"Ah, then you are a lucky commander. Far luckier than th
Sultan himself," said Assen with some irony. "Tell me—tha
is, of course, if you care to—what leads your mind to thin
that you are being betrayed?"

"Among other things, you lead me in this direction," replie
Olivier. "You were too easily captured, too easily brought int
my presence. Actually, you presented yourself to the Doge.
may well be that you speak the truth about your family an
your thirst for revenge—in fact, I am certain that you spea
the truth. I have my spies as well, you see. This is the way o
war as we fight it, and I am not a novice at my game. Th
Sultan Murad slaughtered your family and your village. Yo
were then put under his care and you advanced. This much
have managed to ascertain."

"And so? I told you as much myself."

"You did not tell it to Gian Galeazzo—and yet he know
this. Just as he knows how many men are in my army and hov
many ships will be ferrying us up the Danube to Buda. Just a

1e knows the date of our leaving. And that our aim is none
)ther than Nicopolis.''

Assen no longer pretended disinterest. "He could have
earned this from a close attention to gossip. Men, even loyal
nen, have been known to talk.''

"My men did not know these things. They were told only
o a few—the Doge, the Oligarchy, the Council of Ten. A few
of my most trusted lieutenants. That is all.''

"Except for your secretary, the Maid Julian.''

Olivier waved his hand in a quick dismissal. "Julian would
1ever tell,'' he replied.

Assen said nothing but his brow knit around these new facts.

"So your proposal is?'' he said at last.

Still Olivier's eyes did not falter. "That tomorrow you con-
inue your journey. That once you reach the Court of the Vis-
:onti, you immediately make your way to Gian Galeazzo and
:onfess the story you have told me. Tell him that you were
vying for information and I have given you some. Do not worry,
I will find a juicy tidbit to entice him. It will be truth, so that
1e will then easily credit all you say. Once you have gained
1is confidence, I want you to very quickly discover who spies
for him and inform me of the bastard's name so that I can kill
1im.'' He paused and shook his head in something like wonder.
'For whatever reason, there is someone who wants me to lead
my men like lambs to slaughter. They want defeated that which
is trying to save them. And I cannot do it. I cannot fail again
to protect those to whom I am pledged.''

Assen's laugh was short and to the point. "Gian Galeazzo
Visconti is far too clever to fall for any small ruse. Once
Bayezid knows that I have turned traitor I will have but two
choices before me—to die a slow, messy death at the end of
a silken cord at the court of the Visconti, or to die an even
slower and messier one at the end of the Sultan's sword. I see
nothing else, and no reason at all why I should risk my life—
poor and miserable as it is—to do as you ask.''

"Because it is the right thing to do,'' said Olivier softly.

''Because we—the both of us—were not able in the past to
protect those whom we most loved and cherished. Now, perhaps, we can finally right the wrongness that we feel. Perhaps
after all, it's not too late for us to wash some blood from our
hands.''

CHAPTER SEVENTEEN

"He was my mother's lover," Julian said to Olivier much later, after the rest of the palazzo had fallen into a weary, satisfied, post-Carnivale sleep. "I've known him all my life."

"All of it?"

She nodded. "He even visited us in France—before we went to prison, that is. I was with my mother. The Inquisition let me live with her in her cell."

Olivier nodded.

She had never talked about this part of her life to anyone.

"And then you saw him again in Nicopolis?" he asked her.

"Yes, in Nicopolis. All the time," she said.

They were in the massive hall within the Cá Venier where Assen had first been brought. Now she and Olivier were alone. She knew that at least a few of his soldiers must be near, but she hadn't seen them. She wondered idly what he would do with Roberto and Clemente for letting her into Assen's cell. It had frightened her the way he had so calmly said he would kill his betrayer. She had never seen this warrior side of him before, but it was there. She knew this now, and she fervently hoped the two guards would not be punished overmuch, though she did not regret her actions. Whether or not he had planned to, Assen had told her much.

"All the time," she repeated. "As I said, he was my mother's lover. One of them." She felt the hot blush, but she would not allow herself to turn away from Olivier's probing eyes. "Perhaps he is even my father. And if he is not, I am persuaded that he knows who my own father is. My mother would never tell me—but Assen was her lover. She would have told him."

She heard the bitterness in her own voice. She could force herself to stand still, could force herself to look Olivier in the eye as she told her family's sordid secrets, but she could not stop her hands from shaking. Even balling them together, she could not hold them still.

Olivier reached down and took them and gently splayed them against his chest. She could feel his heart beating, steady and strong, as he covered her hands with his own.

"Did he hurt you?"

She would have made her hands into fists and pushed him away if Olivier had let her, but he held onto her hands, onto her body, as the tears finally came. And without knowing how it happened, Julian found herself holding onto him as well—holding onto him for dear life.

"He slept with my mother—not once but over and over again. He was with her for all the years of my life and yet now he has no thought for her. He doesn't care if she is blinded or in prison, or even if she is alive or dead. It doesn't touch him. He never loved her, never cared. She was always just a witch to him, an easy bedfellow. She was never a woman at all."

"You don't know that, Julian." Olivier had pulled her closer. He was running his hand through her long, dark hair. "You don't know what a man can hide in his heart. He is here, isn't he? He came."

"Came for what?" she demanded through her sobs. "You heard him. He came for revenge against the Sultan. He has been planning and plotting his vendetta since his family died."

"And do you think this is the first opportunity he has found to fulfill it? Do you think a man as astute as Assen, a man who has pulled himself up from an unspeakable abyss, could not have found an earlier chance for vengeance, if vengeance was truly what he sought?"

She said nothing. Olivier noticed that she had stopped crying. He also noticed that he could not stop stroking her hair.

Julian slowly looked up at him. Tears still sparkled like diamonds along her cheeks, but she was beginning to reason once again, to put puzzle pieces into their proper place. "You were outside the whole time," she said quietly. "You followed me."

"I had no need to follow you," he said, still holding onto her. "I knew exactly where you would go."

"And you let me go there."

"I have a crusade to fight and a war to win. I cannot fail the people who have employed me. Venice's trade routes must be protected—that is what the Doge and the Council of Ten have decided. Whether or not I believe battle the best way to achieve this end, I must follow the orders I have been issued. Assen's arrival and his offer of information were too fortuitous to be coincidental. Of course I had to investigate further."

"And so you used me to get to him."

"Tell me the truth, Julian." He was so near to her now that he could feel her breath as a caress at his cheek. "Would knowing my plans have stopped you? Could you have kept yourself away from Assen, even if you had realized that I followed you there?"

"No," she said, and when he said nothing she repeated her words. "No. And I'm not sorry, either. I've told you that already. I don't care that he thinks me a witch like my mother, or even that you do. I'd do it again if I thought he would tell me that my mother lives, or even that she doesn't. I'd go to him again just to know."

For one, precious, crystallized instant, Olivier knew with perfect clarity that he was about to change the whole of his life. He knew that if he reached out for Julian now, there would be no going back—not to a perfect Belvedere, to a perfect Domiziana, to the perfect life he had constructed on his family's ashes.

The thought made him hesitate for just one second. And in that second he saw his life clearly, as it actually was. He saw himself living forever in the lonely splendor of a castle that was no longer his home. Having to remind himself to kiss a wife whom, even now, before their marriage, he knew he did not love. Trying to hold on to a family that had long ago fragmented to find happiness elsewhere.

And worst of all—most frightening of all—trying to do all this without Julian.

He reached out then. He pulled Julian close.

But the witch rose between them. He could see this in the tears on her face, in the wariness of her eyes. She thought he was taking her now because she was easy game, the Magdalene's daughter. Someone who would not know right from wrong. Someone who would use any situation to further her own advantage.

That wasn't the reason. He knew this. And he was determined that soon Julian would as well.

Even if she didn't, he, the great Lion of Venice, the head of his own personal army, found it impossible to put distance between himself and this woman. Right now, he decided, for this instant, with her tears wetting his tunic, he would let himself smell the softness of her violet perfume and let her fragrant hair whisper against him. He felt the peace and the trust that he had always sensed deep within her, and he was determined to hold this peace and trust close.

Never to let them go again.

It had been so long since he had done this—he had made it his sacred business to stay away from Julian since Belvedere. Yet he had wanted her—God, how he had wanted her. The times that he had bedded his betrothed had made him realize, more than anything else, how different he had become since

Julian's return. He could not imagine that loving Julian would feel like rutting in a silken cocoon. But that's how it had felt with Domiziana. As though he thrust with determination towards nothing more substantial than a gossamer void.

And he could not go back to nothingness. Not now, when he held life itself in his arms. He would bargain with Luciano Venier. He would bargain with Domiziana. He would bargain with God Himself if he had to.

He would not let Julian go.

"Trust me." He kissed the words gently, over and over, into the salt of her tears. "You did once before. You can trust me again. I won't hurt you. I promise you that."

He felt her tense in his arms, but this did not stop him. He was a warrior, after all, and used to battling his way through opposition. He wanted Julian, but as his wife. He did not want their first time together to be here on a trestle table or stretched out on some dirt floor. He would tell her this, and declare himself just as soon as he was free. For now, all he wanted was just a little bit more of what he already had—the feel of her breasts against his body; the scent of her perfume, the sweet, salt taste of her tears.

He wanted to kiss Julian. Nothing more.

But it seemed that she did not want to kiss him.

Olivier opened his mouth and lowered his head slowly— oh, so slowly. He would give his intended time to get used to the strength of his touch, to get used to him. And then, very slowly, she opened her mouth to him and he was so tantalized by the picture of her tongue just behind the relaxing barrier of her straight, white teeth that at first he couldn't hear her words. Didn't really want to hear what she was saying, and he moved his hips a little closer to her in order to make this fact perfectly clear.

Still, she persisted with her words anyway.

"I'm not like that," she told him as she looked with her deep, dark eyes into his clear, light ones. He noticed that she was no longer crying. "I'm not a witch. I cannot go with a man who belongs to another."

She could have thrown cold water on him. She did not need to, but her words carried the same effect.

"Of course you cannot," Olivier said, remembering everything and stepping back. Though he had to literally force himself to remove his arms from around her, because so much within him still wanted to hold her close. The distance between them was not insurmountable. He could be patient, because he could broach it. "I will not ask your forgiveness because I am not sorry for what I have done. I could never be sorry for kissing you, Julian. You are my . . ."

No, this was not the time for that, either. Not until he was free again and could give chivalrous voice to his sentiments before the world. Until then, he could not demean Julian by declaring them to her in secret.

You are right," he said. "Quite right. We will speak again upon the morrow, after I have managed to settle certain things. For now, I will have two of my soldiers escort you to your chamber. You will be safe that way."

Julian nodded and moved away.

At the door, just as she was leaving, he stopped her with his voice once again.

"The Carnivale is finished. From tomorrow morning onwards, church bells will toll the hours of Lent. It has been decided—we have decided—that the fleet will sail the day after Easter. It is not certain that our mission will take us to the castle and the city of Nicopolis, but I promise you I will search for Aalyne. I promised you that in the past. Again I promise you now."

She nodded, but did not thank him or turn back.

It didn't matter. Lent would pass quickly. Everything else certainly had.

CRUSADE

CHAPTER EIGHTEEN

"You can't mean it," said Luciano Venier with calm decision. " 'Tis but the stress of putting together your army for war. You will soon come to your senses."

"I am well in my senses. I have just decided that I cannot, in good conscience, marry your daughter. It would not be fair to her. It certainly would not be fair to me."

"How can you speak of fairness in marriage?" Luciano queried. He made a motion with his jeweled hand that took in the wonders of the room in which they sat. He congratulated himself on having chosen such a haven of polished silver and tapestry work and bright frescoes for the meeting with his prospective son-in-law. "What you see around you is what matters. In the end it—and, of course, power—are the only things that count."

"So I once thought, myself," Olivier said. "However, my mother doesn't agree with me, and neither does my sister. Neither did you yourself, at least at one time. You married for love."

"Ah, so you think yourself in love with another?"

Too late, Olivier realized his mistake. He did not want thi conversation pulled into the future. He needed to keep thei talk converged on the present proposition of the imminen dissolution of his betrothal to Domiziana. He needed to accom plish this quickly and with as little harm as possible. But h needed to accomplish it.

"The Lady Domiziana is a fine lady and, indeed, one of th most accomplished women I have ever met. However, the plan of our final engagement had not yet been finalized when yo made the formal announcement. You know that as well as I There was still time for discussing, and coming to terms. Noth ing had been truly decided."

"Yet you did not contradict me," shot back the outrage father. "You did not say out loud what you held in your heart Or did you hold it—or should I say *her*—in your heart tha time?"

"I realize my culpability in this. I always had some doubt about this marriage. I should have spoken them earlier."

"Indeed you should have, but that would have jeopardize your standing here in this city. It would have put at risk you chance to be acclaimed the Lion of Venice. You knew the Lad Domiziana to be the Doge's niece. You saw her as a mean towards your own advancement and power. She was only a instrument to use in the attainment of your overriding ambi tion."

Olivier did not shirk from his own guilt, but he was no fool He knew Domiziana's history. He had heard of the conven threats.

"The Lady Domiziana does not love me," he said. "I know this, even if she does not. It is fear that brought her to me. Sh can barely stand my touch."

"Ah, so you've bedded my fair daughter." To Olivier' surprise, Luciano threw back his head and laughed. "She is cold one, that's a known certainty. Froze out two husband before you came along."

"The Lady Domiziana does not love me," repeated Olivier. "I did not know that before. I know it now."

"Why, because you have found true happiness within the arms of your young ward? Don't you think that a bit much? The Count of all the Ducci Montaldo could do better, I think, than to ally himself with a witch."

A muscle began its work in the corner of Olivier's rigid jaw. He had brought this all upon himself. He should have known from the first time he kissed Julian that it was no use to hang onto the dream of his life that Domiziana represented. Now he both deserved and could endure a few harsh recriminations. He would do his best in this crusade and then be free again to finally begin his life.

It did not matter what Luciano Venier might say to him. Especially about Julian. She was no witch.

"You think it will be simple, don't you?" said Luciano, as though he had been reading Olivier's thoughts. "You have used me and you have used my connections to further your plans, until now you think we are no longer needed and you can leave us and go on as you wish."

Olivier shook his head. "It was not like that and you are aware of this. I had my commission in Venice long before I made your acquaintance or that of your daughter. I thought the Lady Domiziana and I would do well together. This crusade, this coming to Venice, has changed all that."

He stopped. It was useless to try to force Luciano Venier to understand something which he was having great difficulty in understanding himself.

"I am sure the Lady Domiziana, as beautiful and talented as she is, will have no trouble in finding another betrothed." He paused over his next words. "I am prepared to pay generously in order to ensure that this is so."

Luciano sat silently for a moment, his head resting well down on the front of his elaborate tunic. Outside, a bird, a harbinger of spring and the passing of Lent, trilled noisily for a second and then stopped.

"Generously?" he repeated.

"I have no desire to see the Lady Domiziana convented," said Olivier. "There must never be a question of that. She is a fine woman. She should be free to take a husband of her choosing."

"You have a proposal to make?"

"It is you who should propose, Count Luciano. I owe you much, and I am not insensitive to the debt. Tell me what it is that you require of me. Allow me to put some right into what I have done wrong."

"What I propose," said Luciano slowly, "is that you leave the situation to stand as it is; that you carry on as though still engaged to my daughter, at least for the little time that remains to you before the crusade."

Olivier opened his mouth to protest, but Luciano moved relentlessly onward. He would not allow himself to be stopped.

"It is better for you this way, as well. You are thought to be allied with my family, one of the greatest of the oligarchy. If certain people—take, for example, the ruling Council of Ten—were to suspect that this affiliation might be in danger, perhaps they would be less willing to provide sufficient funds for the good maintenance of your men."

"We fight Venice's fight," said Olivier shortly.

"Indeed," replied Luciano. "However, Venice is a fickle mistress. There are other means for her to obtain the good she wants. She might take it into her mind to discover these means at a most inopportune time. You must think of your responsibilities. You must think of your men. You would not want your own personal inclinations to jeopardize your mission."

Olivier shook his head. He did not want that.

"Then take my word that this is the best solution." Luciano even managed a smile. "And in exchange for your indulgence in this matter, I will take it upon myself to explain matters to my daughter, and to my wife."

"I would prefer to talk to Domiziana myself," Olivier replied. "We are both adults, and this is a matter best settled between us. I only spoke to you first because you are her father, the head of her house. It is my duty to personally make my wishes known to her, and I intend to do so.''

"As you wish. As you wish. I only thought you might want to avoid the unpleasantness.''

"It is unpleasantness that I myself have caused. I will, of course, be leaving the Cá Venier. Other arrangements will also be made for my ward. Probably I will send her on to my sister at Harnoncourt Hall.''

"You may do as you wish. One can understand your desire to spend time with your army, but I suggest you leave the Lady Julian where she is.''

Olivier cocked a questioning eyebrow.

"Just so,'' said Luciano. "It is natural that you should be with your army. It is not natural that your ward should leave us as well. This may create talk and Venice is a gossiping city. You would not want anyone hurt by what people say.''

Something deep within Olivier did not like the subterfuge in all he was hearing. He had wanted to break the news to Luciano. He had wanted then to talk to Domiziana and have it done with her. He realized now that he had been naïve. He had expected threats and insults and recriminations—and he still might get these from his betrothed, but he doubted it. Luciano would talk to his daughter first. If there was bullying to be done, Count Venier would be the one to do it.

"Domiziana will be compensated for this,'' he said. "And compensated handsomely.''

Luciano nodded. He was still nodding as the door closed behind Olivier's retreating form.

Indeed, thought her indulgent father, Domiziana will be compensated. This whelp of the Ducci Montaldo has no idea the price he will pay.

"Julian, you have lost your mind,'' whispered a horrified Ginevra. She had come to her friend's chamber to talk about the Knight de la Marche, a topic of which she never seemed to tire, but now her eyes were round with incredulity and consternation. "You could never accompany the army. Only bad women and prostitutes do."

"I am not a prostitute nor am I what you might call a bad woman. This makes no difference. I am going to Nicopolis anyway."

Ginevra was so agitated that she stuck herself with her needle. A drop of blood fell to mar the white purity of her linen work. "The Count would lock you up in a minute if he heard this. And it would be more than right of him to do so. It is absolutely selfish of you, Julian—and truly not like you at all—to think of adding to his worries at this moment. Why, even my sister Domiziana, who is the most selfish person in all of Christendom, has agreed that they should put off their marriage until his return. If even she is willing to think of his welfare, I cannot imagine how you could do less. Forgive me, but this is true. Why, in three days' time he will be off to join forces with King Sigismund of Hungary and the armies of the French at Buda."

Julian knew this already and, indeed, she knew much more of it than the Maid Ginevra possibly could. Though he had left the Cá Venier, Olivier continued to call her to the Veneto when he had need of her translating. He always made sure that she was escorted to him by his soldiers and by nuns from the convent of St. Dominic. He always made sure she was returned to Venice before nightfall. Since the night of Carnivale, Julian had noticed, he had gone to great pains to make sure that they were never alone together.

Gradually, she had grown frightened of his aloofness. She could attribute it to only one reason—that his plans no longer included a care for her mother.

"It is not the Count of the Ducci Montaldo or even the King of Hungary who will lead this crusade. The Count of Nevers has been chosen to march at its head." Julian held her voice neutral. She did not want to worry Ginevra with this information, though she worried about it herself.

"Is the Count a great warrior? Is he as legendary as the Knight de la Marche?" Ginevra's eyes were bright with excitement. She had momentarily forgotten Julian's shocking news.

And Julian did not want to remind her of it. Nor did she want to take away her excitement. She did hesitate an instant before she said, "John of Nevers is young. He was given this command because he is son and heir of the Duke of Burgundy, uncle to the King of France. He was given the command for reasons of protocol. There will be many to help him," she hastily added. "The Comte d'Eu, Sir Philippe de Mézières, the Sire de Coucy, the Knights de Bar and de Boucicaut. Not to mention the Knight de la Marche and the Count of the Ducci Montaldo."

Julian smiled and after a second Ginevra smiled as well.

"You must not think of going," the maiden insisted. "You must stay away until Count Olivier gives his permission for you to return—though I doubt he ever will. But Julian, I want you to tell me what it was like to live at Nicopolis. Tell me about the people and the Sultan Bayezid. My mother says that all the eastern people are infidels or heathens and thus bound for hell, but I've never believed it. I know there must be beauty and good people there as well. And the Knight de la Marche thinks as I do. He told me so himself. He said he made friends and found people to admire even when he was imprisoned at Mahdia." She looked shyly down at her needlework but her hands were still. "Tell me about it, Julian. Tell me about Nicopolis. There must have been something that you loved here."

There must have been something you loved there.

"I loved my mother," Julian began slowly. "I loved the smell of her rose perfume. The Castle of Nicopolis, where we lived, juts out over the Danube and over a plain. Beyond the Balkan Mountains there are roses—valleys and valleys of roses. My mother distilled them down to their essence to make her perfume. She said the Sultan once told her that he could tell she was on the way to him by the scent of roses that fell upon the air."

Julian paused. Her smile was sweet and soft.

"And the Sultan himself?" Ginevra prompted.

"I've heard bad things about him," said Julian. "But he was always kind to me. He was always kind to my mother. He gave her a home and protection when only the stake awaited her in her native land. I cannot remember his palace. I was too young, too unaware, when we passed through before we settled at Nicopolis. They say it is mightily luxurious. What I do remember is that he had a sweetmeat for me always, or a spiced fig. He had them carried by his servants and he would have them give some to me. I had lived with my mother in a cell in Lyon. No one thought to give me anything agreeable there. My memory of the Sultan is of a benevolent man."

"Lord Olivier thinks him highly intelligent," Ginevra whispered. What she said could only be whispered, especially by a young girl in a country intent on Holy War. "He thinks the French underestimate the Sultan's intelligence. I heard him say so to the Doge himself, just the other day. He thinks we will find the Ottoman well equipped to defend what they have taken."

"Indeed they will be," agreed Julian. She, too, had been listening in places where she shouldn't have. And more, she had lived for years under the Ottoman Turks and had grown to know them well.

"The Knight de la Marche says nothing against the duke," Ginevra continued. "Indeed, Burgundy is his liege lord, which means that loyalty is due his son, the Count of Nevers, as well. He does sometimes seem a bit disheartened, though he tries to hide it. Especially from me. Unfortunately, he still thinks of me as a child."

"I wonder why?" teased Julian

Her friend chose to ignore this. "I heard him tell Lord Olivier that the French are overconfident in this battle."

"They might well lose it. Which is why I must find a way to go there and see to my mother."

Ginevra shrugged. "The Count will never let you go—you must accept this fact and make up your mind to it. No one defies the Lord of the Ducci Montaldo," she said mildly but with extreme common sense. "I don't understand why you think you must go as well. The Count is perfectly capable of bringing back your mother. He has given you his promise, his word as a knight."

"She is my mother," insisted Julian. "She is the only family I have."

Ginevra looked at her curiously. The Maid of the Venier had Domiziana's gray eyes, but what was silver on one sister was warmed pewter on the other. Julian knew that if anyone could understand her, it would be Ginevra.

"Yes, I would be that way, too," the girl said. "At least about my mother. I would want more than anything to free her, to bring her back among her own kind. How terrible it must have been for you—must *be* for you—not to know if she is alive or dead. And she must miss you as well. Surely she will come back with the Count if only she is given the chance."

For an instant, Julian wanted to blurt out everything to her friend, to tell someone the truth. That far from hating the East and the life she lived there, Aalyne had loved it. She had chosen it and held onto it when other roads opened, and she would probably not want to leave it now. Yet she must. And she must be forced to see this. Olivier, for all his might and all his power, was still a man. He might not be able to persuade a woman who knew as much about the Power as Aalyne did.

How could she explain anything like this to Ginevra, with her clear eyes and her brow untroubled by any of life's hard choices? Julian opened her mouth, and then shut it again. Something told her that in the end Ginevra would help her, would understand and supply the things she needed, but now was not the time to press her. And besides, Ginevra was already talking of something else.

". . . The witch she brought with her from the village of Sant'Urbano," she said. "The two of them are always together. They *concoct* things together, though naturally I am not supposed to know this. Domiziana thinks no one knows. She is pretending to be newly taken with the healing arts. She says she wants to share the Lady Francesca's interest in this. The Lady Francesca is known to be a great healer—as are you. Domiziana's curiosity has nothing to do with good. 'Tis witchcraft that she practices. She wants her way with someone. She wants to use a witch's fancy."

"There is no such thing as witch's fancy," Julian said, just a little too quickly.

Ginevra arched a pretty eyebrow. "My sister has a strong will and a ready eye for her own best interests. And if she thinks the witch will get her what she wants, she will be bound to use her."

"She *thinks* the witch helps her and this is what gives Elisabetta the strength. The rest is superstition. It is only what you sister thinks that matters," said Julian. She did not at all like the direction that this conversation was taking. She did not want to talk witchcraft with a maiden as young and chaste as Ginevra. Her own youth and chastity had been sullied by it. She did not want this to happen to anyone else.

Ginevra's interest was not so easily put aside. "Domiziana knows what she wants, or rather who she wants, and she works to have him. Something has happened in her life lately—something important that neither she nor my parents have seen fit to share with me. But she is still determined to see to her own interests and to better whatever it is she perceives as an obstacle. You might take a lesson from her yourself."

Julian had long hated herself for being so envious of Domiziana Venier. She envied Domiziana's cool composure and the comforting cluster of her family. She envied her silvery good looks and her fixed place and position in the world. Above all, she envied the fact that Domiziana was very soon to marry the man whom Julian herself loved. But one thing Julian did not envy was Domiziana's entanglement with the witch Elisabetta. She had been involved with witchcraft all her life. She knew where it could lead.

"She is only enamoured of the Strega Elisabetta. It will pass," Julian assured her friend.

"She is not at all enamoured of Elisabetta," returned Ginevra gravely. "However, she is perfectly besotted with someone else. And Elisabetta has promised him to her. Domiziana's witching ways have turned on her and she finds herself in heat for a man who no longer seems to know she exists."

"He will marry her," said Julian. "The Count is pledged to her. He loves her."

Ginevra shrugged. "He seemed to once, if only tepidly, but that time is many months past. She is desperate for him now and Elisabetta is not above feeding her need. And why should she not? The bed is soft, the food plentiful. She seems perfectly capable of seeing a queenship for Domiziana, if this would guarantee a continuance of these things. I've heard you ruined life for her at Belvedere."

"I meant her no harm. The child was dying and her herbs could not cure him. He needed fresh air and something to make him breathe clearly. I used a simple combination of rosewood and pine. Elisabetta was not doing this. The child had no need of witchcraft. Neither does your sister."

"Oh, but she thinks she does. Domiziana has always been barren and Elisabetta sees children for her, and she had convinced my sister that she will indeed bear children. The cards have told her that the bad times are over and that there will be only happiness ahead."

"Sometimes the cards lie," whispered the Magdalene's daughter.

She slept, and as she did, firelight played against her closed eyelids. She felt hands on her shoulders grabbing her from the dream into wakefulness—or perhaps into another level of the dream. She didn't want to leave the peaceful valley of her sleep for what she knew awaited her when her eyes were finally opened.

"Wake, Julian. Come along now."

She shook her head against the waking and pretended to sleep on.

"Pick her up. Carry her." She recognized Aalyne's voice. Julian opened her eyes then, delirious with joy.

"Mama," she cried, and held out her arms to her mother. Aalyne reached over and ruffled her hair. The Magdalene's own hair caught the firelight and shed gold all around her face. Julian was aware of the flames and she could hear screams in the distance and curses. But Aalyne was laughing. She had thrown back her glorious head with the force of her mirth. Julian had never seen her look so beautiful. Once again she reached out her hand.

She could not quite reach her mother. The man was in the way and for the first time, Julian turned to him. She could not see him clearly because his face was shrouded within the folds of his black cape. His walk was slow and he limped. She recognized his gait. He smelled of lightning. Julian recognized this scent as well. None of this seemed to matter to the beautiful Aalyne; not to the Magdalene, the famous witch of the Knights Templar.

"Freedom," she said as she kissed the shrouded man gleefully upon his mouth. They walked out of the prison together. Julian looked back as behind them the screams died and the fire glowed bright upon the horizon. Ahead of them was the sea.

The man was talking quickly. "Go to this place once you have arrived and all will be settled. Take the child. Care for her well. She is our future."

He removed his cloak and smiled down at Julian. His silver eyes gleamed.

"There will be no wedding," he whispered.

* * *

"There will be no wedding," the Lord of the Ducci Montaldo said to the courtiers who had collected around him in the great gathering hall of the Cá Venier. "There is a flux plague in Venice. The Doge himself is sick with it. We cannot hold the festivities of marriage now. We will do that when we come back from this crusade—there will be time then and reason to celebrate."

His voice sounded convincing and there was a murmur of approval from the people gathered around him. The men nodded wisely—few of these Venetians would be going themselves to fight the war—and the women clustered around the Lady Domiziana. Their lips clucked sympathetic words but their eyes told a different story. Could it be that the Lady Domiziana was to lose another husband—and this one through abandonment and not through death?

"It is best this way," Olivier said. "It would be too much of an affront to the Doge to think of even a private marriage when the city itself faces so much. We must put off our personal happiness for the interests of the Venice that we serve."

Indeed, even the Countess Venier was said to be highly indisposed. She was not present at this announcement, but Domiziana was. She sat beside Olivier, dressed splendidly, the serenity of her face unmarred. Her eyes impassive as they stared at Julian Madrigal.

CHAPTER NINETEEN

Julian had known that the sickness ravaged the city. Gatien had been the first to tell her of it. He said that it was not the first time he had seen this particular illness. He called it one of the plagues of war.

"Come and I will show you a case of it. Perhaps you can help."

Julian did not particularly want to help. She liked the work she was doing for Olivier. She liked the pristine propriety of his presence and the careful way he had of including her. She no longer felt herself an outcast, with no place and no home and of no use. His actions told her that she was a benefit to him.

And he did not touch her. Though part of her longed for his touch, another part knew that she should not want to be wanted by a man who was promised to another. She could trust him; she could trust men. She was learning that. Julian liked this new feeling. It was so different from what she had been taught as a child. It felt safer. She thought she could continue in this feeling of safety as long as she did no healing work, as long as she did not touch her Power.

And so she did not want to accompany the Knight de la Marche on his visit to the sick. In the end she went only because he insisted.

"You must see this patient," he said, looking down into her dark eyes with his clear, light ones. "He is one of my men. I know his family well. He is asking for a healer because he knows the time for our leaving grows near. He has not yet earned his golden spurs and is determined to have them at Holy War."

How could she say no?

Julian gathered some of her medicinal herbs and placed them in a flax basket. She sent word to Gatien that she would be ready by the morning nones bell and she was. When he arrived, she put on a new light blue cloak—it had grown too warm for her fur-lined one—and set off with the Burgundian. The sky was bright above them; even the streets of serene Venice bustled in the sun. As usual, her mind was on other things and she did not take his arm.

He led her to the small convent of St. Clare.

There seemed to be no hesitation about admitting the Knight de la Marche. The young novice who answered the door welcomed him quietly but eagerly in French. She led the two of them through winding halls.

The young squire was sitting up in his bed, talking to a woman swathed in white. Julian thought she might have seen the boy before; he looked somewhat familiar, but she had never seen the woman. She recognized from the heavy gold cross at her breast that she must be the abbess of this place. This was odd, because she was still a young woman. Not more than twenty, Julian guessed, but clearly well educated and an aristocrat.

She looked at them without smiling, her clear gaze taking them in. From habit, Julian walked towards the woman and went to kneel before the crucifix she wore but the woman offered her hand instead.

"Do not kneel," she said. "We are not a place that stands on ceremony, but even if we were, it is I who should make reverence to you. You have come to help my brother."

The abbess, too, spoke in French but with the rhythmic accent of Burgundy. There was no welcome in her voice and none in her eyes. She motioned towards the man on the bed.

Julian was surprised at how young he was. His beard lay as soft as peach fuzz on his waxen cheeks, and she could tell that once he'd gained his weight again it would come back as more baby fat than man-muscle. He still had a child's body. His short brown hair, damp from the sweat of his fever, curled in ringlets around his forehead. There were spots of bright color upon his face.

"I am well," he said, struggling up in his bed. "Or I would be if my sister would but let me out of this woman's place so I could join my comrades. Our ship sails from Venice in three days' time."

"You don't look well," Julian said mildly enough. Instinct told her there was something not quite right with this illness, something not quite natural to it.

"If you miss this there will be other opportunities to win your golden spurs," said his sister. "There will always be plenty and plenty of wars. Have we not already lost three of our brothers to battle?" The nun turned her level gaze upon Julian. "It was hard enough for our mother to give her permission for this, her last son, to go on Holy Crusade. She would not have done so had not the Duke of Burgundy himself pleaded the case. He is—was—our father's liege lord. Our castle is near his fortress at Dijon. We are—were—the warrior family de Croyant."

"What do you mean 'were'?" demanded this youngest Croyant. "I am the last of my family, but I will start it again. I spent my paging days under the great duke himself. He took me with him to Paris when his son wed, and now that same son, the Count of Nevers, commands the French troops who will march against the infidel. Tell her this is so, Sir Gatien.''

'' 'Tis so,'' de la Marche agreed, putting a restraining hand on Croyant's thin shoulder. "Yet the Count of Nevers, for all his noble lineage, is still a squire, just as you are. He will hardly be the real leader of this crusade. That role will fall to other older and more experienced allies of his father, such as the Sire de Coucy. Your sister is right when she says that you must not take it amiss if you are forced to forgo this crusade. There will be others.''

"Nevers and I are to be knighted together on the field of our first bloodletting," insisted Croyant with the hard obstinacy of fever. "I was always told it would be so.''

"The Duke of Burgundy has other sons," insisted his sister with just as much firmness. "You are the only one remaining to your mother.''

Croyant's brown eyes gazed out at her, ready for battle. It was obvious that he had heard this reasoning before. "What has that to do with anything? The Croyants are directly related to the kings of France, be they the old Capetians or the present Valois. We have spilled blood on every French battlefield for centuries, since the Battle of Roncevalles.''

'' 'Tis not the spilling that is important, but what is obtained for it," replied his sister. The lines around her mouth had grown set and white. She had aged ten years in ten minutes. "Your blood may have more use for France remaining in your veins and not spilled for a useless battle that is meant only to fatten merchants' pockets and keep a silly king in Hungary upon his throne.''

"There is no better place for my blood to be spilled than in service to my King and to the Church of Christ," answered Croyant. The voices of the brother and his sister had risen. "Tell her that, Sir Gatien. You were knighted when you had few years more than I have now. And your father was before you. You come from a family of legends. Tell my sister the responsibility that my name brings.''

"What is your name?" interjected Julian quietly.

"Croyant." The boy did not even glance in her direction. He was still glaring at his sister. "I've said it here more than once."

"I mean your Christian name. The name your mother gave you as a babe."

"Michel," he said. This time he did turn towards Julian. "Why?"

"Because I will need to know your name if I am to treat you. You want to stay well, do you not? You want to live a long life?"

Exactly," agreed the abbess. She deftly plucked a bottle from the nearest trestle and moved it smoothly beneath the voluminous folds of her habit. "Though 'tis a moot point. You are too ill to go on this crusade and that is that. At least there will be a compromise. The Lady Julian Madrigal is known to be a Wise Woman. The Knight de la Marche has brought it to my attention that she worked miraculously well in effecting the healing of a young child in the Ducci Montaldo village of Sant'Urbano. I'm sure she will be useful in keeping you alive." The woman glanced deliberately at Julian and then pulled the small glass bottle from beneath her robes.

"But first take this, my little brother" said the abbess. "It will make you well."

Julian gazed at her and then nodded in agreement. "It will keep you whole."

"What do you carry in that bag, Julian?"

She felt the comforting weight of her new acquisition as they left the small gray building. She could not tell its secret to Gatien. She had determined that only the abbess should know it. The young woman had been almost pathetically grateful that the Magdalene's daughter had not revealed her subterfuge to young Michel. She had complied without question to Julian's strange request.

Now it was important that the Knight de la Marche not question her, either.

"She is sedating him," Julian said, adroitly changing the subject as they walked once again through the narrow streets of Venice. A barge waited to take them across the canal. The simple gates of the convent slammed shut behind them as a bell started tolling the midday prayer. "Of course you must have already known that."

"I suspected it," Gatien corrected. His guard fell in step behind them. This time, as they walked, Julian automatically tucked her arm through his. "But I wanted your opinion."

Something womanly in Julian suspected that he might have wanted to see her alone again as well, but this was a thought she chose not to pursue. "And now that you have it, what are you going to do?"

He smiled at her, and she was amazed once again at how readily the whole of his face seemed to curve into that smile. It did not amaze her that Ginevra Venier was so totally and completely in love with this man. What truly amazed her was that she, Julian, was not.

But she wasn't. And she knew she never would be. The simple, good life of marriage that Gatien offered could never be hers.

"What would you suggest I do?" he asked.

"Leave him here in the care of his sister. Make out that you think him seriously ill. This war against the Sultan is useless. I think this—but Michel's sister does as well. She protests furiously for this 'War of Conversion,' as she calls it, but at the same time she doses her brother with aloes. This is a most dangerous drug, and she obviously is intelligent enough to know this. It is still rather unknown here in Europe but was widely used in the East, and the Lady Francesca had a precious store of it upon her shelves. It is a mark of both the abbess's devotion to her brother and her desperation that she is using a poison to keep him from this war."

"Do you blame her?"

Julian quickly shook her head. "How can I blame her? You heard de Croyant's story—you know it yourself. All of his brothers dead. He the only one left alive. What surprises me is that you would aid the abbess in this. If you confronted her with the truth—a truth you obviously knew well before you involved me in this—she would have had to put an end to her feint. Did you not always tell me that warring was your family enterprise and thus a Burgundian one as well? Is it not then something for which this boy should be allowed to sacrifice himself?"

Her voice was rising. She could feel agitation in the air around her. She was growing deathly scared of this war.

There was no longer even the clue of a smile at Gatien's lips. "Did not Michel de Croyant remind you of someone?"

"No," said Julian. Then for a second the young squire's eager face rose up straight before her eyes. She saw its soft, almost feminine, eagerness. She saw curled brown hair and eager eyes. Yes, there was something vaguely familiar about him, something that was only coming to her now.

"He reminds me of you," she said finally. "He reminds me of Olivier. He reminds me of Assen the Janizary. He reminds me of each and every one of you who have been doomed, since time began, to fight in some silly, stupid war."

Her fingers tightened around her precious bundle.

CHAPTER TWENTY

Before coming to Venice, Julian had rarely seen her own face. Even in the grand castles and palaces where she had lived, mirrors were rare and the ones that existed were small pieces of glass with silver backing. In them one could see one's eyes or the curl of one's hair, but never both of these things together.

One could see oneself reflected in stream or pond water as well and once she had even chanced upon her face smiling back at her in a sheet of ice at Harnoncourt Hall. At first she had not recognized herself, and thought she gazed upon a wood nymph who had fallen into the ice and been captured in it. It was natural for Julian to think this way. The whole of her life had been built on myths and legends. The one thing that these images held in common was their waving shifts. It sometimes almost seemed to Julian that the more she tried to see just what she looked like, the less she actually succeeded.

Today it was most important that she know exactly how she looked—because she was able to become someone else.

She lifted her hand, hesitated, and then heard the thump of the heavy iron scissors as the two blades met through her hair.

The first cuts seemed to bob very slowly on the air before falling to lie among the stone floor's fresh thyme. It was heavy enough to stir the herb and filled the chamber with fragrance. Julian paused again and stared down. She had never known how much she reveled in the luxury of her hair until now when she was resolved to lose it. She indulged in two tears—she couldn't help herself—and then turned quickly back to her task. Ginevra could come in at any time. And Ginevra would feel it her duty to stop her.

Julian could not see what the outcome of this day would bring her, and for this small grace she was truly grateful. There were so many things that might go wrong, that were out of her control. The abbess might not manage to keep her brother drugged. Julian might not be able to locate Michel de Croyant's appointed place within the Black Fleet. There might be many Burgundians about who had known him. An endless number of things that could go awry with what she was doing. And yet when Julian sat still, when she listened and let the Power work through her, she felt no fear. She was doing what she should be doing and she knew it. The Power told her so.

"No lady would join the entourage of an army," Ginevra had whispered, horrified. But Julian Madrigal was no lady. She was a witch.

And a witch could do what she wanted.

"'Tis horrible that you should be taken sick on such an important day." Ginevra's eyes were filled with true consternation as she stared down into her friend's white face. "The French pope has sent his legate down from Avignon, and the Roman pope has, of course, his own nuncio here. They are both, together, to bless the fleet's sailing. Venice, of course, keeps both sides in this papal schism. As she, indeed, keeps to both sides in most controversies. Anything else would be bad for trade. The different parts of the city have gathered and there will be festivities and dancing to send the Gold Company and the Black Fleet upon their way. Are you certain you are too ill to join us?''

Julian nodded painfully. ''It is my ill luck to be abed on such an important occasion. I had so wanted to go to the Lido, to be part of the blessing of the ships and the soldiers. Instead I will lie in my bed and pray them safely on their way.''

Ginevra clucked sympathetically. ''You are so good,'' she said. She reached to tuck the linen blanket closer around her friend's neck. She also moved to adjust the white sick-wimple that covered Julian's hair, but Julian moved just a little and thus shifted out of her reach.

''It is kind of you to want to stay with me,'' she said, ''but I think you should be on your way. The Doge will want the whole of his family surrounding him on this great day.''

They could hear the sound of festivities echoing from St. Mark's Piazza, where the procession would be. Ginevra had told her there were minstrels from as far away as France, and dancing bears and jugglers. She was going to have her fortune told by a woman who had come all the way from beyond the Balkan Mountains. The woman, a witch for sure, wore impossibly bright colors and was a flash of silver rings and hoop earrings. She had had the audacity to set up her blue flax tent right before the Cathedral door itself. Ginevra was hoping for good news about the Knight de la Marche, she had told Julian, but she was doubtful she would get it.

She laughed. ''Our uncle is not known for great affection,'' she said wryly. ''He will be present because it is his duty and he is a man sternly attached to his duty. My cousin Cosimo, the one for whom the Dogeressa is in constant mourning and prayer, was his son. And he was a good son as well, if perhaps a trifle high-spirited. He did something once—they wouldn't tell me what, I was too young; they only whispered about it amongst themselves when they thought I wasn't paying attention—and he was sent across the Bridge of Sighs and into the prison. There he caught the plague, but it was a light case and there was strong hope of a cure. The Dogeressa pleaded for

her son. She did not ask much, knowing the natural hardness
of her husband. She wanted her son freed just long enough so
that a cure could be effected. However, *Zio* Antonio is both a
stern and proud man. Ours is one of the oldest families in the
Republic, he says, and we must set an example to all the other
folk of Venice. We of the lagoons sit upon no firm foundations,
he constantly intones; therefore, we must construct them within
ourselves. He would not bend to commute his son's sentence
by even a few days, though of course he had the power to do
so. Three days before he would naturally have been set free,
my cousin Cosimo was once again carried across the Bridge
of Sighs—though, of course, this time he was dead.''

It was a horrible story, but Julian knew it to be true. For all
of its play and frivolity, a hard man ruled Venice. And he was
a man who had already shown himself to be hardest of all upon
his own privileged family.

Once Ginevra had left, Julian reached beneath the draperies
of her bed and pulled out the packet that contained Michel de
Croyant's splendid squire's uniform. He was to wear the red
and green of Burgundy and not the colors of the Knight de la
Marche, nor the Lilies of France. The duke, with the aid of a
heavy burden of taxation upon his peasants, had managed a
splendid showing for the nobles who would represent his house
in this, the greatest of all the crusades.

The abbess had given Julian one of her brother's gold-
trimmed silk habards and one of his tunics. She had done this
without asking why they were needed. The abbess had smiled
as she calmly handed over the clothing. She seemed happy to
be rid of them.

Julian dressed quickly and ran through the deserted Cá Venier. Once outside, she could hear sounds of a trumpet and
shouting and she realized that the procession would soon begin.
She would have to hurry. Her shorn scalp tingled, almost painfully so, and she ran a quick hand through the short curl of her

hair. She could feel the tears at her eyes, but they did not
surprise her.

See to it yourself, Assen had told her.

Deep within, Julian knew he was right. Aalyne was her
responsibility. And life had always taught the Magdalene's
daughter that she could trust no one else. Or rather, life had
taught her that until recently.

But, though she loved Olivier, she didn't quite trust him. He
was a man and men could not be depended upon, especially
when they had pledged a woman their solemn word. Julian had
learned this lesson well. No, better to do as she had always
done. Better to rely only upon herself. Better—much better—
to bury her love for Olivier forever and get on with the living
of her own life.

The Lion of Venice, the Venetians called him. She could
hear them crying it now as she ran through the deserted streets
of their city. The morning was cold and damp, as forbidding
as the day that had first marked her impression of Venice. Even
the huddles of pigeons added their grayness to the general
gloom. Rain threatened. Julian kept close to the slick stones
of the inner building, away from the lagoons and the festivities
that fronted them. At least for now. She caught whiffs of incense
from the masses that had been chanted throughout the islands
for the blessing of the fleet and its warriors. Julian stayed
carefully away from crowds. She knew that if she were caught,
she could be sent immediately back to Harnoncourt Hall. There
would be no quarter for her. She had no illusions that Domiziana
would allow her to stay in Venice—and it would be Domiziana
who would be in charge of her once Olivier was gone.

Julian bit her lower lip. She edged closer to the gray wall,
and she waited.

A bright robin stared back at her, his head cocked thoughtfully to one side as he clung to the branch of an espaliered
tree.

"I won't tell your secret," he seemed to say.

The Magdalene's daughter nodded her thanks.

Suddenly even the bells ceased their somber ringing. The continuous trumpeting of paper horns grew silent as well. She ran to the far corner of St. Mark's, then stopped to look around. All of Venice seemed crowded into the piazza that fronted their great Cathedral. The women had dressed in sober black or white and the men also wore the deep colors that tradition and probity demanded on such a solemn occasion. They milled about silently, waiting for the nuncio and the papal legate to emerge simultaneously from the Cathedral. Julian heard the sound of monks chanting and the Latin supplications for the success of an endeavor that everyone was already assured would be a grand success.

All about the piazza, boys too young to be thinking of killing held aloft the banners of their liege lords. As Julian watched, priests began sprinkling the crowd with olive branches that had been dipped in the coolness of holy water. The banners of the various city guilds and the colors of the Ducci Montaldo, the Gold Company, and the bright banners of de la Marche were held high.

Gatien's were the flags that she needed; Michel de Croyant was in his service and so the de la Marche colors would lead her to the right ship within the moorings of Venice's famous Black Fleet.

Once there, she found it surprisingly easy to squirm into the duke's ranks. She wore his colors and, with her hair cropped short, she knew she looked like one of the younger squires. There would be no need for these boys to present themselves to their knights until the fleet was well underway.

The smell of incense and of the sea itself was overpowering. Julian knew that this was a fragrance she would remember forever—just as she remembered the smell of roses past their prime which reminded her of her mother, the sweetness of lavender that was Francesca, and the male scent of cleanliness and fine leather and hard fighting that instantly evoked Olivier. She smiled now as she always did when she thought of him and perhaps it was this secret smile that conjured him. The crowd shifted; Julian was jostled to one side. And there, suddenly, was Olivier standing not more than twenty feet away. His extraordinary eyes seemed to be staring into her.

For a heartbeat, Julian was certain he had seen her, that he knew she was near. She held her breath. She stood perfectly still, only taking time to bow her head slowly. Her dark eyes were lowered and her heart was pounding. She was certain that she would soon be called upon to give a speedy and convincing explanation for her strange hair and her even stranger dress. Her mind started to whirl though various rationales.

When she had the courage to look again, she saw that his head was bent in deep conversation with the Knight de la Marche. He was frowning. Julian could see his mouth and the occasional flash of his perfect teeth. She sighed with relief. In a moment he had turned towards the approaching procession and her own way ahead had cleared as well.

"Dominus vobiscum."

All eyes turned towards the papal legate as he began the solemn intonation of his prayers. Julian eased forward, closer to the ship. Her hands were white against the deep red velvet of her cape and her short hair caught the wind.

Something teased the corner of her vision. Julian stopped, for a second, to stare. A little ship was moored at a far corner of the quay and slyly hidden from the inquisitive gaze of the Legate, the Nuncio, and the good women of Venice. Its cargo had obviously been boarded early and told to stay hidden as well. But obviously the cargo did not want to stay hidden. Parts of it had already drifted back onto the deck.

"What is in that ship?" Julian asked the man who stood in front of her on the wharf. He wore neither the colors of the Gold Company nor those of the Duke of Burgundy. Amulets, charms, and good luck fetishes hung from his neck and his clothing. They bounced against the fat of his chest as he turned her way.

"The women, of course," he said irritably. He spoke with the short, hard vowels of Venice. "Who do you think they are, soldiers? Not even a Frenchman would dress so outrageously. Now move along smartly. You are blocking the legate from seeing me, and I have need of his blessing.''

Julian apologized, nodded, but all the time her eyes were on the little ship. She saw the women moving about on it—at first only one or two, the boldest ones. But gradually more emerged. She wondered how one little vessel could hold so many.

The women. She remembered what Ginevra had said about the type of females who followed the fighting.

They, too, had probably been told not to draw attention to themselves, at least not as long as the legate and the nuncio were near. Yet like the others, they could not resist the temptation to witness the pomp and spectacle of such a solemn blessing. They wanted to be part of it as well. Julian stared at their hair, which had been dyed bright orange or yellow as the laws of Venice demanded. She stared at their dresses, which were striped in yellow or blue. Not one of them still wore her clothes inside out as a mark of her occupation, though Venetian law required this of the city's prostitutes. These women no longer cared for the rules that had previously bound them. They would soon be leaving fair Venice and its moral strictures far behind.

And they were joyous.

Despite her nervousness and her need for discretionary speed, Julian stared at them as they jostled their way to the front of their small ship. One woman whooped that she was truly willing to do her very utmost to see that the men of the Gold Company were kept jolly so that this crusade would be easily and quickly won. The others laughed and shouted back to her. In the past, they said, her utmost had been proven more than enough. Julian looked cautiously around and discovered that these were the only women about.

Except for herself.

Her heart hammered against her ribs so loudly that she was certain the quartermaster could hear it as she hurried over to him. But, like everyone else, his attention was fixed firmly beyond her. He kept his eyes firmly upon the papal legate. The soldier was breathing in the incense and crossing himself against the dark to come. Not that there was much of particular worry. The ships of the Black Fleet were not large. A fair wind and a few good days would see them to Buda. That much he knew. Beyond Buda? Well, they said that this would be an easy war, that the Sultan Bayezid would cower and weep before the might of France. Still, the quartermaster was no novice and neither was he a knight. He had seen his share of wars gone wrong, and he labored under no code of chivalry to keep him from talking of them.

"Name?" he said to the young man before him.

"Croyant. Michel de Croyant d'Eu de Boule," Julian answered. "I am page to Gatien de la Marche."

The voice was high, but then they took the pages young this day. The quartermaster was a good, chauvinistic Venetian. He suspected that anything might come out of France these days. He motioned the page forward and turned his attention back to the prelate and his prayers.

Julian took the precaution of keeping her head lowered as she asked for directions to Gatien's cabin. However, this was not really necessary and she knew it. No one had paid her the least attention since she'd come on board. Her red-and-green livery told the soldiers that she was one of them. These were the colors of the Duke of Burgundy and of his son, the Count of Nevers. She might seem young, but then again that small part of the Burgundian army that was sailing under the command of the Cavalier de la Marche had been recruited from throughout Europe. It was normal that a nobleman would want his son to learn of war under the patronage of a knight as illustrious as Sir Gatien, especially when there would be glory for the taking on the field against the Turk. Michel de Croyant d'Eu de Boule was obviously one of them, and they waved the young squire on.

Gatien's small space was quiet and dark and peaceful. Eve the chests that contained his shipboard necessities were ne and contained. There was a stool, a table with one large flas of wine upon it, and a bed.

Julian sat primly upon it to wait.

CHAPTER
TWENTY-ONE

Julian's eyes took in the three stern faces before her and knew that there would be no recourse but to fight. Olivier's face and the unsmiling one of Gatien de la Marche were bad enough. That Michel Croyant—the *real* Michel Croyant—should also be gazing at her would, under other circumstances, have forced her to swallow hard. Indeed, Julian *did* swallow hard, but only to force words through the blockage that suddenly seemed to be obscuring her throat.

" 'Tis my fault and mine alone. I forced the abbess to give me Michel's squiring clothes," she said.

"I am sure there was not much forcing in it," said Croyant. "My sister has proven herself a disgrace both to her holy calling and to the family name she bears."

He was both so young and so angry that his voice broke twice getting out these few words. What part Michel de Croyant had played in all of this and how he had managed to escape was something no one had as yet seen fit to tell her. In fact, since Gatien had come upon her, no one had seemed willing to talk to her at all. He had come late to his cabin. Both Venice

and daylight had been lost to sight by the time he discovere
Julian and took her to the Count. In the brief time she had bee
on the deck, she had sent a prayer to heaven and looked up t
see the promise of starlight and feel the caress of a breeze.

"My sister, the servant of God," Michel continued with col
irony, "was more than a willing abettor of this duplicity. Sh
may well have initiated it, just as she initiated my illness.
hope she will be speedily and fully punished by her bishop fo
this trickery."

"I am sure she is being punished more than sufficiently b
the knowledge that you are on this ship and no longer safel
in your bed." Julian's voice was mild.

"Whatever could she have been thinking of?" For an instan
there were tears in Michel's eyes. "We have always been s
close. I always thought I could trust her. Why would she wisl
to deprive me of the chance to earn my golden spurs?"

Julian opened her mouth to respond but Olivier motione
her to silence. He refused to stop looking at her and thus Julia
was forced to look at him as well, though God and all Hi
angels and saints knew she would much have preferred not t
do this She had never seen Olivier's eyes so coldly gree
before. If they had been glass shards they could have embedde
themselves in her soul.

"Thank you, Sir Gatien," he said, without releasing his war
from his gaze, "for bringing my ward to me as soon as yot
discovered her. Once again you have shown yourself a loya
friend and a true guardian of chivalry. It was only our ba
fortune that the *Lady* was found after the ships had embarked
She must accompany us to Buda now. There I will make provi
sion for her return."

There was no doubt as to what this "provision" would be
The threat of a convent hung in the air.

"However," continued Olivier, his voice chilling everything
about him, "if you and Squire Michel would excuse us, I think
it best I have a word in private with my ward. I will see to it

hat both you and your squire are suitably recompensed for any
rouble the *Lady* Julian has caused you.''

Out of the corner of her eye, Julian saw Gatien bow and
ake his leave. Michel looked as though he would much have
»referred to stay and hear what promised to be a memorable
.colding. But after a look from the Knight de la Marche, Croyant, too, bowed, turned and left. Julian found that she missed
:ven his quite slight comfort. It would have been preferable to
vhat she had to face alone now. There was no help for it.
She had known that this would happen and she had carefully
»repared.

"I hope you do not think, my lord," she said to Olivier as
;oon as the small oak aperture had closed behind the others,
'that I am easily cowed by the stormy look you have decided
o level at me. I am no silly nit of a girl who is easily frightened
»y the disapproval of a man.''

"Indeed?" asked Olivier with deceptive mildness. "One
vould not readily discern that from the quaking of your voice.
Nor could one easily mistake you for a damsel, silly or otherwise, at least not with the butchering you've done to yourself.
You should have spared your tresses, Julian—bound them up
or hidden them away. Your hair *was* your softest feature.''

The mention of her changed looks stung Julian, but it did
aot deter her. She had reasoned that in order to win this inevita-
»le battle, she must keep herself firmly on the offense.

"You mean to frighten me." She heard her voice waver yet
:ontinued on. "You mean to scold me and communicate to me
:hat I should have left everything to do with my mother in your
:apable hands.''

"Certainly they will be more capable of performing the task
:han yours, clasped in forced prayer as they will be for at least
the next six months. I have already selected the convent of
your destination. You have my honor bound word that it will
aot be to your liking.''

"I am not afraid," said Julian, though her heart scudded
apidly within her chest. "Nor have I any intention of letting

you continue to command my life. I will go for my own mother
It was my promise. I extracted it from you. It is my own
responsibility to see that it is kept. You are released from your
vow.''

For an instant there was only silence between them. Julian
heard waves lapping against the ship's hull as it carried them
to the crusade that lay ahead. The waves seemed very loud.

''You could have trusted me to keep my word,'' Olivier
roared.

His words seemed to rupture forth from some deeply hidden
part of him, a part that Julian had previously not known existed
Her guardian's face had gone quite flushed with rage and Julian
knew that if she let go of her vigilance for even one instant
she would cower before him. She could not do that. Not now
She had gone through too much. She had come too far.

''I will not be threatened,'' she whispered. '' I will retrieve
my own mother. I will honor my own word.''

Olivier's rage shattered the air around them.

''I will not be brought back again to what I said and what
I promised,'' he said. His voice, though pitched low now
vibrated with anger. ''I will not have you speak thus to me
ever again. Do you hear me, Julian Madrigal? *Ever again.*
am not a paging-boy who needs constant reminders as to his
duties. I have acted with honor both towards you and towards
Aalyne. Your mother had what she wanted from me. You were
freed. You have been well cared for and, should you have
needed one, I was prepared to dowry you well. That should
very well have been the end of my responsibilities towards
you. For most men of honor it would have been. I have never
done anything to betray your trust. Indeed, I have done everything to earn it. Why you think me faithless is a mystery to
me.''

''Venice forced you into this crusade. You had no intention
of maintaining your promise.'' Julian sounded childish and
stubborn, even to her own ears.

Olivier's was a small cabin. He was off his high stool and

eside her in three strides. She thought him far too close. She
lmost felt the swish of his suede tunic against the hairs of her
rm.

"Let us not talk about me for an instant," he said softly.
'Instead let us talk about you."

"Me?" Julian scoffed, though again she felt a repeat of that
heart-scud. "There is nothing more to say about me. You have
already touched upon it all. I am the spoiled ward of a pampering
guardian. I have need of nothing more than what he might
deign to provide."

"Ah, we seem to have neglected the subject of your sainthood
in that summation."

"My sainthood?" She was growing wary, moving away.

"Indeed, your sainthood, my dear Julian." He placed a restraining hand upon her forearm and his was not a gentle
hold. "Do you not agree that you deserve nothing less than
beatification for your role in this affair? How unselfishly determined you have been in seeing to the welfare of your mother—
a mother, I might add, who always seemed more than capable
of taking care of herself." He laughed aloud. "Do you really
believe that had Aalyne wanted to leave Nicopolis, she would
not have come with us? Do you really believe me so vile that
I would not have protected and supported the woman who
arranged my escape, just as I have protected and supported you
for all these years?"

"But she couldn't come back to England," Julian insisted.
"She was under threat of the stake."

"She was under threat of burning in France, not in England.
Those two countries have been at intermittent war for more
than fifty years now. And certainly Italy cares nothing for their
rivalry. But I could have sent Aalyne to Harnoncourt Hall—
to Britain where the Knights Templar have not as yet been
outlawed. She would have been safe from the stake there—
safer by far than she would have been in Nicopolis after you
left. But that does not fit into your pious plan, does it, my
little ward?" Olivier's laugh was not pleasant. "You have

generously decided to take your mother to the safe haven tha is Harnoncourt Hall. It is well-known that neither my mothe nor my sister is able to refuse you anything. You will tak Aalyne on to England where the Templars have never beei outlawed—and, indeed, to seek sanctuary with Belden of Har nonourt who was wrongly accused and barely escaped the stak himself. You will rake up all of these old coals again, my littl Julian—not for Aalyne but for yourself.''

Julian shook her head. She did not trust herself to speak.

"You see yourself as so eager to return and keep a promis that you are willing to dress as a man and risk your life upoi a warring vessel—or, at the very least, risk the remnants ol your virtue with its crew. Why, one might ask? Ah, only becaus you are so good—*too* good—a noble and obedient and devotec daughter. You must rescue your mother. She must be brough home to you." He paused. Julian saw something like compas sion in Olivier's eyes, but his voice continued on as relentlessl as ever. "Ah, but to what purpose? For what reason?"

"Because I love her. Because she is my mother. Because have promised her and I must return." The words, long prac ticed, came out of their own accord. Julian could feel the flaming of her face. She could feel the shaking betrayal of her hands.

"For Aalyne's sake—or for your own?"

"For hers—of course, for her sake. She is my mother. want her to be safe." The voice of the Magdalene's daughtei had grown shrill.

Olivier slowly shook his head. "I don't think that is your reason, Julian." His grasp upon her gentled. "In your mind you have constructed a pretty fantasy. You propose to pull your mother from one horror, only to thrust her into another. If you make it to Nicopolis, you can perhaps free Aalyne, if she is not already dead. Perhaps she will agree to come back with you. And if she does, what will happen to her? Why, she will be under your control. You will decide the life she will lead and the work she will do. You will decide the house she will live in. What was it you had in mind? Tell me again. Ah, now

I remember. You want nothing more than a small, gray stone cottage. How picturesque! Aalyne de Lione, the famous sorceress, will spend her days devoutly dressed in black and doing good. She will spend her nights quite alone. Under your stern-willed aegis, she will lead such an exemplary life that soon all rumors of witchcraft and the Magdalene will die for want of nutrition. Not only for Aalyne de Lione, but for her witching daughter as well. That's what you really want, isn't it, Julian? To take your mother back so that she can be purified. So that *you* can purify her. You want to put Aalyne in drab clothes and make her pay and pay and pay. No more men for her then, and no more fascination. No more healing work, or selling charmed futures or making amulets to plant love where it doesn't exist. No more of that nonsense. You will purge your real mother and then purge her again until, in the end, she becomes the mother that *you* want her to be."

Julian snatched herself away and slapped him so hard that the sting of her own hand brought tears to her eyes. "You don't know what you're saying. My mother wants to leave that life. She wants to be a good woman."

"Aye, Aalyne was a good woman." The Count of the Ducci Montaldo spoke calmly despite the livid mark that burned upon his face. "You did not wish to follow her as the Magdalene and she left you free to decide. Once you had reached a decision—your *own* decision—she sacrificed much to see you safely away. In the end she may have died so that you could escape. She would have taken this decision knowingly. She knew the Dogan Bey's castle. She knew its rules. Above all, she had the Power and the sight that it allowed her. But she did not choose to leave Nicopolis. She did not choose to leave behind her identity as the Magdalene."

"How dare you say that?" Tears streamed down Julian's face as she hissed the words at the man she loved. "You are a man and it was men who made her do what she did. The men of the Knights Templar, the strange, black-cloaked man—

my father, whoever he is. They used her and hurt her and left her. They hurt *me*. They left *me*."

"Not all men," said Olivier as he slowly refolded Julian into his arms. "I have never harmed you. And I never will."

Something in what he was saying stopped Julian's anger and her tears. It stopped any mention she might have made of Domiziana, of his betrothal, of his duty, and of his knight's oath. These words did not even rise to her lips. She knew they were not part of this moment and that somehow Olivier had already thought them through. Some power within the Magadalene's daughter whispered that maybe she had found the man she could trust.

She listened, and the first thing she could hear was the steady throbbing of his heart against her own. She heard their hearts beating together, strongly and deeply and well.

Then she listened to his voice once again.

"I love you," he said, kissing each of her tears away. "Have loved you. Will love you. Forever and ever, with all my heart and my soul."

Julian pulled back, bemused. She shook her head back and forth, back and forth, until Olivier lifted his hands to cradle her chin and stop its nay-saying movement. But Julian would not let herself be stopped.

"You needn't lie if you mean to have me. I am not a virgin. I know how men are and what they want of me."

"Do you, now? Do you, now, little Julian?" He murmured his words into the short curls at her hairline, caressed them into the lobes of her ears. "Tell me how men are."

"They want . . ."

She gasped as his mouth opened and she felt his tongue touch against the heartbeat at her neck. His hands had moved her close against him. She felt their heat and strength along her spine.

"They want . . ."

"Yes, tell me what it is they want, Julian. Try harder."

"They want . . ."

"Is this not what they want?"

He kissed her lips then, edging his tongue softly around them until she sighed. Until she opened to him. His tongue was like ilk against hers. It tasted of heaven. She felt the sweetness of a quiver slide through her. She might have been embarrassed, would have been embarrassed, except that she could feel that same quiver run through Olivier as well.

"Is this what men do?" he insisted, as he ran his hands through her newly shorn hair. He let them languidly trace their own way down the column of her neck until they came to rest on the small mound of her breast. "Is this how they touch the woman they love?"

But some dark, hurt place in Julian asserted itself. It pulled her back from Olivier and it made her say, "It is if they want to whore with that woman."

"Or if they want to take her for wife."

Now it was Olivier's turn to pull back, and he did that just far enough so that Julian could read the truth of his soul in his eyes.

"There is no one but you, Julian. No other betrothed."

"But the Lady . . ."

"The Lady of the Venier and I no longer share an intention to marry. I have spoken to her father. I have spoken to the lady herself as well. Luciano Venier has prayed me to keep the new arrangement secret because of this bloody war we are set to fight. He thinks—actually, I do not know what he thinks, but it seemed important to him to have the Venetians believe that things had been left as before. Perhaps this is important to me as well. I have no relatives left in England. It is probably best for my people that control of the Ducci Montaldo estates rests in Count Venier's hands whilst I am away from Italy."

Julian hesitated again, this time because she felt the pull of the Power within. But Olivier's kisses were too strong for her. They called her back to her body and to him.

He tasted her, running his tongue just within the cover of her boy clothes. "I am no longer pledged to another. Tell me,

Julian, will you have me? Will you wed me, as soon as this crusade is over and we can mount the banns at Belvedere?''

It was too much for her, too overwhelming. Julian tried to order her thoughts, to think and to answer, but she was whirled by emotion. Whirled by Olivier's touch as he kissed his words into her mouth.

"Do you trust that I would not harm you and that what I tell you is true?''

"Yes,'' she said, bringing the word up through the deep layers of what seemed her long-ago life. "Yes, I trust that you would not harm me and that what you tell me is true.''

"Do you trust that I will wed you?'' he said. "That you will take me forever and ever. If we will not wed, then we will not bed. Tell me, Julian, what is it that you want?''

"Both,'' she gasped as he drew her forcefully against his excitement. "I want all of you, Olivier. Everything—all of you that I can have.''

She thought he would kiss her then. Thought he would take her immediately to the small bed and have his pleasure with her. This is how it had happened before. This is how she assumed it happened with all men.

But Olivier was having none of that. He took her hand in both of his.

"Then take this and honor it,'' he said, slipping the crested iron ring of the Ducci Montaldo upon her finger. "Know that with it I honor and love you as my wife. I wanted things different for you, Julian. I wanted our first time together to be different—different for you and different for me. I hadn't planned taking you to me on board a ship bound towards God-knows-what-danger. I wish I were stronger.'' His smile was as young and rueful as that of a young boy. "Unfortunately, I am not. You are free to decide if we will be together here, on this small cot. Otherwise, for both of our sakes, I must go to hunt you other quarters.''

"Then love me,'' Julian whispered. She did not need to think. "I cannot bear to leave.''

It had taken her a lifetime to reach this quick decision. She was not a virgin and she knew what would happen next. She knew that it had always hurt her and she expected nothing better now, but she loved Olivier and wanted him anyway.

He kissed his understanding of this into her hair as his hands lowered her deftly onto the bed so he could remove her soft boots. He kissed her again as he searched deftly for the strings and bindings that held her in her squire's habard and her tunic. He kissed her through the thin, chaste silk of her undergarments.

"These are a woman's breasts," he said, slipping lace from her shoulder and exposing the white mound. "A secret Julian, meant for me alone."

He traced the tip of her nipple with his callused hand. Julian surprised herself by dipping her head and kissing his hand as it worked at her. His touch warmed her. She felt pliable and hot.

"No more hurting," Olivier whispered. He leaned her back against his one simple pillow as her nostrils filled with the scent of clean linen and of the man she loved. The feel of his hands upon her were an intoxication. She drew one of them to her and sucked the taste of him from it, running her tongue over and over against his fingers and along the length of his palm.

"Julian." He seemed unable to get enough of whispering her name.

It was then that something—some power—within her started its whisper that things would be different this time. That loving need not hurt. Julian, still remembering other times and still frightened, chose to follow that voice. She chose to let it lead her where it may.

Olivier laid back on the bed and let his gaze roam over her as the ship hove gently around them. He was still dressed in his light wool tunic. She was embarrassed by his scrutiny but the sky was darkening into nightfall and she thought he would take her without looking. The Dogan Bey always had.

Olivier was not the Dogan Bey. He reached deftly to the

trestle table that had been bolted beside the bed and struck fli▪
to one candle and then to another and another. Julian, cheek
flaming, reached to pull the linen around her but Olivier staye▪
her hand. He put her fingers one by one into his mouth.

"Julian, don't hide from me, now or ever. I want to see yo▪
when I love you. I want to see the love as it marks your face.'

He moved to undress himself and to his surprise Julian helpe▪
him, just as he helped her. It was Julian who pulled his la▪
undergarments over his head. It was Julian who whispered t▪
him, "No hiding for you, either. I, too, wish to see love pas▪
over your face."

She thought he would take her immediately. It had been nic▪
so far, all of this kissing, but she knew what came next, ha▪
known since she was twelve years old, and already she wa▪
gritting her teeth against it. She remembered she must ope▪
her legs wide and move her hips when she was told to do s▪

But Olivier seemed to be in no hurry. He drugged her wit▪
his lips and his tongue and his fingers. He kissed her an▪
tongued her, sipping and nipping at her until her skin glowe▪
She felt his hand, then his mouth, trail down her body. Felt hi▪
hand and then his mouth as they entered her. She blushed ho▪
but only for a second before the rhythm of his kisses snatche▪
her up and the wave of his motion swept her along. She fe▪
her body tighten—tighten just as Olivier's kiss deepened an▪
shattered her into a thousand crystalline pieces of love.

Only then did he enter her, slowly and gently. His enterin▪
was like nothing she had ever experienced. It was deep bu▪
slow, full but needy. His thrusting caused her no pain. The fee▪
of him brought her higher and higher, and there was nothin▪
to hurt her, as there had been in the past. Just this wonderfu▪
giving and taking, this natural rhythm that was Olivier and tha▪
she could trust. Julian felt again that hot tightening rise u▪
within her and was frightened of it still, afraid it might was▪
her away. She reached out for Olivier, held him to her, molde▪
their bodies together with her touch. She opened herself t▪
welcome this hot power that Olivier had found and that he ha▪

gnited. She said yes to it; she moaned yes to him. And felt herself shatter and shatter again.

With infinite care and patience he loved her back together again—loving her until she could once again find her body, her mind and her soul. Insinuating himself into the pores of her being. Loving her into the realization that never again would she know just where she ended and Olivier began.

"Olivier."

He was hers now and she was his.

She felt his ring on her finger.

She felt his love in her heart.

Ah, it was different with a woman you truly loved. For a second the memory of his fevered ruttings with Domiziana—or that was how he had secretly always seen them—attempted to push themselves into a dark corner of Olivier's mind. But he pushed them aside. That was not what he had wanted. He now had what he had always wanted and the having of it left him satisfied and complete. It lay well-deep within the woman who slept beside him and who had her hand trustingly in his.

He lifted the sheet and bent down to kiss her bare shoulder. He watched her smile in her sleep. He knew that she did not have a perfect body. She was a bit too thin, her breasts a bit too small. Her short, boy curls were a terrible disgrace. This didn't matter to him. What mattered to the Count of the Ducci Montaldo was that this vision, even now, was beginning to stir beside him, to waken and to smile. And that the only thing she wore, as she opened her arms wide to him, was the Maltese Star of her mother and the crest ring of the man she was to wed.

CHAPTER
TWENTY-TWO

Afterwards Buda would be only a disjointed mingling of senses for Julian—the tranquil blue flow of the Danube beneath wooden bridges, the glimpse of the small city of Pescht on the far shore, the beauty of the Hungarian women, the smell of red roses, the personal magnetism of its young king. These things were all that was possible for her to remember, so overwhelmed was the city by the force of the French. And so overwhelmed was Julian by the force of her love.

Neither the city nor her love was exactly as she had expected them to be. Buda was smaller than London or Paris; it had none of the sprightliness of the Italian towns. It was the gateway to the East, where men wore loose tunics and women bright skirts trimmed in colored bandings. They were darker, livelier, and merrier than she'd imagined. It was not uncommon to see a group of them dancing through the narrow street at midday.

But it was the discovery of love that proved to be a true revelation. Olivier was a real man to her now, and he had a real man's needs. He had proved from their very first night together that he would not be satisfied with the chaste, make-believe kisses she'd always dreamed they would share.

What surprised Julian was that neither was she.

She had trusted in Olivier, trusted in the womanly feelings that he evoked from her. She had followed the voice of these new feelings and not the old voices of the past. Not her own voice that had always told her that men would hurt her, and not her mother's voice that told her men were to be used. Instead, she followed her instincts. She followed her love. She made the conscious choice to open to him—and it *was* a choice. Julian Madrigal was Wise Woman enough to know this. She had always left her thoughts open to him; now she opened her body and her soul as well. What's more, she reveled in this new liberty, reveled in the feeling of womanly power that it roused in her. She found herself sucking at her own fingers in order to taste Olivier there. She had but to move her hands or her body and she could hear him cry out or moan under her touch just as she cried out and moaned under his. They drugged each other with the touching of their tongues. Yet Julian, a true Wise Woman, knew that what they shared had nothing to do with the sorcery of physical intoxication and everything to do with the reality called love.

Shyly at first, and then with more pleasure, she learned to open herself to this thing called loving. She could tell that her inquisitiveness pleased him. She knew that he had not expected the level of intimacy that they shared. He had not hurt her. What they were together carried no pain with it.

She trusted what they shared, and through it she was learning to trust the man who had first opened its wonders to her. She found that she did this more and more readily and in more and more situations.

On the ship and then in Buda, Olivier handled their relationship with discretion but he did not hide it. He had given his word to Luciano Venier to maintain the fiction of his continued betrothal to Domiziana until the end of the Balkan crusade. He intended to respect his promise. But he had made other vows to Julian concerning their future together and he had every intention of maintaining these as well. He *wanted* to maintain them. His was a delicate line of balance—between what he owed a fellow noble and what he owed the woman he loved— but he managed to walk it with grace. Perhaps it would have been better if Julian were not with him, but he knew he could not give her up. Not now. Not ever.

So Olivier did the best he could. He introduced Julian as his ward to King Sigismund of Hungary, who had awakened the western world to this crusade. Though Sigismund's was not a licentious court as was that of Paris, life had taught him to view the world from a liberal viewpoint. He welcomed Julian in any way that his good friend the Count of the Ducci Montaldo might prefer to present her. Though he endeavored to hide his feelings behind a mask of propriety, it was obvious that Count Olivier was quite besotted with her.

Julian found the king both handsome and charming—if a bit harried. As well he might be with the French at his door and overrunning the city where, as brother to the Holy Roman Emperor Wenceslas and a native of Bohemia, he had only reluctantly been welcomed as king.

"Will you look upon this disaster," grumbled the king as he guided Olivier and Julian through a tour of the French camp just outside the city. "They must plan upon drowning the Ottoman in these caskets of red wine."

"Indeed, there are more than enough of them," agreed the Count of the Ducci Montaldo, looking worried. "Though I see nothing else that proves a plan of action on their part. There is not one seize engine or catapult to be seen."

" 'Tis because they go to engage the infidel." Irony was thick as sweet cream in Sigismund's voice. "They think themselves in need of nothing but the grace of God."

"How they can imagine themselves in possession of that is nothing short of wondrous. I doubt very strongly that a serious God would look with anything but dismay and anger at the extravagance of these French."

Julian was distressed by what she saw before her. She both liked and respected Gatien de la Marche and she had thought that his good qualities reflected those of his countrymen. The French she met in Buda did not correspond to the kind image she had formed. They were young and many of them—including the Count de Nevers, their commander—were untried in battle. Like the young Michel de Croyant, they thought of war as a necessary lark. Even their careful stacks of highly polished armor had more glitter to it than menace.

The armor did not look substantial. It did not look as though it would last.

Despite the blossoming of her love for Olivier and the passion of their nights together, Julian woke most mornings to find the pit of her stomach knotted. She felt that they were speeding towards catastrophe. Something deeper even than the Power told her this.

She wanted to share this feeling with Olivier, and sometimes she did. Then Olivier would touch her, he would need her, he would draw her near—and his touch would force all other thoughts from her mind. At least for a while.

He, too, was more than a little preoccupied.

However, the French forces included older, seasoned warriors as well. Olivier introduced Julian to the Sire de Coucy, whom he had paged for, and to Philippe de Mézières, Henri de Bar, and Jean, Sire de Boucicaut. All of them had fought well for France in the past. But there were so few of these, and so many of the others. The young ones drew the tenor of their lives from the profligate Burgundian heir.

"My lady mother always told me that a fish rots from the head down," grumbled Olivier. "This small enterprise may yet prove her correct."

They were bedded together in the small white silk tent they shared. It was pitched on a plain just beyond Buda and discreetly near the allied army's main encampment. Olivier had procured the tent for her as well as the two nuns who served as her chaperonage. They had been specifically warned that the Lady Julian Madrigal's reputation needed no protection from the Count of the Ducci Montaldo. They may not have spoken Olivier's tongue, but they understood his meaning. They disappeared whenever he came near.

Which he did every night and sometimes, if he could be spared from the war council, during the day as well.

"From the head down," he repeated. "And this army proves that to be true."

"In what way?" Julian said. She had moved over to rub his temples with her supple, soft fingers. He had grown tired and preoccupied lately, much more worried than he had been in Venice. She could see it in the new lines etched round his mouth and in his furrowed brow.

"In that it is a foolish Burgundian enterprise, led by the most foolish of all the French counts," he answered simply. 'Nevers is a vain and cunning man who will undoubtedly prove himself to be quite a dangerous one when he inherits his royal father's dukedom. He is also extremely ugly."

"Not everyone can have the glorious looks of the Ducci Montaldo," Julian teased.

"I meant ugly in his soul. Mean and vicious."

"Indeed he is that," Julian agreed. "I can tell."

"Is this my little Magdalene speaking?" Olivier queried as he rolled onto his side and played at nibbling her ear. "Is this your famous Power telling you something?"

She wiggled away from him, her face serious. "I don't know what it is—the Power or else something inside me. But I have bad feelings about what is ahead. It is as you've said. The French have brought no seige weapons or catapults. And they cannot expect to take Nicopolis without them. You know yourself how Bayezid has strengthened the fortress. He has built a tower over it that will enable the garrison to see up the river for miles."

Olivier shrugged. He knew all of this. He had told her these same things more than once.

"Something will happen," he said finally. "Sigismund knows the difficulties. He has fought off Bayezid's nipping for years."

"But French nobles will not pay serious heed to a Bohemian. It is beneath their dignity."

"We are counting upon what we presume to be the rightness of our cause," said Olivier with not a little irony. "We assume that God will forgive all manner of stupidities just because we have launched ourselves against the infidel. We seem to forget that he has not always blessed our cause—in truth, he rarely has. We will be leaving Buda in just a few days and my advance guard sends back word that the plain beyond is just as hot as hell itself. And this mission will end as hell for us—I believe this to the end depth of my soul. But what does Nevers care? He has brought his wine. He has brought his fancy women. He will be content with these."

"Umm," said Julian. "Fancy women. I wonder if they are fancy like this?"

She reached her lips towards Olivier to kiss his worries away.

" 'Tis a grave penance to me that I was designated as your guardian," said Michel de Croyant to Julian Madrigal. The scowl on his face told her that he meant every word.

"I appreciate your care of me, Sir Michel. It was kind of you to respond to the Count's request."

" 'Twas not Count Olivier who asked this of me. Had it been, I would have refused. It was the Knight de la Marche. He knew I could not refuse him."

"Indeed, it was thoughtful of Sir Gatien to spare a full knight as my protector."

Michel had won his coveted knighthood exactly one day ago. The allied army had engaged the enemy, if it could actually be called an engagement, at the Turkish suzerainty of Vidin.

ie city's Bulgarian prince, choosing to deal with the devil at
s gates rather than wait for an intervention by the absent
ultan, had turned Vidin over to the French without a fight.
o blood was shed—unless one counted that of the Turkish
irrison. Each of its men, naturally enough, was immediately
it to the sword. After this bloodletting, the Count de Nevers
id three hundred of his companions, including the young
lichel de Croyant. had been awarded the golden spurs of their
iighthood.

"It is quite kind of you, Sir Michel," she said with a careful
.e of his new title, "to keep company with a lady when you
ight feel yourself better employed elsewhere."

He looked at her from the corner of his eye. "No lady wears
iorn hair, and no lady accompanies an army into battle. But
have been told that the monks will have good use for you
hen the fighting begins in earnest. Not that Vidin wasn't a
:emendous battle," he added quickly. "However, there will
: at least a few more before this country has been redeemed
id you might prove yourself useful. The Count of the Ducci
'ontaldo has employed a great physician for his men. His
ime is Yacopo Moscato and he trained in Salerno."

*"I owe them that much, " Olivier had told her. "I am leading
em into a fool's trap and there is nothing I can do for it. At
ast I can provide the best I can for my own men."*

Julian alone knew that he paid for Yacopo Moscato and the
her expenses of the Gold Company with his own resources.
e had not as yet requested anything from Venice. Luciano
enier, who had charge of Olivier's affairs in his absence, had
iggested that money from Olivier's estates be used now. The
ty would pay it back to him once the crusaders returned
ictorious. Many things will be well-righted, he had written,
1 the wake of your great victory.

Olivier had had no choice but to agree. He had certainly not
lought twice about following Venier's recommendations when
came to the welfare of his men.

"However, despite my own inclinations," said Michel, his

words bringing her back to the present, "my sister said th
one day you would be a great Wise Woman. She said I mu
never call you a witch. She said that you mean to help and ‹
good."

"What do you say to that?" asked Julian, laughing.

"What do I say?" The new Sir Michel wrinkled his bro
in concentration for a moment. "What I say is that you shou
at least put on your veiling. It is hot as fire on this plain ar
the midges are fierce. If you don't take care, they will bite y‹
and mar your face. Despite the harm you tried to do to me
have noticed that you have quite a nice face."

The new Knight de Croyant stopped in his tracks to stare
her. His own words seemed to surprise him. His face turne
red.

Julian wished to relieve his discomfort and she knew ju
exactly the topic that would. "Tell me, Sir Michel, how we
you ever able to persuade your sister to let you free from tl
convent? You've never yet told me."

His bright eyes grew wide with astonishment and then l
laughed. "Oh, I could never have persuaded Solange—that
my sister, the abbess—to let me go. She was determined th
I would miss my great chance." His face turned momentari
hard with anger. "Can you imagine that? A daughter and gran
daughter of famous knights and sister to four more, and sl
would begrudge me my golden spurs?"

"But then how did you persuade her?" insisted Julian.

"Oh, there was no question of persuasion. I noticed th
when she fed me the medicine that was supposed to make n
feel better, it invariably made me feel worse. I determined
stop taking it and would hold it in my mouth and when sl
was no longer looking, I would spit it onto the floor benea
my bed. It took me less than a day to feel myself again.
escaped through the window and ran straight to the ships.
His voice quivered with indignation. "Can you imagine th
my sister would have deprived me of all of this?" He thre
his arms wide to take in the army camped around them, tl

azy sweep of the river, and the stone walls of Rachowa that was their morrow's aim.

"Your sister loves you," said Julian softly.

"How can she love me?" said Michel with a snort. "When he wanted to keep me tucked like a baby with her?"

The sound of a lute and a high-pitched clarion rounded over to them from the front of the lines where the French were camped. There was an accompaniment of clapping and womanly giggles.

"Run on," said Julian. "There is not much to settle and here are the two nuns to help me as well. You go and have your fun now. They say that the ships bring fresh fruits from France."

She was happy when Michel was with her, but he was with her little. He ran away to be with the other knights as often as he dared. Her two chaperoning nuns prattled on together as though she did not exist. She was often totally alone.

Often, when this happened she would walk to a slight promontory, sit with her back to the river, and look out at the army as it stretched out over the fields. It had taken three days to cross from the left to the right bank of the Danube on pontoons. They had done this at the little town of Orsovo, where the river ran exceptionally straight. This had been two weeks and one battle ago.

Two weeks and one battle, Julian thought. And tomorrow they were set to fight another one at the fortress of Rachowa. She remembered that the Janizary, Assen, had come from near this place. She wondered how he was doing and if he had made it to Gian Galeazzo Visconti and come back. No one had heard anything of him since Olivier had released him to seek his fate. She settled back against the trunk of a tree and silently prayed for him. Then she prayed for all the men who were waved out below her, stretching on and on as far as the eye could see.

* * *

"Do you remember?"

She must have dozed, but not for long. The light had shifted just a bit more towards evening but she could clearly make out Gatien's face as she opened her eyes. She smiled up at him.

"I remember everything," she said. "At least everything about you. You brought me from Harnoncourt Hall to Belvedere. You were the first true friend I ever had."

He seemed pleased by her answer and settled down beside her. "That's good," he said. "I wanted to be a friend to you."

They both knew he had wanted to be more, and this was the reason he had kept such a careful distance from her lately. Julian had missed him. She had missed his kind and easy ways.

"I still have the ribbon you gave me our way to Tuscany." She reached into the bosom of her simple blue tunic and pulled it forth. "I carry it with me always, near to my heart."

"And near to the amulet that your mother gave you. You have fulfilled your promise to her, Julian. You are on your way home."

"Home," she echoed thoughtfully. "It's strange, but I never thought that I had a home. Certainly I never thought of Bulgaria, of Nicopolis, as being my home. As being a part of me. Yet they are. I knew it as soon as we crossed the Danube. As soon as I could see the distant mountains and smell the scent of roses once again."

"And Belvedere. That is part of you and it will be your home as well."

"Ah, yes, Belvedere." She paused. "I'm sorry for what happened between us, Gatien."

He smiled the smile that she had always loved, the one that enveloped the whole of his face, including its scars. "I am as well," he said simply. "But it was what had to happen. It was what had to be."

Julian nodded. She knew what he was saying to her: that

heir friendship had changed but that it wasn't ending. She felt
ears of gratitude sting at her eyes.

"It will not go easily for us at Rachowa," he continued.
'Not nearly as easily as at that sham battle at Vidin. No one
eems to know the whereabouts of the Sultan Bayezid. He
:ould be anywhere. He could be ready to attack us at any time.
We would have no way of knowing, either. We have made no
riends among the people we have conquered. Perhaps at the
>eginning, the Bulgarians might have viewed us as liberators.
Certainly they do this no longer. We have pillaged and looted
and raped our way through their country—forgive my blunt-
iess, Julian, but what I am saying has its importance and I feel
must say it now. This is war, and I may not get another
:hance."

Again Julian nodded. She felt her hands clench.

"The Bulgarians hate us for the swath we have cut. We
eave behind nothing but silent peasants with hatred in their
:yes. It is Bayezid who has now become their liberator and
hey will give us no information about his movements. We are
ilone in this strange land and only God knows what will happen
o us."

"Gatien . . ."

"Shhh. Listen to me. Julian, I know that Olivier will make
>rovision for you. Probably he already has done so. He is your
;uardian, and more. But I want you to know that if anything
,hould happen either to him or to me, that you must make your
vay to my castle. It is in Burgundy, near Dijon. Anyone will
>e able to direct you. It is a small place, Julian, not large even
)y Italian standards. Still, you will be welcome there, no matter
vhat happens. You can make it your home."

Tears glistened at Julian's eyes as she nodded. "Thank you,
;ir Gatien. 'Tis nice to know that you have made a place for
ne, should I need one."

"Should you need one," he whispered.

Together, the two friends sat watching the sunset until the
ast of its light had disappeared.

CHAPTER
TWENTY-THREE

"Come, Lady. Hurry. Hurry."

Julian hesitated, frozen within the waning clutch of her dream, still reaching out to the dark man who would show her the secret. He was so close that she could once again have taken the white rose from his outstretched hand. She so longed to know the answer to the secret. She so longed to understand. It seemed in that brief instant between sleeping and waking that the answer to this secret was all that she had ever wanted. But the man was fading, going away, buried in the words pouring over her.

"Wake, Lady Julian. My lord has been dreadfully hurt," said Michel.

Julian stumbled up on her pallet. She was instantly awake to find she was alone in her bed.

"Oh, God, no. Not Olivier. Not my love."

For an instant Michel did not understand and then he quickly shook his head. "The Count of the Ducci Montaldo is well, at least as far as I know," he said. He was far too young to hide

the distress in his eyes. " 'Tis the Knight de la Marche wh
has been grievously wounded."

"Leave me to dress," she told him. "I will need but a
instant."

Julian scrambled from her bed and pulled on the simple tuni
that she wore to tend the sick. She grabbed the flax basket wit
her ointments and tisanes. She ran a shaking hand through he
shorn hair.

It was not yet even full morning. Michel helped her onto
skirted destrier and jumped onto another. The horses' plume
headpieces, in the deep red of the Duke of Burgundy and th
brilliant green of the Count de Nevers, were still fresh. The
caught jauntily at the wind. Now that she was awake, Julia
heard the clang of metal against metal. She heard oaths an
screams. Their mounts seemed to move in slow motion dow
the pocked road.

"Tell me quickly—what has happened?"

" 'Twas the Sire de Coucy's idea," Michel answered. "An
it was a brilliant one. He said that we should take the castl
this morning, and we reached it just as the Turks were comin
to burn the bridge down. Julian, you would not have credite
the look of surprise on their faces!"

He was still young enough to indulge in a wondering chuckl
before continuing. "There were five hundred of us, includin
Count Olivier and Sir Gatien. The best of France was with u
as well—Coucy, Boucicaut, Henri de Bar. We carried the ava
garde magnificently well!"

"What happened?" Impatience caught in Julian's mouth.

"There was stalemate." Michel glanced quickly over at he
"We could not take the city. The Turkish were ready for us
They defended fiercely. In the end it was left to the Hungarian
to come to the rescue. King Sigismund sent his troops hurtlin
up the ramparts and with their help we were able to brea
through the lines. Boucicaut wanted to refuse the air but it wa
desperately needed."

Their horses picked a delicate way ahead.

"But in the end we won." Michel's confused voice faltered for an instant. "The Bulgarians surrendered the town, asking only that we spare their lives and goods. Sigismund, of course, agreed to this. He will be liege lord here when we claim victory, and so he must bear responsibility for the people. But they—we—claimed that we had already taken the town walls and that Sigismund, therefore, had not had the right to set terms. The varlets were allowed their traditional rights of pillage. They—we—seized one thousand prisoners for ransom. The rest were killed."

Julian closed her eyes. She could barely breathe.

"And Gatien?"

"Oh, Julian, it is terrible." Tears flooded Michel's eyes and spilled down onto his cheek. He was no longer a knight. He was once again just a very young boy. "Sir Gatien has been grievously wounded. Yacopo Moscato says he will lose his arm—his sword arm. My God in heaven, how can this terrible thing be?"

How *could* it be?

What could Julian say to him? What were the words? She racked her brain to think of them but they would not come. Probably that was just as well. She could never have forced them out past the constriction of her heart.

So she said nothing. When she reached the spot where they had laid Gatien, she helped Yacopo Moscato with his care. She cleaned her friend's wound as best she could and bathed him. She applied healing tinctures. She held his good hand. She stayed with him all the day of fighting. For both of them, the battle of Rachowa had ended very soon.

"Will he live?"

The smell of battle was still on Olivier as he came into the tent. Again, as at Vidin, luck had held for the crusaders. Maybe ten or twelve of their men had been wounded, and no others as badly as Gatien de la Marche. Not one of the French or

their allies had been killed. Julian heard them celebrating the
victory and talking loudly of God's grace.

"He should live," said Julian. At the physician's suggestion
she had dosed Gatien with aloes and myrrh against the pain.
"But he must want to do so. That is what my mother always
said, and it is what Yacopo says as well. He must want to get
well."

"He is a warrior who has just lost the use of his sword arm.
He is still in too much pain to know if he will want to live or
not. That will come later." Olivier reached over to draw Julian
to him. "But we must get him away from here. Do you think
he is able to travel?"

"No. No, of course he cannot. It would be dangerous for
him. He has lost so much blood."

"It is more dangerous for him to remain here," said Olivier
quietly. "A thousand times more dangerous."

Julian felt herself turn cold. She noticed that it was gloaming
again; she had passed the whole day here with her friend. She
would soon need to light candles and torches. She remembered
watching last night's sunset with Gatien when he had been
strong and whole. It seemed as though a thousand years had
passed since then.

"The Sultan will soon be upon us. We have sent spies and
they have brought word," said Olivier quietly. "When he sees
what we have done here, there will be no quarter for the Christian troops. He will avenge all of the blood spilt in the defense
of Vidin and Rachowa."

"We won both those battles. Surely we should be able to
defeat more of the Sultan's troops."

"We have luckily won battles against garrisoned troops.
They are nothing compared to the *ghazis* that the Sultan will
have in his vanguard. These soldiers are considered instruments
of Allah. They have been trained to fight with the zeal of Holy
War against what they consider to be a heathen invasion and
they will fight with the zeal of Holy War against us. It is we
who are the infidels to them." He paused, and his lips curled

onically. "They will give no quarter. Not after what has appened at Vidin and especially today at Rachowa. My God, nnocent children . . . What has happened to our oaths? What as happened to what we stand for and what we have vowed o protect?"

Julian looked at him, letting herself absorb the horror of vhat he said.

"Women and children," she whispered.

"There are ships leaving tomorrow. We must persuade Gatien to be on one of them. He is a famed French knight who vill not be able to defend himself, and he can do nothing to elp us. He must leave here before it is too late. You must ersuade him of this, Julian. He will listen to you."

In the end, Gatien did listen. It took Julian most of the night o convince him, but on the morrow he was ready to leave. he worked with Olivier to bundle him into his cape and waited s two squires loaded him onto a flax table and carried him own to the river's edge. Julian followed with Olivier at her ide, holding her hand. Behind them came two pages who vould accompany their liege lord to Italy, and young Doctor Moscato. His face, usually animated and lively, looked drained. ir Michel de Croyant carried Gatien's still-bright armor. It attled a bit in the tranquility of early morn. It was still so ighly polished that Julian, gazing into its brightness, could ee a formation of birds overhead—birds that were heading outh.

At the water's edge she heard a noise from behind and turned ack to it. The Count of Nevers with Boucicaut, Coucy, and Henri de Bar—the First Knights of France—stood silently by. here were no pages or squires or bodyguards with them. Neither had they ridden horses. The First Knights of France had made their way on foot. Silently they watched as Gatien vas loaded upon the barge that would take him away. It was only when he was safely aboard that Jean de Nevers detached imself and came near. He carried his personal banner of the rusade; it showed the Virgin and the Lilies of France embroi-

dered against a bright green field. The cloth was encrusted wit
pearls and precious stones. There was no wind to flutter it. A
Julian watched, the arrogant heir of the Duke of Burgund
knelt before his vassal, the Knight de la Marche, and presse
the banner into his hand. The two men looked at each othe
Neither spoke. Abruptly, Jean de Nevers rose again and walke
off as the other knights followed. The jingle of their golde
spurs echoed after them as they made their way back to th
French side of the camp.

It was early September. They had left Buda less than si
weeks ago, but already July seemed a lifetime away.

" 'Tis a nightmare," Julian said to Olivier as they watche
the barge carry Gatien away.

He held her hand tighter as the boat rounded a bend an
disappeared. "You, too, should leave," he said. "You coul
go straight to Belvedere. You could wait for me there."

Julian shook her head slowly—one, two—just as he ha
known she would.

"I have come too far along to turn back," she said quietl

"There will be death at Nicopolis," Olivier said quietly. "
will be just as dangerous for you as for Gatien. If he catche
you, the Dogan Bey will surely want revenge."

"I know that," she answered. She turned her face to his s
that she could love him with the brightness of her smile, an
so that she could remember this moment through all the tim
to come. "Both of us have died at Belvedere before, yet w
rose again from there. We went on. We will continue to go o
now."

"Yes, on," said the Count of the Ducci Montaldo as he be
down to kiss the woman he loved. "We will go on."

Later he lay beside her and whispered into her ear.

"There is no doubt that Bayezid knows our intentions," h
said. "The Sultan has been informed of all our movements–
too informed for this to be simple happenstance. He will surel

come to the aid of Nicopolis if we lay siege to it. It dominates the river at a very strategic point. The fortress is key to control of the lower Danube. Whoever rules Nicopolis rules the Balkans and will have a clear sweep into Hungary—then into Italy and the rest of Western Europe. We know Bayezid is on the march and must be drawing near. Yet we don't know exactly how close he is and when he will attack. We need to know this. The Sultan is counting on this element of surprise."

"So you are going to find him," said Julian.

Olivier noted with wry satisfaction that she neither pleaded with him nor brought out the weapon of her tears. She knew him so well, had always known him well. She had realized what he would do, perhaps even before he had.

"I am leaving this night," he said quietly. "Right away, as soon as I am dressed. It is three days' march to Nicopolis. The Count will start in that direction tomorrow at the morning bells. Once he has arrived, he will lay siege. The citadel will not be able to withstand him without assistance. The Dogan Bey is fiercely loyal to the Sultan and he will resist, counting on succor. Bayezid will not disappoint. I must try to discover how much time we have before that help arrives."

Julian only nodded, but her fingers felt like ice against his cheek.

"Sigismund has promised to be your defender whilst I am away. He has pledged to protect you and you must stay close to him. He will see that you are safely kept, if the battle should start before my return. I do not wish to leave you—you must trust in that. But a massacre may lie before us. I must fulfill my duty to my men."

"It will be dangerous for you," she said.

"Not so dangerous as it will be for you," he said. "Promise me you will take no initiatives. That you will stay near to King Sigismund while I am away."

Julian smiled at him and kissed him.

She promised nothing.

* * *

Once, in an illustrated parchment, Julian had seen a pictur
of the Colossus of Rhodes. The Arabs, great mathematicians
had admired the science that had given birth to such an improba
ble lighthouse. She had heard learned men discuss it with awe
It had fascinated Julian as well. She had stared at that illustrate
parchment for hours and hours, just as she now stared at th
fortress of Nicopolis—the place that at one time had been he
home.

It was no longer home to her, yet she remembered it well
And she remembered it with all the fear of a twelve-year-ol
child. The Danube valley seemed to cower before it, as we
as did the allied army of the west. Nature had formed it t
command. Jutting out above the river from a sheer limeston
promontory, it had ruled this spot since the beginning of time
A narrow road divided the river's edge from the base of th
cliff. The cliff itself was cut in two by the thread of a stee
ravine. Parts of the fortress lay on both sides. Julian had live
in the larger, which had contained a thriving bazaar and bot
Christian and Muslim religious places of worship. It had con
tained the Dogan Bey as well. The governor, Julian's first love
was a man devoted to the Sultan and his interests. He was als
supremely capable. It would take more than one battle to crus
him.

Julian, too, would face battle and she knew its path woul
once again take her into the heart and soul of this sheer limeston
cliff. But for now there were other tasks that begged her atten
tion. Sigismund had asked her to tend the survivors from
Rachowa who were being held for rich ransom. She had wel
comed the duty. Most of these women and children had los
loved ones in the massacre of their city. Many of them ha
been injured as well.

Olivier was gone and Julian was worried about him. Sh
thought that by helping the women of Rachowa with thei
wounds she might be enabled to forget her own.

* * *

It was in the women's camp that she met Saleima.

"I come from Nicopolis," the old woman had told her. She
had been injured but not badly and was being tended by a
young girl. They were the only survivors of a large family.
The young girl had carefully placed the old woman under a
screen of light flax so that she would not be bothered by the
hordes of flies. People complained continually about them and
about the unseasonable heat. The more superstitious thought
both circumstances were preludes to the extinction of the world.

Without a word, Julian examined the woman's forehead and
nails, touched the skin of her callused palms, and looked at the
flesh along the underside of her arms for lividity and bruising.
She looked deeply into the woman's rheumy eyes. Then she
settled back on her haunches to listen.

"This child is my granddaughter," said the woman. She
spoke a strange dialect but Julian could still make out her
words. A cough rattled her small frame and it was fully five
minutes before she could hawk the last of it into the bowl
beside her bed. "We are the remnant of a numerous family. I
am dying, am I not?"

Julian wanted to say no, but she found herself nodding yes.
Saleima seemed satisfied. "I knew from the first you would
tell me the truth. Not that it matters overmuch. I've a feeling
that once Bayezid comes we'll all be dead anyway. He is not
one to ransom women and children. And if he doesn't finish
us, the French will. This is the way of war for poor peasants.
I am named Saleima. You are Julian Madrigal, are you not?"

Julian nodded, surprised that this woman would know her.

"You are the daughter of Aalyne de Lione, the Magdalene."

This was no question, but again Julian nodded. She could
feel her heart scud in her chest.

The old woman shrugged. "I recognized you from the charm
at your neck. I knew you were her daughter from that. They

call it the Maltese Star and there is some ancient story to it
Your mother wore it as well."

"Is my mother alive?" she whispered.

Saleima shrugged, then coughed again "I cannot tell yo
that. I do not know. I had long married and moved to Rachow
when you left. But of course, even there, I heard what ha
happened. Everyone did—though none spoke out loud abou
it for fear of the Dogan Bey. They say he vibrated with fur
on the day you made your escape. I may not have certainty
but I believe your mother is dead. Everyone believes this. Hov
could he not have killed her? She committed a terrible offens
against him."

"I must have that certainty," Julian said simply. "Even i
it means I must go into Nicopolis myself."

The old woman's eyes took on a wary interest. "And hov
might you mean to accomplish that?"

"I have no way of entering. You know yourself how it is
The entrances are all carefully guarded. The secret passage m
mother found has long since been blocked."

"Perhaps I know a way for you," the old woman said. "
was captured by the Turks when I was but a babe and worke
for years inside the fortress kitchens. Perhaps I know a wa
for you to enter. Perhaps we can strike a bargain for it."

The old woman coughed again. "My granddaughter is name
Saleima, just as I am. Remember her name well."

It took Julian longer than she had anticipated to organize he
singular quest. The young Saleima had not wanted to leave he
grandmother. She had cried and clutched, but in the end sh
had been forced to go. Her grandmother had dug surprisingl
strong fingers into her young skin and made her leave. She ha
threatened to rise up and beat the girl senseless should she no
depart.

Julian had soothed and stroked the young Saleima's head

she had cooed to her and told her that everything would be well in the end. She had tried to believe this as well.

The young girl had not been moved by any of this. "My grandmother is dying. She does not want me to see it, but it is better for me to see and to know," she said.

Julian had left Saleima in the care of the nuns. They did not ask if she were Christian or infidel. They seemed grateful to have someone alive and unwounded who needed their love and care. They, too, had seen death in this crusade.

Then there was the note to write supplicating Sigismund's aid. It was a risk to write to him rather than go to him in person to beg for Saleima's protection. Sigismund was, after all, a king, and a king who was necessarily sensitive to the prerogatives of his position after the continuing insults of the French. He was also quite a busy and harried man. Still, Julian decided that it was best to entrust her begging to a note. Sigismund was no fool. He might ask questions should she approach him directly. He might guess what she intended doing and take steps to thwart her.

Julian had no intention of being thwarted, not now. She fingered the hasty map the old woman had scribbled out for her and thanked God.

"I was a servant," Saleima had told her, "and servants must learn to do much in little time. It was a hardship for us going each day down the mountain to the river—and going to the river was necessary. The Danube was the lifeblood of Nicopolis. It still is. But the constant coming and going was difficult, so we had to find an easy way."

What the old woman had found was a cave. She had come upon it quite by chance but it had served her purpose well. She had been able to follow its winding passages—they had taken her straight to the river's bank. In the years that followed she had almost forgotten its existence—almost, but not quite. The memory had just been buried under time's sands but it reappeared now, just when she needed it most.

" 'Tis the gift of a merciful Allah," she had whispered.

" 'Tis the way I can guarantee that my granddaughter wil
live."

Julian had nodded and thanked the woman. She did not tel
her that she would have tried her best to save Saleima anyway
How could she tell the woman this? How would this old woman
the last remnant of her exterminated family, possibly have
believed her? It would have been impossible to make her under
stand. Instead, Julian had run to her tent and brought back
quill and some scrap parchment. Then she had written down
precisely what the woman had said.

But she agreed with Saleima about one thing. Julian, too
believed their meeting to be a precious gift from a mercifu
God.

She waited until the lights shone from the French tents on
the one side and the Hungarian ones on the other. She waited
until the sounds of the nightly festivities rang out in full force
She slipped from the tent, leaving the two nuns with the child
They were tranquilly working at their mending and did no
look up. Saleima did, however. Her enormous, doe-brown eyes
watched Julian as she slipped from the tent. The child did no
try to stop her. She did not say a word.

Julian crept silently down to the Danube's bank, thankfu
that the moon was in its dark phase. In the darkness she could
hear the river busy at its steady flow and the occasional plot
plot of a flying fish rising out from its depths. She stared of
at the allied army's separate camps, then held her breath and
listened. She trusted in the Power. It would guide her. Only
when she was certain that the time was right did she turn
towards the city of Nicopolis and its hidden cave.

It called to her and she was suddenly moving towards it
Running towards it.

Running, running, running for dear life.

* * *

It was worse than he could possibly have imagined. Olivier unkered down and gazed across the dark, grassy expanse as n ocean of men flowed past him. Only an occasional torch marked their silent path. He knew he was staring at death.

Bayezid's men, infantry and cavalry, had crossed over into Bulgaria and were advancing, at forced march, straight towards Nicopolis. In the distance he could see them passing by in recise formation. Olivier could not help but contrast their discipline with the confusion that marred the allied armies. His warrior's eye told him that this juggernaut would reach its destination in less than one day's time.

Oh, my God. Julian.

But he had his duty to attend to before he could go back to er. Death was on its way, and he must try to save as many f his men as he possibly could.

"Michel," he whispered. The young knight was instantly at his side. "Head back through the lines and warn the Count de Nevers. Above all, tell King Sigismund. They must both know f this danger whilst there is still time to ready their armies. It is most important that you carry this word to them—it is our *duty*."

Croyant nodded. "And you, my lord?" His voice was barely a whisper. He, too, had seen the endless waves of humanity round them and, though he was young, he was warrior enough to treat so much strength with the respect it was due.

"I will cover you with my sword for as long as I can," replied the Count of the Ducci Montaldo "Then I will join forces with the Sire de Coucy. He has brought his advance guard near. They must number five hundred men. He is a capable leader. Perhaps, working together, there is some way we can stave off this catastrophe."

He did not think for an instant that they would be able to do this. But this was not said to the young Sir Michel.

Croyant opened his mouth to protest, then thought better of it and nodded again. It was his duty to return to warn the allied armies; there was no argument. Then he suddenly thought of something.

"Tomorrow is September 29, the feast of St. Michael the Archangel," he said in a bright whisper. "And St. Michael is my patron saint. Surely he is able to save us."

Olivier smiled and nodded. "Happy feast day," he said. "May St. Michael keep you safe. And if on the morrow you chance upon the Lady Julian Madrigal, you will tell her for me that she is to have care."

"God go with you, my lord," Croyant whispered.

He could not quite see it, but he could feel Olivier's quick smile as it flashed in the darkness.

"God go with you, my son," the commander of the Gold Company said.

And then, much to the astonishment of the new knight Sir Michel de Croyant d'Eu de Boule, the great warrior Count Olivier Ducci Montaldo bent over and hugged him fast.

It was here and she knew it. Julian was determined not to strike flint to her one candle. She did not want to notify the French of her presence, nor did she wish to come to the attention of some Turkish sentry who might be gazing out onto the bank. In the darkness she could not seem to fix upon the opening, yet she knew it was here. Saleima had not lied to her. Of that she was certain.

She felt once again along the underbrush that fronted the river. This was the only place where a cave could possibly be, the only area in the whole massive wall that was not part of the jut of limestone. Besides, her instincts and the force of her Power were telling her she was near. She must only be calm and listen to what the rock was trying to tell her. She must only hold still.

She thought she heard a swish of movement beside her.

ulian froze, stopped breathing. Her hands gripped a patch of
undergrowth that covered the slime of the wall. She waited for
what seemed an eternity but the sound did not come again. She
could not see even five feet ahead. The sounds of revelry from
the French camp echoed down to her. Without stars or moon
was impossible to tell the hour but she knew it was late.
Experience had taught her that the late night usually found the
army well into its tankard. In the past the nobles had often
grown careless; they had even forgotten to post sentries or
guards.

She hoped that this would be the case this night. She must
strike flint or she would never find the hidden entrance that led
into Nicopolis.

Her hand shook as she reached into her flax sack and pulled
the flint out and unwrapped it. She sat perfectly still, willing
herself into the heart of the night so she could learn from it.
So that it could warn her. She sat like this for many long
moments. Then she gingerly rasped the flint and caught its
spark. Light from the candle illumined her small part of the
river's bank.

The man was sitting directly before her. She could have
reached out and touched him. His legs were crossed in the
Turkish manner that she knew well. His eyes were dark, his
smile triumphant.

He held a large scimitar that curved out dangerously near to
her throat.

CHAPTER
TWENTY-FOUR

Once again, she was in her mother's cell and, oh, her mother *as near. Despite the squalor and the roving rats and the stink* *nd the damp of the witch-prison, Aalyne was smiling at her.* *he Magdalene held her daughter close. With gentle hands* *he brushed Julian's damp hair back from her forehead. She* *nderly wiped the garish paint from Julian's twelve-year-old* *ace.*

"Ama!"

How she loved her mother. How she had always wanted her *ear.*

Me and my Ama. My Ama and me.

"Come with me, Ama," Julian whispered. Her voice was *rgent with joy. "I've searched so long and hard for you. I* *ought I'd never be able to get back. I've found a place for* *s, Ama. A place where we can be together forever and ever—* *place where we can be safe."*

"Shhh," said Aalyne. The sweetness of her rose scent envel- *ped the room. "We will talk of that place later. But tell me,* *o you hold the man dear?"*

*Julian's smile welled up from heart-deep within her. N
longer was she a child. She was a woman, and fully so.*

"Yes," she answered simply. *"I love him well."*

*The Magdalene looked at her daughter closely. Betwee
them the Power that had united and then ultimately divide
them crackled and snapped. Julian watched as it seemed .
crystallize, floating just above Aalyne's beautiful head.*

Me and my Ama. My Ama and me.

Julian heard angel voices singing her song.

*"Good." The Magdalene's smile was radiant. "Then th
is enough, maybe more than enough. The love is what final
frees us. The rest has no power at all. Stay with that lov
Julian, my daughter. Follow where it may lead."*

*Something in the way Aalyne said this wiped Julian's swe
smile away. It made her reach out with cold, rigid hands .
hold onto the strength of her mother. To hold onto her an
never let her go again. They could be together forever an
always. She had come so far. She had gotten so close.*

*But already, as she watched, her Ama was fading, gettin
fainter. Going far, far away.*

*Until the only thing left was the man dressed in black,
man she had come to recognize and know so well. His smi
was triumphant as he held out his gift of a white rose.*

"She is long dead," he whispered.

"Long dead," repeated Dogan Bey. He was delirious wit
triumph—not only for what he had done in the past but fo
what he was doing in the present as well. He could barel
believe that in the space of one day an ever-gracious Allah wa
not only delivering Nicopolis into the hands of the Sultan, b
that He had brought back this little snit of a concubine as we
so she could be punished. "I killed Aalyne myself."

Julian struggled back into consciousness. They had drugge
her, of course. She felt its heavy pull. It had been in the wate
Water was the only thing she had been given since coming

is dark and lonely cell. Yet she knew that drugging had not
caused that perfect vision of her mother; it had been pure and it
had been real. Julian could still smell the sweetness of Aalyne's
roses. She could still feel her mother's soft hand at her hair.
She could still hear the Ama song.

"She was dead within six hours of your leaving," Dogan
Bey continued. "I had no choice. Not that I would have taken
another. She admitted what she had done, and she knew its
penalty was death. She pleaded only that the nurse be spared."

Tears welled up in Julian's eyes as she stared across her
prison cell at this man whom she had once known intimately.
He was still very much alive after all these years, though Aalyne
was dead. She wondered if he had taken other wives, other
concubines. It didn't matter. She tried to hate him for what he
had done to her and what he had done to the mother who had
saved her. Somehow, either because of the drug or because of
her tiredness, she could not bring herself to do it. She could
hear the sounds of battle seeping through the dungeon walls.
She could hear the screams of the dying, and she could not
force herself to hate. She had seen what hate could do.

She knew with great clarity that what the Dogan Bey had
done he had done from pride and not because he truly cared
for her. He had wanted her but he had never truly loved her.
Julian was loved now and she had learned the difference between the two.

She smelled her mother's roses. She heard the Ama song.
She thought of Olivier, and she prayed to God to keep him
safe.

But it was impossible to think that anyone could be safe in
the inferno that lay beneath the fortress of Nicopolis. The Dogan
Bey had dragged her to the precipice to witness just exactly
what her God had wrought. She wanted to keep her eyes tightly
closed, wanted to hold on to the roses and the Ama song.

Wanted to come to terms with the thought that her mother w
dead.

He would not let her. She had to be punished. But the Doga
Bey was determined that she see the end of what he called t
French madness. He forced her to look.

In the end she saw it all.

The French knights had not waited for death to overtak
them. They had galloped out to meet their enemy and ha
engaged him on the plain. They had been awesomely outnum
bered, and they remained outnumbered even in death. But the
were not going down easily. As Julian watched she saw group
of them thrust and fight and thrust again into the Sultan
strength until the ground was covered with bodies from bo
sides. She heard the sounds of their agonized screaming. Sh
smelled the stench of their blood.

Olivier, thought Julian with horror. My God, Olivier mu
be deep within all of this death.

"You are monsters," she whispered to the man who ha
been her first lover.

"Monsters?" Dogan Bey repeated. His voice was playful
ironic but there was nothing playful about his eyes. "I doub
indeed, that we are the monsters in this little tableau. Perha
you do not know what your own good Christians have don
When they heard that the Sultan came on forced march
attack them and that he drew near, they panicked and kill
the hostages from Rachowa. All of those women and childr
are now gone. Even the Christians among them were killed.

"Surely you do not speak the truth," Julian whispered.

"Oh 'tis true. They are all dead," he repeated "They a
all gone. Just as you yourself will soon be."

She swayed, but just then she saw movement and saw
faraway spot where the French still fought. As she lean
beyond the parapet, she saw the Saracen soldiers advan
toward one last small group of the French. She saw the brig

gleam of their armor falling as the Sultan's soldiers hacked their way through.

Then she saw soldiers fall to their knees, not in death but in supplication. They surrounded one last figure. Julian squinted closer and recognized the Count of Nevers. She waited, not daring to breathe, not daring to hope. She followed the eyes of the French to the one man she knew—waiting, as they did, to see what this man would say.

She saw the Sultan Bayezid, the same prince who had once given her sweetmeats and candies, nod that the Count's life should be spared.

And Julian Madrigal, a woman no longer just the Magdalene's daughter, knew that this last, long battle in this short and dreadful war had finally come to its end.

In years to come, troubadours would sing of Julian Madrigal. They would tell the tale of her birth and how she had escaped but had come back to rescue her mother. They would sing of Aalyne de Lione and the outlawed Knights Templar. They would write lyrics about how the Dogan Bey had captured Julian when she came back to Nicopolis again and they would tell of what had happened next. Olivier Ducci Montaldo would be immortalized with her. Their love, and the great sacrifice that based it, would make up the stuff of myth and legend. In time its glory would eclipse the tradition of the Magdalene and leave this tale of witchcraft to be hidden, and then forgotten, in the vagaries of time.

But now, as the Sultan triumphantly entered to take possession of his liberated citadel, no one felt like singing songs of glory. Even the vanquishing Turks mourned the price that victory had required; it had been far, far too high. Bayezid entered Nicopolis to the solemn sound of both mosque and church calling their faithful to prayer. Aside from this—and the screams of the dying—there was only silence.

*   *   *

She must be strong. She must be strong. There were people who needed her, people she had the skill to help. He would expect her to do her duty. He would expect her to keep putting one step before the other.

Julian knew that Olivier would expect her to go on.

But it was so very hard.

Bayezid had decreed that she should not be kept in a cell. He had dying men, thousands of them, and he needed all the help he could get to save them. Julian was Christian and not Muslim. She was free to move among the men.

"And my men need her help," said the Sultan as he placated his great and faithful ally, the Dogan Bey. "We have won this battle but our losses were terrible. Greater than those suffered by the West. I wept when I saw the field where my men lay. I cry when I think of the slaughtered women and children of Rachowa. I am tired of this killing. I will richly reward you for your loyalty and strength, but give me Julian Madrigal now. She is a strong healer, as was her mother before her. There is only one more person on this earth that I would see dead and it is Sigismund of Hungary. He is the one who initiated this catastrophe. There are thousands of men dead out there on the plain. I would strangle the King of Hungary with my bare hands if ever I found him again."

Indeed, it was known by all of Nicopolis that the Great Sultan had spent his first hours of victory walking through the corpses, searching for Sigismund of Hungary so he could quarter his body and feed it to the dogs. But the French had claimed the avant-garde, had insisted upon it, and so had left the Hungarians and their allies to hold the rear. But the rear had seen little action. It was the avant-garde that had paid. Many feared that the King of Hungary had managed to escape.

"Strangle him with my bare hands," repeated Bayezid vehemently.

The Dogan Bey, looking around at the devastation of his city, agreed wholeheartedly.

"Thousands dead," he said without triumph. "Thousands upon thousands. You must give me Julian so she can help to save what she can."

Julian did what she could. She was grateful for the work. It kept her mind off other foolish thoughts. It stopped her from thinking, *Until I know for certain,* or the much worse, *He is dead. I know he's dead. I feel it in my heart.* She could trust neither. Her mind was far too tumultuous for her to be certain that she touched the Power. She could not tell if it was truly the quiet voice within her that spoke. She would have to wait in this moment of not-knowing, wait for the return of calm and certainty.

And she still had her mother. She still held to the comfort of her vision, and the knowledge that Aalyne was near. Her mother had promised that in the end she would know all that she needed to know, and that enable her to wait. As for now, she would work hard at using her skill.

Julian welcomed the exhaustion of her body. She welcomed the use of her skill.

"We meet again," the voice said. It spoke, as it always had, in perfect French. At first Julian thought the sound an illusion of the intense heat. The streets of Nicopolis were awash with the Sultan's sea of wounded, sweltering under the sun. How could she have found Assen here? Yet she had.

"Assen." She bent towards him, looked at the mace wound in his chest and knew it would soon prove fatal. "I thought you had escaped to the West."

"I came back," he said simply. "I found I had grown quite fond of my men. In the end I could not betray them. It must be a weakening of my will in old age." He paused. "I prayed to see you once again."

"I thought you didn't pray," she said, pushing hair back from her forehead and settling near him.

"For this I did." He managed a quick smile. "I have something to tell you."

She thought it would be something about the battle, or that he had finally learned who had played traitor to the allied army's plans. But Assen had other things to tell her.

"I knew Aalyne first in Lyon," he began softly. Julian had to strain close to hear. "I knew her in the deep sense of that word. I don't know if she had already met the dark man. He is—was—a prelate, a cardinal, though a badly corrupted one. His name is—was—Archangelo Conti. The Sire d'Harnoncourt knows his evil intimately, as does the Lady Francesca. He was their nemesis, a man determined to do them damage. A dog sent straight from hell. But he's dead now." Assen sighed. "They killed him."

Julian wasn't so sure. She remembered the man on the bridge; she remembered her dreams. But she would not trouble Assen's last moments with these doubts. She would not let the memory of that cold, dark man intrude upon what he had to say.

He wanted to tell her about her mother.

"Aalyne was beautiful when I first met her, as well as poor. She had a certain gift. People could see it in her. That man saw it. I saw it. But of course I was a man already married. My future depended on the Sultan's whim. Aalyne was beautiful and I loved her but she could do nothing for me. She could not further my plan for revenge. Nor could I further her ambitions—and she had many.

"She never knew her own mother. She had been taken in by an old woman who slaughtered pigs. The man was dressed well. He smelled better than anything she had ever before smelled. He promised clean linen, good food, and fine wine. He promised that she would eat from silver plates. He promised the Power. Aalyne would have been willing to sell herself for a great deal less. The Inquisition was beginning to sniff at the herbal help she offered to the poor. The priests did not like the harms she fashioned or the amulets she wore. She was a woman without family, alone and without help. She had no power. She had no choice.

"But she knew you," said Julian softly, though she could feel a roil of rage begin to grow. "Could not you have helped her?"

Assen saw her anger and did not turn away from it. A cough spasmed through his body, causing fresh blood to seep through the bandage that bound his chest.

"She had no money," he said finally. "She had no power. I had vengeance in mind and I needed and wanted both."

"So you left her," said Julian softly. "You left me."

"You were not yet born when I left but it is true I knew of your coming. She had told me. She had begged." Again he coughed. "But I had a duty to my family. I had promised to avenge them. I had responsibilities."

"But we were your family as well."

"I know that now," said Assen softly. "I did not know it then."

"So you allowed it to happen."

"I allowed it to happen. I knew the Cardinal would take care of her. I had seen him before with the Sultan. I knew he had studied in the East and that he knew the Turkish language well. I knew he shared a secret with the Sultan, though Bayezid does not wear the Maltese Star. I knew she would be safe as long as she had Conti's protection."

"But she wasn't safe. The Inquisition sentenced her to the flame."

"Because of what he had taught her? Perhaps. But Aalyne was an eager pupil. Do not sell your mother's will short. She was determined to pull herself up, to have a better life. Cardinal Conti gave her the means and the story. She took the legend of the Magdalene and its relation to the Knights Templar. She made it her myth and her glory."

"But is the story true?" insisted Julian. "Were we born witches?"

Assen looked up but not directly at Julian. His eyes wer
fixed upon the golden six-pointed star at her neck—the sta
her mother had given her. Julian could feel the metal warm.

"Are you a witch, Julian?" He sighed. "That is somethin,
you must decide for yourself. Just as Aalyne decided for her
self."

She knew it was shameful, but she was angry with this dyin;
man. Furious with him for tantalizing her once again with half
stories and legends and lies.

"Then you have told me nothing," she said. "Just as yo»
told us nothing in Venice. You could have prevented all o
this, if only you had told us the name of the traitor. Why hav
you called me over to add more mystery to my life?"

"Haven't you guessed?" Assen had stopped coughing. Hi
gaze had shifted from the Maltese Star to look at her directly
"Because you are my daughter—the only fruit from the onl'
true love in my life. I have never held one of my children.
have never comforted any of them—none of them has ever
sought to comfort me. I want to hold you, my child, before
die."

Julian hesitated. She felt her rage bank and die down. She
had come back to Nicopolis far too late to help her mother
but not too late to help her father. Julian, the Magdalene'
daughter, did not believe in happenstance. Aalyne was at peace
Julian knew this. Perhaps Assen could find peace as well.

The only fruit from my only love.

Julian reached out. She drew her father near.

She felt the tears overwhelm her then. Tears she had no
shed for Gatien de la Marche or for Michel de Croyant or ever
for Olivier—her own dear love, Olivier, whose breath and lov«
and heartbeat she had shared.

The flood of silent tears was so strong that she almost misse»
her father's dying words, his parting present to the daughte
who had forgiven him and whom he loved.

"The traitor of Venice is Count Luciano Venier."

CHAPTER
TWENTY-FIVE

"The Sultan will see you now."

The guard made a reverence to Julian. She took this as a good sign.

Bayezid was exactly as Julian remembered him. Short and stocky, powerful and handsome. He had lost none of his vitality in the years she'd been away. He had also, she noticed, lost none of the charm that had caused him, the greatest and most ruthless man in the East, to carry sweetmeats to a young child. Julian was the only girl not in his harem. She had been allowed to run rampant—because she was Christian and because he had long ago given his word to Archangelo Conti to protect the Lady Aalyne and her child.

Cardinal Conti had driven a hard bargain but the young and ambitious Prince Bayezid had been more than anxious to pay his price. Safety for the child, protection for the woman, that was all. Though in the end, no one had been able to protect the Lady Aalyne from herself.

Bayezid thought of all this as Julian knelt in deep obeisance before him. Maybe some day he would be able to tell her what

had really happened that day ten years ago at Kosovo whe
his father was killed and he, Bayezid, had strangled his ow
brothers to ensure the crown. Maybe one day he would be abl
to tell the secret of the Maltese Star.

He gave his hand to her now and helped her to her fee
What had happened had certainly not been her fault. He ha
always liked Julian. He intended to keep the promise he ha
made long ago.

"Ah, I see they've cut your hair in the West, my child," h
said. "Does this mean they think you a witch?"

"I cut my own hair, Majesty," she answered. "No one di
it to me. I ruined it myself."

"Ah, then you are your mother's daughter." He settled dow
before her on his makeshift throne. The rich gold embroider
on his tunic rustled a bit as he moved. "They have told yo
of Aalyne, I trust."

"She is dead. I know that now."

"She was dead within hours of your leaving. There wa
nothing I could do to prevent it. She was under my protectio
but you both lived in the household of the Dogan Bey and wit
those women he could take his own revenge."

Julian nodded. "My mother knew that she would die fc
what she did. Just as I know that I will die for coming bac
for her."

Bayezid shrugged. With an army lying decimated on th
plain below him, he was not overly fond of the subject of deatl

"You will not die," the Sultan said simply. "I have take
you back under my own care. The Dogan Bey was not in favc
of this shift. He had already devised quite a singular punishmer
for you, but in the end he acquiesced to my wishes. He ha
no choice. You will be returning to the West."

Julian's heart thumped at the thought of freedom. She ha
begun to think of herself as already dead. This new idea of lif
came as a surprise.

"You will be sent over with the man I have chosen to tak
my terms of ransom to Venice and to France. There are riche

to be had from these Latin fools. Coucy, Boucicaut, de Bar—some of the greatest names of France are in my hands. Not to mention the Count of Nevers. Burgundy should pay well to have his precious heir back.''

He had not mentioned the Count of the Ducci Montaldo. Julian knew that this meant Olivier was dead.

''You will be given one day's safe passage. It was the best that even I, the Sultan of the Turks, could do. But that should be enough. They say that blackguard Sigismund of Hungary has managed to escape back down the Danube. You should be able to make your way to him. I would give half of my empire for the death of that one scoundrel. But never mind. We will meet again later. We take turns in our mutual flagellation—first he tortures me and then I torture him. Life is long and I am a patient man. I know that Allah will give me his life in the end.''

The Sultan seemed lost in his own thoughts for an instant. A smile—not a very pleasant one—marred his face.

''But that doesn't matter now,'' he said, coming back to himself. ''You will be accompanied by the man whom I have chosen to carry the terms of ransom to the West.''

He clapped his hands and Julian heard a door open and close. She did not turn towards it. She could not turn her back upon the Sultan. Instead she listened to the slow sound of leather boots coming towards her. She heard the jingle of golden spurs.

''My Lady Julian Madrigal,'' said the Sultan, waving a jeweled hand. ''I believe you have already made the acquaintance of the Count of the Ducci Montaldo. I captured him before the battle. He will take my ransom demands to Venice, but you are the reason I am allowing him to escape.''

She held his hand as they ran through the valley. Held tight to him and would not let him go. They had one day of freedom and in that day they must escape from Nicopolis, just as they had in the past.

Blessedly, they had been released from Nicopolis after night-fall. Julian could not see the death and wreckage she was leaving behind. She knew that by some miracle she had been spared and by an even greater miracle Olivier was alive and holding her hand. They were leaving the horror of this Feast of St. Michael the Archangel far behind them. They were going on. Julian could feel a thought deep within her start to rise through the horror and the shock. She could feel the Power trying to tell her that everything would be all right.

When the thought of Luciano Venier came to mind, she pushed it aside. In the end she would have to tell Olivier everything her father had told her. She would have to name the traitor of Venice. But she could not do it now—when Olivier's face was set so rigidly white.

Not when she, the Magdalene's daughter, could see that the thirst for vengeance had sucked all the love from his heart.

He was solicitous of her. He found water and scoured what was left of the harvest fruit. The Sultan had seen that they had provisions—simple cheese and brown bread. Olivier insisted that she take more than her share and she forced herself to eat what he offered. Her body felt tender and her stomach queasy. She was starting to think they were being caused by more than the heat and the war's harsh conditions. She could not tell her suspicions to Olivier, not with the way his eyes became vacant and he looked away from her. He had worn this same look of implacable vengeance the other time when they had left Nico-polis and traveled back to Belvedere; he had worn it as he told her of the deaths of his father and his brother.

They found King Sigismund just as the Sultan had said they would. He was happy to see his old friend Olivier, one of the few allied commanders who had foreseen the disastrous ending of this crusade. Eventually Sigismund would recover, but he was heartbroken now.

"There were survivors," he said to them that night in the open under a tree. There were no longer silk tents with this small remnant of the allied army, even for its kings. "We were saved by our position in the rear. The French who insisted upon the avant-garde were decimated. It was a massacre on all sides.

hope never to see its like again." He paused. The air around them filled with the cheerful singing of cicadas. "I was dragged from the field by my friends. We conscripted a fisher boat and this eventually brought us to the allied vessels. In all, there were ten of us who escaped."

"A few others made it out. One Polish knight managed to swim the Danube in full armor," said a burly German whom Julian had never seen before. "But there were few enough. Many drowned in the attempt."

"And the Sultan killed everyone left behind," said Olivier. "He was enraged over the death of his men. He gave no quarter. Except for those held as slaves or for ransom, all the rest of the allied warriors who fell into his hands were massacred."

"We lost the day by the pride and vanity of those French," cried Sigismund bitterly. "If they had only listened to my advice—we had enough men to win. We fought bravely and well. We could have taken the day."

Olivier had his own opinions as to the reason for Bayezid's victory, but he kept these to himself. He could make no accusations without proof, but he would get this proof if he did nothing else in this life.

Sigismund turned to Julian. "When we first had notice that the Sultan had arrived, I sent the child Saleima and the two nuns on the allied vessel that carried word to Buda. They should be safe there, awaiting our return. I sent Michel de Croyant as their escort. He protested vehemently but could not refuse. The Knight de la Marche had appointed me as his liege lord."

Julian thanked him, tears in her eyes. The old woman, Saleima's grandmother, had been right. All of the prisoners of Rachowa had died. But Michel, the only male left to his warrior family, had been saved on the feast of his patron saint.

The men let her cry for all of them.

"You have been sent to carry the Sultan's demands to Venice and to the Duke," said Sigismund finally, turning to Olivier.

"And to raise money for my own ransom as well." Again Olivier's face tightened. "I gave Bayezid my word of a knight on it and it is a word that must be respected."

"They will be hunting culprits in Venice," said Sigismund mildly. "They will be burning witches wherever they are found."

Again there was silence. They all knew that the king spoke the truth.

"The price of their ransom will be high," speculated Sigismund.

"It has already been that," replied Olivier as he reached across the darkness to take Julian's hand.

Sigismund said, "We sail to the Black Sea and eventually to Buda. You are welcome to accompany us for as long and as far as you wish. I am sure that at Buda you will find a vessel to take you to Venice. That will be your destination, will it not?"

"Aye, I go to Venice," said Olivier softly. "But first I must take the Lady Julian home to Belvedere."

CHAPTER
TWENTY-SIX

It took them until Christmas. Actually, past Christmas and into the birth of a bright new year. Julian and Olivier journeyed with Sigismund as far as Constantinople, then went on, just the two of them, to Genoa and inland from there. The news of the slaughter at Nicopolis traveled before them. All through Europe church bells tolled in continuous mourning as the continent cried for its unshriven dead. Olivier traversed his grieving country with Julian by his side. Still, they made it through and topped the last hill that separated them from their destination on a crisp, cold winter's day.

"There is a legend," he said as they stopped to view Belvedere's chaste beauty in the light of their changed lives. "One of many concerning my family. They say that since their deaths, my father—the local people called him the Old Count—and my brothers haunt this place. They say they enchant stray folk by offering more than a night's hospitality. They offer them a home." He paused. "But I am not one to believe in legends. I have no faith in fairy's tales and happy endings."

Julian glanced over at him, and her hand moved protectively

to just beneath her heart. Olivier's bitterness had not faded on
their voyage, as had that of the King of Hungary. Instead, the
Count of the Ducci Montaldo seemed to be once again the hard
and driven man who had reluctantly saved her from Nicopolis
and even more reluctantly brought her home to Belvedere. It
seemed almost as though nothing had happened to them in the
interim, at least nothing that Olivier now found to be important.

Julian had not told him what her father had said about Luciano
Venier. She had tried to do this over and over again in the
months that they had spent traveling home to Belvedere. He
had the right to know. She knew it. Still, the words had not
come.

She had no proof of her accusations. She did not *know* that
what Assen said was true. He had always been an embittered
and vengeful man, a man who could say or do anything just
to have his revenge. And Julian could not aid and abet this.
She had seen at Nicopolis the harm a vendetta could do. Even
if Luciano had traitored the allied armies, then Venice—
Europe—would not make him suffer alone. There would be
Domiziana and the Lady Claudia and Massima and Sofia, and
most of all Ginevra—Ginevra, her good friend—who would
all be made to suffer as well. They could be burned for sorcery,
even if Luciano were proved innocent in the end. Julian could
not make up her mind to condemn them. She kept her silence
as they spurred their horses into the last valley that separated
them from their longed-for destination.

"They will be hunting culprits in Venice," King Sigismund
had told them. *"They will be hunting witches wherever they're
found."*

She remembered her mother. She remembered the torture
and the witch's cell. She knew she could not condemn the
women of the Venier without more proof than she had.

The portcullis of the castle opened on squeaking hinges. No
pages sprang out to gather their horses, no sound of trumpets
on the air. Only Giuseppe, the ancient bailiff, emerged. Julian

oticed that his livery had been mended. It was no longer
-eshly new and bright with hope.

Olivier waited until he had handed Julian from her horse
efore he turned to his bailiff. He seemed reluctant to hear
/hat the man said.

But Giuseppe's news burst out as from a dam.

"'Twas Count Venier who did this," he said. "He came
⅋st after the Feast of St. Michael, at the very beginning of
⅌ctober. He said that you had been captured and that your
⅋nsom was great. He said that everything must be taken from
⅃elvedere and sold to raise the money. Everything. Even the
⅋ings that the Lady Francesca had managed to salvage after
our father—after the death of the Count."

Olivier nodded. Slowly he gave his arm to Julian and escorted
er up the stairs.

"And in the village of Sant'Urbano as well," Giuseppe said
⅋s he followed them. "They've taken everything. All the fruits
⅃f harvest and the slaughtered pigs. All of the wine. Count
⅋enier said he needed everything, every last morsel, to send
⅋n to the Sultan. He said you had given the Ottoman your
⅋ord. But, my lord, the peasants are starving through the winter.
⅃hey have prayed night and day for your return."

The empty hall rang with the sound of their footsteps and
⅃he jingle of the Count of the Ducci Montaldo's golden spurs.
⅃livier did not look around at the devastation of his castle. He
⅃id not look at the white spaces where once great tapestries
⅋ad hung or at the ghost marks of scrolled leather chairs on
⅃he stone floors or at the brittle light of late afternoon that no
⅃onger flashed against silver or pearls.

Instead he kept his eyes studiously on Julian. He kept his
⅃houghts on her as well.

"You must be tired," he said. He patted her hand.

She knew he watched her closely and so she kept the tears
⅃ack—forced them back with a will and a strength that only
⅃he, the new Magdalene, could use. There would be no tears.

A lifetime of tears would surely await her, but she could no
begin shedding them now.

That night he placed her again in Francesca's virginal cham
ber. It was the first time, since they had first begun to love
that he had chosen to sleep alone. He had work to do, he said
He would be working through the night, and he did not wan
to disturb her. Julian nodded. She could not begrudge him hi:
secret thoughts. She hid hers as well.

Instead she looked up at him and smiled. And vowed alway·
to carry him deep in her heart.

"Wait for me here," Olivier said on the morrow. "I'll come
back to you. I have business in Venice. I must see to my ransom
I must see what awaits me there. But I will come back to you
I promise you that. I have sent to San Mario and Padre Gasca
is on his way here. But I will return as well."

Julian nodded, still smiling. Still loving. But in her heart she
knew he would not come back.

He bent down low in the saddle of his great destrier in order
to kiss her, then, in a flash of gold and black, he galloped away

And Julian Madrigal, daughter of the Magdalene, used none
of her knowledge and none of her Power to stop him.

She waited for him through the rest of the winter. She waited
as her belly grew and as her motions slowed. The Count of the
Ducci Montaldo sent back money, both to her and to the village.
but he never sent back a word. Julian knew what had happened
He was a man bound first to his duty—to the remnant of his
army, to his peasants, to the city of Venice he had vowed to
protect. The breaking of his betrothal to this wealthy woman
had not been made public. In the end Domiziana would have
him, just as she had planned. She would prevail.

Julian, the Magdalene's daughter, certainly did not need the
Power to know this.

* * *

Still she waited with dwindling hope until April, but when
[s]he felt the first movements of her child she knew that she
[mu]st go north. There was someone who had invited her to
[co]me to him if ever she were in need. Someone she might be
[abl]e to help as well. Someone she could trust.

"The snows have melted," she said to Padre Gasca as they
[ro]de side by side on their small donkeys along the road that
[wo]uld lead them first to France and then on to Burgundy. "The
[Kn]ight de la Marche waits for us at his castle. He offered to
[sen]d an honor guard to escort us or to come for us himself.
[Bu]t he is still convalescent. I could not have had him move."

The priest had his doubts about this journey. He had voiced
[the]m over and over to Julian. Was it not right to tell the Count
[of] the Ducci Montaldo of his child? Was it not right to give
[hi]m the choice?

But for Julian the choice was quite simple. Olivier had sent
[he]r no word. She could have sent word to him, she knew. She
[cou]ld have told him about their child. But she knew she would
[ne]ver do either of these things. She had had him once in love.
[Sh]e would not have him now in duty.

She smiled over at the small, wizened priest as a flock of
[no]rth-flying birds appeared overhead to point them a way.

"This is what had to happen," her father had once told her.
["T]his is what had to be."

BELVEDERE

CHAPTER
TWENTY-SEVEN

It had been five years since he had last seen his castle, and those five years it had changed once again. Perched on its top, pristine and beautiful, it seemed as eternal as the march hills that stretched Tuscany out towards eternity. It looked peaceful as the sun that had always beamed down upon it. But it wasn't, thought the last Count of the Ducci Montaldo. or had it ever been.

Changes had taken place within this castle. Memories and osts now ruled Belvedere, in place of real flesh and blood. e turned his horse down the hill.

Welcome home! Welcome to Belvedere!

For an instant Olivier was certain he heard his father's voice. e Old Count called to him and bade him draw near. Olivier t tears sting at his eyes. Almost all that he loved had died him, but still some fate had kept him alive.

Julian.

Her presence was strong in him in this, the place she had so ved. He could smell the sweet, spring smell of her violet rfume. He could hear her laughing again with the Knight de

la Marche. But Julian was lost to him, had been lost to hi
for years. He had not sent her word. How could he have?

But, then, neither had she sent word to him.

He was so deep in his memories of Julian that at first he d
not see the young child sitting upon the stone wall. But tl
child had seen him. She stared at him. She studied him. A
something in her clear, bright face caused the last Count of tl
Ducci Montaldo to stop his desultory canter towards hom
Something familiar in the long sweep of her hair caused hi
to halt and then dismount and come near.

"What are you doing here?" he said to the child. But l
knew. He knew. His heart was pumping the message into h
brain even as he spoke the words. He knew.

"Waiting for you," answered the young girl. She star
back at him with his own wide turquoise eyes, eyes that ha
made his mother famous, bright chips of turquoise that ha
signaled the Ducci Montaldo fate. She seemed to be all of fi
years old.

"Why are you waiting?"

"Because the Old Count told me to expect you here."

It was not necessary for Olivier to ask which Old Count.

His instinct was to reach for his daughter and hold her, b
he held himself back. She was staring at him with his eyes o
of Julian's clear face. He saw her mother's Maltese Star catc
the waning sunlight and wink at him from the slim golde
chain at her neck.

"What is your name?" he asked, determined not to frighte
her or cause her to bolt. She had already been away from hi
too long.

"Alix," said the girl. "I am Alix Madrigal. My mother
the Wise Woman here."

He reached out then and gathered her to him. "Come wit
me, Alix, and let us find your mother. It is time we were goir
home now. The hour grows late."

Julian was not in the castle main, but in its village. She wa
surrounded by people, and she was laughing. She looked tir

d sweaty but jubilant as she held out a carefully swaddled
ndle.

"Our fine friend Sabata has delivered herself of a third
apping son! One day she will be a great Wise Woman her-
lf!"

Her joy seemed contagious. The people caught it and laughed
 they gathered around the small stone house built into the
ves. Someone brought forth a small kettledrum and began to
ck out a tune. Julian turned without seeing Olivier and went
ck into the cottage. But the others saw him and one by one
ey stopped their dancing and turned in curiosity to their lord
til, in the end, even the kettledrum stilled.

It must have been this silence that brought her curious face
 the window. He saw her look out over the red blush of a
st-bloomed geranium. He saw her look out and around and
en over to him.

Watched the astonishment on her face as it turned into wari-
ss. He saw no love for him there.

She thought he looked somehow younger and freer as he
od holding their child in his arms. Younger than when she
d first seen him in the caves under Nicopolis, and that was
 long ago. He was Olivier and so he was still dressed in
ack, still carried his jeweled sword. He was a warrior, so his
rse was ever near. But his eyes had changed since she'd last
en him, enough to let the blue that had always been in them
ine through. No longer were they the hard green chips she
membered.

And he was smiling at her. Olivier, her love, was loving her.
Julian felt the tears well up, splash down, disappear.

"Why didn't you tell me?" he said. They were in Julian's
ug little cottage. Their child slept peacefully between them
 they talked.

"It seems so long ago, so impossible now. But then I had
y reasons. I couldn't trust what Assen said. He was so filled

with hatred. I thought he might be lying, even upon his dyin
bed. I could not risk telling you that it was Luciano Venie
who had betrayed you.''

"But in the end I found out the truth myself."

Julian said nothing. She did not move, but she could n
quite force her eyes not to ask the question.

"My lady mother once told me that left to himself, the dev
will always divulge himself in time. She said that he will alway
exaggerate. He cannot help this. Luciano Venier exaggerated.
Olivier's laugh was short but no longer filled with bitternes
"He was already here at Belvedere pillaging on September 2
the Feast of St. Michael—the very day that had been fixed f
Bayezid's attack on Nicopolis. But when he came there wa
no way he could have already heard of the French defeat. H
greed was his downfall."

"He was also the only one who knew which road you wer
taking from Venice to Belvedere on the night you were attacke
I remembered this later," Julian said. "Did you confront him?

"He was already dead by the time I made it to Venice. H
died suddenly. There was much talk of poison. The Dog
too, is not a stupid man and he is strong on family principl
Thousands of men died on that crusade. The Doge had let h
own son die for a much lesser offense against honor. The lo
of a cousin was nothing to him."

"Was he denounced?" Julian whispered.

"No, but his family was exiled. Their goods were confiscate
and divided among the widows and children of the men he ha
caused to be killed."

"Poor Lady Claudia." Julian found that she meant what sh
said. "Poor Domiziana. Had you married her by then?"

Olivier stared at her in true astonishment before letting o
an explosion of laughter that caused Julian to frown and motio
towards the sleeping child.

"Domiziana needed no husband. She was quite capable o
looking to her own best interests. When news came of th
defeat there was much talk of witching. Someone found doll

for this woman was palpable. Alix could feel it scintillate the air around her. She could taste it on the bile in her throat. She knew that this love was not a dream and that it would not pass with time.

If anything, Robert's passion for Solange had grown through the years and especially after the birth of their child—his child. Any woman would have been able to see the signs of his passion. Especially a woman who loved Robert as much as Alix did. Who needed him as much as she did. She watched as Solange automatically reached to brush a wayward leaf from his cloak and smooth back a curl in his crisp dark hair. Wifely gestures.

Except that it was she, Alix, who was this man's wife.

The Count de Mercier has ever but one love.
His heart forever. His childhood flower
Solange
His life's one quest.

How easily troubadours and jongleurs gossiped in their witty tunes about the passions and the sentiments of life, not thinking that what was love for one was often heartbreak and humiliation for another. Or not caring. For years musicians had earned bright silver half-coins by warbling on and on about the great love Robert, Lord de Mercier, bore his peasant mistress. Certain sensitive noblewomen, safely cocooned within the steel clauses of their own carefully arranged marriage contracts, had been known to sympathetically swoon at the mere mention of so great a passion. The scandalously impossible *liaison* between a peer of France and one of his serfs could only be rationalised by thinking of it as the truest of true loves. Love was the basic gossamer intertwined within all of chivalry's most resplendent myths. It was deemed as important to life as bread, and almost as necessary as battle and conquest. Thus, everyone in France, be it the humblest Parisian glover or the king himself, knew of Robert's passion for Solange. But unfortunately—at least

CHAPTER ONE

It was just a dream and Alix knew it. But it was also real, and she knew this as well. In her dream or out of it, the man and woman were in love. One could tell this. *She could tell this*, as she stood within her dream, just a little away from them and staring at their shared dark beauty through her clear turquoise eyes.

They fit so well together, almost as if they had always been in love and always would be. Alix would have had to be blind not to see this, and she was not blind. It was evident in the way the man took the woman's hand and tucked it around the safety of his arm, the way his dark eyes smiled down into her even darker ones, the way he gifted her with the last wildflower that remained on his path. Alix had heard that he'd always been like this with this woman. He could not help himself. Since their shared childhood, whatever his hand fell upon, whether it was a diamond or a dandelion, he gave it to Solange. He, Robert de Mercier, one of the mightiest nobles in France, wanted to give her everything that belonged to him. Even after all of their years together, and the birth of their son, his love

he makings of a great Wise Woman. One day, like her mother, he would be a good healer.

Just as they turned their horses towards the east, Alix, sitting on the saddle before her father, smiled and clapped her hands and pointed up, up.

''I see the Old Count upon the ramparts,'' said Alix, laughing. 'He is saying Good-bye and God Speed!'

Olivier looked over her head and caught the eye of the woman he loved. They both laughed, too, as they turned their horses away from the castle and towards their new life in the north. Belvedere's heavy portcullis clanged shut behind them, but the last Count of the Ducci Montaldo did not look back.

as they said? When I tracked you, that is what they told me. That you lived in his castle. That you were his wife.''

''Indeed, the Knight de la Marche has married.'' She reached across the small trestle table and took both of his hands into her own. ''But he did not marry me. He married the woman he loves.''

Olivier felt his heart thump but he had to make her say it, had to hear the words.

''And that woman was not you?''

She looked at him with well-deep tenderness. ''How could I marry another, when you were always my true husband?''

''As you,'' he said, reaching over to kiss her, ''were always my wife.''

The Count of the Ducci Montaldo had things to see to at his family's castle but there was no question that he could stay.

''Sigismund needs me. He fights the Bohemians. He fights the Germans. His brother, the Emperor Wenceslas, is a drunkard and his kingdom is in terrible array. Unfortunately, for his sake there will always be employment for a warrior with Sigis-mund.''

Olivier's work was soon finished and he would have his wife and child with him as he left Belvedere forever to journey to the far reaches of Germany. Sigismund had given him a small but important castle. It would be their new home. Padre Gasca would come with them. He had decided this himself after he had married his two old friends.

'' 'Twill be good for me,'' he said. ''Nothing to do in Germany but live a life of contemplation. I cannot possibly get into trouble there.''

He laughed but Olivier saw him wink at Alix, and knew that she was the real reason for his sudden interest in the north. He had taught Francesca and Julian. Now he would teach Alix. She had the Power and her father knew it. He did not know where her path would lead her but he did know that she had in her possession, and charms and amulets. Rather than accept the responsibility, she turned upon the Strega Elisabetta and denounced her loudly and long to the Inquisition. The witch was tried and burned before the Cathedral of St. Mark.''

''Dear God,'' said Julian, crossing herself.

''They say she cursed the family for thirteen generations, just as Jacques de Molay did when the Knights Templar burned him.''

''But what happened to the Lady Domiziana?'' Julian said almost shyly.

''She has been convented in Picardy. For her this will be a worse fate than death.''

''Then you did not wed her?''

''How could I ever wed her?'' asked Olivier simply. ''When you were always my true wife?''

Alix murmured something in her sleep and Julian instantly bent over her, grateful that Olivier could not see her blush.

''She wears the Maltese Star,'' he said. ''Did you ever learn its meaning?''

Julian shook her head as she turned to face him once again.

''I stopped searching for it. I knew it no longer concerned me, because after I had returned to Nicopolis, after I had faced the truth of my life there, the man with the white rose no longer haunted me. I was free from him and what he meant.''

''But you have passed the Star on to your daughter.''

''Because it is hers by right, and I cannot keep it from her. Just as my mother could not keep it from me. Perhaps one day she will discover its secret. Or else she will make up her own mind as to what it means.''

For a moment they sat in silence before the remains of the simple meal that the Wise Woman had made. Olivier watched the flames dance in the fireplace before him. He did not want to ask the question—did not want to hear its answer, not now when he was so close to having all that he would ever hold dear.

''And you,'' he said. ''Did you marry the Knight de la Marche

or Alix—there were too many other tales to carry in these
warring days for the story to have worked its way throughout
he rest of Europe. It would have had to be startling indeed to
 have travelled as far as King Sigismund's court in Hungary.
No one knew or had time to care about the niceties of a French
ove story there. Life was too real and too rugged. It had to be
seized quickly and on its own terms. Which is why Alix's
loving but unsuspecting parents had betrothed, dowered, and
married her into this nightmare.

Alix herself had learned the truth soon enough. It had been
waiting in the courtyard of her husband's castle to greet her
two years ago, when she had arrived fresh from her marriage
at the Cathedral in Buda. She had been all of sixteen years old.
The truth had been dressed in rich blue velvet and pearls. It
had been dark and graceful and full; not thin and light as Alix
herself was—the kind of woman who, even now that she was
wedded, could easily have passed for a boy. The truth had
taken Robert's hand and smiled at him and led him away.

"He had no choice." For an instant, in the dream, Solange
turned to face Alix, her eyes filled with something that might
well have been compassion. "He needed to make a noble
marriage. He needed to produce a legitimate heir, or else his
lands would have been forfeit to Lancelot de Guigny. You
know that. He told you so himself. Robert did not marry me
because he could not, but he has always loved me. He will
always love me. I am the mother of his only child."

Even in her sleep Alix felt the pain as she clinched her hands,
digging her fingernails deep, deep into her own flesh. Any
mention of the son Robert had fathered upon his mistress
brought out the same shameful reaction. Alix could not help
herself. She fought against it, but she hated Solange's child.
She hated the child.

Above all else, she hated the child.

Soon after their arrival and the meeing with Solange, her
husband's visits to her chamber—never frequent or especially
ardent even during the early weeks of their marriage—had

ceased completely. Alix had heard chambermaids snickering
behind their hands as she passed through the cold and friendless
halls of her new home. Yet she knew that one day Robert must
return to her. He had no choice. He needed an heir—a legitimate
heir—or else his lands would be confiscated and devolved upon
his cousin, de Guigny—or worse upon the new upstart warrior
lord, Severin Brigante Harnoncourt, who claimed them from
his fortress in Angevin, Italy. It was a universal truth that in
this, the year of Our Lord 1414, a legitimate heir could only
be begotten upon a legitimate wife. The Duke of Burgundy's
threats had been enough to make Robert marry her. Surely in
the end they would be enough to make him bed her once again.
Especially now that Burgundy had taken the particularly risky
step of siding with the English against his liege lord, the King
of France. Alix, never particularly prayerful in the past, prayed
each night that Robert would come to her. She loved her husband. She had never loved anyone before him, and in her heart
she was certain that she would never be able to love anyone
else. Despite everything, she must continue to love Robert.

Yet that did not mean that she loved his son. She fought
against it; she prayed against it. She had to continue reminding
herself that the pain in her life was not the fault of a two-year-
old boy. Nothing mattered; no argument helped her. Robert's
child should have been hers.

Things were different now, however. They had changed.
Robert would not be able to refuse her much longer, not with
the Duke of Burgundy turned traitor. Not with Guigny and that
upstart Harnoncourt both threatening his lands. The very air
they breathed was filled with the scent of war and usurpation.
It was only a matter of time now. Robert must come to her.
He must put her to bed with his heir.

Alix shivered in her sleep and snuggled more deeply into
the shelter of her fox fur blankets. In her dream she watched
Robert as he took his mistress's hand and as they crossed
toward the dense, dark forest that lay beyond his castle. Alix
had seen them do this a thousand times before in the reality of

vakefulness, but she frowned now in her sleep. Something was vrong. Something was missing. But then Alix saw the two of hem turn back and smile at the young child who toddled quickly to catch up. For an instant time stopped, and the three of them were framed in a golden glow of falling autumn leaves. The child giggled rapturously, and the sound of his happiness ippled upward, into the sky and the clouds that were just beginning to form upon its surface. Even the ravens flying wiftly south and away from the threat of winter, stopped to quawk and flutter, obviously wanting to be part of the pretty cene playing out below them. The beautiful, loving parents; heir perfect, happy son. Alix heard the boy's laughter ring hrough her dream and she winced.

Then, from her place just outside the circle of their love, Alix sighted her husband's young squire rushing toward them. He ran forward with the intense slow motion that one saw in a dream that was just about to deepen. But this was not what had attracted Alix's attention. Her forehead crinkled in perplexity as he stared at the running, flaying youth, as she tried to piece together what was wrong. And then she recognized his livery. Robert's squire no longer sported the crisp silvery blue of the Counts de Mercier. His tunic was a blaze of bright scarlet, and in his hand he carried the standard of a scarlet flag that rippled and undulated over his head. Both in her dream and on her bed, Alix frowned at this. What could it mean, all this red? All this running? Whose colors did he wear? Who called his allegiance now? But then she heard Robert call her name and she turned back to him—as she always had and doubtless always would—only to look upon the child she hated instead.

The two-year-old was alone now, and he was no longer laughing. His parents had moved far, far away, almost to the very edge of the forest. At the tree line, they turned to look at him with sad, reluctant faces, but they did not come back. They did not motion for him or wait for him. They moved on.

Alix shivered again and as she lay dreaming, she automatically reached to touch the Maltese Star that hung at her throat.

It was the same small golden six-pointed star that had belonged to both her mother and her grandmother. Alix felt the amulet grow warm and move just slightly beneath her fingers. She felt its power. For the first time in a very long time she let it call her back to Belvedere.

That is when the screaming started.

Merlin's Legacy

A Series From
Quinn Taylor Evans

The Queen of
Romance
Cassie Edwards